Darkest Truth

Catherine Kirwan grew up on a farm in the parish of Fews, County Waterford. She studied law at UCC and lives in Cork where she works as a solicitor. *Darkest Truth* is her first novel.

Darkest Truth

Catherine Kirwan

CENTURY

1 3 5 7 9 10 8 6 4 2

Century
20 Vauxhall Bridge Road
London SW1V 2SA

Century is part of the Penguin Random House group of companies
whose addresses can be found at global.penguinrandomhouse.com.

Penguin
Random House
UK

First published in the United Kingdom by Century in 2019

www.penguin.co.uk

A CIP catalogue record for this book is available from the British Library.

ISBN 9781529123814

Typeset in 11.75/17.25 pt Times New Roman
by Integra Software Services Pvt. Ltd, Pondicherry

Printed and bound in Great Britain by Clays Ltd, Elcograf S.p.A.

Penguin Random House is committed to a sustainable future for
our business, our readers and our planet. This book is made from
Forest Stewardship Council® certified paper.

MIX
Paper from
responsible sources
FSC® C018179

For Michael and Breda Kirwan

PROLOGUE

She hears the bus, the hiss and chug of it, behind her. The 203 from Lehenaghmore. Two minutes early. An omen, she thinks. She sticks out her right hand, shoulder high, one half of a crucifix. The other she plunges into her anorak pocket. She left her phone and purse at home, but her bus pass is where it always is. Palming it at the driver as she boards, she keeps her head low. No chat. No reply to his 'how's it going?' No acknowledgement of his 'suit yourself, love'.

The bus is almost empty. You don't go into the city centre on a damp Tuesday night in January unless you have to. She chooses a seat in the middle, equidistant from the other two passengers. They take off after a minute's dawdle, and the lights are in their favour for the first couple of junctions. Another omen, she thinks. But at the end of Summerhill South, the light is red. Doesn't matter, she thinks, nothing does.

In town, at the last stop, she waits. The other two passengers say 'thanks' to the driver as they get off. She wants to say it too, this final courtesy, but silence is safer, and the driver is busy anyway, filling in a form. He hardly notices her, she thinks. She doesn't see him watch her cross the street to the river. She doesn't see him shrug and tap his breast pocket and step off the bus and light up a cigarette. She doesn't know that he'll remember that smoke. She doesn't know that he'll regret it.

She reaches Patrick's Bridge. At the pedestrian light, she almost looks north, towards MacCurtain Street and the Everyman Theatre. She looks east instead, towards her destination. As soon as the road is clear, she makes for the other side. One more crossing, she thinks, and I'm there. She speeds up, then slows again, recalling that she'll have to pass the Opera House. Don't think, she says aloud. As the glassy bulk of it looms into view, she registers that the place is dark tonight. For a second, she's glad.

At the Christy Ring Bridge, she pauses, barely, then crosses, weaving her way through the cars. Nobody bothers to hoot. Everyone jaywalks in Cork. At the Half Moon Street opening from Lavitts Quay, she stalls and looks south. She pushes down her hood. Around now, her parents will be watching the nine o'clock news on RTE. They won't have noticed yet that she's not in her room. She shuts her eyes and swallows hard. This is it, she thinks, this is the only way.

Walking on, the mist is cool on her face. She breathes through her nose and something like a smile rests briefly on her lips. She snaps open the fasteners of her anorak, methodically, deliberately, one by one. She touches her right hand to the quay wall. The stone feels rough against her skin.

Near the footbridge, she stands and bows her head, breathing as slowly as she can. She hears the blood pulsing in her ears. Then, quickly, she slides her coat off her shoulders. Checking that her bus pass is still in the pocket, she folds the coat carefully and places it on the wall. She takes off her trainers and socks and puts them on top of the anorak. She pulls her sweatshirt over her head and drapes it across the pile.

Barefoot, in black leggings and a thin black T-shirt, she's ready. She steps on to the stone staircase and descends three steps. On the fourth step, her left foot breaks water. She flinches, but takes another step. There's something hard and sharp under her feet. She gasps, though what she's feeling now doesn't seem like pain.

With the next step, she's in up to her knees. She has to cling on to the wall to steady herself. But it's slimy. She takes her hand away for a moment, then grips the side again. When she's up to her waist, she feels the sway of the river, the size of it. She hears shouts from above. She has been seen. She lets go.

And the current takes her.

1

November 2013

With high tide due at 18.42, I needed to move fast. I saved the document I was working on, logged out and felt around with my feet under my paper-strewn desk. Nothing. I'd forgotten my wellies. Which meant I had to move really fast. The city is built on a bog, and when the tide is high enough, and the rain is heavy enough, and the wind is blowing in the right direction, Cork can do floods better than anywhere else in the country. The streets that once were rivers revert to watery highways, and there's an eerie beauty to it all, if you don't have to mop out a flooded shop or dump a sodden carpet. And if you have the right footwear.

'Shitfuckbollocks,' I said.

I hate having wet feet, and my way too expensive leather-soled work shoes were going to die in the rain.

They would have to do. Shrugging on my charcoal raincoat, I tied back my hair with an elastic band grabbed from my desk. Not ideal, but better than having a thick dark curtain blowing over my eyes and blocking my view as I walked. I pulled on black leather gloves as I ran down the four flights of stairs to the street door, the one we use at night when the main entrance is closed.

'Everyone gone?' I shouted.

The echoing silence told me I was alone. Mostly, I like this place better when it's empty and dark and cold. But I was feeling shaky that night. A flood warning will do that to you, will fool you into thinking there might be safety in numbers.

I keyed in the alarm code, hauled the flood barrier out of the ground floor cupboard and wedged it into the steel grooves on the door frame. The council had made a sandbag delivery. I heaved three in front of the door. Lastly, I hit the button on the shutter remote control, pulled up my hood and walked away, towards Barrack Street and higher ground. It was too late to take the low footbridge from the Grand Parade, so I made for the South Gate, built high enough from the water to withstand the tidal surge. It was only ten past six. I had enough time. If the wind didn't blow me away first.

Glancing back to check on the shutter's progress, I saw a short, portly figure in a flat cap and an old-man rain jacket standing in front of the office, staring up at the unlit windows. Just then, he looked in my direction. He shouted something I couldn't hear, and rushed towards me, and grabbed my hand like he wasn't planning on letting go.

'Miss Fitzpatrick, isn't it?' he said. 'I need to talk to you. It's an emergency.'

Mid-sixties or older, the man's accent was local, but he was a stranger. If he knew who I was, it was thanks to the firm's website. I've been a solicitor long enough to know that new clients who come to the office without an appointment late on a Friday, any Friday, and especially wet Fridays in November, are to be avoided at all costs. Normally, I give them a business card, suggest a meeting the following week and, usually, the so-called urgent business evaporates over the weekend.

'Sorry. Not now,' I said. 'I'm finished for the day. And it'll be high tide in less than half an hour. Come back Monday?'

'It has to be now, Miss Fitzpatrick,' the man said. 'Finola. Please.'

I tried to pull away, but his grip on my hand tightened. At the same time, his other hand grabbed my forearm. I looked around in panic. The street was deserted. Not good. Not good at all. I'm five foot eight, and fairly strong. The old man was smaller than me, but he was solid and stocky. Though I tried pulling away again, he held me still. I thought about pushing him, which might have had no effect. Or, worse, might have toppled him like a skittle. I looked down again. After a moment, I realised that the man was weeping.

'I have to show you something. I-I-I'll explain everything but there isn't much time,' he said. 'It's about my daughter.'

'Come on,' I said. 'But we have to cross the river *now* or we'll be in trouble.'

*

We trudged through the darkness and the driving rain, heads down, battling the gusts. As we crossed the bridge, the black water slapped violently against the quay wall.

'We'll go into Forde's,' I said, shouting over the roar of the river.

I pushed open the door and we fell into the warm gloom. The storm meant that the pub was quiet for a Friday, but Forde's is never raucous, it's a place for respectable drinking. The table nearest the door was free and I made for it, peeling off my sopping raincoat. The old man went straight to the bar and I joined him after a moment.

'What'll you have?' he asked.

'Just a pot of tea, no milk or sugar, please,' I said.

'I'm after ordering a hot whiskey,' said the man.

'Barry's Tea will do me grand,' I said.

Get this over with fast is what I thought.

I returned to the table and sat, back to the wall, with a view of the room. After a few minutes, the man came and sat opposite me. He had taken off his cap. He was bald with a semicircle of tufty grey hair.

'We can't do much tonight, not here,' I said. 'But I can take a few preliminary notes and give you an appointment to come into the office next week.'

I was thinking about the whiskey, wondering if it was his first of the day. Whether it was or not, I wasn't going to be acting immediately on any instructions he gave me. My professional indemnity insurance doesn't stretch that far. I poked in my handbag and dug out a small black notebook, a business card and a biro.

'Now,' I said. 'Let's start with your name, address and contact details, and here are mine.'

I slid my card across the table.

'Though obviously you know how to find me.'

The man stayed silent.

'Look,' I said. 'I know you're nervous, but you're the one who said it was an emergency. And you said it was important, something about your daughter?'

He was looking past me, his eyes half closed, and saying nothing. Finally, he took a slug of his whiskey, and started to talk.

'My name is Sean Carney and I live at 54 Lee Valley Rise, Turners Cross. I can't remember my mobile number off the top of my head. But it's in the phone.'

I wrote down the name and address.

'Deirdre. That was her name. She was my beautiful baby. And she's dead.'

'I'm so sorry, Sean,' I said, and I meant it.

But, simultaneously, I was calculating and weighing what the emergency might be, half hating myself for doing it. This is the job. This is how it is. People tell me their secret stories and their deepest fears, and I box and package and strategise and, somehow, try to hold on to the humanity in all of it. I knew it couldn't be an inquest he was talking about, not on a Friday. And, if foul play was suspected, that would be a matter for a Garda investigation. Or was his daughter's death recent? Something he wanted to get off his chest? Something he needed to tell to someone who couldn't tell anyone else? The hairs on my arms stood up, and I braced myself for the worst. I was expecting a confession.

And I was wrong.

'Deirdre died by her own hand, ten months ago now. You might have heard – or maybe not. There's been a fair few suicides in Cork the last couple of years. They pulled her.'

He paused.

'Her body, I mean, from the water down near Blackrock on the 31st of January. Two nights she was in the river. Our Deirdre. She came to us on the 1st of December 1982, the happiest day of our lives. She was just gone thirty when …'

He cleared his throat, and I looked away, giving him a chance to compose himself. It gave me a chance to do the same. Stories like the one Sean was starting to tell were the last thing I wanted to hear. But after a time, I felt the silence change to something else. I looked back and found him watching me, and it struck me that there was something altered in his expression, something unexpected, though I couldn't have named it. And then it was gone, whatever it was, and Sean was talking again.

'My daughter had been troubled for a long time,' he said. 'Depressed. Hurting herself. It's unbelievable what happened to her, how she went downhill that way. Barely finished school. Couldn't go to university. Never did much with her life.'

He shifted in his seat.

'It's strange being here with you,' he said.

'Talking about all of this must be awful,' I said 'We could leave it to another …'

'It's you,' he said. 'You remind me of her, of how she used to be. The black hair, and fair complexion. And the way you …

'What I'm saying,' he went on, 'is that our Deirdre was confident, like you are, she used to be. At one stage, I had it in mind that she might go for law as a career. I thought we'd be going to her graduation up in the college one day. But there was nothing like that. Not that we put any pressure on her about school, or anything. There was never any need. We were only delighted to have her, and whatever she wanted to do was fine with us. She was a good girl, a great girl. All we wanted was that she'd be happy, you know. She worked in Marco's, the chipper down the road from us, on and off. That's when she was able to work.'

His voice was weaker now, but he kept talking.

'A lot of the time she was in her room or going into the hospital for treatment, psychiatric treatment. When I think of what she must have suffered … Until she was fifteen, she was sailing through life. A grades – six of them – in her Junior Cert, no bother to her. She loved art and English especially, and music, of course. She loved life – and she had such promise. Was in the school plays – always the best – and in the musical society. I know I'm biased, like, but everyone said it. She was tall for her age, beautiful, and she had a great voice. She got the part of Liesl in *The Sound of Music*, at the Everyman Theatre, even though she was a bit young for it at the time. Look, here's a photo of her in it. You can keep it. The reviewer from the *Examiner* said she was "one to watch". But it was films she was really interested in.'

I took the photo, and placed it between the pages of my note-book. I didn't want to look. Couldn't. Not yet.

'She was like an angel from heaven,' Sean said.

He smiled. He looked like he was out of practice.

'We're ordinary people, us. I'm a lorry driver – was – and my wife used to work as a shop assistant in Roches Stores before we got married. But Deirdre was special – extra special because she was our only child. Deirdre was our first and last, the way it went. But she was enough, more than enough.'

'Then, she turned fifteen, was in Transition Year and doing that film project. I can see it now. That's where it all went wrong. And that's why she's dead today. I blame myself for not seeing the danger.'

I blame myself for not seeing the danger. I blame myself.

'I heard a fair bit about you from my neighbour Tom Broder-ick,' Sean continued. 'You helped him out getting access to his kids when he was away from his wife. That's right, isn't it? Though they're back together now that he's off the drink. And aren't you involved some way with the Film Festival, as well as being a solicitor?'

He didn't wait for my reply.

'I saw in the *Evening Echo* this afternoon that the festival, that it's starting tomorrow, so there isn't much time.'

I remembered Tom Broderick. I was surprised that he knew anything about my work with the Film Festival. And then again, I wasn't. Cork is small, with all kinds of hidden connections. Infor-mation is currency here, and news seeps through the cracks in the broken-down pavements. But I still had no idea what Sean wanted.

'I'm sorry,' I said. 'I don't understand. Somehow doing a film project was bad for Deirdre and you're here to see me because of something to do with this year's festival?'

'Not the project,' he said.

He thumped the underside of his closed fist on the table.

'It was the man she met because of it. A man who hurt her. Abused her. Destroyed her. And he got away with it and became so famous he thinks he's untouchable. Deirdre didn't make a complaint to the Gardaí. She couldn't, she said she hadn't a chance of being believed. Wouldn't even tell us who he was. But I know his name now and I've told the guards but they say they can't take it further.'

'Unfortunately, they're right,' I said. 'It's—'

'It's the law,' Sean said. 'It's too late. Go home, they say. Rest. Take it easy. Tell me, how can I ever take it easy while that man walks free?'

'I understand your frustration but legally—'

'*Legally*, because Deirdre is dead, there's nobody to make a statement or go witness against him.'

'Yes,' I said.

'And the Child Protection social workers say I can't do anything either,' Sean went on. 'They say I have no records, no proof, not even a name. Anyway, they think I'm imagining it, they think I've gone mad. But I haven't gone mad. I know who he is.'

He sucked in a breath. Then he took something out of his shirt pocket and laid it on the table. He unfolded it. Inside a clear plastic bag was a sheet of white paper. He turned it over without a word and passed it to me. I left it in the plastic and read:

Mam and Dad
He's too strong now. But the academy wouldn't like him so much
if they knew.
Sorry I wasn't brave enough. Sorry for everything.
Love
Deirdre xx

'You see now who it is,' Sean said.

I didn't, but said nothing. The way he was, he mightn't have heard me anyway.

'The nominations in January must have been the final straw for her,' he continued. 'It was the day following the announcement, on the 29th of January, that she left that note in her room and went to the river. Though at least she wasn't around to see him winning, and the press coverage. All that glory, after what he did to my daughter. After what he did to my girl. I didn't know what the note meant until he won, when I heard his acceptance speech. He was everywhere on the telly and radio for weeks and the clip from the speech was played over and over again and eventually I realised what Deirdre meant by the academy. If he hadn't won, I might never have copped on.'

I had an inkling now who Sean was talking about, but it was so unimaginable, so unspeakable, that I needed to hear it from him.

'Can you say his name, Sean? Can you say the name of the man you think it is?'

'I don't *think*. I *know*. It was Jeremy Gill,' he said.

Biting my lip, I laid my pen on the table and sat back in my seat. Jeremy Gill, the most successful film-maker Ireland had ever produced, was an icon, a national hero. There were a few critically acclaimed Irish film directors, and one or two Oscars here and there, but he was in a different league, a Spielberg kind of league. Gill's films made hundreds of millions of dollars. And they weren't just popular, they were good. Last March, *Seeing Things* had won five Oscars, including Best Director and Best Picture. After all that, and the viral BBC chat show appearance, and the hour-long stateside television special, and the round of homecoming radio and TV interviews, and the front page newspaper and magazine photos, everyone in Ireland knew who he was. The pool of A-list celebrities is small in Ireland, and Gill was that rare thing: an enormous talent, and a massive international commercial success, who retained an appetite for frequent appearances on Irish TV and radio. People liked that he hadn't forgotten where he came from. People liked Gill. I liked him.

I had been holding my breath. I sat forward again and wrote 'J Gill?' in my notebook, though it wasn't a name I was likely to forget, and drew a box around it. Then I asked if I could photograph the suicide note with my phone. Sean blanched, but agreed. When I had finished, I gave back the note and fixed my eyes on him.

'That's some allegation, Sean Carney,' I said. 'Can you back it up?'

'Are you saying you don't believe me?' he asked, too loudly.

'Shhh, keep your voice down, we're in a public place and we have to be careful. Only for the weather, we wouldn't be having this conversation here at all. I'm not saying I don't believe you.

I don't know enough to say anything at this stage. But I need you to explain why you believe it's him, and what the emergency is.'

'Well, her note, for one thing. Deirdre wrote about the academy, and all he was doing after he got the Oscars was thanking the academy, in his acceptance speech and on every chat show after. The academy this and the academy that.'

'You think she was talking about the Academy of Motion Pictures. But, from what you tell me, Deirdre was dead a couple of months before he won.'

'Yes. But, like I said, she knew about the nominations – it was the day after they were announced that she left us.'

'Right. And you're convinced it was *the* Academy Deirdre was talking about. Not a school of some kind, even a stage school?' I said.

He shook his head.

'No? Okay, I get that, But, Sean, you've told me nothing about how she might have met him, let alone anything else.'

'I know, I know. I haven't that much to go on. But it all goes back to the film stuff she did. You know how in Transition Year they're encouraged to branch out and choose projects to work on that they're interested in as a future career, before they start working for the Leaving Cert and all that. Deirdre chose films, film studies, that sort of thing, and got into the Film Festival doing work experience. The festival was held in October back then. I know she was involved in helping them to choose short films for something to do with the schools' part of the festival – she was coming home with stacks of videos to watch. And she was raving about a short film by a fella from Dublin called, well, it was him, Gill ...'

He picked up his whiskey glass, but didn't drink from it, and put it back down.

'She kept talking about him, about how he was definitely going to win a prize. And he did – he won three. It meant nothing to me, but our Deirdre was over the moon about it. She said it was the first time someone had won the audience award, the best Irish and the best International short film. And, if you remember, he was nominated for the best short film in the Oscars after – he didn't win, but it got him noticed.'

I remembered. Fifteen years ago I was twenty-two, working as a trainee solicitor by day. What Sean didn't know was that I was also working for the festival as a volunteer, evenings and at the weekend, in return for a season ticket. I didn't meet Jeremy Gill, though. Never even saw him, except on stage. And Sean seemed to have no evidence that Deirdre had met him either. The probability was that she hadn't. Even in 1998, Cork Film Festival was careful to ensure that schoolkids in on work experience or attending the education programme screenings were well chaperoned, by their own teachers usually, and that they'd gone home long before the late nights in the Festival Club at Cork Opera House.

'Sean, along with thousands of others, Deirdre and Jeremy Gill were both at the same film festival. But, in all likelihood, they never even met.'

'They met, they had to have met. That's what I'm trying to tell you. He was a man of the world by then, working in Dublin, and the short films were a sideline for him.'

'He was in advertising, very successfully, as far as I know,' I said. 'But …'

'He was about thirty or more when he made the short film that got him on the road to where he is now. I can't remember the name of it.'

'*Another Bad Day at the Office*,' I said. 'And you think they met because …?'

'I don't know,' Sean said. 'I don't know how they met, all right? I just know that my wife Ann took Deirdre and her friend, Jessica Murphy from her class at school, to the closing night at the Opera House, the prize-giving and the closing film.'

He pointed at my notebook. I wrote down Jessica's name and other scant details. Cork Film Festival. 1998. Short films. School/education prog. Oscar noms. January. Deirdre Carney. 29th Jan 2013. Suicide.

'She must have met Gill during the festival or in the Opera House, maybe even on the stairs, or something,' Sean said. 'Ann remembers that she went to the toilet at one stage on her own. Ann didn't think to go with her, thought she was safe. You'd think at fifteen, in a public place like that …'

'So are you saying that something happened that night?' I asked.

'No, no, I don't think so. But some time during the festival, either that night or some other time, he saw her, targeted her. He was way too clever to do anything then – but he met her after-wards. Trust me. She changed after the festival, got more distant from us, and from her school pals. Was growing up, we thought … And then we knew that something serious had happened. Ann first. And the blood ... on the sheets ... and the bruises. That was the 12th of December 1998, nearly two months after the festival, a few weeks after her sixteenth birthday. A Saturday night, Sunday, it was, when Ann ... But we never knew who it was.'

Sean stopped.

'She never said. Never would. But I know now. I know it was him.'

'Okay,' I said. 'And the emergency?'

'It's what I read in the *Echo* today. That he's coming back to Cork, next week. For the Film Festival,' Sean said. 'I want to make sure the bastard doesn't do it again.'

2

'So, what do you think?' Sean asked.

It was tenuous, at very best, is what I thought. Sean had a broken heart and was searching for answers: the 'emergency' was no more than a poignant attempt to atone for not being able to save his daughter. I had seen it before, relatives replaying the incomprehensible so often that insignificant occurrences garnered meanings invisible to outsiders. And, after a while, two and two no longer added up to four. I knew that what Sean was suggesting *could* have happened. Anything was possible. But, with a deceased complainant, and no evidence whatsoever, this allegation looked like a non-starter in every way.

And now wasn't the time to tell Sean any of that. His only daughter was dead by suicide. He had to wake up to that knowledge, and to her absence, every single day. I couldn't reject him straight away, not after the effort he'd made to find me, though I knew that there was little or nothing I could do.

But I could respect him, and respecting him meant giving what he had told me the time and the consideration it deserved. I would send him home to his wife and, later, when he was rested, I'd let him down gently. There would be no need to mention the probability that Jeremy Gill was completely innocent. I reckoned that, deep down, Sean knew that already.

'I'll need to do a bit of thinking about this,' I said. 'Give me your home and mobile numbers and I'll give you a ring to arrange a meeting as soon as I know more. One thing I forgot to ask, does your wife – Ann is it? Does she know you're here?'

'She does, but she thinks that there's nothing you can do. She thinks I'm only upsetting myself more. She says that whatever I do, I can't bring her back.'

Sean paused.

'I know that too,' he said.

I couldn't think what to say in response, so I asked him for his phone number again. Then I shepherded him out the door, checking how he was getting home, and was he all right. Goodbyes take a long time in Cork.

I walked up the hill and into the gale, though at least the rain had lightened. A few minutes later I turned off the wind tunnel street into a sheltered lane lined with with tiny cottages. At the end of the lane stood a high stone wall with a dark grey door. My door. Inside, there was a yard with a narrow path to a second door, and inside that, a winding staircase that emerged in an open loft with an oak floor and views on all sides. Whenever I hear myself complaining, I remember this place, a contemporary tower house, midway between Elizabeth Fort and Cat Fort. I had bought the small vacant site and gone through the exhausting design, planning and building process, having seen the potential of the old stone wall and the privacy it afforded. Almost landlocked, with pedestrian access only, even at the height of the Celtic Tiger, Ireland's doomed property bubble, the site had had had limited appeal. Nevertheless, on my income, I couldn't have afforded the purchase and build except for the questionable banking practices of the Tiger times, where the normal salary multiplier was a tiresome detail, easily overcome by obligingly inventive bankers and brokers. So it had been, and so it was no longer. Now, my mortgage was a stretch, but doable, and I still had my safe place, even after the carnage of the crash. I was grateful for it every day.

And 'Rapunzel' always was my favourite fairy story.

I hung my coat on the bannister to dry, and kicked off my shoes. I unzipped my damp skirt and hung it beside the coat, but my tights were beyond saving. I rolled them down over my thighs and calves, packed them into a soggy ball, and threw them down the stairs. They landed on the stone floor below, close enough to the door to remind me to bin them the next day. I propped my shoes at each side of the top step, letting them take their chances. Another night, I might have stuffed them with paper and massaged them back to health.

I crossed the room slowly, using only the yellow glow of the city to light my way. I took down *Pieces of the Sky*, moved the needle to track 4, and lay down on the sofa, pulling my burnt orange and buttermilk Foxford wool blanket over me.

When 'Boulder to Birmingham' finished, I let the album play on, Emmylou's voice pure and clear like a cooling balm.

After a time, I stood, and switched on a lamp. I took out the photo that Sean Carney had given me, laid it on the kitchen worktop and glanced at it, quickly at first. Deirdre had dark hair and brows, pale skin, red lips and lively, mischievous eyes. Sean had said that we looked alike. I could see what he meant: her colouring, her hair, her blue eyes were the same general area as me, except Deirdre was stunning.

And now she was dead. And that was a tragedy. And there was nothing I, or her parents, or anyone else could do about it.

Though there was food in the fridge, my appetite had disappeared around the time Sean Carney had mentioned his daughter's body washing up in Blackrock. But as I filled the kettle, and willed myself to nibble at a snack of cheese and oatcakes, I kept coming back to look at the photo, wondering how long it would take before I went downstairs, to where I knew there was a stack of old Film Festival catalogues.

Ten minutes later, I was crawling on the floor of my study, trying to find 1998. And there it was. I ran my finger through the index and turned to page 67: *Another Bad Day at the Office*, a twenty-four-minute short film by Jeremy Gill. Also produced by Jeremy Gill and a production company called Gill/Direct Productions. Seemed like a one-man show.

I got up off the floor, rolled my chair into position, flicked on my desktop and did an online company search on Gill/Direct Productions. The company status was normal, which meant that he'd kept filing accounts and making annual returns on it all these years. The directors were listed as Jeremy Gill, and a trust company called ProGill Trust, which showed up, along with Gill, as director of a raft of other companies. I forced myself to stop after clicking through to the twentieth company. Searches like these are addictive but they eat time, and to no end, in this case. It was of zero consequence that Gill had a web of investment vehicles. That was how the film business worked. Applying for government incentives and taking advantage of tax avoidance schemes meant that there was usually at least one company for each project, and often more. The only *slightly* odd thing was there were no women listed anywhere on any of the documents. I googled details of his agent, lawyer and business managers: all male. And in the 'About Us' section of jeremygillproductions. com, there were no women listed either. Maybe Jeremy didn't like working with women. Or maybe women didn't like working with Jeremy. There was nothing much to any of it, but I opened a Sean Carney file on my desktop anyway and saved the results of the search into it.

Next, I did a search of the *Irish Examiner* archive for Cork Film Festival 1998. I found a large colour shot of Jeremy, holding his three trophies. He was smiling, dark hair tied in a ponytail, brown eyes. I had forgotten about the teeth, the slightly crooked, slightly off-white Irish teeth, that he'd subsequently had fixed to Hollywood dayglo perfection. I reckoned they'd looked better before he'd shelled out for the replacements, but I was probably in a minority. I saved the photo and the accompanying article into the Carney file.

Then, I read the Wikipedia entry on Gill. There was a piece about his education at UCD in the late 1970s, how he had been a classmate of the writer Christopher Dalton, who had scripted two of Gill's early features, though they hadn't worked together after that. Dalton had gone on to be a successful literary novelist. I had a quick read of his Wikipedia page. It looked like he hadn't allowed any of his later works to be adapted as films. He might have had his fill: some liked the collaborative process of film-making, some didn't.

There were various references to Gill's stellar career in advertising, working for Thomson AdGroup, and footnotes on a few of the campaigns he'd been involved in.

But, in relation to his personal life, there was remarkably little. He had never married. A legendary workaholic bachelor, Gill was famous for taking his mammy to premieres. In fact, now that I thought about it, I had always assumed he was gay. I copied the Wikipedia entry into my file and googled 'Jeremy Gill gay' but nothing of significance came up, except that, as with a lot of people in show business, there were unsubstantiated rumours about his sexuality. If anything, there seemed to be less about Gill than others. Maybe it didn't matter as much if you were a gay director, maybe people were less interested. I googled 'Jeremy Gill love life'. There were thousands of photos of him with myriad different actresses, and articles where they both protested that they were 'just good friends'. Yet the 'friendships' seemed to last only as long as the films they were promoting and, even from a distance of 8,000 miles, or however far LA was from Cork, they looked like fake dates. And all of this information was utterly irrelevant to Deirdre Carney and her unfortunate life and death.

Nevertheless, I went into IMDb and scrolled through Gill's entry, refreshing my memory on his film-making history. He had made a lot of good films, across various genres, since his time in Cork in 1998, and I had seen all of them, mostly on the big screen.

Though I hadn't seen the prize-winning short film for years. I checked the credits and cast list on IMDb – no names I recognised, apart from Jeremy Gill. He had played the male lead himself, as well as directing, and had used various other unknown actors, I guessed, for budget reasons. They were probably people he worked with or friends of his. There was a teenage girl in it, too. According to IMDb, her name was Rhona Macbride. She was talented, from what I remembered, and I would've put money on her having a career as an actress but she hadn't, or at least I hadn't heard of her. She didn't have a profile on IMDb, and showed up as a cast member on just that one film. I googled her. There were a few Rhona and Rona McBrides, and several Rhonda Macbrides, but no Rhona with that spelling of Macbride. She'd be over thirty by now. Maybe she'd married and taken her husband's name.

I found the short film on YouTube. *Another Bad Day at the Office* told the story of a world-weary, overworked businessman, with a failing career, who develops a platonic friendship with a fifteen-year-old girl he meets in a park while she's on her school holidays. The joke of the film, and probably what appealed so much to young viewers like Deirdre Carney, is that the girl, played by Rhona Macbride, is much more mature than the Gill character. She becomes his counsellor and business adviser and, as a result, he turns around his flagging career and becomes hugely successful. Until the girl goes back to school after the holidays, when he starts to flounder again and has 'another bad day at the office'. The film was brilliantly made, with a light touch and extraordinary comic timing.

And, with the benefit of hindsight, was the storyline just a little creepy? Maybe. Though nobody had thought so at the time. Even if it was, it wasn't evidence of anything. Still, I would talk to the Film Festival about their Child Protection arrangements. I wouldn't mention Jeremy Gill by name but I'd remind them that the festival could, and should, take appropriate precautions, as the law required. It had policies in place, I knew, but it might be a comfort to Sean Carney to hear that I had double-checked.

It was time for bed, long since. I logged out and picked up the 1998 catalogue again, intending to put it back in the pile on the floor. Before I did, I turned to the Schools section of the catalogue to see the selection of films Deirdre and her schoolmates would have seen, though I knew already that one of them was Gill's film.

But, underneath the Schools listing for *Another Bad Day at the Office* was a photograph of Deirdre Carney and a piece of text which read:

Another Bad Day at the Office was championed by youth jury member Deirdre Carney from Transition Year at St Finbarr's Catholic University School.

If Deirdre had been on the youth jury, there was a chance that Gill had met her during the festival, especially as she had 'championed' his film. At the very least, he would have received a copy of the catalogue. And, if he had the catalogue, it was inconceivable that he wouldn't have checked every mention of himself in it.

Even if they hadn't met during the festival, Gill would've had to have known Deirdre's face and name.

And where she went to school.

3

I crawled out of bed and into the shower. I had spent much of the night awake, thinking about what Sean Carney had said and what I should or shouldn't do with the feeling I had that he might be right about Jeremy Gill. But even if Sean *was* right, from a legal point of view, pursuing Gill made no sense. The wisest thing I could do would be to tell Sean that I wouldn't be able to help. His daughter was dead: case closed. I would follow up with the Film Festival, make sure their procedures were fit for purpose. Leave it at that. Yet, even as I was thinking it, I knew that I couldn't let it drop. And that it wasn't something I could let sit till the following week, not with the festival starting on Sunday. Besides, it could do no harm to investigate a little, surely? To reassure myself there was nothing to it?

I combed through my wardrobe. I rarely work weekends, but this wasn't a normal Saturday. I might be meeting Sean at some point, who was a sort of client, so I was going to have to wear something half decent. I chose a grey wool dress, with wool tights in a darker grey, and pulled on my knee-high flat black leather boots. I twisted my hair into a messy bun, rubbed tinted moisturiser on my face and looked at myself in the mirror. Black circles around my eyes. Skin the colour of sour milk. Something that might turn into a spot on my chin. The tinted moisturiser wasn't going to be enough. Yawning, I sat at my dressing table and clicked open my Mac foundation. On the way upstairs, I slid silver hoops into my earlobes.

I revived a little after a bowl of Flahavan's organic porridge, made with milk, and a mug of Cork Coffee Roasters' Morning Growler blend. Over breakfast, I messaged my friend Alice Chambers, the Film Festival manager, to say that I needed to see her this morning and would it be okay if I called into the office around nine?

Alice replied: 'if u must!!! don't expect much of a welcome!'

I laughed, and replied 'short visit, will bring u capp.'

'Okay,' replied Alice.

With the Film Festival starting the next day, Alice was working at full throttle and probably getting by on four hours' sleep, but her usual cappuccino would win me a five-minute window. I checked the local news online. For once, Cork had had a reprieve. The centre of the storm had bypassed the city, and the rain hadn't been as bad as expected. But the air was laden with moisture still, and bloated grey clouds crouched barely clear of the rooftops.

Though water wasn't spilling from the sky at that exact moment, it would, and soon.

I pulled on my candy-pink wool coat, then took it off again. I should never have bought it: most of my clothes are in dark colours, and anything bright feels scratchy and wrong. I still have the coat, though. Can't bring myself to throw it out, or take it to a charity shop, and not just because I bought it in Brown Thomas and because it cost the best part of my Visa limit for the month.

I felt last night's raincoat. More me. Charcoal grey. And dry. Nearly. I wound a long grey and black striped wool scarf around my neck and reached for my bag and phone just as it pinged.

'Where have you been lately?'

'Oh God,' I said.

It was a message from my good friend and sometime personal trainer Davy Keenan. And I knew why he was calling.

'Busy, sorry, talk soon :-),' I replied, hoping it would be enough to hold him off.

It wasn't. I was walking out the gate when the phone rang.

'Don't you know it's Saturday?' I said.

'Hello, stranger,' Davy said. 'You're up early. How's your fitness plan going?'

'It's not, Davy, okay, it's just not. This is harassment,' I said. 'Have you nothing better to be doing?'

Davy laughed.

'I'm concerned for you, Finn, that's all it is.'

'Yeah, right. Or has one of your yummy mummies cancelled on you?'

'Naw,' Davy said. 'Client due in at nine, very un-yummy daddy, in fact. Just thought I'd check in on you. When you coming to see me?'

'Soon, Davy,' I said. 'I'll call you this week, make an appointment, promise, okay?'

'I'll hold you to that.'

I could hear a note of smugness in his voice that I decided to ignore.

'Bye,' I said and rang off before he had a chance to say anything else.

I had first met Davy seven years ago when he had been a client of mine, charged with drink driving and cocaine possession offences. After one of Davy's later court appearances, I had bought him a coffee and had a long talk with him. I'd explained how close he'd come to prison and we'd talked about him going into rehab. At the time, I knew he was humouring me in talking about it, but I told him that if he needed my help getting a place in a programme in the future, I'd do what I could. It took another year and a half, but he came back to me for a referral letter and I made a few calls for him. Later, after he came out of treatment and retrained, I gave him legal advice and organised the lease on his gym space.

Davy applied the same devotion to sobriety and work as he had in the past to getting wasted. His gym was a success. Even during the recession he'd expanded and he seemed to have a knack for sales and pricing. I never asked how he'd acquired such expertise, though I had a fair idea. He'd given me a voucher for three personal training sessions as a gift and I had felt obliged to go, after numerous calls from him, with a plan to sustain a minor injury during session one and never to return. I'd reckoned that I was as fit as I needed to be. I walked most places, most of the time, and I was tallish; not skinny, admittedly, but not over-weight by any normal standard.

It didn't matter, apparently. Davy had delivered a terrifying lecture on weight-bearing exercise, muscle loss and osteopor-osis. 'Use it or lose it in your thirties,' he'd said and signed me up for a series of classes and training sessions. He emphasised fitness and strength rather than weight loss but, almost despite myself, I had dropped a dress size in a year and was fitter than I'd ever been. Which entitled me to take a break, I'd thought, and, to my surprise, Davy had agreed. But he was back on my case again, and I knew it was only a matter of time before I would have go back to the gym. I would, definitely, but not just yet.

I walked down Barrack Street, turning right at the bottom to go over the Nano Nagle footbridge. The river was mud brown and fat with flood, broken tree limbs rushing by, reminders of how bad the storm had been. The day was dull and quiet, nothing unusual for November. Except that it was a Saturday, and I was on my way into town to start an unofficial investigation into an Oscar-winning film director. If I stopped to think about how unusual that was I might come up with other words, like deluded, misguided and foolish. I didn't stop.

The Film Festival office occupied the upper storeys of a plush interiors shop on Emmett Place, opposite the red-brick Crawford

Art Gallery. The festival, Ireland's oldest, has been running annually since 1956, and prides itself on its commitment to short films. Winning one of the main shorts prizes at Cork is prestigious and has the added bonus of getting the film on to the Oscar longlist. I had been a board member for three years. Together with the rest of the directors, I had a duty to supervise the festival's management and operation on behalf of the Arts Council and the local authority. The role is unpaid and, at times, the commitment can be considerable. As a result, more often than not, board members are drawn from film fans and regular attendees at the festival.

I climbed the stairs. Open plan, the main room was filled with bleary-eyed, worried-looking people, the same as every year: last-minute hitches, difficult guests, organised chaos and a sense of impending doom that dissipated as soon as the opening film was under way. Holding the place together for the last decade was Alice Chambers, a tiny woman with stylishly cropped grey hair, Clark Kent glasses and a work ethic that put most of the lawyers I knew to shame.

'Gimme that fast!' Alice said. 'I'm gasping.'

She grabbed the coffee from me.

'You're welcome, Alice,' I said.

'Shut up, you big eejit, and come into my room for a sec, if you can find a space.'

Alice's office was piled high with stacks of boxes and reams of paper. With some difficulty, the two of us managed to get in the door and close it behind us.

'Now,' Alice said. 'What's so urgent?'

I had to be careful. I needed to keep what Sean had told me confidential, even if he might have been happy if I'd spread it to the four winds and ruined Gill's reputation.

'I was lying in bed last night, Alice, and it came to me that it's a couple of years since I reviewed the festival's child protection policy. I just wanted to make sure that everything's still going all right. A bit of a pain, I know, but could you run through it with me briefly, how you're applying it, what you're doing this year, etc.'

'It's the day before the festival. And you're coming to me with *this*? Jesus, as if I haven't enough to be at.'

She paused.

'But I know you'll sit there and I'll never get fucking rid of you unless I ...'

She had a thousand things to do. I was relying on her trademark conscientiousness. Along with the fact that I was asking as a member of the board of directors.

'Okay, okay,' she said. 'I need this like a turkey needs Christmas, but here goes.'

She summarised the policy from memory. 'No under-eighteens at education screenings or workshops unless accompanied by enough responsible adults to ensure appropriate safety and supervision. No festival staff on their own with students at any time. Any under-eighteen guests to be chaperoned. And all staff and volunteers had been taken through the rules, along with their Health and Safety training, a week before the festival. Don't worry, I'm on it.'

'Sounds like you are,' I said. 'Knew you would be. Just one of those 3 a.m. thoughts, sure you know, yourself.'

I was reassured, but needed to move the conversation on to Gill without arousing Alice's suspicions. Not an easy thing to do. She's one of the smartest people I know.

'Anything else?' Alice asked. 'Do you want to check that we have enough loo roll? Or paper clips? How about fucking paper clips?'

I laughed.

'I'll be back to you about the paper clips tomorrow so, just before the opening film. Seriously, though, thanks for that, you've set my mind at rest. I have to go into work for a while this morning so I thought I'd drop in now, get it out of the way.'

I made as if to get out of my chair, but sat down again.

'Hey, the festival made the paper yesterday I see. Jeremy Gill's visit.'

'Yeah, it's great,' Alice said. 'All the Gill events are sold out, hope you have your tickets.'

'Think so. What's his schedule like while he's here?'

'Busy. Arriving at the airport on Tuesday afternoon, I'm going to meet him, then to City Hall, meet Lord Mayor, then Opera House for reception with sponsors and funders, usual rent-a-crowd wine-guzzling liggers *not* invited, though we can make an exception for you,' she said, and smiled angelically at me.

'Too kind,' I said.

Alice knew that I don't touch alcohol, though she didn't know the reason.

'Then he's on stage at 7 p.m., says hello to audience, quick chat about the new movie with yours truly, then roll movie and I take Jeremy and entourage to Paradiso, for fine food and glug

glug, unless he's off the drink as well. God, I hope not. He's gone vegan, apparently. I had to tell Paradiso. No butter or cream for Jeremy. They said they'd put on some extra options for him.'

'Where will he be staying?'

'Muskerry Castle,' Alice said.

'Needless to say.'

Muskerry Castle is Cork's finest hotel. Backing on to an oak wood and overlooking the Lee valley, with a top tier golf course, and private salmon and trout fishing, it is world famous for its legendary hospitality.

'He's been before, apparently. Loves it. I'd love it too, if I could afford it. But he offered to pay his own bill, in fairness to him, though Muskerry agreed to sponsor us anyway so we didn't have to argue about it. Anyway, the next day at noon, he'll be doing a public interview with Tiernan McDevitt, again in the Opera House and, unbelievably for a Wednesday in the middle of the day, that's sold out too. And then in the afternoon a workshop with film students and young film-makers. End of official programme. He's booked to stay on the Wednesday night in the Castle again but his assistant said he might go to Dublin to visit the mammy instead so they're not sure yet.'

Film students and young film-makers.

'That's a bit of a coup, him doing the workshop, isn't it? How did you swing it?'

'He was the one who suggested it, wants to give back to the city and the festival. He's really appreciative that ours was the first award he ever got. We wouldn't have dared to hope for such commitment. I mean, can you imagine the opportunity it'll be for those kids? It's just amazing. Fair fucks to him, is all I can say.'

He was the one who suggested it.

'Tell me more,' I said.

'Not much more to tell. It came in an email. Limited numbers. No more than twenty film students, wants an even gender balance and has a special interest in film fans from local secondary schools. So generous of him, no sign of any ego at all so far. I was blown away. We all were.'

'Wow. Fantastic,' I said.

Young people, young girls, and Jeremy Gill. Potentially hazardous? Or not? But I needed to make sure it was safe for those kids or I'd never sleep again.

'Hey listen, Alice,' I said. 'Any chance I could go along to the workshop, maybe as some sort of steward or board of directors' representative or something? You know I'm a big fan, I'd give anything to be there and you're going to need some responsible adults, right, remember our child protection chat earlier? Not that there's any concern or anything but still, huh, what do you say?'

'You're shameless, you know that?' Alice said, getting up from her desk. 'Yeah. All right, I'll sort it for you. And actually having a board representative there is a good idea. Now please get out of my office or we will have no Film Festival to put on.'

'I'll buy you a drink,' I said.

'Just one?' she said, and pushed me out the door.

Running down the stairs, I felt guilty about being less than honest with Alice. At least, I thought it was guilt, and I thought it was about Alice. But standing outside on the street, I shivered, though I wasn't cold. I told myself that whatever happened, things were about to get interesting, and that that was good.

And then I thought about the Chinese curse. And started walking. And tried to stop thinking for a while.

4

I headed in the direction of my office. I needed to check my diary for the upcoming week and do enough to clear Tuesday afternoon and Wednesday. After what I'd heard from Alice, I intended keeping a close eye on Jeremy Gill while he was in town. And I wanted to arrange another meeting with Sean Carney, and to meet his wife Ann.

There was no time to waste, but I did anyway. Crossing Patrick Street, I cut down Marlboro Street as far as Liam Russell's bookshop and circled back on to Princes Street. I thought about the mix of optimism and bravery and foolishness that had led people to settle and build and trade in this damp place. I thought about how, every so often, the water rose fast from the marsh beneath the streets and, just as fast, drained away leaving ruin in its wake. And I thought about the city's narrow escape overnight, about how it was luck, and nothing else, that had saved it.

I swung past the grand cast-iron gates, and into the English Market, busy already, though it was not yet ten, with the usual weekend foodie crowd stocking up on provisions for their Saturday night dinner parties. Taking a left at the fountain, I passed the wooden steps to the Farmgate restaurant on the balcony, went through the arch, and got an Americano with milk from Mary Rose.

I was at 17–19 MacSwiney Street two minutes later. The flood barrier was still in place on the lower door, but there were lights on in the reception area. I walked up the front steps to the main entrance. At this hour on a Saturday, it could only be one person, Gabriel McGrath, founder and managing partner of the mainly commercial law firm of McGrath Lynch Cleary. Housed in a trio of converted eighteenth-century town houses, MLC had seven partners and fourteen associate solicitors, including me. I had worked there since being recruited by Gabriel as a trainee in the late nineties. I would always be grateful to him for taking a risk on me. I didn't fit at MLC, I knew it and he knew it. But I was adaptable and discreet, useful for doing the messy but necessary work the other solicitors didn't want to do. The partner's daughter caught with twenty-seven Ecstasy tablets. The valued secretary's brother fallen from improperly guarded scaffolding after drinking three cans of cider at lunchtime. The corporate client with marital problems on account of his inability to keep his hands off any woman under eighty. None of my workload conformed to the glossy image MLC tried to project, which didn't bother me one little bit. The job pays the bills and some days are better than others.

I met Gabriel as I was going up the stairs.

'You're in bright and early,' I said.

Gabriel was *always* in bright and early. Late fifties, and permanently anxious, he worked a lot harder than he needed to at this stage of his career.

'No earlier than usual, Finola, as well you know. I've been in since half seven, wanted to get a bit of a head start on next week and to check on the flood situation, but it's all grand, thanks be to God.'

That was another thing about Gabriel. He was always thanking God for things that, as far as I could see, wouldn't have been a problem if God had been a bit more thoughtful in the first place. But I didn't say that, or that I didn't believe in God; not Gabriel's traditional Irish Catholic version anyway.

'What brings you in on a Saturday?'

'New client late yesterday evening, after everyone else had gone home,' I said.

'What kind of work?'

'Hand-holding. Advice. That kind of thing.'

'Hmmm. Right,' Gabriel said. 'Don't waste too much time on it now. You know that you're a valued employee and that you play an, em, important role for us but, of course, your fee income is, em, a concern, all the same, and, er, well, you know yourself.'

'I know, Gabriel, I do,' I said.

'Don't worry. I'm all over it,' I added, knowing that nothing would really change, that I'd keep getting the time-consuming, low-paying, miscellaneous work I always got and that Gabriel knew that too. But at the next partners' meeting he'd be able to say that he'd had a word, and I would go back to the bottom of the agenda for another while. Hopefully. I knew that I wasn't popular with some of the other partners, Dermot Lyons in particular. I made a point of avoiding him, though I kept a low profile at work generally.

'Good girl,' Gabriel said.

I had stopped cringing at the 'good girl' comments from Gabriel a long time ago. He didn't mean to patronise, and wouldn't have understood if I'd complained. Did that make me a bad feminist? The short answer was yes. But some day I'd crack and sit him down and give him a comprehensive education in gender politics.

Gabriel waved goodbye, and took off at speed. I didn't need to ask where he was going. His migraine-inducing yellow golf jumper gave me all the information I needed. I watched him go, short legs working at the double to keep up his pace. Half man, half whippet, he never walked when he could run.

I had family law district court on Monday, so there was no chance of putting that off. But by noon I had phoned my clients with Tuesday and Wednesday appointments and rescheduled them for later in the week. Next, I reviewed the information I'd gathered last night, did a short note of my meeting with Sean Carney, and rang and arranged to call out to their house to see him and Ann at half past one.

I had time to spare so I worked through my inbox and did some prep on my Monday caseload. I glanced out the window at the blue-grey slate of the rooftops. It isn't Cork's best view. It might even be one of the worst. The city centre is in a hollow. You have to climb the streeted heights on either side to get the views, go northside for the full panorama. My office would be claustrophobic if it weren't for the light. It might have something to do with the proximity of water, the double river, the enormous harbour beyond, but no two hours look, or feel, the same. I've thought about leaving this town, thought about it often. And then I walk around a corner, and see something I see every day made new against the sky, and the notion of living anywhere else loses purchase.

Turning back to my desk, I did a last run through my pending work, and dictated instructions for Tina Daly, my secretary of six years. Twenty-eight, whip smart and totally reliable, but quirky enough to want to stay working for me rather than one of the other solicitors, she had been bored rigid during the short time she had spent in the Commercial Department. Like me, Tina liked variety.

There was just enough time for me to have lunch before going to the Carney house. I thought about picking up a salad and coffee from the Rocket Man, but I needed time to think, and the trouble with Cork was that I'd be bound to bump into someone I knew, either there or on the walk over. I decided to go home and reheat the remains of the butternut squash soup I'd made during the week. As I trekked up the hill, every step I took told me that I had no space in my head, or my life, for the Carneys and their tragic story, and that I should cancel the appointment, say what I had to say on the phone, and not go to see them at all.

I went anyway. I told myself it was courtesy. Truthfully, though, I wanted to know more. About Jeremy Gill? Sure. But mostly I wanted to know about Deirdre, about how she had come to decide that dying was better than living.

The house in Turners Cross was a modest semi-detached two-storey, sixty or seventy years old, with a Ford Focus parked outside. I rang the bell. Within seconds, Sean Carney opened the door.

'Thanks for coming, Miss Fitzpatrick, Finola, thanks a million. You don't know how much it means.'

'Call me Finn, Sean,' I said, 'Only my boss calls me Finola.'

The front room was spotless, though it was less of a living space and more of a shrine, with photographs of Deirdre on every wall and surface. There she was, making her communion, being presented with a medal for some kind of sporting event, baby and toddler photos, but none of her as an adult, nothing that showed her beyond mid-teens.

They wanted to remember the good times.

'I don't know where herself has got to, give me a minute,' Sean said.

As he was getting up to look, the door opened and a stern, grey-faced woman came in, carrying a tray. She wore a chunky brown fisherman's-rib wool jumper tucked inside a sludgy tweed skirt. The clothes looked ten, or twenty, years old, and the skirt gaped at the waist. She hadn't always been this thin.

'I thought you might like a cup of tea,' Ann Carney said.

She laid the tray on a small coffee table that Sean had magicked out of some corner without having to be told. I was impressed by the double act, the telepathy of a long marriage. And the Carneys would have had to rely on one another even more than normal, each propping up the other through the agony of watching their only daughter wither and die.

Ann poured tea for the three of us and, with something approaching a glare, offered me a biscuit, which I took, thinking it would be unwise to refuse, despite a lifelong loathing of custard creams. I sipped my tea and waited for Ann to sit. Instead, she walked over to the fireplace and turned around to face me. She scanned me and our eyes met fleetingly. For a second I thought I detected a softness in hers, but it didn't last.

'I didn't want Sean to go and see you,' Ann said. 'I can't see what good will come of us raking through this. Our lovely girl is gone, and there's nothing any of us can do to change it. Sean came up with a notion that that man is the one to blame and that he wanted to warn people about him. But he got short shrift from the guards and the social workers. And he got a warning about defaming a public figure from our family solicitor, Frank Mannix, I'm sure you know him, and Frank is no fool. But that wasn't enough for Sean so he went to you, thinking you could do something. But you can't. I know you can't so there's no point letting on you can.'

She stopped, raised her hand, bones and blue ropy veins protruding from the sparse flesh. She put her palm to her cheek and let out a hollow breath.

'I suppose you're here now,' she said. 'You may as well say your piece.'

She lowered herself slowly into one of the armchairs in front of the fireplace. I had the impression that she was conserving her energy, preparing for round two.

'I think you're right, Ann,' I said. 'I think there's probably very little I can do. But I've double-checked on the Film Festival's child protection policies, in case Sean was right about Gill, and I'll keep a watch on him, insofar as I can, while he's around. It's a short visit, mostly public engagements. As far as I can see, the danger to anyone is minimal.'

I had held back on telling them that Gill had sought out an opportunity for contact with teenagers during the festival, and that my preliminary researches had thrown up more questions than answers. I'm not sure why I did that, though I told myself that I wanted to avoid stoking their fears. The other reason that came to me, that I was trying to keep control of the situation, made no sense unless some part of me knew that I needed to.

'So that's more or less it,' the sensible side of me said, acting as my cue to leave.

But seeing Deirdre's early life chronicled in the room's many photographs had only made me more curious about her.

'There's something else. If I could, I'd like to look through Deirdre's things, her room, if possible, to see if there's anything there that might help. Maybe, I don't know, some kind of evidence ...'

It sounded lame, I knew, and ghoulish. They were bound to say no. Mentally, I was out the door and nearly home. But Sean darted a glance at Ann, then at me, then back at Ann again. To my surprise, she nodded.

'Come with me,' she said.

At the top of the stairs, she pointed at a door but didn't open it. Instead, she turned and descended towards her husband at the foot of the stairs, his hands gripping the bannisters like they were prison bars.

If the sitting room was a shrine, the bedroom was a time capsule, a perfectly preserved late 1990s teenage museum. I flicked through a rack of CDs: Robbie Williams, Oasis and the Fugees. Cuddly toys stacked on the bed, stickers on the furniture; there was even a Furby. Though she'd lived another fifteen years, it was as if Deirdre's life had stopped in 1998.

I batted away the questions that came to me, about why I was spending my Saturday afternoon playing Poirot in a dead woman's room when I could have been doing anything else with my weekend, and sat on the bed. Being a solicitor contains elements of detective work – figuring out what your client isn't telling you, and why, or divining what the opposition is planning to do – but this was different. I was trying to feel my way into who Deirdre had been – and where she might have hidden something that she didn't want her parents to see. She had spent much of her time on earth in this room. She must have left traces of herself, and of the monstrous attack that had marked her short life.

I got up and began to work my way through the wardrobe and the chest of drawers, both of which were emptier than I had expected. Though the surfaces of the room displayed the

trappings of a teenage girl, the interiors held drab and shape-
less adult clothes, the shrouds of the woman Deirdre had
become.

But there was nothing that signified her interest in film and
theatre, and nothing hidden under the bed, around the back of the
wardrobe, or taped underneath the drawers. I got down on my
knees and moved along the wall, feeling the edges of the skirting
board and carpet as I went, checking for a loose section or corner,
but there was none. Deirdre had stripped her physical surround-
ings of every item that might have reminded her of Jeremy Gill.
Was that significant? According to her father, at one stage she
had been his number one fan. Or was that just Sean's version?
Maybe Gill was a lot less important in Deirdre's life than Sean
imagined. Yet she had left a coded message apparently identifying him in her suicide note. If that's what the note meant, she had
to have done it deliberately. And, if it *had* been deliberate, there
was a chance that she had left something here too.

I sat on the floor, in the corner at the end of the bed. In front of
the window, there was a cheap wood veneer desk, where Deirdre
had probably done her schoolwork. The desk had two drawers
that I'd already checked: empty, both inside and underneath. I got
up again. I slid out the top drawer and laid it on the desk. I did the
same with the second drawer, and got down on my knees and felt
around at the back of the opening. There was something wedged
there. I shone my iPhone torch into the aperture. It looked like a
mechanical instruments box. I took the ruler out of the drawer
and used one hand to prise out the box with the ruler and the other
to pull the box from its hiding place. Finally, it came free.

I laid the box on the desk. It was battered, dented and scratched with the initials 'DC' but, more than anything else that I had seen of her so far, it was the box that brought Deirdre to life for me. I could almost hear her laughing in school corridors, almost see her passing notes in class.

From my handbag, I took a roll of small plastic bags that I had brought from home. I tore off two and put a bag on each hand, improvising gloves, not wanting to contaminate or damage whatever I might find.

I opened the box.

5

I had been hoping for something written, a diary or a letter, and not this collection of meaningless detritus. But I told myself that what was inside the box had to have been important to Deirdre, things she had wanted, or needed, to hide away and keep; and that I owed it to her to give the objects my full attention.

There was a blue circular metal badge, about an inch across, with a cartoon-style picture of a white, round-edged boxy desktop computer, broken into two pieces, down the middle, with jagged black-outlined edges along the break. The badge looked old, but it was probably no older than the rest of the objects in the room. Maybe it had been publicity material for some nineties band that Deirdre had liked. But which one? And why keep the badge? What significance did it have for her?

The second object was a name tag, the temporary kind, with a safety pin on the back, given out at seminars. The name 'Deirdre' was handwritten in marker, with a smiley face over the 'i' instead of a dot. It should be easy enough to check if it was in Deirdre's handwriting but, apart from the signature, the name tag was blank.

The final object was a drinks coaster with scalloped edges, bearing the name and logo for Muskerry Castle. Originally white, age had turned it yellow, and the absorbent top was coming away from the plastic underneath. There was a dark ring stain that looked like cola but could have been red wine. *Muskerry Castle.* My thoughts leapt to what Alice Chambers had said: that Jeremy Gill would be staying there during the festival. And that he'd been there before. Which might be a coincidence. I'd have to ask Deirdre's parents if they had had any family visits to the hotel, and if there was a reason Deirdre might have kept the coaster, a special occasion of some kind.

I heard voices, and what sounded like the front door closing. I checked my watch. I had been in the room for almost an hour. I put each object into its own plastic bag, and the box into a fourth. Then I put all of the bags into one and put it, along with my phone, in my handbag and went downstairs.

The fire had been lit, and Ann Carney was sitting in the armchair to the left of the hearth. She was alone but, in the crook of her left arm, she cradled a framed photograph. There was a gap on the mantelpiece. She had taken the picture from there: the communion one. With her right hand, Ann gestured towards the other fireside chair. I sat and she began to talk.

'I wanted to speak to you on my own. I wanted to know why you're here.'

I shouldn't have come.

'Because you asked me,' I said. 'I mean, your husband did.'

But he hadn't. Visiting the house had been my idea.

'You're here in my front room on a Saturday afternoon,' Ann said. 'You've said nothing since you arrived that you couldn't have said in a text message. So you've checked the festival's child protection arrangements? So what. You hardly came here for a clap on the back. You came to see my daughter's bedroom. Why?'

I rubbed a piece of my dress between my thumb and forefinger, avoided her eyes.

'Talk, for God's sake. Talk or go,' she said. 'But I don't think you want to go.'

I looked at her.

'No,' I said. 'I don't.'

'Right,' Ann said. 'We'll start again. Why are you here?'

I had to be careful. She was an intelligent woman, wouldn't be fobbed off easily. I let go of my dress, pressed both my hands into my lap, felt the muscles in my thighs, drew strength from them. Tried to.

'It's got to do with something ...'

My coat was next to me on the arm of the sofa. I could get up and walk out and never look back. Instead, I found myself telling the story I had never wanted to know.

'My mother died.'

My voice sounded strange to me, had the hiss and crackle of an old record.

'My birth mother. I'm adopted,' I added.

'How? How did she die?'

'The river. Like your Deirdre.'

After a silence I continued.

'When I was sixteen my adopted mother told me what had happened.'

'And you came here because?'

'I'm not really sure,' I said.

I was finding it hard to swallow, a lump the size of a peach stone in my throat. Not crying, though. No fucking way was I crying.

And all the time, Ann was watching, assessing me and what I had said. Then she went to the door and spoke into the hallway.

'You can come back now,' she said.

Sean Carney came into the room again and Ann returned to her seat.

'You were right,' Ann said. 'She knows nothing.'

I leapt to my feet.

'What the hell is going on?'

'I'm sorry, Finn,' Sean said. 'We haven't been completely honest with you.'

'We?' Ann Carney said.

'Me,' Sean said. 'I haven't. You see, there was another reason I contacted you. It's about your birth mother. After you, a few years after you, she had another baby she gave up for adoption, and we ... Well, what I'm saying is, our Deirdre was your sister.'

6

For a time, the only sound in the room came from the fireplace, the coal and logs collapsing into ash. Then Sean Carney started talking again.

'We met her, your mother, via the Adoption Society, while she was pregnant with Deirdre. We met her a few times, she wanted that before she'd agree to us. We had long talks with her. She talked about you too, about how much she loved you, wanted the best for you. She said she'd wronged you, but she'd make it up to you. Sadly, well, she, as you know …'

I know.

'She didn't want any contact with Deirdre after the adoption. She kept saying she wanted Deirdre to grow up without baggage. And that she wanted her to have a good life. She said that's what she wanted for both of you.'

'We kept our word, never told,' Ann said. 'And, especially after our lovely girl got sick, we thought we were shielding her from the pain of knowing how her mother had died. Deirdre never knew a thing about that. For all the good it did in the end.'

'She didn't know she had a sister either,' Sean said. 'We regretted that later. Maybe if she'd known you, she'd have seen a way forward for herself, she might have been able to ... I don't know what would have changed, maybe nothing, but we should have tried. That's why, when I found out about Jeremy Gill, I thought about contacting you. I'd kept an eye on you over the years, saw that you'd become a solicitor and I knew you had an in with the Film Festival. When I saw that Gill was due back in town, I was sure that it was meant to be, that I was meant to contact you.'

'I didn't agree,' Ann said. 'We'd made a promise. I didn't want to break it. And then when he told me you were coming to the house, I thought you knew. But then you didn't seem to know anything after all. And I wondered if Sean had the right girl, or if he'd made some mistake. You look a little like Deirdre, though not much. But it's the way you have about you, how you hold yourself. You're her sister all right. There's no doubt in my mind.'

I thought of all the things I should have said when I was halfway down the street; things like if I'd wanted to know more about my mother, I'd have gone looking; and did I fall asleep and wake up in an episode of *EastEnders*; and what gives you the right to lure me out here under false pretences and blow a giant hole in who I thought I was; and how dare you spring on me like it's nothing that I had a sister I knew sweet fuck all about and, by the way, she topped herself too, just like her mother, so my all-new sibling is dead as well; and what am I to do with that; fast-forward through a non-existent relationship, do not pass Go, proceed directly to bereavement, speed mourning, is that what you fucking expect, is that what you want?

I said none of that, muttering instead something about fresh air, pushing my way past Sean – who was he to me now, some kind of relative? – slamming the door behind me, that at least, and talking to myself, walking as fast as I could, putting distance between them and me.

When I came to, I found myself on Pearse Road. For want of a better idea, I took a right on to Connolly. The streets around there are named for the executed signatories to the 1916 proclamation. Too injured to stand, James Connolly was shot by firing squad while strapped to a chair. He had had a daughter called Nora, I remembered.

All around me, it was Saturday afternoon. Cars drove by, and people went in and out of the corner shop, oblivious. I couldn't bear the regularity, the din, of normal life but my legs wouldn't carry me home. I thought about calling for a cab. And then I saw the sign for St Joseph's, a short distance east of the roundabout.

I stumbled down the hill.

'NO WOOD', the sign by the entrance said, 'STONE ONLY'. The cemetery was crammed with it, tall thin pointed slabs and high Celtic crosses, carved angels and obelisks, and decorative ironwork, rusted and vulnerable, footpaths and tracks snaking through the vastness of the place, and silver birch trees, their papery bark peeling like forgotten elegies. Most of the graves were old, recalling lost merchant fortunes and extinct surnames, all tightly packed, money and social status irrelevant now. The only open space was the smooth grassy mound, bordered by a rough stone retaining wall, that held the bodies of the Great Famine dead, fever and cholera victims and those who had starved. In the middle, on its own, was the grave of Father Mathew, who had preached temperance to the Catholic poor; fresh offerings set by his headstone.

I thought about my birth mother then, and how little I knew about her, and how little I had wanted to know. And I thought about my birth father, his name unknown to me. Did Deirdre and I have the same father? There was an age gap of six and a bit years between us. It was unlikely that we did, but not impossible. And I thought about family, and blood, and what that might mean, the thoughts I had spent my life avoiding.

Yet something had shifted for me when I'd met Sean Carney. I hadn't sent him away, hadn't dismissed him. He had led me to Deirdre, to my sister. And she had suffered and died, and that was wrong, about as wrong as anything could be.

I kept walking, tracing and retracing my way among the dead. Time passed and the short grey day dwindled into dusk. I left as the gatekeeper was locking up for the evening.

'You cut it fine, love,' he said. 'Are you not afraid of ghosts?'

He was a squat tank of a man in a tight fleece jacket, a bobble hat and all-white trainers that glowed like fresh snow in the half-light.

'Depends on the ghost,' I said.

On the road outside it came to me that, from what I had seen of the Carneys and of how they had loved her, Deirdre had had a good childhood. And that she would have grown up to have a life, and whether that would have been good or bad, it would have been hers to do with as she wanted, were it not for what had happened to her, either at the hands of Jeremy Gill, or someone else. I couldn't do anything about her life: that was over.

But maybe I could do something about her death.

7

Night had fallen by the time I reached the Carney house again. Ann opened the door before I had a chance to ring the bell.

'I wondered if you'd come back,' she said. 'I'm glad you did. I'm sorry for earlier,' she added. 'We were wrong to dump all that on you.'

'It's okay.'

'Still,' she said, 'it wasn't right. But when Sean gets an idea in his head, he can't let it go. I went along with it for the sake of peace, but I shouldn't have. He's not here, by the way. I sent him down to the pub to watch the soccer match. It was either that, or kill him.'

I laughed.

'I'm not joking,' Ann said.

But, for the first time since we'd met, she was smiling and, for those few seconds, I glimpsed who she had been before.

'Will I make more tea? Or maybe wine? I'm sure there's a bottle somewhere.'

'No,' I said. 'No thanks. A glass of water would be good, though.'

I followed her into the kitchen. A square pine table with four matching chairs took up one corner. In the other, an old television kept watch over two well-worn armchairs. This was where they spent most of their time, I realised, the place they tried to keep going. The front room, with all the photographs, was where they went when the trying got too hard.

Ann was at the sink, letting the tap run, filling a glass, handing it to me. I drank it off quickly and gave it back. She filled it again.

'Come,' she said.

We sat quietly together at the table and I sipped at my water and it felt like I didn't have to say or do anything.

'Is there anything you'd like to ask?' Ann said after a while. 'About the adoption or Deirdre growing up, what she was like? I have the family albums in the top of that high cupboard over there. It would be no bother to take them down and—'

'Thanks,' I said. 'Maybe I'll take you up on that offer some day. I think I have as much as I can handle for now.'

Ann nodded.

'You need time,' she said.

'Time doesn't always heal, in my experience,' I said.

'Nor mine,' she said.

'Especially where a wrong's been done.'

'Yes,' she said. 'People talk about closure. Whatever it means, we never got it. We were left with so many unanswered questions. And now this Jeremy Gill thing that Sean has dreamt up. He's been looking for an excuse to contact you for months. Gill's visit for the festival gave it to him.'

'I don't understand,' I said.

Ann looked at me.

'You don't?' she asked. 'Well, you wouldn't, but Finn, I know him. Whatever he says, this is a lot less about Jeremy Gill and a lot more about Sean wanting to meet you, wanting to have a link to Deirdre to—'

'I thought it was because he wanted to warn people about the danger,' I said.

'It's that too,' Ann said. 'And he has some notion as well that because you're a solicitor you'll find some legal way of punishing Gill. If it *was* Gill. But so what. Whether it's him or someone else, they got away with it, and there's nothing we can do.'

'The thing is,' I said. 'Maybe there is.'

'Look,' I went on. 'If Sean's hunch is right, Gill deserves to pay for what he did. There's no chance of bringing a criminal prosecution. As you know, the DPP is the person who decides whether or not somebody should be charged. Here, because the main witness, Deirdre, is deceased, no prosecution is possible.'

'So that's it, then,' Ann said. 'Same as what the guards told Sean.'

'No,' I said. 'There *is* another possibility. You could pursue a civil case; in other words, a claim for damages for the loss you've suffered, though any case would be extremely difficult for all sorts of reasons. But there's a lower standard of proof in a civil case. It's called "the balance of probabilities", rather than "reasonable doubt", as it would be in a criminal case. That helps.'

'Even so, it would be nearly impossible to bring it home,' I continued. 'To succeed we'd need evidence – a lot more than Deirdre's mention of the Academy in her note.'

'I don't know,' Ann said.

'It wouldn't be easy. We'd have a huge hill to climb in proving the link between Gill and Deirdre's death – proving that he caused it, I mean. It's not that expensive to issue proceedings, though costs climb very quickly. To start, we'd need to have a stateable case.'

'I'm not sure I'd be interested in taking any case, when most likely it's hopeless,' she said. 'Anyway Deirdre never wanted the law involved. And I don't know how this turned into a case against Jeremy Gill. I don't know how it turned into a case at all.'

Ann was right. The impetus was coming from me. And if Sean's main reason for contacting me had been to find an excuse for him to have a link with Deirdre, why did I have to do anything? Any action would, in all likelihood, never get to trial. Gill had enough money to employ an army of lawyers who could tie us up in forensic knots for years to come. But Deirdre Carney was my sister. And she hadn't died of cancer, or in an accident. Someone was to blame.

Still, I couldn't run an investigation, or issue proceedings, without the Carneys. As her parents, they had the necessary legal and moral standing. I was sure Sean would support my efforts. It was Ann I had to convince. I felt myself managing her, knew how it would go. I'd release information in pieces, and guide – manipulate – her towards the decision I wanted. A part of me squirmed at what I was doing; another part, the part I liked less, didn't care.

'First of all,' I said, 'I want you to know that I agree with you. On the face of it, we have little or no chance with this case, legally speaking. But I want to try to find evidence, if it's there, against Jeremy Gill. It's possible that Deirdre was pointing a finger at him with her note, and with the timing of her death in the aftermath of his award nomination. The way I'm thinking is that there have been some civil cases taken in the States by the surviving relatives of people who have committed suicide. It's that kind of action I have in mind. To do that we'd need to show that Deirdre and Gill met, that they had been alone together, at the very least. After that, we'd need as much as we could get. We'd have to find witnesses. And we'd have to show that the deterioration in Deirdre's mental condition started at that time and continued, so that her death was directly linked to the event. I'd have to look at the coroner's report and we'd need psychiatric expertise and reports and—'

Ann interrupted, shaking her head.

'There's a big difference between being alone with someone and rape.'

'You're sure that's what it was?' I asked.

'I'm sure. But to prove it now? I don't know how you could.'

'You're right,' I said. 'We'd need to find something fairly big on Gill to get anywhere. But if we can find that, or a combination of things, we could threaten to take a civil case. Once proceedings are issued, the allegations against him would become public. He won't want that. Bear in mind that his main area of operation is the States. A lawsuit like this isn't common our side of the Atlantic, but it's better known over there. If it got picked up on by social media or news outlets – and it would – Gill would be damaged. Badly damaged. That's why I think that, if there's any truth to the allegations at all, he'll want to settle with us.'

'Settle?' Ann spat out the word. 'You mean pay money? Money couldn't replace Deirdre. *If* there was a case, it would have to be about justice.'

'I know. It's not about money. But money's the only way to get to him. I explained already about the DPP and why the criminal courts' route is closed to us. What I'm saying is that if we want to hit him where it hurts, we have to hit his reputation – and his pocket.'

'You can't just go around making accusations against powerful people like Gill.'

'No,' I said. 'That's not how it would be. I'd be careful. Nobody would know about my personal connection to the case. And we would only issue proceedings when – if – we had the evidence. Which we might never have. Or we might find out that somebody else was responsible. We'd have to be prepared for that to happen.'

'I see what you're saying,' Ann said. 'Though it's not what I expected from you. After what you found out today, I expected you to be …'

'Looking through the photos?' I asked.

'I suppose,' she said.

'Not my style,' I said. 'I wish it was. I might be more well adjusted.'

'You're all right, girl,' Ann said. 'Don't run yourself down.'

The sudden kindness unmoored me. For a moment, all I wanted was to find a dark place and sleep for a week.

The moment passed.

'Ann, this is what I know how to do. It's all I know. In my job, I look for cause and fault and blame, for the thread that runs through things. I mightn't find every answer, but I'll find some, I'm sure I will.'

'I kept a lot of it from Sean,' Ann said. 'How much she'd changed, and it's all a muddle in my head what happened, so long ago, only yesterday too it seems like ...'

'I know you say it's all a muddle,' I said. 'But it's my role to sort through it for you.'

After a long silence, while the tap dripped and the ancient fridge groaned, Ann spoke.

'I'll tell you what, we'll go with it,' she said. 'For a while, anyway. See what progress you make. But I want to make one thing clear before we start. We're not taking any stupid risks. Sean might sell the house to fund a case, but I won't. Does that sound selfish? Maybe it is. But we have to live somewhere, if you'd call it living. The guilt never goes, Finn. I keep thinking, even still, that I could have stopped it if I'd done something, if I'd known what was in her head, if I'd picked up on the signals. Don't say anything, none of the stuff about it not being my fault. It's what people say, and I'm worn out from hearing it, from telling it to myself and not believing. Makes no difference.'

'Tell me what you remember,' I said. 'No matter how silly or insignificant it seems.'

'I'll try,' Ann said. 'Well, somehow, she got involved in the Film Festival, during her Transition Year at school, doing what exactly I'm not sure but it was short films coming out our ears for a long time, I can tell you. It was arranged by her art teacher at the time, Mr O'Donnell, Colm is his first name but he was always Mister in this house. The week of the festival she was off school and was in at the festival all the time. She had a couple of pals that she was close to, Jessica Murphy and Aifric Sheehan. And there were a few boys she was friendly with too, Joey O'Connor was one of them. I don't have addresses for all her friends, though I have Jessica's. And there could be more of them, maybe, from other schools.

'I saw very little of Deirdre during the week of the festival – she was gone in the morning and back in the evenings exhausted, with nothing to report about what she had been up to for the day. I put it down to the teenage thing, kind of let her off to spread her wings a bit. She told me that everything was none of my business and that she was grown up and well able to take care of herself ...'

At that, Ann smiled ruefully and shook her head.

'Try living with that, Finn. You see, at the time Sean was away a lot, driving the lorry, doing as much overtime as he could get away with. We were still thinking of university for Deirdre at that stage. He had a run to Dublin, would collect up there again and would head for Letterkenny after that so he could be away three or four days on the trot and when he came home Deirdre was always on her best behaviour, no cheek for Dad.'

She smiled again.

'Deirdre could wrap him around her little finger. And me too, if I'm honest. She was so precious ...'

I would have to press harder if I was to get any useful information.

'Was there a time before the attack when you noticed anything different, maybe something that made you uneasy?'

'I'm not sure,' Ann said. 'It was gradual, a kind of a moving away from me, from us. I noticed after the Film Festival that she was keeping a secret. She'd got one of those Ready To Go pre-pay phones for her Junior Cert results that September. She hardly used it at the beginning because very few of her friends had mobiles then, they were only just coming in, but Deirdre was an only child, we spoilt her, gave her what she wanted. Anyway, after the festival she was getting a lot of calls or she'd get a call on her mobile and would run out to the hall and take a call on the landline and talk for ages on that. Ringing mobiles was very expensive at that time so she used the landline for longer calls. Sean didn't know the full extent of it, still doesn't, no point. I gave her privacy, though of course I regret that now. But thinking back it could have been Gill, maybe. I answered it one time when she had left it out of her hand, gone to the toilet or something, and it was a male voice but she came back in and grabbed it from me before I had a chance to ... And you asked about something that made me uneasy. I don't suppose it means much but I remember that before and during the festival she was all talk about Jeremy Gill and his short film, and then after it she stopped talking about him. I did think it was strange, even at the time, that she suddenly didn't want to know, said nothing about him ever again. I thought he was a reminder of how she had been before. But I see it differently now, that Sean might be right, that it could be *him* she was trying to forget.'

'Tell me about the 12th of December 1998.'

'Yes,' Ann said. 'The day it happened. It was a Saturday. I should have twigged there was something fishy going on. In retrospect I see that. As far as I was concerned she was going on a sleepover to Jessica's, there were going to be a few other girls there, all normal but she was extra-excited that day, that week. I *did* notice it, I'm not imagining it. Anyway, there was no sleepover, she never went to Jessica's. She arrived back here the following morning early and went straight to bed. I didn't even see her going up the stairs. I was in the kitchen. But later on I heard her bawling and I went in to her. And she told me to get out and I did at first but I couldn't stay out and I went back in. She was all curled up in the bed. So I sat down beside her and talked to her and eventually I persuaded her to tell me what was wrong but all she would say was that something bad had happened to her, and that it was her fault. And that was all she ever said, really, down all the years until her . . . until we lost her. That someone had hurt her and it was her fault. And I asked her, of course I did, if we would call the doctor, and the guards, and she said to call nobody, and that come hell or high water she wasn't going to ever call the guards or let us ever tell anyone and that if

I did tell anyone she would never talk to me again and she'd leave and run away and all sorts like that. And by then Sean had come in, he'd heard the commotion and he said it too at first, that she should report it, but then he went along with her, that we would keep it to ourselves what had happened. I wasn't happy but I went along with it too, thinking, I suppose we both did, that we could talk her around later and that she would tell us, tell someone, who had hurt her. But she never did. If it was now, well, I would do everything differently. We know all about trauma and counselling and DNA now. But that was new then, new to us anyway. So I washed and cleaned her, I had to be careful not to hurt her any more than she was already ...'

'She was physically injured?' I asked.

'Bruised mainly, like she'd been held down. Her upper arms, her shoulders. All over her legs, thighs, belly. She'd been battered, my baby girl, everywhere except her beautiful face. But that was changed too. Pale as a corpse she was. It was like she'd been dosed with a lethal poison. Her eyes were dead, even though she was breathing.'

'Ann, I know she didn't tell you who hurt her, but did she say any more about what had actually happened?'

'She didn't have to say the word for me to know that she had been raped. She was torn, and bleeding from inside her, bleeding too much for it to be normal ...'

'And you didn't call a doctor?' I said.

'I wanted to, but I didn't. She said that she'd die of shame if anyone knew. I understood what she meant, though it makes no sense to me now, but back then, and with herself and Sean against me, well, I was weak. It was a mistake, the biggest one I ever made. I was her mother. I should have done better by her. I failed her when she needed me most.

'And I threw out the bloody sheets and the stained clothes that she'd been wearing and I dressed her in her pyjamas like she was my baby again. That means there's no evidence, doesn't it? Nothing. The mobile phone she was using is long gone. Sometime after, she put it in the sink and covered it in water to destroy it. I threw it away. Thought it was useless. If I'd kept any of the stuff there might be some hope of tracing him from phone records or DNA, I'm sure, even now, wouldn't there?'

'Hard to say,' I said. 'And what's done is done. We need to work with what we have. Any idea where she went that night?'

'Not a clue. And the way it was, that we couldn't tell anyone, I couldn't ask Jessica or I was afraid … I don't know … Maybe the truth is that for a while I might have thought it was Deirdre's fault too. And that's the worst thing, that I thought badly of her.'

'Her attacker groomed her,' I said. 'Whether it was Gill or someone else, Deirdre was led into a situation that turned into something she didn't want.'

'I know. But I wish I had seen it at the time, or even that I could help in some way now,' Ann said.

'You might be able to help me with these things,' I said. 'I found them in at the back of the desk drawers in her room. Did you know there was something hidden there?'

Ann shook her head. I took the bagged box and contents out of my handbag and handed them to Ann, one at a time. First the coaster from Muskerry Castle.

'Do you have any idea why Deirdre would have this?'

'No,' Ann said. 'You'd need to be half a millionaire to go to a place like that. I'm sure Deirdre was never there.'

The next item was the badge. Ann shook her head again.

'I've never seen this before,' she said. 'I've no idea what it is.'

The final item was the identity tag.

'It's Deirdre's handwriting all right, but as to what it was for, I don't know. I don't remember her ever being at a conference. She was a schoolgirl, and after she left school she didn't have any education worth talking about. Unless she did a course when she was in St Michael's having treatment? But I think I would have heard about that ...'

'Think, Ann,' I said. 'Did she ever go to anything where she might have needed a name tag like that, a seminar or a school debate, maybe?'

'There was nothing like that,' Ann said. 'Nothing at all.'

8

It was almost eight o'clock when I left the Carney house. I walked past the football ground, home of Cork City FC, shuttered and silent now. The streets were empty, and the night air was murky, and the footpaths were damp and slippery underfoot. Around the corner, on Evergreen Road, the giant concrete slants of Christ the King Church menaced.

I pressed on, picking my way through the mist. Ann had said that Deirdre's school friend Jessica Murphy was married with a couple of kids, so there was no hope of a meeting at this time on a Saturday evening. I would ring her in the morning. By then, too, Ann would have phoned Jessica and told her to expect my call, which might make for an easier first contact. There was no legitimate excuse for going back to the Film Festival office twice in one day and, though I was even more convinced now that I needed to examine the 1998 archive, there was nothing else to be done tonight. I would go home, absorb and process all that had happened. That was the appropriate thing to do.

And I couldn't do it. I hurried down the narrow steep incline of Nicholas Street, and around past the Red Abbey, and across the river on to the city's central island.

The festival office was quieter than it had been that morning. There was no sign of Alice, but there were a few junior staff members and, as I had hoped, Sarah-Jane Dooley. In her late twenties, Sarah-Jane had a carefully curated look that changed with every hairdo. Recently, she'd gone for a pixie crop that made her look like Jean Seberg in *Breathless*, though she was too chatty and smiley to pull off the required ennui. Sarah-Jane handled the in-house publicity for the festival and in planning this year's campaign she'd be bound to have dug out the festival archive of Gill's previous visit.

'Hey, Sarah-Jane, how is it going?' I said.

Sarah-Jane raised her eyes towards the ceiling, its paint flaking and grimy: arts funding cutbacks left no room for a decoration budget.

'I'm demented, Finn, trying to get on to someone in TV3, they're supposed to be running an item in tomorrow evening's news and I'm organising the meeting time and about a hundred other things simultaneously – sure you know, yourself. If you're looking for Alice, she's gone – she was in since half five this morning and she was dead on her feet.'

'I kinda was looking for her,' I lied. 'But maybe you could give me a hand if you have a minute? It's just that I'm supposed to be meeting Jeremy Gill on Wednesday for the workshop as board representative, I was in this morning talking to Alice about it, and I realised afterwards that I really needed to look at the records of his 1998 visit to the festival so that I'd be fully up to speed. I was wondering if you had the archive handy?'

'Em, sure, yeah,' Sarah-Jane said, staring at her computer screen. 'I'm a bit busy right now, I ...'

'Just point me in the right direction and I'll take it from there,' I said.

My conscience itched with the knowledge that I was using my position on the board and my friendship with Alice to worm my way in. But, as I cleared a corner for myself and sat with the five box files that comprised the 1998 archive, I pushed all squeamishness aside. It would be worth it if I found something.

The first three boxes yielded nothing of interest: posters, flyers, guest attendances, audience records, copies of the catalogue and publicity materials. The fourth one was all Jeremy Gill. Somebody had realised early on that Gill was going places and had preserved everything they could about his time at the 1998 festival, including his original handwritten entry form for the short film competition, the original videotape that he'd submitted, a thank-you card that he'd sent afterwards, numerous press clippings, many of which I had seen online, as well as a note of the prizes he'd won and the judges' comments. There was a bundle of photos, too, mostly duplicates or alternate versions of the prize-giving ones that had appeared in the *Examiner*.

But wrapped separately in a white page were two other photographs. The top photo showed Gill standing in a posed shot with a group of teenagers in various school uniforms. I took a closer look. The teenagers were wearing white name tags. I would need an enlargement to confirm that the tags were exactly the same as the one I had found at the Carney house, but they looked similar.

I recognised Deirdre immediately from Sean's photo. As well as Gill, there was another adult male in the photograph. I'd need to find out who he was. The second photograph was another posed shot, this time a foursome: Deirdre, Gill and two other teenagers, both boys, wearing different uniforms which meant that they were from different schools. I didn't recognise the uniforms but, as they had name tags, I could find out who they were and talk to them.

In the four-person photo, Deirdre was standing beside Gill with the boys on either side of them. Deirdre and Gill were standing close to each other. They looked happy, and the boys looked happy. It seemed like everyone was having a great time. I took both photographs, the large group and the foursome. I would write a note on the page that had wrapped them confirming that I'd borrowed the two of them to get them copied. But I stopped before I wrote anything. The page wasn't blank. Created on a computer and not specially printed, it was an A3 promotional poster publicising a schools workshop which read:

Darkest Truth

The poster didn't mention Jeremy Gill but, given that the page was filed with the rest of the Gill memorabilia, he could have been the one giving the extra schools-only workshop. The education officer of the time – whoever that was I didn't know but I'd find out – would be able to say how it had come about. I photocopied the poster and slipped the copy and the two original photographs into my bag. I was fairly sure nobody in the office had noticed.

As I placed my note in the file I told myself that that was nearly the same as getting permission. And that I'd return them on Monday. Then I put everything back and had a quick look through the fifth box. But there was nothing more: all the Gill material was in the file I'd checked already. I re-stacked the boxes on the shelf where I'd found them, said goodbye to Sarah-Jane, and left. I had a photo of Gill and Deirdre Carney together. That was better than I could have hoped for, though I still had nothing directly on him and I knew it.

As I walked home, I repeated to myself that I had to keep an open mind, that Jeremy Gill might not be the one who had attacked Deirdre, and that there must be other suspects. There was no need to remind myself of what else I'd learnt that day, but it was hard to take in, all the same: a surprise sister found and lost.

I barely remembered my birth mother, though I had lived with her full-time until I was four and started school, until the teachers had noticed me and made a report of neglect to the Southern Health Board. The assessments had started, then, though I didn't learn the lingo until later when I started going to court for my job: the temporary care orders, the supervised access, the foster place-ment with the Fitzpatricks that had become permanent when I was nine, old enough to be told that my birth mother had gone to heaven, old enough to go to the funeral; not old enough to be told everything.

That came later, when I turned sixteen and started asking about my history, and talking about looking for my father. Except that there wasn't a father to look for: that section on the original birth certificate had been left blank, my adopted mother Doreen had said. She had told me about my birth mother's suicide at the same time. And one other thing: that my birth mother had been drunk when she threw herself in the river.

It would have been more of a surprise if she had been sober. She had been on and off the drink numerous times by then. I wouldn't see her for ages, and then she'd reappear, back from holiday or hospital or whatever her euphemism for rehab was at the time. It must have been when she was away on one of those extended absences that she had had Deirdre and given her up for adoption.

On my way up Barrack Street, through wooden blind slats and net curtains and clear glass, I glimpsed other people's lives, like a succession of short films. In one of them, a group of friends sat easily together on a sofa. A TV was on and they were half watching it, half talking to each other, checking their phones, too, but sharing the same space. In another, two men in sportswear stood in a kitchen, drinking bottles of beer, trading stories, laughing.

I was starving and exhausted but kept walking, past the turnoff for my house, as far as La Tana. When it comes to emotional eating, sometimes only pizza will do.

Back home, I went straight to my ground floor study and sat at my desk. The room was small and cramped, piled high with books and the prints and posters I'd bothered to get framed but hadn't bothered to hang up yet. Somewhere underneath everything there was a futon I'd used for guests, before I'd been able to afford a bed for the spare room, also on the ground floor, along with a laundry and storage space and a small shower room. I'm a 'keep it just in case' person; not so severe that I'm going to end up on a TV show, but a hoarder nonetheless.

Between bites of pizza, I turned on my computer and began logging my progress into the file I'd opened the previous night. I checked through my notes of the meeting with the Carneys and did a file memo. I set up an exhibits file, saved my photographs there and listed the items I'd found. Then, I recorded my attendance at the Film Festival office, did a note of Gill's itinerary while in Cork, and saved copies of the photos retrieved from the Film Festival box file and a scan of the workshop poster.

Next, I opened a new document and called it 'Connections'. For now, all I could do was list the connections, or possible connections, between Gill and Deirdre and see where they led next.

There was the suicide note, referring to the academy, that I'd photographed and saved, and the time coincidence between Gill's Oscar nomination and Deirdre's suicide a day later. And that, according to the festival catalogue, Deirdre had championed his short film at the 1998 Cork Film Festival. I knew for sure now that Deirdre had met Gill: I had incontestable evidence of their meeting. I knew too that, in the aftermath of the festival, she had developed a telephone relationship with an unknown male. But there was little hope of getting phone records of any kind so many years later and I reckoned I'd waste too much time looking for them. I needed to concentrate on what I had.

I clicked on the scanned photo and expanded the PDF as high as it would go. But the resolution was poor and it was hard to see anything. I'd need professional help with it. Though if I expanded the original ...? I rifled my desk drawers. There was a magnifying glass somewhere that I could use to examine the photographs more closely, to see if the name tag I'd found earlier was the same as the one Deirdre was wearing at the workshop.

I found the magnifying glass in a drawer that also contained two ancient Nokia mobiles, which I should have taken to recycling, along with the old Hoover and broken toaster that clogged up the bottom of the wardrobe in the spare room.

With the benefit of the magnifying glass, I saw that the name tag in the photo and the one I'd found in Deirdre's room looked the same. They *were*, I was sure of it. I'd have to get the hard copy photo enlarged properly and the name tag analysed by an expert, if I was going to be able to use it as evidence. It had to be significant that Deirdre had saved and hidden it all these years since the time she'd met Jeremy Gill. I would need to talk to the others in the photos. Maybe they had seen or heard something.

But, as I was squinting at the photos with the magnifying glass, I saw that they showed even more than I'd realised. I had been too stuck on the workshop connection to notice at first, but the students in the photos were wearing more than name tags on their school jumpers. It was hard to see but most of them had badges and in the four shot, with the magnifying glass, I saw that they were the same as the cartoon-style broken computer badge. Whatever that badge was, it was nothing to do with a band Deirdre had liked, and must have something to do with Gill because he was wearing one too. But what was it? I had been around the Film Festival in 1998 as a volunteer. Was it something he gave out at his workshop? Something to do with his job? A logo? Or free advertising for something? I drummed my fingers on the desk. What did the broken computer symbol mean? Back in the nineties, most references to computers had been positive: people raved about the information superhighway, and it was long before cyber-bullying or online privacy had become issues of concern. I turned it over and over to see if there was a 'made in' or 'made for' mark on it – any clue to where the badge might have come from. There wasn't.

Yet the more I looked at it, the more I felt that I recognised it. It would come back to me, I hoped. Though not if I kept staring at it. I put the badge and the other exhibits into my desk drawer, locked it and put the key on my key ring. This was never going to be a criminal trial. I was never going to have to prove a chain of evidence for a jury, but I didn't know where the case might go ultimately. In the meantime, I'd have to keep the items exactly as I'd found them and free from interference. When an exhibit is used in a trial, you have to be able to show who handled it. A locked desk drawer would have to serve as my evidence room for now.

Quickly I ran through the documents again and sent them to my work email. I couldn't open a work file on my home computer so I'd get Tina to sort that on Monday in the office. I binned the pizza box in the wheelie bin outside the door, locked up for the night and went upstairs, checking my phone as I went. There was a message from Davy.

'You out or at home?'

I flicked on Radio 1, made a pot of camomile tea, and switched off the lamp. It was a little after eleven and *Country Time* was just starting. I sat and gazed over the lights of the city. I heard George Jones sing 'He Stopped Lovin' her Today' and lost myself for a while. But, after a time, my mind drifted back to the case. I had forgotten to check the name of the education officer in the programme – I'd do that tomorrow. And I needed to contact Jessica Murphy in the morning. See her then too, if I could, because I had other plans for Sunday afternoon, plans that involved Davy Keenan, though he didn't know it yet.

I picked up my phone and texted Davy back: 'Home. Doing nothing. You?'

He must have had his phone in his hand because within seconds he'd texted back 'Nada'.

I wasn't surprised. Careful of his sobriety, Davy avoided Saturday nights in town. I wondered, not for the first time, what would happen if I asked him to come over. There, in the dark, I could admit that I was attracted to him, and not only because he was gorgeous-looking and funny and smart. I had enough insight to know that Davy, an ex-addict, was perilous territory, an emotional minefield. I knew about repetition compulsion, how we are programmed to seek out the familiar. Davy was a push–pull for me: something in him spoke to something in me, something I had to keep under control.

'Want do something tomorrow afternoon?' I typed.

'Could be persuaded maybe, what is it?' Davy replied.

'Muskerry Castle? Afternoon tea? My treat. Dress up – what you think?'

'Sounds good,' Davy replied.

'Fab. Will phone for reserv, will text you time. PS you're driving,' I wrote.

'Guessed I would be,' Davy replied.

'Hmmm. See you tomorrow. Night night.'

'You will. Sleep tight,' Davy replied.

I left my phone on the side table and went to my bedroom, on the middle floor of the tower house, and undressed for bed. I was regretting my trip to La Tana. Delicious at the time, the pizza lay like a boulder in my stomach.

I fell asleep quickly but was awake again after ten minutes, drifting in and out of consciousness for the second night in a row.

As I lay in the darkness, I went over and over what had happened that day, what I knew, and what I didn't, puzzling still over the broken computer symbol. At around 4 a.m., I remembered, or thought I did, where I'd seen it before.

I got out of bed, went downstairs to the study and searched YouTube again for the Gill short film. I was right. The opening titles and credits were in a comic, cartoonish script. And the name of the film showed through when an animated desktop computer broke in jagged half revealing the words *Another Bad Day at the Office*. The badge was publicity material for Gill's short film. That's why the kids in the photos were wearing them. Gill must have distributed them at the workshop. And that's why Deirdre had kept it. It was another connection. I wrote it up and, as I was awake anyway, checked the identity of the 1998 education officer – he had to be the other adult male in the photos. The name in the catalogue was Daniel O'Brien. I didn't know him, so he had to be long gone from the festival.

I put the computer in sleep mode. In the hall, I glanced at the full-length rectangular window to the side of the front door. My reflection made it look like a dark figure was skulking in the tiny garden outside.

I went to the top floor. I pulled the Foxford blanket from the back of the sofa and walked to the armchair. I sat in the dark, facing due north, as I had earlier. No music played, and the room felt the wrong side of chilly, but I was too cold to get up and turn the heating back on. I curled my legs beneath me and arranged the blanket so that it covered me from the neck down.

Darkest Truth

First memory? Awake in the middle of the night, like now, but noisy, people sounds from the next room.

Laughing. Shouting. Doors slamming. A party?

Her voice.

Her.

My mother.

Me, a baby.

No. Bigger than that.

Not in a cot, in a bed, chairs lined up along the side. To keep me there.

Not so big.

Must keep eyes closed.

Must be asleep.

I heard my breath, mouth breath, shallow, and quick.

'May I be safe,' I whispered, the opening words of the Loving Kindness meditation.

'May I be safe,' I said again and again until my breath slowed and deepened. Then I remembered the rest of the mantra.

'May I be safe, may I be healthy, may I be happy, may I live with ease,' I said, repeating the words as I got up from the chair and got my yoga mat from the nook at the top of the stairs. I unfurled it slowly, and sat on the mat, cross-legged, eyes closed, breathing, *nadi shodhana*. As my strength returned, I moved through the quietening *asanas*, ending with *savasana*, corpse pose.

Then I went back downstairs and slept till morning.

9

Clarity came with the dawn. Whatever progress I'd made, I was a long way from proving anything. And the Film Festival was starting this evening. As I gulped back my Morning Growler, I began to scribble my priorities on a sheet of paper. Top of the list was to talk to Jessica Murphy today, if possible. I needed to find out what she knew about what had happened to Deirdre – and if she knew anything about Jeremy Gill. Though I wouldn't lead with him. I didn't want to put words in her mouth. I had to keep open the possibility that Gill wasn't the one, had to look for evidence of his innocence as well as his guilt. But I'd bring along my iPad with the photographs of the workshop on it and the pictures of the items that I had found in Deirdre's room and see what Jessica had to say. She'd recognise Jeremy Gill, anybody would, so that was a way in for me. Ringing someone before ten on a

Sunday morning was a no-no, even a mother of young kids who was most likely up since before seven. I had to wait. And waiting has never agreed with me.

I moved to the next item on my list: Muskerry Castle, but here I was a lot vaguer about my aims. I had been there twice, once for the wedding of a college friend, and again for the Law Society annual conference in 2010, but I had never stayed over, or seen it during its normal working day as a hotel. Afternoon tea was a good excuse, and bringing Davy along was good cover. Nobody goes for afternoon tea on their own, and the hotel was too far from town, and too exclusive, to permit cheapskate solo coffee-drinkers.

What I hoped to find out, I didn't know, other than to check the coasters they used and compare them with the one I'd found in Deirdre's room. If they had changed them at some stage, maybe I'd be able to date the one I'd found, though I hadn't much hope of it. But Gill liked the hotel and he'd been there before, so it was worth a look.

I checked my phone. It was 9.15 and I had a text from Ann, saying that she had phoned Jessica and told her to expect to hear from me. Next, I rang Muskerry Castle and made a reservation for afternoon tea at 3.30 p.m. I texted Davy to let him know the time. No reply. He was probably out running or doing something equally torturous.

My phone pinged. It was a message from Sadie O'Riordan asking if I wanted to go to a film. Any other Sunday, I would have. We often met up to go to the cinema while her husband

Jack Lehane went to a match (hurling in summer, rugby in winter, the Premiership on telly, if he was stuck). Sadie was a detective in the Garda Síochána, based at Detective HQ in Coughlan's Quay. She had been in my law class at UCC. Our closeness was situationally inevitable: she and I sat in the back row at every lecture. By the end of week one, we were friends for life.

After college, Sadie had opted for Garda training in Templemore instead of going into legal practice. It was a decision I hadn't understood at the time. I had always seen the law from a defence rather than a prosecution standpoint. But, based on my behaviour over the last few days, I was beginning to understand that we were more alike than I'd realised. I would have liked to have shown the evidence I had to her to see what she thought. As I was bound by client confidentiality, I couldn't do that unless the clients permitted the disclosure. Though why wouldn't they? I'd check it with them. I texted Sadie to say I couldn't meet today but that I'd call her during the week to arrange something else.

Along with the messages from Sadie and Ann, I had a voice-mail from my mam, Doreen, wondering how I was, as she hadn't heard from me for days and didn't know was I alive or dead, let alone if I was coming around for the dinner and should she put on spuds for me or not and would I please phone soon or my father was going to have to drive over and see what was wrong. I groaned as I listened. Then I rang her.

'Finn! At last. Thank God. We were worried,' Mam said.

'Sure wasn't I only talking to you Friday afternoon? Anyway, how are things?'

My mother went into an animated recital of local news, weather, sick relatives, dead neighbours, funerals attended and upcoming medical appointments, ending with 'So we'll see you later on?'

'Not for dinner, Mam, but I might be able to call in – or during the week. I've been busy, sorry, working all weekend as it happens so ...'

'I *knew* that's why we didn't hear from you. Your father wants to talk to you.'

I heard muffled voices as my mother summoned Jim, my dad, to the phone. He's not a phone person and would have been a lot happier saying whatever he had to say when he saw me next. But if Doreen wanted him to talk to me now, he would. Otherwise he had no hope of a quiet read of the Sunday papers.

'Ah, Finn, how are you at all?'

'I'm grand. How are you, Dad?'

'Grand altogether. Listen, don't be working too hard now, sure you won't?'

I laughed.

'No, Dad, don't worry, I won't,' I said.

'Grand altogether. Sure we'll see you soon so, will we?'

'Yes, Dad. Listen, I have to go, I'll talk to you. Say goodbye to Mam for me.'

It was 10 a.m. I rang Jessica Murphy. She told me that she'd sent the kids out with their dad, and that it would suit her best if I called over right away.

Jessica's house was a twenty-five minute walk from my house. On the way, I went back over the phone conversation with my parents. Overprotective was putting it mildly when it came to how Mam was with me. Though she never said it, I knew that she watched for signs of the damage done to me in my early years, the harm that she and Dad had done their best to repair.

After I had found out about my birth mother's suicide, I abandoned whatever interest I had had in my roots. I had never even seen my original birth certificate. I knew as much as I needed to know. My legal parents were Doreen and Jim Fitzpatrick. My legal name was Finola Fitzpatrick. My previous identity no longer existed unless I allowed it to. I locked all of it away.

But, no matter how hard I tried, at times the pictures and sounds and feelings of that other life took control. It wasn't something I could predict, though usually I tried to avoid – and at the same time was drawn to – anything that might trigger me. Things like this case. Whatever I did, occasionally it was like a switch flicked inside me. I had learnt how to handle myself, had a whole toolbox I used to put myself back together: music, meditation, yoga. Often I was tired of the effort.

Before yesterday, what had I known about my past? There had been a lot of alcohol, I knew that. And depression. I knew that too. Assumed it, given my birth mother's suicide. And there had been chaos and neglect and terror. I felt that, a shadow barely glimpsed at the edge of me, a darkness, unknowable, at the core of me. I had faint memories, like scenes from an old TV show. The rest was burnt into my brain like melted plastic, the true shape of what happened long gone. I had read up on the theory, and putting a label on it helped a little. I had been exposed to relational trauma, certainly. And 'Big T' trauma, probably. Though there had been love, too, some warmth, some care. And now I'd found out that there had been a secret sister. What effect would this new information about my background have on me? Were there other secrets? And, if there were, did I want to know?

Jessica lived near the church in Ballyphehane, one of the necklace of churches built around Cork during the 1950s, at the height of the Catholic Church's institutional power. At the time, some of the women in the surrounding area had donated their engagement rings to fund the enormous and, these days, mostly empty church. But the hierarchy's influence on Ireland had declined over the intervening decades, precipitously so after the revelations of recent times: the Mother and Baby homes, the priests and Christian Brothers convicted of serious sexual offences, and how Church institutions had colluded in serial cover-ups. I wondered what those women would think of their sacrifice now.

By 10.35, I was knocking on the door of an ex-City Council end of terrace, an ordinary home that was becoming more extraordinary with every passing year. Most of the houses in the area had been built when the State was young and poor and had had many faults but had, at least, cared enough to house those of its citizens who hadn't been forced to emigrate. But for a long time now, government policy had decreed that large schemes like this one were a source of social problems, and publicly funded housebuilding had more or less ceased. The resulting homelessness crisis, a spectacularly serious social problem in itself, hadn't yet led to an effective change in policy.

I rang the doorbell, and stood down off the front step again. I saw that the house had been renovated and extended. The work looked less than ten years old and, with a ramp and handrail, there was a granny flat with a separate entrance built on to the side.

'Coming,' a voice said from above.

Feet clip-clopped down uncarpeted steps and a scrawny woman, with fine dyed blonde hair pulled into a thin ponytail, opened the door. She looked a lot older than thirty or thirty-one, which was all she could have been if she was in Deirdre's class. Her pale skin had a matt dullness to it, and a deep cleft had developed between her over-plucked brows.

'Sorry,' the woman said. 'I was upstairs doing a few bits while I've peace.'

I introduced myself, and handed her my business card.

'You're Jessica?'

'God yeah, sorry, that's me, I should've said.'

She smiled, and put her hand to her forehead.

'Come in out of the cold, for God's sake.'

She showed me into the front room, which had been turned into a play area. The floor was almost entirely covered with a jigsaw-style rubber play mat, littered with plastic toys and picture books in varying states of repair. *The Very Hungry Caterpillar* had survived best, but I feared for *The Gruffalo*: the front cover had come loose and was holding on by a hangnail. I thanked Jessica for seeing me at such short notice, and sat on the sofa.

'Did Ann say anything about why I wanted to see you?'

'Nothing, only that it was about poor Deirdre's death and that you were looking into the background. That's about it. C'mere, I never asked if you wanted a cuppa?'

'I'm grand, thanks, Jessica, I'm only after it. You knew Deirdre well, I hear?'

'When we were kids, we were best friends, in the same class all the way up. But I didn't see much of her after we left school. And when we were there, she was out sick a lot, scraped through the Leaving, nervous breakdown, but you know that, I suppose. I tried to keep in touch, called in occasionally. Believe it or not I hadn't even seen her for a few years before she died. But strange as it sounds, you know, I think we would've grown apart no matter what, even if she hadn't got sick. We were on different roads. She was heading to university from nearly the day we started primary. I was only dying to finish school myself. I went to the College of Comm after, did a book-keeping and secretarial course, and never looked back. Met Paul, had the smallies and, sure you know yourself, moved on, like.'

She frowned.

'Between work and the kids and Paul, I hadn't a minute. Still haven't.'

She paused again.

'With everything, I had no time left for Deirdre.'

'I never forgot about her, though,' Jessica added, willing me to believe her. I didn't. I reckoned that plenty of time had gone by when Deirdre was alive that she never crossed Jessica's mind. And that she thought about Deirdre a whole lot more these days.

'When she died, it brought it all back, you know, how close we'd been,' Jessica said. 'I was so sad. But I suppose life's like that, and it's nobody's fault and that's it.'

She looked at me, waited for me to agree. I couldn't. Somebody was at fault, I just didn't know who, not for sure, not yet. But maybe Jessica did.

'Was there a trigger for the breakdown, the change in Deirdre, do you think?'

'Not as far as I know,' Jessica said. 'Some people are more susceptible to that kind of thing, aren't they? Around the time of the Film Festival, she broke up with her boyfriend and—'

'Boyfriend?'

'Yeah, Joey O'Connor, mind you when I say boyfriend it was all very innocent. She was only fifteen and we were all in the same class at St Finbarr's. Joey was a rich boy, from the Blackrock Road. Gorgeous, in his day. A bit like Colin Farrell, but tall as well. Played rugby, too.'

She laughed.

'He couldn't *believe* it when he got dumped.'

'Deirdre broke it off? Why?'

'I don't know what happened. I wasn't surprised she got tired of him. He thought he was God's gift. He was crazy about Deirdre, though.'

'Any idea where he is now?'

'As far as I know he's working in the family business, they have that big car sales place on the Kinsale Road.'

'Ann Carney never mentioned a boyfriend,' I said. 'Do you think she knew?'

'No way. Deirdre didn't tell her. No point. And the dad would have had a canary.'

'I see. It's interesting that the break-up with Joey happened around the time of the Film Festival. The Carneys trace the change in Deirdre to then.'

Jessica put her head on one side and looked at the ceiling. I followed her gaze upwards, towards a paper globe with a map of the earth pattern on it, and a small hole where Buenos Aires should have been. I looked at her afresh, and at the furrow between her brows. I wondered what had put it there. She started talking again.

'That's right. Now that you mention it, she was never the same after the festival.'

'You went to the closing ceremony with Ann Carney and Deirdre, is that right?'

'It was a long time ago. All I remember is being in the Opera House, and it was boring, at the beginning anyway, loads of speeches and giving out prizes, and all that.'

'Jeremy Gill won that year, didn't he?' I said.

'God, yeah he did. Cork really put him on the map.'

As far as the local population was concerned, whatever about his talent, Gill's later success was entirely due to the fact that Cork had discovered him. 'He'd be nowhere only for us,' taxi drivers said, too often for my liking, even before I'd heard about Deirdre.

'I was volunteering that year. I did it for a few years back then. I didn't meet Jeremy myself, unfortunately. Did you?'

'I did of course,' Jessica said. 'We did the workshop with him.'

'Oh yes, the workshop. I have some photos of it. Didn't know you were at it.'

'Well, to be honest, it wasn't really my thing. But Deirdre was doing it and at that stage we were joined at the hip. And it was a day off school, of course.'

I took out my iPad and got up the scanned photos, the group shot first. Jessica squealed.

'Oh my God, look at me, I was so fat,' she said.

She pointed to a round mousey-haired girl, and looked at me expectantly.

'I wouldn't say fat exactly,' I said. 'But you look a lot different, that's for sure.'

'I took up running down by the Lough to get out on my own for half an hour a couple of times a week. And the weight fell off me. Mind you, it's a struggle to keep it off. I nearly have shares in Special K. But look at Deirdre, God help us, may she rest in peace. She was so pretty, such a star. No wonder Jeremy Gill was mad about her.'

'Really? How do you mean?'

'Just asking her opinion and things,' Jessica said. 'And if he had to demonstrate anything, he got her to help him, all that. Teacher's pet. But we were used to that with Deirdre. Everyone loved her. Mr O'Donnell the art teacher *adored* her. Even after she got sick and gave up art in school and dropped down to doing all pass subjects, he kept asking about her all the time. We used to say that he was in love with her.'

'Was he?'

'Dunno. Doubt if it was love, really. But it happens, doesn't it?'

I'd need to talk to Mr O'Donnell, find out more.

'I suppose. But tell me, do you recognise anyone else in these photos, Jessica?'

'Well there's Joey,' she said.

She pointed to a thick-necked, surly youth in the second row.

'And Aifric Sheehan, she was Deirdre's friend more than mine. Aifric's still around. I bump into her occasionally. She went on and did teaching. Works in our old school, would you believe? I don't think I'd send our two there, though I don't know, they're still young. But from what I hear, the school's changed a lot since our day. Less mixed, more exclusive.'

I had to get her back to the case.

'I don't have kids myself so it's not really on my radar. Em, the two boys in the other photo? Any idea who they are?' I asked.

'They were on the youth jury with her, as far as I know,' Jessica said. 'But don't ask me their names. I only met them that one day, at the workshop.'

'What about the other guy, the adult who isn't Jeremy Gill?'

'Oh he worked for the festival, what was his name again? He was really nice to me, I should remember him. I felt out of place, didn't know much about films, the rest of them were way cooler than I was, but he looked out for me. Hang on, was it Donal or something like that?'

'Could it have been Daniel? According to the programme, the education officer was called Daniel O'Brien.'

'Yeah, it could have been,' Jessica said. 'He was something to do with education, I'm nearly sure. Yeah, it could have been Daniel.'

'That's good to know, Jessica, thanks,' I said. 'And do you remember the badges you were all wearing? Anything about them?'

'I don't even remember seeing one, let alone wearing one.'

'Okay. And, one more time, any joy on the two jury boys' names?'

'Not a hope,' she said. 'Not even a glimmer.'

It didn't matter. If they were on the youth jury, as Jessica had said, their names would be in the catalogue. And she had confirmed my suspicion that the other adult male in the photo was probably Daniel O'Brien, the education officer.

But I hadn't bargained on having two new suspects in the mix: a jilted boyfriend and a besotted teacher. I had intended being open-minded about Gill's culpability but this new development was, most definitely, not part of the script.

10

Back home, I went to my study to log what I'd gleaned from Jessica. In my 'Connections' file, I noted that Gill had known Deirdre well, that she had been something of a teacher's pet to him at his workshop. But, as far as Jessica was concerned, Gill was a celebrity they were lucky to have met once, a public figure with no significant connection to Deirdre. If Jessica was telling the truth, she knew of no subsequent contact between Gill and Deirdre after the festival. Even worse, the clues that I had been so excited about, the badges and name tags, meant nothing to her. Jessica didn't even recall wearing them.

But one of the others might. I checked the catalogue for the names of the youth jury members and saved them to my file. One of them was Lorcan Lucey from Presentation Brothers, a famous rugby school universally known as 'Pres', though bespectacled skinny Lorcan didn't look like he spent much time on the pitch. The second boy was Patrick McCarthy from a boys' school in Bishopstown. Patrick was open-faced, athletic and enthusiastic-looking, like the star player on the school hurling team.

With a sigh, I opened a new document labelled 'Other Possibilities' where I typed two names: Colm O'Donnell, art teacher and Joey O'Connor, ex-boyfriend. Then I left my study and went upstairs to my bedroom. It was after two. I needed to get ready. Davy would be around to pick me up soon.

I had intended to wash my hair but a mane like mine takes too long to dry and I hadn't left enough time. I pinned it up and went for a 30-second shower, keeping my head out of the water. Then, quickly, I pummelled my skin dry and slathered on Summer Harvest body lotion that I'd bought in the Burren Perfumery in Clare the previous August. Next, I shook out my hair, put my head upside down, and sprayed on my old music festival staple, Batiste Dry Shampoo. I smelled nice and my hair didn't look too bad, but at twenty to three I still had no clue what to wear. Eventually I settled on a purple seventies vintage dress, with a high neck and long sleeves, and high-heeled Mary Janes. And too much black eyeliner and mascara, forgetting that I was going to Muskerry Castle for work reasons, and not on a date with Davy Keenan.

My phone pinged. It was Davy.

'Your carriage awaits.'

Which probably meant that he was stopped in the middle of Barrack Street, blocking traffic. I'd better leg it.

But when I got to the end of the lane and on to Barrack Street there was no sign of him. I looked down the street, in the direction of town. No sign either. Then I heard him call my name. Parked to the south of the turn-off, he was leaning against his car, a black BMW. A drug dealer's car, I'd teased, when he got it, asking if NA didn't have some kind of a ban on black BMWs?

'You're only jealous, Finn,' he'd said at the time, unfazed. And maybe I was, a little, though cars don't interest me usually. Davy gave a little nod and a smile and I strolled towards him, trying to look casual, which was not easy when he looked this good, sandy hair and beard, six foot two, slim but strong, wearing a vintage brown Donegal tweed jacket over jeans and an open-necked white and blue cornflower print shirt.

'You look nice,' Davy said.

'So do you,' I said.

He opened the door and I got into the car as fast as I could. I needed the seat.

We drove west from the city, past the Lee Fields, out the Straight Road, where they used to run land speed record attempts back when people were interested in that kind of thing. Then, instead of continuing along the main route, Davy chose the narrow winding road that tracked the river, high above it, a shimmer of water visible intermittently through the hedgerows.

Once or twice I felt him looking at me, but he said nothing. He always knew when I wanted to talk and when I needed quiet. As we turned on to the mile-long tree-lined driveway to Muskerry Castle, the BMW earning us an effortless wave through gate security, I tried, with limited success, to drag my mind back to why I was here.

The hotel was as beautiful as I remembered: castellated limestone, carved oak and stone interiors, Turkish carpets, open fires, pastoral views from every window. It had been the landed estate, the 'big house', of the area, not burnt out as many like it had been in the 1920s, or demolished, or fallen into ruins, as others had been after their farms were compulsorily acquired by the Land Commission; death duties had crippled even more. Almost by default, the house had survived intact until one of the less useless members of the family, a daughter, had stopped yearning for a vanished *Downton Abbey* idyll that had never been, and turned the place into a hotel. She had done well. It was part-owned by an international group now, but the family was still involved in the running, and it was one of the few places in Cork that the recession didn't seem to have affected, except to make hiring staff a lot easier.

'Is it a special occasion, madam?' the waitress asked as she led us to our table. Thrown momentarily, I looked to Davy for help.

'It might be,' he said and flashed a smile in her direction.

As we sat down, he asked 'Why *are* we here anyway, Finn?'

'It's a work thing, Davy. I can't tell you too much about it, you know, client confidentiality and all that. But I really appreciate you coming along.'

I watched his expression change and settle as I spoke, from curiosity to resignation, with a hint of disappointment somewhere in the middle.

'Excellent,' Davy said. 'You know me, always up for a bit of legal work.'

'That's what I thought.'

But it felt like I was using him and, when they came, the perfect mini-sandwiches and cakes tasted like cardboard in my mouth. I had to salvage something from the afternoon, and got my chance when a florid, silver-haired man in Muskerry Castle livery, royal blue, for the kings of Munster, and red trim, for Cork, stopped at our table.

'Davy Keenan, as I live and breathe, how *are* you?' the man said.

Startled initially, Davy made a quick recovery.

'Edward, how's it going, boy? I'd forgotten you worked here. I wouldn't have known you in the outfit anyway. In all fairness, you look like a reject from the Opera House panto. Buttons, is that his name?'

They laughed.

'And who's this lovely lady?' Edward said.

Davy introduced me as his friend Finn and Edward introduced himself as Edward 'Call me Ned' Foley, concierge of this fine hotel for more years than he cared to remember.

'Would you like to join us, Ned?' I asked. 'It's my first time here for afternoon tea, and only my third time ever. I'd love to hear more about the hotel. Is it okay to have a look around, do you think?'

'I can't join you, I'm afraid,' Ned said. 'The curse of the day job. But if you call by the concierge desk on your way out, I'll be only delighted to give you a tour and to tell you what little I can about the place.'

'Hey, what's the story with you and Ned?' I asked after he'd left.

'Sorry, can't say,' Davy said.

'Now who's gone all secretive?'

What I didn't say was that I liked the man of mystery act he was putting on; liked it a lot. I leant across the table towards him and whispered, 'It's from NA, I'll bet. That's how you know him.'

I knew that members weren't supposed to tell who else went to meetings.

'Come off it, Buttons in NA? Hardly,' Davy said.

'AA so. That's it, isn't it?'

'I never said it, okay, so you can stop right there. But he's a good guy, believe me. Though I can see you have every intention of bleeding him dry for information, whatever you're up to.'

'Don't worry,' I said, calling for the bill. 'I'll be the soul of discretion.'

Not as discreet as Ned. For all his apparent friendliness, he was giving nothing away. He showed us the ballroom, and the bar, and gestured dramatically up the stairs in the direction of the bedrooms, and the various suites named after the ancient clans of Munster, the O'Briens, the McCarthys and the O'Sullivans and so on. I could have learnt as much, or more, from the hotel website. And when I mentioned Jeremy Gill arriving on Tuesday, dropping in that I was a Film Festival board member, I got an arctic reception.

'Oh, Finn, we *never* talk about our guests,' Ned said as he ushered us into the bar for a complimentary drink. I ordered a grapefruit juice and Davy a still water. At least I'd be able to check what kind of coasters the hotel used.

But there weren't any.

'You don't use coasters any more,' I said.

'We've never used coasters in the bar, Finn,' Ned said.

'But I have one,' I said. 'Small and round with fluted edges and "Muskerry Castle" printed on it.'

'I thought you said you'd never stayed over?'

'I haven't.'

'We only use those coasters in the bedrooms. In the bar, we've always used a cocktail napkin, American style.'

'I must have picked it up when I was at that wedding, maybe, or I'm not sure, I ...'

'I believe you, thousands wouldn't,' Ned said, with a quizzical glance at Davy, and a 'Byeee' as he went back to his duties.

'Well that was weird,' Davy said. 'What was it all about?'

'Davy, I can't say,' I said. 'I told you, it's something to do with work.'

'You're a solicitor with a sudden professional interest in coasters?'

'In a way, yes.'

'Give me a break. All I know is, the minute Ned mentioned "bedroom", you got very uncomfortable.'

'Don't be ridiculous,' I said.

'I'm ridiculous now, am I? Thanks.'

'That's not what I meant.'

'It's what you said, though. Are you going to tell me what's going on?'

'I can't. You know I can't.'

'Oh, come on. Don't give me this "client confidentiality" shit. I don't believe for a second that this is about work.'

'Well you'd better fucking believe it because it happens to be true.'

'This is all about a case?'

'I already said that it is.'

There was silence until Davy spoke again.

'Let's go,' he said. 'I've had enough.'

On the drive back to town, I felt Davy's annoyance in every gear change and engine rev, but he didn't say anything, and neither did I. He said nothing either as I got out of the car on Barrack Street. Every others time he had dropped me off, which wasn't all that often, he had got out and given me a hug. Or leant across and kissed me on the cheek. Not today.

I watched him drive away. He wasn't just annoyed, I realised. He was hurt.

In my bedroom, I tugged off my shoes without opening the buckles and dragged the purple dress over my head, leaving it crumpled on the floor where it fell. I pulled on pyjamas, sat in front of my mirror, and scrubbed at my eyes with make-up remover and cotton wool. Then I went upstairs to the living room, and paced. A lot of the reason I liked hanging out with Davy was that he didn't ask questions. Maybe he knew not to: today, the one time he had asked me anything, I had lied to him.

Darkest Truth

I was too wired to watch TV or read. I needed a minor project to occupy me, nothing too demanding, but enough to tire me out and quiet my thoughts. I went back downstairs to the study and checked the 1998 programme again. I typed 'Daniel O'Brien Cork Film Festival Education' into Google.

Nothing showed up so I tried 'Daniel O'Brien' on its own, then 'Dan' and 'Danny'. Lots of hits, but the photos didn't match. Then I remembered that Jessica had said she thought the man's name was Donal, the Irish for Daniel. Maybe there was a typo in the programme? I tried 'Donal O'Brien Cork Film Festival Education'. Then I tried Domhnall, the other way of spelling Donal. Nothing.

I tried Domhnall and Donal with the surname in Irish too, O'Briain, instead of O'Brien. Still nothing on general searches so I tried all the names on LinkedIn, Twitter and Facebook. And got nothing. There were numerous men with the same name but no matching photographs, and no mention of Film, Education or Cork Film Festival in the work histories.

I poked out the 1996, 1997, 1999 and 2000 catalogues. No Daniel O'Brien. No anybody O'Brien. It looked like he had only worked there that one year, 1998, and there was nothing in the printed 1998 programme about him except his name listed as education officer. I didn't know if he was originally from Cork, but if he had only worked there for one year it made sense that the festival didn't appear in searches against his name. What made less sense was that he wasn't showing up at all. Daniel O'Brien, the other adult male in the workshop photograph with Jeremy Gill and Deirdre, seemed to have vanished.

You can find anyone on the internet. People don't just disappear. Unless he was dead? At his age, it was unlikely. But if he *was* dead, he might show up on rip.ie. He didn't.

There was bound to be a simple explanation. All I had to do was talk to someone who had worked with him in 1998: fifteen years ago. None of the staff listed in the 1998 programme were still employed by the festival. Even Alice, who was almost an institution, had only been there for ten years, so there was no point in asking her. Not that she would have had time to talk. It was after 8 p.m. With the opening film starting at 8.30, she was sure to be busy.

But I had worked as a volunteer in 1998, organised by a co-ordinator who might remember the Education Officer. Marie was her first name, I remembered, but I had to check the catalogue for her last.

Thankfully, she had a slightly unusual surname: Wade. If she'd been called Murphy I could be here till morning and never find her. She showed up on a gratifying number of searches as living in Cork. Even better, she worked in the accounts department at the Opera House.

I logged out. I was fed up with the former Education Officer, who could probably add nothing to what I already knew. It was more comforting to review the progress I *had* made. Unexpectedly, earlier that day, I had gained potentially useful information: that the coaster Deirdre had hidden away had come from a bedroom. Ann Carney was sure that Deirdre had never been to Muskerry Castle.

But what if she had?

11

My assistant poked her head, and then her ample form, around the door, a Danish pastry with a bite taken out of it in her right hand.

'You've been diligent,' Tina said. 'In over the weekend and working from home too by the looks of it. I've *piles* of work waiting for me before the day starts. I was mighty impressed for about two minutes until I remembered that the Film Festival is on. You're obviously only working the weekend so's you can doss off loads during the week.'

I laughed.

'It's kind of to do with the festival,' I said. 'But there's more to it than that. Close the door and sit for five minutes. I'll give you a quick rundown.'

I walked her through my initial meeting with Sean and told her the results of my weekend researches. At the end of it, Tina said 'Feckit, Finn, that's got to be the dodgiest case you've ever taken on. Exciting, though. What did Gabriel say about it?'

'Well I haven't exactly told him. I half mentioned a new case to him on Saturday but didn't give him the details.'

'Hmmm. You have to tell him. The sooner the better. He might say no.'

Tina was right. I had to tell Gabriel about the case. But I hadn't told her about Deirdre's connection to me, and I hadn't figured out yet how I could get away with not telling Gabriel either. Though part of me knew that I should, most of me wanted to stay silent. If he knew anything about the case, the question would be sure to come up: why in the name of God was I taking it on? If I answered truthfully, he'd be bound to say that I was too close, and that my judgement was impaired. More than likely, he'd demand that I hand the file over to a colleague who'd see it immediately for what it was, a doomed pursuit that made sense only to me, and the case would be quietly dropped. No, I couldn't tell Gabriel.

'I need to put a few more things in place first. I think it'll be okay. I won't be spending office funds. And I've done everything so far on my own time. I want to have something concrete before I talk to him. That's where you come in.'

'If you're sure you know what you're doing?'

'I am,' I said. 'I need you to open up a file for Sean and Ann Carney, set them up as clients, check what information I need that I haven't got already. I know I didn't get their identity docs – they'll have to bring in that stuff this week. You can prep the client contracts for them, the standard litigation ones, and do up all the Section 68 bumph. And make an appointment with them to come in tomorrow afternoon and tell them what to bring along.'

'Say 3.30 or 4?'

'Make it a bit earlier, 2.30 if you can – but 3 p.m. is fine at a push. And I need you to make some calls for me, find a few people, get their contact details.'

'The boys from the youth jury first, I s'pose, what were their names again?'

I smiled. Tina could read my mind.

'Yes, smarty pants, Lorcan Lucey, who went to Pres. I reckon we should concentrate on him. It's hardly worth our while looking for the other boy. There must be hundreds of Patrick McCarthys in Cork, that's if he still lives here, and thousands around the country. As well, can you see if you can track down Joey O'Connor?'

'The boyfriend.'

'Exactly. Used to go to St Finbarr's School, now possibly working in the family motor business, somewhere on the Kinsale Road.'

'What about the two teachers?' Tina asked.

'Aifric and Mr O'Donnell? Yeah, I'm wondering how best to get to them. I'm thinking that the best thing to do is for me to make an appointment to see the school principal first. Might be hard to get talking to them otherwise – I presume they're teaching classes most of the time. And I'll drop the photos into Camera World to get copied and enlarged on the way to court. Oh and where could I buy a lockable box, do you know?'

'Ronnie Moore's?'

'Marlboro Street. On my way, sure, so I can do that too,' I said.

I locked the exhibits into my office desk drawer and grabbed my bag, double-checking that my files were in it, along with a pen, a barrister's notebook and the photos for copying.

'I'm gone. Talk later,' I said. 'Thanks Tina.'

It was an unwritten rule that the really easy cases, the ones that looked most settleable, were the ones that ended up causing the trouble. And often the troublesome cases ended up being easy. But not always. And if the tough cases went wrong, they were the worst of all. So, over the years, I had learnt to expect the unexpected, to suck up whatever happened and move on, with the minimum of fuss and as few backward glances as I could manage. Which didn't mean that I was relaxed, or anything like it. My default setting for court was anxiety, varying from low to high, and averaging out usually, like today, somewhere in the middle. And if I wasn't worried, then I'd worry for sure, about losing my edge or what I wasn't seeing. An older colleague had told me when I was starting out that being a solicitor was like being at war: days and weeks of dullness interspersed with moments of terror. He had had it right, I reckoned but, however I scanned them, today's cases were routine, and I was glad. Immersing myself in other people's problems had never been a more welcome prospect.

I dropped the photographs into Camera World and arrived outside the Family Court a little before ten for the 10.30 list. I had a few minutes to spare so I rang the Opera House and asked to speak to Marie Wade. But Marie had a day off so the search for the former festival education officer Daniel O'Brien would have to wait.

Inside the courthouse, I embarked on a hunt for my clients and the opposing solicitors. It was a small place but with two waiting rooms, a couple of possible hallway loitering zones and an exterior smoking area, it was often hard to find who you were looking for at the exact moment you needed to find them.

It was nearly a quarter past ten, with the callover of the judge's list approaching at half past. I had managed to meet and have a preliminary word with both opposing solicitors, yet my clients still hadn't appeared. I hung by the door and started to fret, imagining that I had given the clients the wrong court date by mistake. But, after another while, they had arrived, one of them complaining about parking problems, the other stinking of the previous night's alcohol and saying little apart from a mumbled 'Sorry about that, Finn'.

I dived into the morning's work.

By twenty to one, I was done. I took the opportunity, in the quiet of the solicitors' room, to google Deirdre's old school. I rang the phone number on the St Finbarr's University School website, which was light on other details, teachers' names or the hours of the school day. I gave my name and profession but no other details to the secretary who answered.

I was put straight through to the head teacher. Sometimes 'solicitor' has a magical effect. Schools are universally obsessed by insurance costs and claims and, once he'd heard that I wasn't planning on suing him and that his premium was safe, the principal, Eoghan MacGiolla, agreed to see me that very afternoon. He also said that he would ask Miss Sheehan and Mr O'Donnell to make themselves available. I told MacGiolla that I would be at the school by 3 p.m. at the latest.

As I crossed City Hall Bridge on to the South Mall, I rang Tina and arranged to meet her for lunch. Then I turned right into Marlboro Street and bought the cash box.

Next, I collected the photographs from Camera World. The enlargement all but confirmed that the name badge was the same as the one I'd found at the Carney house.

Now that I had copies of the photographs, I could return the originals to the Film Festival, somehow, preferably without attracting attention. Or was it best to walk in brazenly and say that I'd borrowed them as if it was no big deal? I'd decide later.

I looked again at Daniel O'Brien, the education officer, in the enlarged picture. Jessica had said that he was a nice man. He looked it. He had a round face, a big smile, ill-advised Harry Potter glasses and a small potbelly, the expansion of which seemed inevitable. He'd be mid-thirties by now, and his hair looked light brown or dark blond, though it was hard to tell from the photo. The fact that I hadn't been able to find him was niggling me, and I'd talk to Marie Wade when I got a chance, but I wouldn't spend much time on him.

From the Grand Parade, I turned down Tobin Street, more of a lane than a street, and passed the Triskel Arts Centre. Gulpd Cafe, my destination, was on the left. Opposite was the Hubert Bookbindery on the ground floor of Hatfield House. The building was named for Hurd Hatfield, an American actor who had lived in the County Cork countryside in his latter years. Hatfield, a local celebrity and a regular attender at the Film Festival, though I had never met him, had played the narcissistic deceiver Dorian Gray in the 1945 movie of the book. Which made me think about Jeremy Gill again.

I needed lunch.

Spotting Tina at a table in the corner, I waved. Then, I ordered my usual, a chicken baguette, at the counter and went to join her.

'So, tell me, what have you got?' I said.

'General, or new case?' Tina asked.

'New case,' I said. 'Unless there's anything major I need to know about?'

'Naw, all's grand,' Tina said. 'But on the new case, first of all, and easiest to find, Joey O'Connor is definitely working at the family car sales business. I have a printout of the address and the location for you back at the office. I talked to him on the phone and he said he'd be there till six this evening if you want to call out. He assumed you'd be going to see him about buying a new car, and I didn't bother correcting him.'

'Good woman. Anything else? The jury boys?'

'Not so good. Neither school would give out their addresses without authorisation. I did a general search. There are about ten million Patrick McCarthys, as you can imagine. But I *was* able to find Lorcan Lucey, or somebody I think is the same guy. He's working up in UCC in the philosophy department as a lecturer or tutor or something. He's on their web page anyway. Here's a printout: same guy, right?'

'Looks it. Okay, let's abandon Patrick and concentrate on Lorcan. By the way, I realised earlier that I should've asked you to do up written authorities for the Carneys for Deirdre's education and medical records. Prepare drafts, would you, please, Tina, and we can refine them before tomorrow afternoon. They *are* coming in, aren't they?'

'Yep, half two, it's in your diary,' Tina said.

'Thanks,' I said. 'Now please eat your lunch.'

We walked back to the office together. Up in my room, I gave Tina a few more files to work on and threw myself into my chair.

'You've done loads, Tina,' I said. 'I'll race through my messages and do a couple of attendance notes on court this morning. But then I'll scoot off, see if I can get anywhere with the school and Joey O'Connor later this evening. If you've time, you might see if you can get Lorcan Lucey's work number and text it to me.'

'Got it already, needless to say, being the wonderful secretary that I am.'

'You *are* the best, and so modest too,' I said.

'Modest to a fault, girl,' Tina said.

She was laughing as she left the room.

I ran through my calls list to see if there were any I couldn't ignore. And I decided that, for the moment, the handwritten notes I'd made of this morning's cases would suffice – the orders would be in from the court office in a day or two, anyway. The only work I wanted to do for the rest of the afternoon was on the Carney case, and that meant neglecting other essentials. But Jeremy Gill was going to be in Cork tomorrow and I needed to have as much knowledge as I could before he arrived. I tried calling Lorcan Lucey, got voicemail, and left a 'Finn Fitzpatrick, Solicitor' message and my mobile number, hoping it would pique his interest enough for him to call me back.

'Back to school time,' I said aloud.

Almost instantaneously, I was out of my chair, taking the stairs two at a time and on MacSwiney Street, walking at speed in the direction of Deirdre's old school. I'd think about what I was going to say when I got there along the way.

But five minutes later, I was back in the office. I had forgotten to put the exhibits in my newly purchased lockable box. And I'd forgotten, too, about returning the photos to the Film Festival. No matter, I thought. The photos could wait. I put them, and the exhibits, into the box, locked it, and locked everything into the desk. It wasn't anything to worry about, I told myself. The photos weren't of interest to anyone except me.

Most likely, nobody had even noticed they were gone.

12

Built in the late nineteenth century, with more than a nod to the neo-Gothic splendour of William Burges's St Fin Barre's Cathedral, St Finbarr's Catholic University School was something of an oddity. Co-ed since the seventies and, despite its title, an independent school from its inception, it had been founded by a Catholic merchant prince family determined not to be outdone by the city's numerous Protestant benefactors. Legend had it that the 'Finbarr' in the school's name referred not to St Finbarr of Cork's first monastic settlement but to Finbarr McCarthy himself, the school's founder, he of the charity and good works, and never shy when it came to publicising them.

'Sure you probably know our history, Finn,' Eoghan Mac-Giolla said, ushering me into his shockingly palatial office overlooking the Lee. 'And you're most welcome to visit, let me add, most welcome indeed, *fáilte*, but I'm wondering, now, what can I do for you?'

Short and wide, with tightly cut brown hair and a well-fed, fleshy face, Eoghan looked like a man who had a hard time controlling his temper. His back teeth clenched, his mouth faking an unconvincing impression of a smile, I could see that he was having second thoughts about his eager co-operation but tried to smarm my way through his doubts.

'Thank you from the bottom of my heart for being so generous with your time and your help – I can't tell you how much Sean and Ann Carney will appreciate it. Do you know them yourself?'

'Not at all, unfortunately, though I'm aware of them, of course. I wasn't working here when Deirdre, God rest her, was a pupil, but the school sent a representative to her funeral. Two, actually, the two you've asked to see. Miss Sheehan and Mr O'Donnell.'

'Perhaps it's best if I see them so, rather than taking up too much more of your valuable time? And I'd like to see them individually, if that's all right?'

'Individually?' MacGiolla asked. His smile was even more strained.

'Essential,' I said. 'Everyone has their own recollections, and I know that Aifric, Miss Sheehan, knew her as a friend rather than as a teacher so it might be inappropriate to see them together.'

'Well, of course, you're right, yes, inappropriate, yes.'

He stood and moved quickly towards the door.

'Come with me,' he said. 'I have the Student Counselling Room set aside for you down the hall.'

*

Broom cupboard might have been a better description. The tiny room held three mismatched lumpy armchairs, a box of Tesco Value tissues and a musty-smelling bunch of dried flowers on a Formica-topped coffee table. It looked like pupil mental health wasn't top priority.

'Mr O'Donnell, the art teacher, I presume,' I said, and shook hands with the lean, handsome, shaven-headed man who came in a few minutes later. Dressed in black and well groomed, he looked like an architect.

'For my sins,' he said. 'Colm's the name. And you're Finn, here to talk about Deirdre Carney.'

'That's right. Deirdre's parents have asked me to look into what happened when she was a pupil here. They trace her mental breakdown to her Transition Year at St Finbarr's. You knew her well, I believe?'

'Yes,' Colm said. 'Though she gave up art for the Leaving Cert, so I saw less of her in fifth and sixth year. And she was absent a lot too, of course.'

'You had a fair bit to do with her around the time of the Film Festival when she was in Transition Year?'

'The Film Festival?' Colm asked. 'Well, yes, I suppose I did.'

'You seem surprised at the mention of the festival,'

'I am. I'm surprised you're here at all. It's kind of out of the blue, isn't it?'

I ignored the question.

'Could you tell me about the lead-up to the Film Festival, how Deirdre came to be on the youth jury?' I asked.

'Well, I put her in for it, nominated her. She had to write an essay about why she wanted to do it and, needless to say, she was selected. She was my first really excellent student. I was fairly new to teaching when she started in First Year, and it was great to see her progress. I had high hopes for her, wanted to do what I could to help her on her way.'

'Sounds like she was a favourite.'

'Favourite? Oh yes, you could say that. We're not supposed to have them but we all do. It was easy to love Deirdre Carney.'

'Love? Isn't that an odd choice of word?'

'It is if you want it to be,' Colm said.

He paused.

'Or it could be the most normal thing in the world.'

Jesus Christ. Was he confessing to a relationship with Deirdre?

'I spoke to Jessica Murphy, Deirdre's old school friend too. Do you remember her? She said that they all thought you were in love with Deirdre,' I said.

He laughed.

'Hardly. I've never been in love with a girl, or a woman, in my life. I'm gay. Not that I'd be broadcasting it in this place, mind you. It's "don't ask, don't tell" around here, as you can imagine, though I'm sure that everyone knows by now. No, Deirdre was like a younger sister, or a daughter, to me. And she was a student of mine. It would be unthinkable to cross that boundary with her, or with any of my students, male or female.'

I believed him. I liked him too, had done from the moment he'd walked in the door. Maybe I could be more direct with him than I had been with Jessica Murphy.

'Tell me anything you know about Deirdre and Jeremy Gill,' I said.

After a pause, he spoke.

'Confidentially?'

'Yes,' I said.

The time might come when I would have to ask him to drop the confidentiality. But for now, yes, anything he told me was confidential.

'There's something not quite right about that guy Gill,' Colm said. 'He's flavour of the month and super-successful and all that, but from what I saw of him during Film Festival '98, he's a complete shit and a fucking pervert too.'

I hadn't expected anything this explosive from him. It took me a moment to respond.

'That's a damning verdict,' I said. 'Did you see him do something?'

'No, I'm just going on how he was with me. He didn't know I was gay so he was talking to me about the girls in the workshop group, while they were doing whatever task he'd set. To be fair to him, the workshop was excellent. But he was going on to me about how there was nothing like a school uniform and how did I keep my hands off them, all that – you can imagine. And he didn't hold back on the graphic language either. He gravitated towards me; all the other teachers were women. They might as well not have existed, and some of them were good-looking too. I thought he was a sleazy oddball who'd end up going nowhere, to be honest. I mean his short film was great but even that had a schoolgirl in it, for God's sake. Shows what I know. I can't say I saw him doing anything wrong. I didn't. If I had, I'd have done something about it. I saw that he took a shine to Deirdre, sure, but there was no risk. I was there all the time, and there were plenty of other adults to supervise. He was all about her, though, charm itself, really. It kinda made me gag, knowing what he was really thinking, after what he'd said. Yeah. I made sure to get her and my other students out of there hotfoot as soon as the workshop was over. So ...'

'It's stayed very fresh in your mind, for something where nothing happened.'

'Yes.'

'You think something *did* happen,' I said, leading him.

Colm leant forward.

'She had a mental breakdown,' he said. 'That's what the parents told us. I know they submitted sick notes from the GP. I know that she spent time, a lot of time, later in St Michael's, with severe depression. I called round to the house, asked after her, tried to get her to talk to me. She wouldn't. But I suppose I knew there was more to it, or thought I did, than depression. It descended so suddenly on her. I arranged a meeting between the school counsellor and Ann Carney, to talk about her, see if we could do anything to help. But nothing came of that. I wondered if there was something odd about the family; her parents were older than most, and I knew that Deirdre had been adopted. But there was no real sign of anything wrong there. And bear in mind this was a long time ago. I think if it happened now, that sudden change, I'd make a call to the social worker helpline. There would almost certainly be an investigation. But times were different then. And she was sixteen, not six ...'

He trailed off, then looked hard at me.

'Is this about Gill? An investigation?'

'It's about Deirdre,' I said. 'Do you think it should be about Gill?'

'Something happened. Something sudden and catastrophic. All I know is that she was never the same after the Film Festival in 1998. And I know she met Gill there. So if you're investigating Deirdre, you have to look at Gill. I only wish I'd looked more closely.'

I felt buoyed by Colm O'Donnell's hatchet job. Before he left, I took his contact details, asked him to say nothing of what we'd spoken of to anyone, and to phone me if he thought of anything else. But as I waited for Aifric Sheehan to come into the room, my critical faculties kicked back in. If O'Donnell had been trying to distract me from looking at *him*, he couldn't have done a better job. I had lapped up his attack on Jeremy Gill. It was called confirmation bias, wasn't it – hearing something that accorded with your personal prejudices and giving it extra weight, as a result? It wouldn't have taken a genius to figure out that I was after Gill. I'd as much as said it. Colm O'Donnell had given me what I'd wanted, without saying very much at all. And I had believed him. Still did. But if he had reason to question Gill's behaviour, to link him to Deirdre's breakdown, why hadn't he said anything at the time? He had had well-formed suspicions. Maybe he didn't want to draw attention to himself – or was there was some other reason?

I'd have to keep an open mind about Mr O'Donnell. And I'd be more circumspect with Ms Sheehan.

'Call me Aifric.'

Blonde, she was dressed all in pink, with dazzling laser-whitened teeth. But, to my disappointment, she remembered little about the Film Festival.

'It was more Deirdre's thing than mine, to be honest, though at that age I'd have done anything for a few days off, anything for a laugh! And the irony of ending up as a geography teacher and I never even liked geography!'

She said that she had lost touch with Deirdre completely after she got sick.

'Like, you know, we all tried to keep up the old friendship for a while but she wanted to be left alone, that's what she kept saying, and if you keep saying it often enough, people take you at your word.'

There was a callousness to Aifric Sheehan, for all her Rose of Tralee looks. But I played along, thanking her at length for all her help and commenting on how upsetting it must have been for her to see Deirdre so unwell.

Aifric nodded.

'You've no idea, Finn, you've absolutely no idea.'

'You all met Jeremy Gill, didn't you, at the Film Festival – what was he like?'

'Octopus,' Aifric said.

'What do you mean?'

'All hands.'

'Jessica Murphy never said that.'

'Ah now, in all fairness,' Aifric said, 'poor Jessica wasn't the prettiest so he'd hardly have bothered with her, would he?'

I didn't think attractiveness had much to do with the behaviour Aifric was describing, but I smiled anyway.

'Do tell me more,' I said.

'Nothing to tell. Coming in a *little* too close to check on the work I was doing, hand on the shoulder, hand on the back, drifting down a bit too far, brushing up against me as I passed. You know yourself, you can't say anything because it's not visible to anyone watching, might even be accidental, though you know in your heart and soul it isn't. Dirty article. Probably fits right in in Hollywood. But, yeah, actually, that's the funny thing, I remember now. I said it to Deirdre at some stage, maybe on the way home, something about Gill being, I don't know, a creep or something, but she was having none of it. Maybe he hadn't done any of it to her. Though he gave her a lot of attention, all right. I remember that. I forgot about him. Next creep came along, I suppose.'

'But you didn't forget.'

A shadow passed across her face.

'No,' Aifric said. 'We don't, do we?'

I shook my head.

'Did you ever see Gill again?' I asked after a moment.

Other than in the media, she hadn't. He had made no attempt to contact her and she wasn't aware of any contact with Deirdre either.

*

After, I replayed what Aifric Sheehan and Colm O'Donnell had told me. Both of them had portrayed Gill as vulgar, obvious and intrusive, grist to the part of me that wanted him guilty.

But Jessica Murphy hadn't seen any of that. And when Aifric had said to Deirdre that Gill was a creep, she had disagreed vehemently. I had to admit that Jessica's story and Deirdre's reaction evidenced a very different narrative, one I liked a lot less.

A pitched battle was going on inside me, I realised, between a reasonable rational lawyer and an Old Testament avenger.

And that thought scared me a lot more than Jeremy Gill did.

13

After several tries, I had finally managed to get my hands on the most valuable document in Cork – the City Council Residents' Parking Permit sticker. The proofs needed made getting a passport look easy but meant that, for a tenner a year, I could park for unlimited periods on the streets near my home. I walked most places so, most of the time, my black Golf stayed parked. But I needed it now for the trip to the O'Connor motor dealership on the Kinsale Road.

I got into the car. Checking my phone, I found a message from Tina. She had been googling. It turned out that Joey O'Connor had form. She had emailed me a link to an *Evening Echo* article and photo: '*Rugby star in Roid Rage Rampage.*' Eight years ago, Joey had been convicted of dealing in anabolic steroids and of seriously assaulting two of the guards who had come to arrest him. The photo showed an expensively suited, baby-faced athletic-looking Joey, in his early twenties by then. The article recited the plea given by his barrister (injury, temptation, bad mistake, inexcusable, deep regret, out of character, new leaf, working in the family business, promising rugby career derailed, charity work) which had resulted in a suspended sentence. It was a middle-class tragedy that might have ended a lot differently if he had been from somewhere less leafy. Well done, Tina, I thought but texted back only 'Ta', focused already on what I'd say to Joey.

He was outside the door smoking a cigarette as I pulled into the front of the gleaming glass and steel showroom. He wasn't on steroids any more, that was clear. Somewhere along the way, Joey's life had taken a wrong turn and instead he'd gained a permanent frown, an air of bitterness, and about sixty pounds. He didn't look like he sold many cars, but then nobody had sold many cars in Ireland in the last five years and, as the boss's son, he would have been insulated from the risk of redundancy.

Joey greeted me with a nasal, '*How's* it going?'

I introduced myself and gave him my card but, before I could say why I was there, he was in with the patter.

'What had you in mind, Finn? We've a great range here, both new and quality used. You look like you're ready for a change anyway,' he said.

He gave my battered ten-year-old Golf a pitying glance, turned back to me, and smiled. The smile stopped at his mouth.

'Keep her outside, do you?'

'Yeah, but I—'

'I suppose the rust is a bit of a giveaway. On the street?'

'Yes.'

'No danger of anyone stealing her, anyway. What area of the city do you live in?'

'Off Barrack Street. But actually I'm not here about a car, Joey.'

I handed him my card.

'I'm here about a case, nothing to do with you, specifically. I represent Deirdre Carney's parents. They've asked me to look into her death. They think something happened to her when she was in Transition Year'

'What the fuck?' Joey said. 'What's this about?'

He backed away, shaking his head. I didn't know if he was mad or sad. Maybe both. But at least he was backing away. He was huge.

'I'm sorry, Joey,' I said. 'This must be upsetting. I know you and Deirdre—'

'Fucking right. She killed herself. I think you might call that upsetting.'

'Yes, of course, Joey. I apologise if this brings up bad memories. I—'

'What exactly are you trying to suggest?'

This time there was no confusion. He was angry and he was walking towards me. I stood my ground. Whatever he felt like doing, I had to hope that he wouldn't do it here, in full view of his workmates, and probably on CCTV, too.

'I'm not suggesting anything,' I said. 'I'm just here to ask you about Deirdre. I've already spoken to Jessica Murphy, and she told me you were close to Deirdre. And that sometime after the Film Festival in 1998, she changed, and was never the same after. And that's it. I'm just here to see if you know anything about why she changed.'

'What are you saying? Why should I know anything about that?'

Anguished-looking, he took in a couple of deep breaths. His voice was quieter when he started talking again.

'She ... she got sick. Did what she did. I don't know any more. I tried to get back with her, even after she was in and out of the mental ... I mean St Michael's. She never answered my calls, never came out with me when I asked her. I even tried to visit her in hospital. But she wouldn't see me. She was like a stranger. When she broke it off with me after the festival, she said there was another guy so ...'

'I've seen a photo of you all back then, a group shot, at a workshop with Jeremy Gill. And then a shot of Deirdre with two other students and Jeremy. She looked happy.'

'Yeah, I thought she was. It was later ...'

He paused.

'Later ... ?' I asked. 'You mean that it was after the Film Festival she ended it?'

'Yeah,' he said, after another pause.

'Do you know the name of the other guy?'

'No,' he said. 'No, I never found out who he was, the fucking bastard. All I know is, he didn't last. There was no one calling to see her. I'd have known if there was.'

'What was Gill like, do you remember?'

'Oily fucker,' Joey said. 'Deirdre was impressed. I wasn't.'

'Did that make you jealous?'

'Jealous? Are you *joking* me or what? He was ancient and I was bored stupid. I was only there 'cause of Deirdre. Films weren't my thing. I was into rugby, and I was into her. Now, please go, would you? I don't like talking about her. Brings it all back.'

I knew I'd get no more out of Joey today. And I couldn't think of a way to ask about his convictions, though I was keen to see his reaction. I tried one last question.

'Thanks for your help, Joey. Will you call me if you remember anything else about Deirdre after the Film Festival, anything that might help?'

'I *told* you to leave,' he shouted, hands by his side, fists clenched.

Shaking, I drove off. Joey had a vicious temper and a history of violence. And he'd cared about Deirdre. Loved her, probably. What might he have done as a teenager, his desires thwarted? Deirdre had kept saying it was her fault.

Might she have been talking about Joey?

I had taken a few steps forward with my investigation into Gill, but this was a giant step back. Impulsive, brute-strong, and with a proven disregard for the law: if you were casting a violent rapist in a TV crime drama, it would be hard to look beyond Joey O'Connor. He had loved Deirdre, was crazy about her, Jessica had said, but the flip side of love is hate: for proof, sit and listen to the proceedings in any courtroom anywhere any day of the week.

And what about Jessica? What if she had known more than she'd said? Had she been jealous of Deirdre's relationship with Joey? Why hadn't she told me about Joey's convictions? She must have known. What if he had sought comfort with her after Deirdre had rejected him? Might Jessica have been protecting Joey by pretending to dislike him?

None of it felt right, but in the end the only reason I could come up with for eliminating Joey as a suspect was that I wanted Gill to be the guilty one.

It was another night of broken sleep, my sense of unease about Joey and my concerns in advance of Jeremy Gill's imminent arrival in Cork made worse by the fact that Davy wasn't replying to my messages. I had sent him two texts during the day. My iPhone told me he'd read them. But he hadn't replied.

By 3a.m. I had had enough. I deleted the conversation from my messages and put my phone upstairs in the living room, on silent. Back in bed, when I wasn't thinking about Davy, Deirdre went around and around in my head, along with the old voices, and the blurred pictures I'd failed to delete.

Her coming to collect me for a visit, coming in a taxi, her at the gate, Doreen walking me out to her, us getting the smell.

'I don't think Mum's well enough to take you out today, Finn. Go back in while we have a chat.'

Me watching from the door.

Her shouting.

'I am not drunk, how dare you, give me my child!'

133

Doreen closing the door on her.

Her hammering on the wood, her face peering through the bubble glass.

Her, and not her.

The noise, that's what I remember most.

Breaking glass.

Shouting.

Crying.

The quiet with Jim and Doreen.

Me starting to call him Dad.

Me starting to call her Mam.

Me wishing it was true.

Me wishing something bad.

14

I got up at six and, with massive effort, went to my study without checking my phone to see if Davy had messaged me. I reread the information I'd logged the night before, concentrating on Joey O'Connor. He had said that Deirdre had told him there was someone else and that, if she had had an ongoing relationship, he would have known. I realised that I should have asked *how* he would have known. If he'd talk to me again, what he had to say might help my case against Gill. But I'd be a fool if I allowed myself to forget that Joey was a suspect too.

And I'd be late if I didn't hurry. This case consumed time like nothing I'd done before. I raced up the two flights of stairs from my study to the kitchen, grabbed an apple from the bowl to munch on the way, shoved a Glenisk yoghurt in my handbag and ran back down one flight and into my bedroom. One of the advantages of being a solicitor is the uniform-like dress code, which is boring, but takes all the effort out of weekday dressing. I grabbed one of my black skirt suits and one of my many white shirts and, with a slick of red lipstick, I was out the door – unshowered, admittedly, and wearing no earrings.

I was in my office fifteen minutes later, just before nine, dead on my feet, distracted as hell, but ready for work. When I'd checked my phone. I did. Still no message from Davy.

'Fuckfuckfuck,' I said, and threw the phone in a drawer.

A groaning inbox, and a list of missed calls from the previous day meant that I barely greeted Tina when she came in with the post.

'Talk later,' I mouthed, on hold at CIE Legal and simultan-eously rereading a medical report on the eighteen-year-old son of an important client of Gabriel McGrath's who had been knocked off his bike when he'd either wobbled into the path of the 214 bus or been the victim of a sudden swerve, depending on whether you believed the bus driver or the plaintiff. It was a good sign that the defendants were the ones who had rung me, a signal that they wanted to set up negotiations. Settle-ments meant fees. It would be a long time before the Carney case got anywhere, if it ever did. Meanwhile, Gabriel and the other partners expected me to pay my way in the firm. And the pressure on me was bound to increase after I told them about the Carney case.

It was almost noon before I realised that I hadn't eaten my yoghurt, warm now, but I ate it anyway. Then I rang Tina and asked her to bring up coffee for both of us. I had already forwarded her my updated notes for saving to the office case management system. I guessed that Tina would have read them and that she would have an opinion on Joey O'Connor.

'The way I see it, Finn,' Tina said. 'Either Jeremy Gill did it or we have nothing. The only reason we're doing this loopy case is because the dad thinks it's Jeremy. He never mentioned Joey to you. Never asked you to go near him. Now, have a Jaffa Cake, it's the best brain food there is.'

I took the biscuit and ate it in two bites. Tina had a point. I had to bear Joey in mind, and any other signs of Gill's possible innocence. But surely I wasn't obliged to give equal weight to every lead? Sean had come to me with his concerns about Gill, and Gill alone.

'I wish I'd had you to talk to at four o'clock this morning,' I said. 'I was tossing and turning half the night trying to sort it out in my head. Though if you'd met Joey ...'

'I don't have to meet him,' Tina said. 'He sounds like a complete langer altogether.' I couldn't have put it better myself.

I was waiting by the bike stand on Emmett Place when Marie Wade emerged at three minutes past one. I had called her at work at the Opera House accounts department. She had agreed to meet me at lunchtime: she took a stroll every day and had said I was welcome to tag along.

'Now I remember,' Marie said. 'I couldn't put a face to the name on the phone earlier. You all set to go?'

'Ready when you are.'

The North Face waterproof jacket and serious walking shoes should have been a portent. She took off at speed over the Christy Ring Bridge, but it was only when we got to the top of Coburg

Street that the full horror of her lunchtime regimen became apparent: repeated trips up and down Patrick's Hill, Cork's meanest slope. Though the view made it a worthwhile slog any time, that wasn't why Marie did it.

'I'm going skiing in January,' she said. 'I go every year. This is great for the muscles.'

At the top, with the green of Bell's Field dipping towards Blackpool, and the houses heaped to the summit of the hill opposite, and Cork's shabby magnificence laid out before us, she paused long enough to examine the photo of Daniel O'Brien I had saved to my phone.

'I remember him,' Marie said, as she started the descent. 'Nice guy.'

'So I hear,' I said. 'Any word from him after he left?'

'Not a sausage. I didn't know him all that well – I was only in for a few weeks managing the volunteers. He was fun to be around but we weren't super-pally.'

'Was he from Cork, do you know?'

'Let me think,' Marie said.

'No,' she said after long while. 'Not Cork. I think he was from County Clare. Is it important for you to find out?'

'I don't know,' I said. 'It might or might not be. If you remember anything else, will you let me know?'

'Of course I will. Ready for the next one?'

We were at the bottom.

'I might forgo that, I think.'

'You should give it a go some other day,' Marie said. 'You'd be surprised how quickly you'd get into it.'

Yeah, I thought as, five minutes later, I sat slurping a latte in the window of Cork Coffee Roasters, I'd be truly amazed. Even Davy had never tried to make me take on Patrick's Hill.

Back at the office, I had enough time to try Lorcan Lucey's number again before the Carneys arrived for their appointment. There was a possibility that he hadn't heard the first voicemail. Whether he had or not, he hadn't bothered to call back. I left a second message and phoned the Philosophy Department at UCC. The department administrator, Noreen, told me that Dr Lucey was at lectures all afternoon and that she'd pass on that I was looking for him, though she didn't know when she'd see him and couldn't possibly say when he'd be in his office. I didn't know if she was telling the truth or being evasive.

'That's a pity,' I said. 'I have a visitor coming to stay from the Philosophy Department in Bangalore University and I know that he's keen to attend some lectures in UCC. He mentioned Dr Lucey's work in particular. I'm not sure what it's about but he was talking about an exchange programme and foreign students or something like that.'

'Oh. That sounds important.'

'It might be, Noreen. You'd be the expert on that kind of thing. I'm just thinking, I wonder would it be possible for you to email me Dr Lucey's timetable? It would make everything a lot easier, less hassle, and we could leave them both to their own devices.'

In less than a minute, the timetable was sitting in my inbox. Lucrative foreign students opened doors at UCC, and at all the universities, but I was shocked at how easily the lie had come to me.

By the time the Carneys had produced their identification documents and proofs of address and had signed the client contracts and the various authorisations that I needed so that I could get Deirdre's medical records, most of an hour had gone by. They looked exhausted and I had started to sweat. Yes, Sean had initiated the complaint against Gill. Yes, he had told me that Deirdre was my sister. But I knew that he and Ann were going through this rigmarole because of me. Whether I hoped to forge a permanent connection with Deirdre or whether it was something else that was driving me, I had invented a civil case that no reasonable lawyer would have pursued. If it ended up being a wild goose chase, which it well might, I was afraid of what that might do to them.

But I was even more afraid of them changing their minds about pursuing the case, and of what that might do to me. Catching Gill, avenging Deirdre's death, was starting to feel like the most important thing I might ever do.

And if I failed? I couldn't bear to think about it.

'We'll be looking forward to a progress report,' Sean said.

I won't have news for a long time. Maybe never.

'It's going to take a bit of time, Sean,' I said. 'It might be a little while before I have anything major to say.'

'Of course it will, love,' Ann said.

'I had a good chat with Jessica, though,' I said. 'She was helpful. And I visited Deirdre's old school and met Aifric and Colm O'Donnell the art teacher.'

'Did you meet the boss?'

'Eoghan MacGiolla, the headmaster?'

'That's him,' Sean said.

'Yes. He told me he wasn't working in the school when Deirdre was a pupil.'

'No,' Sean said. 'But he was a neighbour. Used to live in Lee Valley Park. He knew Deirdre her whole life and then he got the big job in St Finbarr's School and moved to Maryborough Heights and he couldn't find one couple of hours in his day to come to her funeral.'

'What has that to do with anything?' Ann said. 'Finn, Sean spends his time finding people to give out about and it does him no good.'

I was only half listening to Ann. I'd have to check my notes but I was nearly sure Eoghan MacGiolla had led me to believe that he had never met Deirdre. He told me that he didn't know her parents either. Though maybe I had it wrong? Either way, there was no point mentioning it now. By agreement, I put a reminder in my diary to call the Carneys for an appointment to come and see me in two weeks. Meanwhile, if anything urgent cropped up requiring their input, I would contact them immediately.

'Before you go, there's one last thing,' I said. 'It's not to do with the case itself, it's just that by its nature this is a situation where the Gardaí have a lot of expertise and, even though no prosecution is possible, I think it might help if I showed the file to a detective Garda I know well, and trust. Her name is Sadie O'Riordan, from Coughlan's Quay Garda Station. She was in my law class at UCC, actually. Would you authorise me to talk to her about the case?'

'I talked to the cops and it was a complete waste of time,' Sean said.

'Do if it helps,' Ann said, giving Sean a poke in the arm. 'Don't mind this fella.'

'Oh sure if the boss says yes, then who am I to question?' Sean said. 'Good luck.'

I'd need luck, and plenty of it, if I was to earn the trust the Carneys had placed in me. For a while after they had gone, I stared out my window at the darkening sky, my stomach swirling. By now, Jeremy Gill had arrived in town. He might even have reached City Hall. Soon, he'd be making his way to Cork Opera House.

And I would be there to welcome him.

15

If I craned my neck, I could see the spot where Deirdre had stepped into the biting January waters of the Lee's North Channel. I was standing in the bay window on the top floor of the Opera House, high above the river where my sister had floated on the way to being dead, her suicide a tragic mirroring of her own history. Our mother had gone with the river too, though Deirdre had known nothing of that, and I had never looked beyond what little my mam had told me, had never sought out the inquest records or Garda reports, had never investigated what the newspapers had said, had tried to suppress all of it.

And yet I had leapt at the chance to investigate Deirdre's life and death. What would a psychotherapist say?

'Are you thinking about jumping in?'

I jolted, then turned around. It was Sarah-Jane Carey, the Film Festival PR.

'They say it's cleaned up since they did the main drainage, but I wouldn't fancy a swim all the same, would you?'

'Sarah-Jane, you gave me a fright! But hang on, I'm not in your way, am I?'

The window, with clear northern light and the river in the background, was a popular location for PR photos.

'Nah, calm down, you're grand,' Sarah-Jane said. 'It's dark now and anyway we got great shots over at City Hall. Jeremy is a dream, honest to God. So obliging for the cameras. Total pro. But, hey, come on in, you're here for the reception, right? I was just out at the loo. I was dying for a wee, hadn't a second all day.'

I was glad of Sarah-Jane's company and stream-of-consciousness babble as we walked together into the bar. There were no more than fifty guests, a string quartet playing classical arrangements of movie themes and a selection of juices and sparkling wine instead of the usual Château de l'Opening plonk. Jeremy Gill was on the far side of the room, his back to me, deep in animated conversation with a woman I didn't know who looked like she might be a commercial sponsor. She was dressed in the kind of 'office to cocktail party' outfit beloved of fashion features around Christmas: a black trouser suit with a red silky camisole and an enormous shiny pendant that she kept fiddling with.

The atmosphere was charged, and everybody was either looking at Jeremy or deliberately not looking at him. I scanned the room, planning my route. At least the small size of the crowd increased my chances of getting to talk to him. And Alice was hovering close by so, if I went to talk to her, I'd be bound to get an introduction.

I felt a tug at my sleeve.

'Sorry, Sarah-Jane, I was miles away,' I said. 'What were you saying?'

'Just about the photos,' Sarah-Jane said. 'I saw that you took some photos from the archive. I was a bit surprised, to be honest. I was wondering ...'

'Oh gosh, Sarah-Jane, I completely forgot to tell you and even worse, I forgot to bring them back. I have them in my office at work and I'll drop them back to you tomorrow. It's just that I'm a massive fan and I wanted a copy for my collection.'

She didn't believe my explanation, I could tell. If only I had returned the photos on Monday, as I had promised myself I would. But I saw that a gap had opened up near Jeremy Gill, and that he was walking in my direction, phone in hand. Tall, tanned and well built, with shoulder-length glossy too-black hair, he wore an open-necked white shirt and a dark blue suit. Even if he wasn't famous, you wouldn't miss him in a crowd: age and success agreed with him, and he was far better looking in real life than I had remembered, though I'd only seen him at a distance in 1998. A waiter passed, bearing a tray. Gill grabbed a glass of fizz without breaking his stride.

'Sorry, Sarah-Jane. I'll catch you later, okay?'

I pinned on my biggest smile and walked up to him before he could get waylaid by anybody else.

'Welcome to Cork, Mr Gill. I'm Finn Fitzpatrick from the Festival Board. We're delighted to have you back.'

'Wonderful. I've just been talking to the most boring woman in the world and I had to escape. Told her I had an important call to make. And I've lost my assistant. But you look like you know what's happening. When do I go on?'

'The film's listed to start at seven so you'll be on stage at about 7.05 or so, I reckon. You probably haven't seen the huge crowds below, but it'll take the staff a while to seat them.'

'Ah, the great Irish public,' Gill said, and laughed. 'But, c'mere to me, I don't know what they're coming to see me for, do you? Anyway, what are the plans after that?'

'Alice Chambers introduces you on stage and you say a few words about the film and then they're taking you to Paradiso.'

'Oh yeah, what's that like?' Gill asked. 'I'm vegan now, I hope they know that.'

'They do,' I said. 'It's a really good place. But before you go I wonder would you sign something for me? I *love* all your films, going right back to the beginning. I was here in 1998 as a volunteer when you came to Cork with your first film.'

'Oh come now, you don't look old enough.'

I found myself blushing. After all I'd heard about Gill, after all I'd imagined him to be, my conversation with him couldn't have been more pleasant. He was funny, obliging and self-deprecating. Draining his glass, he left it on a ledge beside him.

'Now, what do you want me to sign? Though why you'd want my oul' scrawl . . .'

I scrabbled in my bag and took out my 1998 programme, dropping the bag in the process. Gill dipped and caught it before it hit the floor.

'Oh my God, thanks so much, Mr Gill.'

'It's Jeremy,' he said. 'And it's no bother. Did you never hear that I used to be a goalie?'

'I did *not* know that.'

'Oh yes. Parnell United. Under-12s.'

I laughed, and Gill winked at me.

'I don't like to talk about it. I'm not the boastful type. So, what about that autograph of yours?'

I had bought a new pen the day before, one with a rough grip, surmising that there was a better chance of DNA residue being left on such a surface. My hands shook as I tore at the packet and I was starting to feel foolish. He asked for my name again, took trouble with the spelling, and signed the front of the catalogue, as I'd asked.

'Takes me back,' he said, as he handed me the programme and pen. 'Good days.'

I took the pen from him and held it delicately by its end.

'You enjoyed the festival in '98?' I asked.

'Fantastic,' he said, smiling broadly, but colder now. Though he remained standing beside me, he had moved on: my allotted five minutes of charm had come to an end.

'You would have met Deirdre Carney. Such a pity about her,' I said.

'Who?' Gill said, smiling still but with an almost imperceptible movement in his eyes that led me to believe he knew exactly who I was talking about.

'She died in January, but I figure you would have met her during the '98 festival,' I said. 'She was on the youth jury. Championed your film. Look, here's a photo.'

I had the page marked. I flipped it open and held it in front of Gill.

He inclined his head slightly.

'I don't remember meeting her. She was ill?'

'Mentally ill for a long number of years. Since 1998, actually.'

'I'm sad to hear that,' Gill said without a pause. 'Are you a relative?'

'Oh I didn't know her. Just heard about her death and came across the photo when I took out the old programme in anticipation of your visit.'

'I see,' Gill said.

I allowed Gill's 'I see' to hang unanswered. His eyes bored into mine, and he kept smiling that perma-smile, but I was certain that he was scrutinising me to see if I had an agenda or if it had been an innocent remark.

'I hope Finn's being nice to you?'

Alice Chambers was by my side. I didn't know how long she'd been there, or how much she'd heard. Gill broke his gaze. He turned his body to her and it was as if I didn't exist. He had a magnetic power and a way of turning his attention on and off that left me feeling as if I'd been dropped from a height.

'Couldn't be nicer,' he said, his smile a fixed grin. 'Showtime?'

'Showtime,' Alice said. 'It's this way.'

With a look at me that could have meant anything, Alice made for a side door marked 'Staff Only' that I knew would take them down a descending warren of back stairs and corridors before they re-emerged eventually in the glare of the lights on the huge yawning blackness of the stage. Though I had a ticket for the screening, I'd never be able to sit through it: there was too much to think about. I'd go and watch the introduction, though. I dropped the pen into a fresh plastic bag and made my way down the main stairs to the lobby.

The house lights were down as I slipped into the stalls. The theatre was packed and I waved away an usher with a torch, signalling that I was only staying five minutes. I had a ticket, so they couldn't throw me out, but hopefully I'd get away with standing at the back. There was a stifled cheer and a half-hearted round of applause as Alice walked onstage: they weren't here to see her.

'Ladies and gentlemen, we have a very special guest here this evening …'

The audience erupted with laughter as first a leg, and then an arm, poked out from the wings; as Alice turned around to see what was happening, they were just as quickly withdrawn. After it had happened a second time, she realised what was going on, laughed and abandoned all attempts at speech-making.

'Ladies and gentlemen, the one and only Jeremy Gill.'

Gill emerged to wild applause and a standing ovation. Hugging Alice as if they were old friends who hadn't met for years, he took over the presentation, making a flawless, touching speech about how much Cork meant to him and how grateful he was, and would always be, to the city that was the first place to give him a prize, which had allowed him to be nominated for a short film Oscar and that although that shower over in Hollywood hadn't taken much notice back then they'd seen the error of their ways later. More thunderous applause. Gill ran his hand through his hair and shook his head like he was in a shampoo ad. Without a flicker of nerves, he held the crowd captive and docile. Looking around, I was reminded of those photos of 1950s cinema audiences wearing 3D glasses.

Alice quizzed Gill on his new film (getting its first showing in Ireland tonight and he couldn't be happier that it was happening here and there'd be a Dublin premiere later, but the first showing in Ireland was here and that was really important to him). Throwing in the thing about Dublin was pure genius, appealing to the Cork/Dublin rivalry and superiority complex. I thought back to what Sarah-Jane had said, and on my own encounter with him, how he'd been with the 'most boring woman in the world', whoever she was: all chat to her until he'd had enough and walked away. Gill seemed to have the extraordinary ability to be whoever he needed to be in any given situation; and that tallied with what Aifric Sheehan and Colm O'Donnell had said: a groper, or a pervert, by their accounts – yet, according to Aifric, Deirdre had experienced a very different side of Gill.

He handed back to Alice and she told the audience that they were going to show Jeremy's prize-winning short *Another Bad Day at the Office* before his new feature. There was more applause and another ovation as Gill and Alice exited the stage. I stayed and watched the short film that I'd last seen on YouTube a few nights ago. Now that I knew, or thought I knew, about Gill, it was deeply disturbing.

As the credits rolled, I left the dark theatre. Leaning against the wall at the bottom of the staircase outside the door to the stalls, I felt nauseous. I was thinking about Rhona Macbride, the short film's teenage star. Seeing her talent and youth light up the big screen had crystallised my vague feelings and latent suspicions. What had he done to Deirdre? And what if it wasn't just Deirdre? What if Gill had hurt Rhona too? And what if he hadn't stopped with Rhona? What if he had never stopped?

I walked out of the Opera House, on to Emmett Place, and turned left on to the quay. I crossed the road and walked west along the river to the Shandon footbridge. On the far side was the stepped path that led to Shandon steeple, the four-faced liar it was called, though I could never remember why. A raw north wind was blowing and the water was high and restless and choppy. And as I stood, gripping the handrail, above the spot where my sister had walked to her death, I felt bereft. More than that, I felt utterly powerless.

16

It took sleet to rouse me from my lonely vigil. I looked skyward and stuck out my tongue to taste the icy slush. How long had I been standing there? Ten minutes? Twenty? It was time to move. I turned away from the river. With each step I took, the bridge lit up beneath the handrails. Not magic, it was the architect's joke. It made me smile, usually.

I crossed the Coal Quay and passed the Bridewell Garda Station – which reminded me that I needed to call my friend Sadie O'Riordan to arrange a meeting. I had the Carneys' permission to talk to her now. But I couldn't do any more on the case tonight. I had hit a wall. In the days before Sunday, at a time like this, I would have called Davy and we would have gone for something to eat or watched a film together and I'd have talked a little, never much, about what was bothering me. He had a way of

listening that made everything seem okay again. But I was starting to see that my friendship with him was an unfair bargain. I
called him when it suited me, avoided him when it didn't.

On North Main Street, I took shelter in Bradley's doorway. I
reached into my bag to check my phone. Still nothing from Davy,
no contact from him since Sunday, though I had two text messages from my mother, one from Sadie and another from Alice,
all asking me to call. I'd leave them till morning. Without thinking too much about it, I texted Davy, one word: 'Sorry'.

Aimlessly, I went into Bradley's. I hadn't had anything since
the latte at lunchtime and, though I didn't feel like it, I knew that
I needed to eat. I wandered around, failing to decide on anything,
eventually picking up a Gubbeen salami, one of the finger-thin
skinny ones, a box of penne and six tomatoes. I had onions and
garlic at home and a few ends of Parmesan. I could make some
kind of a sauce out of what I had. Whether I'd eat it or not, I'd
decide later. I grabbed a bag of West Cork mixed winter leaves
before I went up to pay. Not exactly salad weather, but I wasn't
up to preparing vegetables. I glanced down the back of the shop.
Bradley's has the best range of premium drinks and craft beers in
the city. Sometimes I wondered what it would be like to get
drunk, to forget everything for a while. Mostly, I was glad I didn't
know what I was missing. Maybe, like my birth mother, if I
started I wouldn't stop.

Back home, I brought the groceries upstairs and left them on the
kitchen worktop while I selected music to play. Though, feeling
this lonely, it had to be wall-to-wall Gillian Welch. I'd start with

Revival, its opening track 'Orphan Girl' never more apt, and work my way through. From the moment Dave Rawlings's guitar started, I began to feel calmer. I took two onions and a head of garlic from the press and poured olive oil into a saucepan. And tried not to think about Davy and Deirdre and Jeremy Gill.

Hearing a ping, I grabbed my handbag from the sofa where I'd thrown it.

'What exactly are you sorry for?' Davy's message said.

How about that I was sorry for using him? Sorry for being a bad friend? But I wasn't going to say any of that by text.

'We need to talk. If you're still talking to me?'

Pause.

'Might be.'

A sliver of light.

'What you doing?'

'Just out of meeting. Need food.'

Pause.

'Come here. Just home. Making pasta.'

Pause.

Pause.

'You sure?'

'Sure,' I typed, though I wasn't.

'We can talk and eat,' I added, and pressed send.

Instant reply: 'See you in 10.'

I could get the sauce on before he arrived if I worked fast. I chopped the onions and put them on to soften while I crushed garlic and cut the salami into rounds. I put the garlic and the salami into the saucepan with the onions and turned down the heat, giving the fragrant mixture a quick stir. I roughly chopped the tomatoes and left them on the chopping board while I ran down to the yard to get rosemary. I had just broken off a couple of fronds when the doorbell rang. I went to the gate and opened it. Davy had been expecting to be buzzed in from upstairs and my sudden appearance surprised him, though he said nothing at first, then:

'Hey, how's it going?'

'I was getting herbs,' I said.

I waved the rosemary at him in greeting.

'I ... I mean, hello, hiya, em, come in.'

But Davy made no move and I wondered if he'd changed his mind.

'It's dark here in the lane,' he said. 'You should get one of those security lights. If I didn't know where the door was, I'd have a hard time finding it.'

'That's the idea.'

That came out all wrong. It sounds like I didn't want him to find me.

Silence. Then Davy spoke.

'What you said in the text. Well, I'm sorry too, you know. I shouldn't've just gone off like that on Sunday.'

The sleet had turned to drizzle and my white shirt was getting soaked as the two of us stood in the circle of light cast by the garden lamp. I felt the buzz between us. It was always there, that electricity, but it seemed stronger now.

'I missed you,' I said, after a time.

I turned to walk into the house, afraid I'd said too much. And then I felt Davy's hand on my shoulder and turned back to him. We were centimetres apart, and I looked up into his eyes, and he looked down at me. For a moment I thought he was going to kiss me.

'I missed you too,' he said instead.

I could hardly breathe.

'Now where's me dinner, missus?' he said.

I laughed. And caught my breath.

'Caveman,' I said, heading for the stairs, Davy following along behind.

'I try,' he said.

He was laughing too. It was going to be all right. But something had changed between us, though I didn't yet know what, or how much.

Upstairs, I threw the chopped tomatoes in on top of the salami-onion-garlic mix and stirred it all together. I used a mezzaluna to chop the rosemary spikes, and added them to the saucepan along with a little sea salt, a few twists of black pepper and a pinch of sugar. Then I put a pot of water on to boil and put some of the washed leaves into a wooden salad bowl.

'Not long now,' I said.

'Smells great,' Davy said. 'You're listening to Gillian. Things must be bad, so, are they?'

'Yeah, kinda bad all right. Change the music if you want?'

'Nah, Gillian's good.'

Spending time with me meant that Davy inevitably heard a lot of Americana and country music. He tried to like it, though he didn't get rhinestones and dog songs and Tammy Wynette. And he definitely didn't get Willie Nelson.

Without a word, I handed cutlery and napkins to Davy and he brought them to the table, while I followed with glasses and a jug of water. I had positioned the table where it was likely to catch the best light for the longest amount of the day, on the south-west side of the living room. Oval and made of Irish oak, it had been hand-carved to fit the space by Jack Lehane, Sadie's husband. A matching bench ran along the outer edge of the table, and in summer the windows behind the bench folded back giving access to a balcony, a metre-and-a-half-wide perforated steel ledge with a glass wall and a steel handrail, that circled the tower. On the room side of the table there were four wide oak stools, one at each end and two along the length. The table seated six. It was fully occupied once or twice a year.

I went back to the kitchen area, a curved island of cupboards, worktop, sink, cooker and fridge. I put on the penne and made a dressing for the salad. The air in the room felt thick and heavy and the pasta was taking for ever. I walked to the far side of the island and looked south-east, towards Douglas and Rochestown and Monkstown and Cork Harbour and the open sea. After a time, I turned towards the stovetop again.

'A watched pot ...' I said, breaking the silence

'It'll cook. Anyway, it's only twenty to ten. Imagine we're in Seville or somewhere. We'd be eating early, if we were,' Davy said.

'*Gracias*. Though, hang on a second, it might be done, I think. Take the salad there and I'll be over with the pasta.'

The salami had added substance to the simple sauce. After a couple of bites, Davy said, 'Tasty,' like he meant it, and kept on eating. I ate too, more than I'd expected. The rain was heavier now and the drops hammered like warnings on the glass. We had hardly said a word to each other during dinner but I was the one who had asked Davy around, and I had said that we needed to talk. I got up from the table.

'Thanks for calling in, though, well, what I mean is that, like, now that you're here I don't know what to say.'

I walked to the sofa and sat on the arm. Davy got up from the table and went to the far side of the room. Facing me, and backlit by the city, he had a golden aura. He was wearing a long-sleeved white T-shirt under an open blue and white checked shirt and his hair was still damp from the rain. And maybe sometime, or somewhere, I might have seen him looking better than he did right now, but if I had, I couldn't remember.

I got up and walked to where Davy Keenan was standing. I stood in front of him and put my hands in his hair, and pulled his mouth towards mine.

17

Davy wasn't in my bed when I awoke at 6.30 in the morning. He had gone to work, probably. He often had early morning personal training sessions. Maybe he hadn't wanted to wake me. Or maybe he regretted what had happened. Maybe I did too, though it hadn't felt like a mistake at the time. Being with Davy had felt natural. And something else, something I couldn't identify. I stretched myself full length, arms above my head, and let out a moan. How was I going to get any work done today?

'*Finally* you've stopped snoring,' Davy said.

He was standing in the doorway. He had his phone in his hand and, though I couldn't see his face, his body was lit by the phone's glow. He was naked.

'I don't snore,' I said, and threw a pillow at him. He side-stepped it easily.

'Pathetic effort,' he said. 'Anyway, how do you know you don't snore?'

He jumped back into bed beside me.

'So I've just cancelled my 6.30 and 7.30 clients but I have to teach a circuits class at 9.00. Can you think of anything we could do to pass the time?'

'How about a game of Trivial Pursuit?' I said.

As we lingered at the table after breakfast, I explained, withholding names and all identifying information, that I was working on a case that involved a hurt being done to a young girl over ten years before.

'Some kind of abuse, you mean?'

'Something like that,' I said. 'You know I can't tell you.'

I could have said more, but more revelations might have led to more questions.

'I know,' he said. 'I *do* understand. You'll get there, I know you will.'

'I hope so.'

'When we were out at Muskerry Castle, was that to do with this case?'

'It was.'

'I'm feeling *really* bad about all that now.'

He wrinkled his nose.

'I thought we were … I mean, if you'd said it was a work thing, I'd still have gone, of course I would've. But when I realised it wasn't what I thought it was, I felt, I dunno …'

'Used?'

'I wouldn't put it as strongly as that, in all fairness. Don't beat yourself up about it, please. Most of this is down to me, how I handle it when shit happens. Which has always been badly. Disastrously, in fact, as you know.'

'I do.'

He laughed.

'You needn't have agreed so readily,' he said.

We both smiled and said nothing for a while. Then Davy spoke again.

'Anyway, what I'm saying is that I ran for the hills, when I should've stayed and talked it through. Since I've been in treatment I've been trying to do things differently. But it's not always easy. On Sunday, I reacted. Badly. Like a fucking arsehole.'

I laughed.

'Fucking arsehole is a bit strong.'

'Is it?' he said. 'I don't know. Anyway, what do we do now?'

'About what?'

'About us.'

'You're asking *me*?'

'Yeah, I am. Like, what *was* that, last night? And this morning?'

'It just happened, I suppose, I mean ...'

'A case of, you could resist my charms no longer and just had to fuck my brains out?'

'That's kinda true, actually,' I said.

Davy reached across the table and took my hand.

'You know, in rehab they tell us not to get into relationships until we're, not recovered exactly, we never recover fully, but until we're secure in our new way of life. A lot of people ignore the advice.'

'Yeah. AA seems to be Cork's top dating agency, as far as I can see.'

'Exactly,' Davy said. 'For a lot of people. Not me. I haven't exactly been a monk ...'

I laughed.

'Okay, okay. I know what you think about me and the yummy mummies. But I haven't been in a relationship since I left Tabor Lodge four years ago. Haven't felt ready, I s'pose, but now, this thing with us ...'

I wrenched my hand away, leapt up from the table, and grabbed my coat.

'I totally agree. We're not relationship material. Last night was great, but it's not to be repeated. We're friends, Davy, nothing more. Take your time, finish your coffee. Pull out the door after you when you're leaving. I've got to run.'

18

By 8.45, I'd already fielded a call from my mother. Yes, I was all right. No, I wasn't working too hard. I'd tried calling Alice Chambers but got her voicemail. And I'd texted both Aifric, Deirdre's former schoolmate who worked in St Finbarr's School, asking her to call me, and Sadie O'Riordan, asking if we could meet up that night. By then, I would have had two more opportunities of seeing Gill and I intended to use them well: once he left Cork, he'd become unreachable. And it would be good to review the evidence with Sadie while it was fresh.

Though calling it evidence was overstating it. What I'd found were fragments, signposts, no more than that. But the previous evening I had been sure that Gill was guilty, as sure as I'd ever felt about anything. This morning, I was even more sure. I remembered some of Davy's words ('I know you'll get there') and tried to forget the rest, what he had said, and what we had done.

And then I remembered the sense that I had that Gill was a chameleon, that he changed his personality to suit his own ends. There was something about power too, not the power that came with his position in life, though that was part of it. Meeting him had left me with the feeling that whatever Gill wanted, he felt entitled to take.

But at 17–19 MacSwiney Street, real life, and the work I'd been neglecting, got in the way. It was Wednesday and I remembered that, while I was in the office on Saturday, I had moved all my client appointments into Thursday and Friday. That meant that, if I didn't make some shape at getting control of my workload today, I'd be left with mayhem by the weekend. When Tina came in with the post at 9.30 exactly, as usual, I barely saw her but gave a quick wave. She replied with a mock salute.

'Normal service has resumed, I see,' she said.

At 10.55, my mobile rang.

'Wasn't expecting to be talking to you again,' Aifric Sheehan said.

Snap. I wouldn't be calling if I didn't have to.

'Um, something came up, Aifric. Can you talk?'

'I'm round the back of the bike sheds having a quick ciggie. Strictly out of bounds for students, positively essential for teachers. But there's nobody near me. Talk away.'

'It's about your boss, Eoghan MacGiolla. I found out that he might have been a neighbour of Deirdre's in Turners Cross but I'm nearly sure he told me he didn't know her.'

'That's the impression I had too.'

'Would you mind checking for me?'

'Any particular reason?'

'Not really. I probably got my notes wrong and I just want to make sure, but I don't want to make a big deal of it by making another appointment to see him.'

'I get you,' Aifric said. 'I'll *easily* find out, don't worry.'

'Thanks so much, Aifric. And you'll be, what's the word? Subtle?'

'Finn,' Aifric said. 'Subtlety is my middle name.'

They wouldn't open the doors for the public interview until twenty minutes before the start so I needed to time my arrival for after the long queue of enthusiastic movie nerds but before the more casual Film Festival patron. They are the ones who don't go to see a film for the rest of the year but during the festival go to everything, from worthy documentaries about rainforest loss in Brazil to feature-length subtitled Czech stop-motion animation. I *definitely* needed to get there before them. Ten to noon would be about right, and would give me time for a coffee at the House café.

Or it would have, were it not for the crowd. I bypassed the coffee queue and went into the auditorium, finding a single seat, seven rows back and three in from the edge, that gave me a decent view of the stage. Glancing around at the audience, I saw, and waved at, the many familiar faces, the curse and blessing of small town life. What would they say if they knew what I had been up to for the last few days?

I checked my phone before putting it on silent for the duration of the interview. I had a text from Sadie O'Riordan: 'off at 8 – could meet for food?'

I texted back: 'Ramen @ 8.15?'

I'd check later but I knew it would be a yes: Sadie loved Thai food.

At 12.05, the curtains parted to reveal two comfortable arm-chairs and a superfluous lamp on an even more superfluous coffee table. We're here for a bit of a chat, the tableau pro-claimed. It would be interesting to see how much chatting there was. Gill liked the sound of his own voice and I reckoned that poor Tiernan McDevitt, the arts journalist doing the interview-ing, would be lucky if he got a word in. After a moment, Alice Chambers came onstage to do the introduction. She was working her way through an impressive range of outfits, I noticed. Having a special guest in town must have sent her on an anticipatory shopping spree. Today she was wearing a striking-looking red dress that finished at the knee. It was probably from Zara: the clothes there always suited her. Tragically, they never looked good on me.

Tiernan McDevitt came onstage first to warm, though muted, applause. He was average height, had average looks, and seemed averagely nervous. Even his clothes were average, I thought, sand-coloured chinos and a blue shirt, the kind of thing a medical student might wear to look professional on ward rounds. Tiernan sat down, then stood again quickly, clasping his hands in front of him as he waited.

After a few long minutes, Jeremy Gill walked onstage. He was greeted with deafening cheers and another standing ovation. What does that kind of adulation do to a person? Even if they start out half-decent which, according to Colm O'Donnell, Gill hadn't. And what would happen if someone tried to tell a different, less praiseworthy, story about him? I remembered what Deirdre's note had said: 'He's too strong now.' It was up to me to prove her wrong, to show that, with enough evidence, even the most powerful can be beaten. It hit me that I had strayed very far from my initial plan: to seek evidence of Gill's innocence as well as his guilt, but I shelved that thought as Tiernan signalled for quiet.

He opened by listing Gill's films in chronological order, with the audience clapping and hooting to varying degrees, according to their favourites. I had been expecting to learn something about Gill by being here but he had hardly said a word so far, apart from mouthing thank-yous and nodding and doing the joined hand *namaste* sign. My mood was sinking into seriously pissed off territory when, at last, there was a diminution in applause, and the interview began.

In many ways, Gill's behaviour was nothing I hadn't seen before, on TV chat shows or in promotional interviews. There was a recital of well-worn facts, and well-practised anecdotes, that the audience hailed as if he were Moses conveying tablets of stone from the mountain top. No matter what the question, Gill was in control at all times, but the long format of the interview meant that, for those watching closely, and it seemed to me that I was the only one who was, there was useful information to be gleaned.

He was wearing the same suit as the night before, but today he had on a plain black T-shirt, unbranded but expensive-looking, under the suit, instead of last night's white shirt. He looked slick but, even so – observed at length, in all his pomp – Gill was downright weird: a combination of hubris and petty cruelty that, had he not been rich and famous, would have rendered him friendless. It got even more interesting when the Q & A started. An audience member asked Gill about *Another Bad Day at the Office*.

'Mister Gill, I remember seeing your first fillum here in Cork back in 1998 and we all knew then that a star was born. But how hard was it to get that fillum made and do you have any advice for young fillum-makers? I'm sure there's loads of them here today.'

'Well I don't know anything about *fillums,*' Gill said, imitating the man's heavy Cork accent and not getting much of a laugh from the audience for a change. 'But if you want to know about my first *film*, ask this guy.'

He pointed at Tiernan McDevitt.

I had read the credits and there had been no mention of Tiernan. He paled. He looked like he'd rather be anywhere else on earth.

'Em, I think, Jeremy, the gentleman would, ah, probably prefer to hear from you.'

'Look at him,' Gill said, pointing again. 'He's gone all quiet now. You see, myself and Tiernan have known each other a long time, haven't we?'

Gill's voice had taken on the hectoring tones of a schoolyard bully.

'Yes,' Tiernan said, so quietly that the microphone hardly registered the sound.

'I first met this guy when he was just out of UCD with first class honours in something or other, English, I think. And he wanted to be a film-maker, as I recall. How's that goin' for you?'

'Ah, not great, Jeremy,' Tiernan said, to the sound of a few nervous laughs from the audience.

'All together now "Aw".'

To my astonishment, most of the audience went along with it, as if Gill was the pantomime Ugly Sister to Tiernan's Cinderella.

'Well, yeah, to cut to the chase, he wasn't up to much. You see, I had those years in ads behind me – a crap degree from UCD, mind you, but experience of the world. That's what really counts. We had to put Mister Top o' the Class here making the tea. That's what I put in the credits, actually – d'you remember, Tiernan? Tea McDevitt?'

'Oh yeah, I remember all right,' Tiernan said.

'Good for you it was, I'm sure,' Gill said.

'Good enough to make sure I never worked on another film, anyway. Went down a different road. And it seems to be working out okay ...'

It was excruciating to watch. Before Gill had a chance to say anything else, I started clapping for Tiernan's last comment and the rest of the audience joined in. Gill realised that he was losing the crowd. Instantly, he was warm and avuncular again, the version of Jeremy he had been on stage the previous night. After a few minutes, the audience settled; mollified, it seemed.

There was nothing else of significance until the final question. A young woman who said she was a recent drama graduate from UCC asked Gill about the casting process: if he used casting directors, what he thought about them, and if they were an important part of his crew.

'No,' Gill said. 'Totally overrated as far as I'm concerned. I do my own casting, prefer to develop a relationship with the actors myself from the beginning.'

'Is that 'cause of the casting couch, Jeremy?' a wit shouted from the audience, to general hilarity but to the embarrassment of the unfortunate woman who had asked the original question.

Lightning fast, Gill replied in a broad Dublin accent:

'I gave up on the casting couch years ago. 'Twas doin' me back in.'

Everybody thought it was a joke. Everybody except me. As the audience roared with laughter, I kept watching Gill, his face blank, a benign mask.

His eyes told a different story.

19

Now that the festival was under way, the action was elsewhere, with most of the staff deployed at locations all over town, at workshops and screenings and at the various box offices. I had another missed call from Alice and I had a feeling that she wasn't calling for a friendly chat. Had Sarah-Jane told her about the photos? Or had Alice overheard my conversation with Gill? Either way, it was better to try to mitigate the damage. I had taken the photographs from my desk drawer earlier. If I hurried, I could sneak them back to the Film Festival office before the workshop. I introduced myself to the young staffer on duty (Dylan, his name tag said) and told him I was a board member and needed to replace something I'd borrowed from the 1998 archive.

'Oh grand,' Dylan said.

I got the impression he'd have said 'grand' even if I'd told him I planned to burn the building to the ground. He looked about eleven, though he was probably a recent graduate. But it took a while for academic smarts to turn into usable workplace skills. I thought back to my days as a trainee, more of a hindrance to the operation of a law office than a help. At least nobody had put me on tea duty. As I took down the 1998 archive and removed the note I'd left and replaced the photographs, I thought about Tiernan McDevitt. What a bastard Gill was, for what he had done to Tiernan back in the day, and even more for what he did to him onstage earlier. Still, Jeremy had unwittingly given me a useful lead. If I could get talking to Tiernan, I might be able to find out more about Rhona Macbride, and how to contact her. After seeing her on screen last night, I knew I had to meet her.

I sidled over to where Dylan was sitting.

'Thanks a lot, Dylan,' I said. 'You know, all of us on the board really appreciate your work. The festival couldn't run without people like you.'

'I'm just an intern. Graduated this summer. Hoping to do a master's in film next year, filling in here meanwhile to build up credits for my application and stuff.'

'Well you're making a valuable contribution, Dylan, I want you to know that,' I said, which would have been true even if I didn't have an ulterior motive. 'But, actually, maybe you could help me more specifically?'

'Course I will, Finn, if I can, like.'

'It's just that I need to meet up with Tiernan McDevitt and I just can't remember what I did with his number,' I said. 'You wouldn't have it there on the system, would you?'

'I don't know if we have it but I can have a look. I'll check under contacts first.'

'Oh *that's* a good idea, Dylan,' I said. 'And you know, as you've the system open there you couldn't get me Daniel O'Brien's number as well, could you? He's an old mate of mine from his days working here and I seem to have lost his contact details. If you knew the number of times I meant to ask Alice or Sarah-Jane. That's D-A-N-I-E-L, Dylan.'

'Gotcha,' Dylan said. 'Em, no phone number for Daniel, but there's an email, if it's the same guy. Though the address might not be current. But we definitely have Tiernan's mobile number and email. Will I print the two of them for you?'

'That'd be great.'

Subterfuge was getting easier, and lying was bothering me less.

As I walked in the front door of the Opera House, I saw Tiernan McDevitt standing by the box office in conversation with another man. I took a table by the window with my back to the river and watched. The man with Tiernan was slim, blond, tanned, possibly fake-tanned, and dressed in light grey trousers, a fine-knit pink cardigan and a collared T-shirt. He was slightly too old for the boyband look, but he had it down. While I was waiting, I sent an email to Daniel O'Brien. Dylan in the festival office had been right: nobody used '@ireland.com' any more. Predictably, the email bounced back. Meanwhile, Boyband man appeared to have left. I waved to catch Tiernan's attention, and he came and sat opposite me.

'Thanks for this,' he said. 'I'm on the 3.20 train so it suits perfectly.'

'The least the board of Cork Film Festival can do is buy you lunch,' I said. 'Who was that you were chatting to, by the way?'

'Oh that's Jeremy's assistant. He was trying to console me, telling me how well the interview had gone. Which was a big fat lie, obviously.'

The waiter came along then and I ordered the mushrooms on toast, Tiernan the omelette and a glass of Rioja.

'You didn't go for lunch with Jeremy?' I said.

'Ah, no, no, I didn't,' Tiernan said.

'I don't blame you, to be honest. I wouldn't have gone either,' I said.

'It's not that. He was meeting people from the film studies department in UCC, so I wasn't ever supposed to be eating with him. Alice said she'd organise someone to take me to lunch, but I had the intention of going down early to the station and doing a bit of work there so I said no and then you called and I changed my mind.'

'I wasn't impressed with Gill, I must say.'

'No?'

'With the way he treated you, I mean.'

'Oh that? That was only a bit of banter. That's just Jeremy,' Tiernan said.

But he looked stricken, as if he'd lost something precious. Gill was all powerful now that he had his five Oscars and I suspected that it was more than Tiernan's career was worth to bad-mouth him. I needed to change my approach.

'Fair enough,' I said. 'You know him better than me, I s'pose.'

'Yeah, yeah, I do. Known him fifteen years. His bark is worse than his bite. He doesn't suffer fools, but that's a lot of why he is where he is. Total perfectionist, like.'

'Absolutely. His films are amazing.'

'Aren't they?'

He sounded like a little boy, in awe of Gill's talent, in spite of everything.

'And was he a perfectionist from the beginning? What I mean is, was he like that during the film you worked on with him?'

'Always,' Tiernan said. 'He had an actor lined up to play the male lead in *Another Bad Day at the Office* but he fired him at the last minute and took the role himself. And it worked brilliantly.'

'It *so* did. He has such a gift for casting, doesn't he? That young girl in it, what's her name again, Rhona something, is it? She was fabulous.'

'Rhona Macbride. Wonderful,' Tiernan said.

'How did he find her? Some drama school, maybe?'

'He got her in the school where we did the filming, the Sisters of the Blessed Eucharist Convent in Neale Place, near Dorset Street. Did you not know?'

'No!'

'Yeah, it's Gill legend at this stage. He went into the convent and charmed the head nun, Sister Bernadette, I think she was, and we had the run of the place. They were making us sandwiches and all. He auditioned loads of the schoolgirls and picked Rhona for the lead. The park in the film is actually the nuns' garden, would you believe?'

'Wow,' I said. 'That's some story. And did you ever hear what happened to Rhona? She was so talented.'

'Never heard of her again. She just continued on with school, I presume. I'm pretty sure she lived locally. Probably just got on with her life.'

I wondered if Tiernan knew more than he was saying. But he wasn't going to break *omertà* just because I'd bought him lunch. I decided not to push any further. I could talk to him again if I needed to.

I crossed the bridge and climbed the steep, curving hill from the river to the northside. On my right, I passed the Maldron Hotel. Rumoured to be haunted, for two hundred and fifty years until the late 1980s, it had been the North Infirmary, used to treat fever patients during the famine in the 1840s. And, whatever layers came later, that grim history would remain, under the thin skin of the renovation. But the hotel, just below Shandon, had good rates and was always busy. The ghosts only added to its attractions, it seemed.

I walked to the top of the hill. The workshop was in the Firkin Crane, a circular building constructed and used as a weigh-room and butter market in the time of sailing ships. Now it was a choreography and dance centre, though its rehearsal rooms and performance spaces were also hired out to festivals and for special events. I was first to arrive, apart from the Film Festival staff on door duty checking the attendance list. In the ten minutes since, a succession of young people had slunk into the workshop room and scuttled out again immediately on seeing me.

'Is it something I said?' I murmured to myself, and went out again to the front of the building. The sun had come out for the first time in weeks and everyone knew it wasn't going to be hanging around long. Apart from the teachers in huddled discussion near the shaded north-facing entrance, the workshop attendees were across the road, every south-facing step, sill and leaning space occupied. I counted ten school uniforms, five boys and five girls, and ten university-age students, four female and six male. I went up to the teachers, introduced myself as a board representative, and asked if they could get everyone to come inside. That way, I reckoned, I'd have a better chance of monitoring the situation.

I sat with the teachers in a row down the back of the room and the young people sat in a circle of chairs. The room divided along school and college lines and there was no interaction between the two student groups. It hadn't been a great idea to mix them.

Gill arrived ten minutes later, along with Alice Chambers, and Boyband, the blond man I had seen talking to Tiernan, now carrying a clipboard. He looked cold in his California outfit. There was a second man with them, muscle-bound, younger than Boyband, who seemed to have no particular role. I realised that he was probably a bodyguard. Had he been around for all Gill's time in Cork or had he just arrived? Alice moved towards the front of the room, intending to do another introduction and thank-you, but Gill waved her away. Boyband stationed himself, looking attentive, on a chair midway up the room and Security guy took up a menacing pose by the door. It was ridiculous, overkill, completely unnecessary and, if he started talking to his wrist, I was in danger of laughing out loud.

Or maybe not. I could see that the students were impressed by the show of power and importance, and that Gill had them before he opened his mouth.

He was dressed very differently now. It looked like he'd gone to a costume store over lunch and hired a movie director outfit. Instead of the dark suit, he was wearing board-shorts that came to mid-calf, and an oversized grey marl *Seeing Things CREW* sweatshirt. All of the students knew that *Seeing Things* had won five Oscars. Some of their mouths had fallen open. Gill's long hair was tamed by a blue and purple bandana, worn like a kerchief and tied at the nape of his neck, and he carried a vintage brown leather flying jacket – sheep fleece lined – on one finger, over his left shoulder. He threw the jacket on a chair, and his eyes surveyed the room, and the people in it, in a lazy, knowing arc. He rubbed his right hand back and forth across his mouth. The room was so quiet I could hear the scratch of his stubble.

Then, Gill started to talk, in a low voice at first. The students leant forward, as one, to hear better.

'Ah, I'll introduce myself, first, I guess. Though I think that maybe you all know me, am I right?'

Nods, shuffles and few muffled 'yeahs' from the students.

'Maybe I've gone deaf,' Gill shouted. 'Do you fucking know me? Yes or no?'

'Yes,' they shouted back, eyes shining and smiles wide, like a litter of golden Labrador puppies who'd got hold of an entire of roll Andrex.

'That's more like it,' Gill said. 'Now, tell me why you're here. You, the pretty one in the green uniform, you, missy, what's your name and why are you here?'

The St Al's girl went pink.

'Um, Carmel, here to learn, like,' she said.

'Excellent answer, young lady, sorry, Carmel, I mean. Now don't be shy, I'll be back to you later.'

He walked up to her, rested his hand softly on her head, then turned to the rest of the students and shouted, 'Now, what about the rest of you? Do you wanna learn? Yes, Jeremy?'

'Yes Jeremy,' they shouted.

'Let's do it,' he said.

For the next fifty-five minutes, his accent more Americanised than I had heard it before, Gill ran through a presentation on his films, how he'd made them, triumphs and successes achieved, hiccups and disasters overcome, at each stage engaging with individual students, getting them up to demonstrate shots or camera angles, asking their opinions, listening to their answers as if he truly believed they had something interesting to say.

'Why do you think I did that?'

'What do think happened next?'

'Good answer.'

'Interesting.'

Every time Carmel, the schoolgirl in the green uniform, spoke, Gill gave her a smile or a wink, no matter how inane the comment. Apart from that, Gill's attentions were evenly spread through male and female. Except for Carmel at the beginning, there was no touching of any of the students. Though Gill's language had been overfamiliar and borderline inappropriate throughout, the workshop was drawing to a close and I was assailed by doubt again. What did I know, ultimately? Only that he was an egotist – which was probably a prerequisite for being a successful film director. He had given no sign of having noticed me in the back row. Maybe he hadn't thought of me since our encounter the previous evening. Why should he? In the end, I had nothing on him. Was that because there was nothing to get?

'Film is a visual medium,' Gill said, then. 'It's about the moving image. Break that down. The first part is technical, about how our brain processes what we see. You're smart kids – I don't need to go into the science of it. But the image. What the camera sees. Action or stillness. Landscape or people. What about sound? Crucial, of course. But secondary. The image is primary. Some of the most powerful scenes in cinema history have been silent. Hitch – Alfred Hitchcock – knew that.'

Gill paused, steepled his hands in front of his mouth, put his thumbs under his chin, and started to rub the sides of his index fingers up and down on the tip of his nose.

'This is my thinking face,' he said, and the group laughed. 'No, honestly, ask my assistant, whenever I get this face on it means I've had an idea, am I right?'

Boyband made a half grimace, half smile, and said, 'Oh yeah, I mean, yes, Mr Gill.' He sounded like he was off the set of *90210*. The group laughed again, more loudly this time.

'You,' Gill said, talking to the girl in the green uniform. 'Carmel, isn't it?'

'Yes,' she said.

'Well, *Carmel*. You're the one giving me ideas. Any idea why?'

Carmel blushed, shook her head.

'Anyone get the connection? What was I just talking about?'

'Uh, maybe Hitchcock?' one of the boys said.

'Ex-*act*-ly,' Gill said. 'What we have here with the very beautiful Carmel is a Hitchcock heroine, an ice blonde, a Grace Kelly, a Kim Novak, before she piled on the pounds.'

Gill threw back his head and laughed, and the group laughed too, even more loudly. Most of them hadn't a clue who Kim Novak was, I could tell, but Gill had shown them that it was okay to laugh at her, and they did.

'So, *Carmel*, are you up for a bit of acting today? I mean, I know you've done some acting. I'm right, aren't I?'

'Um, yeah. A bit, like, just school stuff.'

'What age are you? Fifteen?'

Carmel nodded.

Fifteen, I was thinking: the same age Deirdre had been when she met Gill.

'Sweet,' Gill said. 'Sweet.'

The students laughed, but Carmel didn't. She kept her eyes on Gill. Rapt, she waited for what he was going to say next.

'What the *fuck* do you mean *just* school stuff? *Everyone* does *just* school stuff, has to, even me. Even Bobby de fucking Niro.'

Carmel giggled.

'I'll take that as a yes. Good, Carmel, Step forward, great, you're great.'

He put his arm around her and brought her to the front of the room, put his right index finger on her nose, and stared, a beat too long, into her eyes. I looked around at the teachers. All of them were smiling. They had suspended judgement, were as seduced by him as Carmel seemed to be. But they were adults, in positions of responsibility. She was fifteen, a child. She was in danger, I was sure of it.

And then, I wasn't sure at all. I kept quiet and I kept watching. In retrospect, I see that I was every bit as useless as the rest of them.

'Stay there, gorgeous,' Gill said, and turned to face the room again. 'Now, do we have a leading man? Or am I going to have to play that part myself?'

The girls squealed; the boys sat up in their chairs. Gill walked along in front of the group, like a sergeant inspecting dress uniforms before a parade.

'Up hands who's done some acting? All of you? Great, like I told the lovely Carmel, it's a good way to learn.'

He stopped in front of one of the college students, a slim, dark-haired boy with full red lips.

'You, I like,' Gill said. 'You want this?'

'Definitely,' the boy said.

He stood, tall and straight.

'Good attitude. How old are you, soldier?'

'Nineteen, Mr Gill. Twenty next month.'

Four, five years older than Carmel. Was that why Gill had chosen the mix of college and school students – because he wanted an age gap? But what was he planning?

'An older man, Carmel,' Gill said, and looked back at her.

She smiled.

'You like that?' he asked.

She smiled again, but less surely.

'Nice,' Gill said.

His tongue played along his lower lip. For a moment or two, his attention seemed to drift. Then, quickly, he turned to the boy again.

'So what's your name?'

'Stephen, Stevie.'

'Great, Stevie,' Gill said. 'Step forward to the front of the room.'

Gill positioned the two students, Carmel at the front of the circle of chairs, Stevie just inside the room door. He spoke quietly to each of them separately, checked back to see that they knew what they were doing, and spoke to the group again.

'Okay,' Gill said. 'I've just been directing my actors, telling them what I want from them in this scene and, because I like you guys so much, I'm going to let you in on it too, and I'm going to talk you all through the scene, and I want you to watch along with me. Now, to do that, I want you to make little rectangles with your fingers to see what the camera sees. I want you to go in for a close-up on what you like, on what looks good, to read the scene, to see what it's saying, what it means. You all ready? Great. But before we start, does anyone know why I picked Stevie here, instead of one of the other guys?'

'Cos he's *only gorgeous*,' one of the other boys shouted, to great hilarity.

'You're all equally beautiful to me,' Gill said. 'But, no, seriously, anyone?'

'Em,' Carmel said. 'Might it be the contrast between us?'

'Say more,' Gill said. 'I knew I liked this girl. I can pick 'em, you know.'

'*I can pick 'em.' Like he picked Deirdre?*

I shuddered. Should I say something? But what was there to say?

'Go on,' Gill said.

'Uh, well, like, what you were saying about the image, like,' Carmel said. 'So, em, the, like, visual contrast would look good on screen, like, maybe?'

'That's right, Carmel. I sense you have a talent for this, and I'm never wrong about these things. This is going to be great. And remember, audience, this scene is silent. No dialogue. Let the actors and your imagination do the work. Now, scene 1, take 1, and action.'

Gill slapped his hands together in imitation of a clapperboard. I heard the sound echo around the inside of my head, but I didn't say a word, and the truth is that, by then, he had me too. I was waiting to see what happened next, just like the other sheep in that room.

'Okay, Stevie, turn, you see Carmel, you wave, that's good, she sees you all right, oh yeah, but she's pretending she doesn't, that's good, Carmel, you're the ice queen, remember?

'Now, Stevie, you're getting a little frustrated, you want her to acknowledge you, but she's still ignoring you.

'That's right, Carmel, I like that thing you did with your hair just then, and now maybe, give him a quick look and, that's right, look away again. You like him, don't you, that dangerous older man, but you're not going to show him, are you?

'And, Stevie, you're disappointed, yeah, that's it, she's raised your hopes and dashed them again, that's women for you, but you can't help it, you like her, you're attracted to her, it's something you can't control, and you move a little closer, casual, like, but hey, fuck her, you're a good-looking guy, let her beg, that's good, Stevie, and yeah, that's right, you're drawing her in.

'Her head turns, and she looks at you for longer now, that's good, Carmel, and turn away, and I'd like you to open your mouth now, Carmel, just a little, that's great, and close it, and now, you moisten your lips with your little pink tongue ... that's perfect.

'And then, Stevie, come closer, and closer still, and step behind Carmel, put your arm around her waist, this is really good, you two.

'And, Carmel, you've got mixed feelings now, things are moving *fast*, maybe too fast, and he's what you want, he's what you desire, but you're afraid too, that's good, Carmel.

'No and yes, Carmel, no and yes, and Carmel, that's *so* good, and Stevie, you know what you want, we all know, and you know she wants it too, even though she's pulling away from you now, but you know what she really wants underneath that fear, you have to push through that.'

'And do it *now*, Stevie,' Gill said, and took a step closer to them.

With force, Stevie put his hands on Carmel's hips, one at each side, then pulled her suddenly and violently towards his pelvis. She gasped. She hadn't known this was going to happen. I looked at Gill. He had stopped talking and he was watching Carmel, her every breath and movement, appraising her as if she was a horse he was buying at an auction.

He spoke softly to her.

'Carmel, you are so, so good at this,' he said.

He swallowed, then continued talking in the same soft voice.

'And, now, Stevie, like we planned and, remember, softly.'

Stevie bent his head to Carmel's ear, and whispered. She blushed pink, and her eyes closed, and stayed shut.

There was silence until Gill spoke again.

'Carmel, let's see that little pink tongue again ...'

She opened her eyes, looked at Gill, did as he asked. He smiled, like he was the one holding her, like she had become his.

'And. Cut,' Gill said.

'You guys, that was amazing.'

Gill walked up to the actors, stood between them, took their hands, and held them overhead while the rest of the class applauded. Then Gill gestured for quiet and spoke.

'They were brave, these two. That's the kind of bravery I'm always looking for in actors, people who are willing to step into the unknown, to get in touch with their animal feelings. We can't deny what's natural. I truly believe that. But, hey, come on, another round of applause for our actors, and especially for Carmel.'

He turned and spoke to her during the applause. I couldn't hear, but I saw him mouthing the words 'amazing, you're amazing'. And I watched as he took her hand and brought it to his lips and kissed it, and kissed it again, all the time looking deep into her eyes. Then he turned and nodded at Stevie, and let go of his hand. He went back to his seat, while Gill walked hand in hand with Carmel to hers. She seemed to grow taller with every step. Whatever doubts she might have had about what had just happened, they were gone.

I sat dumbstruck in my chair, only remembering to clap as the applause was ending. What had I seen? What had we all seen? I looked at the teachers. Many of them seemed uncomfortable, as if they were aware that a line had been crossed. But they weren't sure. And, for all my concerns about Gill, neither was I. We were privileged to be here, weren't we? To have this once in a lifetime access? To bear witness to the master at work? And who would dare to question his generosity?

But the scene directed by Gill had come close as made no difference to saying that no means yes, and that consent was irrelevant, a hurdle to be overcome. Was that Gill's personal philosophy? And yet, most of what had happened, most of what I had found so objectionable, had happened in my own head. My imagination had done the work, as he had planned. There was no denying Gill's directing talent, but the scene had also given me a close-up of his power over people, his power over me, and that was what sickened me most.

The workshop had moved on to a Q&A, I realised. Most of the questions were of the 'who's your favourite/least favourite actor?' variety, and the atmosphere in the room had lightened again. I checked my watch. We were well over the hour scheduled for the workshop; it had to be coming to an end any minute. He would be gone soon, and I would be able to breathe again.

But before the end of the workshop, Gill showed himself a second time. He announced that they had been a remarkable group. I had been listening – they were nice kids, but he was being excessive in his description of them, and in his thanking of the teachers and the Film Festival for their marvellous work.

A warm fog of self-satisfaction settled over the room. At a nod from Gill, his assistant stood up from his seat. Almost too late, I realised that Gill had been softening us up for something.

'In fact, you're so wonderful,' he said, 'that I've decided I want to keep in touch with you all, let you know how I'm doing, send you a newsletter, details of upcoming internships. And there's going to be a premiere in Dublin, a little red carpet thing, in a few months so maybe I can meet some of you again there. My assistant will pass a clipboard with a sheet of paper around to all of you and I want you to sign your names, give me your email addresses and phone numbers and we can keep in touch that way. We'll do a few photos now as well. And of course you can follow me on Twitter, if you're not already.'

The students fizzed. Their teachers and the festival staff looked puzzled initially, then more sanguine. This was beyond what any of them had expected, but Gill was seeking only the kind of information needed for a mailing list, wasn't he? And everybody had mailing lists, didn't they? Even big-time film directors, apparently. So far, so ordinary.

This was it. His entire visit had been leading up to this moment. I got to my feet and started talking, before Boyband had a chance to move, and before I had time to think.

'I'm sorry, Mr Gill, I'm afraid it won't be possible for any of the under-18 students to give you their names and contact details without parental permission,' I said. 'I'm a board member and a solicitor. Finn Fitzpatrick's the name, we met last night, briefly, though you may not remember ...'

'I remember you,' Gill said. 'What's the problem?'

'The festival has rules. What I mean is that it must follow its own guidelines on child safety, and ...'

'What are you saying?'

'I'm saying it's a matter of trust, parental trust.'

'Wait a minute, are you saying you don't trust me?'

'I'm not saying that.'

'That's what I heard. *You* don't trust *me.*'

'It's not you I don't trust. It's not personal.'

'Oh come on. What could be *more* personal? I've been all over the world and I've *never* been treated like this, *never* had my integrity called into question like this. I'll tell you who *I* don't trust, *I* don't trust *you.* You wouldn't recognise talent if it stripped to its tighty whities and danced a jig in front of you.'

The students erupted with laughter. Alice Chambers got to her feet and tried to intervene, but Gill continued.

'No, no, wait, let's hear what the *lawyer* has to say. Because we all know how trustworthy lawyers are, right? Any of you lawyers?'

'No,' the students said.

'I didn't think so. And make sure you keep it that way,' Gill said, and winked. 'So, what's this about?'

'It's the rules, Mr Gill,' I said.

'Do you think anything great was ever made by people who stuck to the rules? Do you think I'd've won five (yes, five, not four, not three, *five*) Oscars, not to mention the BAFTAs and the Golden Globes and the DGAs, if I'd stuck to the fucking rules?'

'Well, Mr Gill, we stick to the rules around here,' I said.

One of the students booed, and a couple of others took it up. My right leg started to shake. I leant a hand back on my chair to steady myself.

'Rules are made to be broken,' Gill said.

'Let me explain,' he added. 'You see, the reason I came here, the reason I asked the festival to organise this event, is because I knew I'd find talent here. And I did, more than I could ever have hoped for.'

He stretched his arms wide, embracing the circle of students.

'The film business would keel over and die without new blood. And you, and your rules mean that I'm going to be walking out of here today with no means of contacting *any* of the bright young people I've met here, and bonded with; yes, bonded, it's true. You know, if I hadn't had a mentor, I wouldn't be here today? I got my first break in ads from Billy Thomson, me, a snot-nosed kid from the shittiest flats in the inner city of Dublin, a guy who couldn't talk proper, even after three years on a grant in UCD, where I never fitted in, by the way. I never fitted in anywhere, until I got into the movies. And, yeah, Cork Film Festival was a big part of that for me, a *huge* part of my growth as an artist. And, you know, that's what matters: having someone who believes in you. That's all I wanted for these kids, these fabulous kids – to listen to them, to care for them, to give them *hope*.'

He brushed his right hand across his eye, as if wiping away a tear. The girl in the green uniform got up from her seat and offered him a tissue. He took it, said, 'Thanks, Carmel,' and continued.

'But I'll do what you want, I'll follow your so-called rules. And I'll go now, and *leave* you to your rules – my God, if you had any understanding of the talent in this room, but you don't, all you people care about is fucking red tape – so, yeah, I'll go, but you're not off the hook, Fitzpatrick. These kids deserve an explanation from you. You need to tell them just what's wrong with Jeremy Gill, and with Jeremy Gill what you see is what you get, *giving his time* to them. You know, the trouble with you people, you fucking *bureaucrats*, is that you strangle creativity. It's never "yes you can", it's always "no you can't". I really thought Cork was better than that. You know, honestly? I think it *is* better, but there are bad apples everywhere, kids, remember that. It's up to people like us to fight for what's right.'

He turned to Alice Chambers. He spoke slowly, and with great control.

'I will be writing a letter of complaint to the board. And I will be telling them that I will never, as long as I live, visit Cork Film Festival again. Not only that, I won't let any of my films come here again.'

He nodded at his security guard and made for the door, followed at speed by his assistant. Alice Chambers scurried after them, but Gill stopped her, hands up, shoulder height, both palms facing the room.

'Damage done. Too late. I'll send a car to the hotel for my things, but I'm leaving right now. If you knew the opportunities I've passed up, if you only knew how hard it was to make time in my schedule so that I could come to this festival. And you know why? Because it means so much to me. But no more. No more. I'm out of this city right now, and you have that, that stupid *lawyer bitch* to thank for it, I'm sorry about the language, but it's the only word that truly fits. I know you'll forgive me, kids, and, hey, meeting you guys, it's been a blast, a total blast.'

He stood for a moment longer and swallowed. He still had Carmel's tissue in his hand. Now, his fist closed tightly around it. He looked down but, after a pause, he looked up again, stared straight at me, and shook his head. Then he waved at the students, and left.

After Gill had gone, there was a gasp, a collective intake of breath. Then came uproar. Confusion quickly gave way to anger and, despite his questionable behaviour, it was clear that Gill wasn't the students' target. I heard a girl's voice, one of the students, I didn't know which one.

'Lawyer bitch,' the voice said.

'Yeah,' another voice said, male this time.

I knew that I had a choice to make: to go, or stay and fight it out. I decided to stay but, within seconds, I felt a firm hand on my left shoulder. I turned around. It was Alice.

'A word,' she said, and walked out of the room.

I followed, and when we were both in the corridor Alice closed the door behind us. I started to talk but she put her index finger to her lips and spoke in a voice that was barely above a whisper.

'Shhh. I don't want you to say anything, I just want you gone. I don't know what you think you're doing, or what your fucking fixation on Jeremy Gill is, and I don't want to know. Ever. I heard you talking to him last night, I mean what the fuck was that about? No, don't answer, I don't give a flying fuck what it was about, actually. And then I hear you've been "borrowing" photographs from the archive. Photos of Jeremy Gill. And fuck knows what else you've been doing. All that matters is, you've just landed me and the festival in the middle of a shitstorm and, let me tell you, Gill won't have to write to the board about you, I'll do it myself. Now get the fuck out of here, Finn Fitzpatrick, and you know what, don't even think about coming back.'

20

When something unforeseen and previously unimaginable happens, and there are no rulebooks, and no professional guidelines to follow, the best thing to do is nothing. Let the dust settle. See how things pan out. That's what I tell my clients, and that's what I was frantically telling myself now. It was time to regroup, take deep breaths, lick wounds, a whole shedful of platitudes and clichés that were easier to dispense than to apply. I felt sick, and sorry too, for the error I'd made in confronting Gill like I had, and for what Alice had said, the shitstorm I had brought on the festival and on her: decent, hard-working Alice. She had always been a good friend to me. It was no wonder she felt angry and hurt and betrayed.

Back in my office, I opened my file and started a note on my conversation with Tiernan, highlighting the names of the convent in Dublin, and of Sister Bernadette. There was no guarantee that either of them were still there but, right after I completed my note on the workshop, I'd try to find out.

A short note it was. Though what had happened at the Firkin Crane had seemed momentous, had *been* momentous, there was little of substance to say about it, and even less to follow up on. I didn't even know the real names of Gill's people, Boyband and Security guy, didn't know what I'd do with them even if I did. They would never talk to me after this.

And the scene that Gill had directed for the kids and his actions in seeking contact details for a mailing list? Both had looked highly suspect. But with a little distance, half a mile and half an hour since I'd been unceremoniously ejected, I was starting to see that I might have overreacted or, at least, that I could have handled the situation at the workshop differently, handled things differently all along, maybe. I was thinking about what Alice had said, that I had damaged the Film Festival, and her too, because of what looked like an inexplicable obsession with Jeremy Gill. Maybe if I had been less of a lone wolf, if I had sought advice from my boss at the start, if I hadn't raced headlong into the investigation, if I had thought it through first, maybe that would have been better? To have ended the case before it began?

But, deep down, I didn't believe any of that. If I was right about Gill, he had to be stopped and it seemed like nobody else was even minimally concerned about him. From what I had seen of his behaviour over the last couple of days, it was extraordinary that nobody had raised queries about him before. How was he getting away with it? In public, he had shown himself to be a bully and a misogynist. But, after it all, I was the one in the stocks, not him. If I believed in conspiracy theories, I *might* think there was a conspiracy of silence about Gill. At the very least, he seemed to inspire a sort of groupthink. What was it Tiernan had said? 'That's just Jeremy.' No matter what he did, he had people around to explain and excuse him. And that was how Deirdre had felt too, wasn't it? That she'd never be believed?

I refused to be one of the enablers. I had regrets about the consequences for Alice, and for our friendship. And I was concerned about the festival, about the bad reputation it might develop if Gill started mouthing off about it to other people in the film business. But I had to keep going. The way I saw it, I had no choice.

Just then, there was a knock at my office door. It was Tina.

'Em, sorry, Finn, I just thought ... em ... I should tell you ... what I mean to say is ... em ... like, sorry, but do you know you're trending on Twitter?'

I could hardly bear to look, but I logged into my Twitter account on my desktop. It looked like every one of the students at the workshop had tweeted their disapproval of @Finnfitz and @corkfilmfest, #WTF, #lawyerbitch. And their approval of @JeremyGill, #weluvujezza. Which @JeremyGill had retweeted, #couldntpossiblycomment. Along with 483 of his three million followers. Not a huge number. But enough to get me trending.

I was appalled.

And things were about to get worse.

My desk phone rang.

'Boardroom. Now,' Gabriel McGrath said.

21

Pale and skinny, with bobbed brown hair pulled back in a messy half-up, half-down ponytail, and wearing black jeans and a baggy black T-shirt under an ancient GAP hoodie, Sadie O'Riordan didn't look much like a detective Garda. But she had a brain as sharp as a drawer full of knives. And she had a way of looking a different kind of nondescript every day, though some things were a constant; the disposable work clothes, for one. She never wore anything that couldn't be torn, or dirtied, or dumped. And she never wore scarves, or jewellery, or anything that could be dragged from her, a tiny silver scar in her left earlobe testament to an elementary error she wouldn't make again.

After some queuing, we'd managed to snag the booth. The remainder of the place had long tables and benches and the kind of retro/industrial/hipster look that had been unusual in Cork until recently. Located in what used to be a no man's land for restaurants, between the city centre and suburbia, Ramen had been full out the door since the day it opened, and had spawned a multitude of imitators, some more successful than others. For a while, every greasy Chinese in the city was rebranding itself as Asian street food, even though Chicken Maryland was still on the menu in a couple of them. I knew. I made a point of checking. And I have no idea what that says about me.

Sadie had had no food since breakfast and attacked her dinner like she hadn't eaten in a year. I used the time it took for her to eat her starter and main course to tell her about the Carney/Gill case and the afternoon's events, almost without reply, apart from an occasional grunt. Nothing unusual there. Sadie never spoke until needed, though once she started, she usually had plenty to say. I hadn't mentioned Davy Keenan, partly because he was off topic, but partly, too, because I had a feeling Sadie wouldn't approve. She was my best friend. But she was a cop, and Davy's past was too much of a grey area. I hadn't mentioned Deirdre's relationship to me either. I needed to know more about how I felt about her and the whole situation before I told anyone.

'So, are you suspended?' Sadie asked. 'You done with that, by the way?'

She had finished her noodles and was eyeing my green curry.

'No and no. Oh go on, eat it,' I said.

I pushed my dinner across the table. I had no appetite, and it was never wise to get between Sadie and food when she was hungry.

'You'll be back at work tomorrow so, will you?' Sadie said.

'Not exactly.'

'Go on.'

'I'm on an unplanned holiday.'

'Sounds like a suspension to me,' Sadie said.

'Yeah,' I said. 'But the partners hadn't a clue what had been happening, didn't know anything about the case. I argued that I had no control over other people's social media activity, that trending on Twitter couldn't be considered misconduct absent any supporting information, that I appreciated that the firm was embarrassed but that fair procedures were required nonetheless and, given that they hadn't carried out any investigation whatsoever, that they couldn't suspend me. Not legally, anyway.'

'Too right,' Sadie said.

'So I offered to take a week off with pay and they jumped at it. Turns out Gabriel had got a call from one of his golfing buddies, who just happens to be the festival board chairman, saying he wanted to meet Gabriel, to talk about me. Then two minutes later, he got a call from a journalist asking for a statement and how he felt about me trending on Twitter. The journo had to explain to Gabriel what that meant. He lost the plot. Started ranting, gave me a complete carpeting. I was in bits, but held it together till I got out of there. I got Tina to cancel my client appointments and gave her work to do while I'm gone. But it felt like moving deckchairs on the *Titanic*, Sadie.'

'What do you mean?'

'If they want me out, I've given them enough ammo. I've been acting way outside my job description, taking on a case without authority, a case that by any standards is unwinnable.

Been behaving more like a detective than a lawyer. They'll get the procedures right next time, and if – when – they do, I'll be out on my ear. And unemployable. Nobody's going to give a job to hashtag lawyerbitch, the woman who disrespected Ireland's uncrowned king. I could lose everything I've worked for, Sadie. No job, no mortgage payments. I can only barely afford my house as it is.'

'Any chance of suing for … anything?'

'Not yet, not that I can see. There's been a heck of a lot of vulgar abuse, but nothing defamatory so far. Gill has said nothing publicly, and neither has the Film Festival, it's just been the disappointed, angry kids, upset because I deprived them of contact with their hero. They don't know why, or what my suspicions are, and I can't tell them. I'm only able to tell you because I got the Carneys' authority.'

I paused.

'I still can't understand why they didn't do something about it.'

'Who?'

'The Carneys. They knew Deirdre had been raped and they told no one, not even a doctor. For fuck sake, she was their daughter.'

'Finn, you *know* that the vast majority of sex crimes – between two-thirds and four-fifths, possibly even more than that – are never reported. And of those cases that *are* reported, most aren't prosecuted and even fewer reach a successful conviction. There could be any number of reasons they didn't pursue it at the time.'

'I know, I know, but it's so wrong.'

'Which bit?'

'All of it. I keep thinking about Deirdre. How awful it must have been for her ... if only she'd been able to do something. I'm not blaming her for not, not at all, I just wish that she could have. For her, for herself. For nobody else.'

'None of us knows how we'd react in similar circumstances. All the system can do is make it as easy as possible for victims to make complaints and, when they do, ensure that adequate supports are in place.'

'*Are* there adequate supports?'

'No – but there's a greater understanding of the issues than there was back then.'

'It was 1998, Sadie, it wasn't a hundred years ago.'

'The last Magdalene Laundry, where so-called fallen women were more or less imprisoned for the crime of being sexually active, closed in 1996. The Supreme Court case, where the Attorney General of this state took action to try to prevent a pregnant suicidal fourteen-year-old from leaving the country for an abortion, was in 1992. The nineties in Ireland might as well have been a hundred years ago. Why are you surprised the poor girl didn't report it?'

Sadie was right. In law and politics, gynaecology was ever-present.

'I'm not remotely surprised,' I said. 'I'm sad for Deirdre, that's all.'

'You're 100 per cent convinced that it was Gill who raped her?'

'More like 99 per cent. Or 90. I shouldn't be as sure as I am. I don't actually know.'

'No you don't,' Sadie said.

'I *think* I'm right, though, or I feel I am a lot of the time. But Gill's like an eel. Every time I have a hold of something, or of him, he slips from my grasp. Even what happened today at the workshop, it seemed so clear at the time that he was targeting that girl Carmel from St Al's. But she's one of the loudest voices on Twitter, she seems to have started the lawyerbitch hashtag. I just don't know. I don't know who he is. Or what I'm doing. Maybe I've gone a bit mad over the last few days. And now I'm going to be mad and jobless and homeless too. It's too awful for words.'

'Could you issue a statement? Defend yourself?'

'I want to – but issuing a statement only fuels the fire and gets me nowhere. I said that to the partners' meeting at work. The best thing is to let it die down and, if asked, say something like "not in a position to comment at present". I'm expecting some press interest, I know it's already made breakingnews.ie and I'm fairly sure it will hit the papers. But if they're not fed, the press will tire of the story. And Twitter will move on. That seems to be the approach being taken by the festival too. But there's an added complication for me, something dire altogether.'

'What could be worse?'

'I got a letter by fax, and an email, this afternoon from Gill's solicitors. Elliott Phillips, the biggest and baddest in Dublin, offices worldwide.'

'What does it say? Just tell me.'

'It tells me to cease and desist my campaign of harassment and intimidation of their client, one Jeremy Gill, in default of which the appropriate further action shall be taken against me without further recourse to correspondence, which said action shall include, without being limited to, civil proceedings for defamation, including all and any damage to their client's impeccable reputation, and/or complaint to the Law Society of Ireland seeking to strike me off the roll of solicitors for misconduct and/or complaint to an Garda Síochána in respect of their client's fears and concerns for his personal safety, and the letter taxes me with the costs of all and any proceedings.'

'Ouch,' Sadie said.

'It looks bad, really bad, and if they were to carry out even a tenth of it, I'd be ruined for ever. A lot of it is bullshit – completely unsustainable, the criminal complaint in particular. He might, at a push, a big push, be able to argue innuendo in a civil case though I'm sure I said nothing defamatory. But, with his money, he could issue proceedings anyway, for the sheer hell of it, and whether the proceedings were sustainable or unsustainable, it wouldn't matter. The fact that they existed would be damaging enough. Or he might take the economical option and decide to report me to the Law Society for unprofessional behaviour, or conduct unbecoming, or some crap like that. And, if he does, they have to investigate and that can go on for months – years, even. Meanwhile, I'm in professional limbo and fired for sure. Worst case scenario, he sues me, gets me struck off and pauperises me. Best case, it's an idle threat, calculated to terrify me with shock and awe tactics that he'd never carry through on.'

'All you were doing was taking standard precautions for child safety, surely?'

'That's true. But I went for a public confrontation when I should have approached Alice privately afterwards, even Gill himself. Instead I set myself up as his public enemy, and made a complete show of myself and the festival – and dragged the firm into the mess. *And* there's the fact that I took the photos out of the archive in advance of Gill's arrival. It looks like I had an agenda.'

'You did.'

'I did.'

I paused.

'My gut says Gill is guilty. If he takes any kind of action against me, I have an opportunity to defend myself in some forum or other, and he won't want that. What I have on him amounts to diddly squat – but Gill doesn't know that. That's what I hope – that it stops here, because otherwise his own reputation would suffer too much. And, if you think about it, this is a total over-reaction to something minor. I mean, I'm a complete nobody in his world. The fact that it *is* such an extreme reaction means, I think, I hope, kind of, *almost*, that I've struck a nerve. That he's rattled. Maybe he didn't know about Deirdre's death until I told him. Maybe he thinks she told me, or someone else, about him.'

I paused again.

'But I'm shit scared, Sadie, about my job, about my life. If his intention was to frighten me, it's working. And even if he doesn't sue my arse off, what else might he do?'

'Maybe if you apologised,' Sadie said. 'Threw yourself on Gabriel's mercy, got a doctor's cert, blamed stress or something, promised to drop the case? Would you do that?'

I grimaced, closed my eyes, put my head in my hands. I remembered Ann's words: 'If there was to be a case it would have to be about justice.' Deirdre, my sister, deserved justice. I looked at Sadie again and shook my head.

'I got Tina to send a letter to Jeremy's lawyer saying that I'm out of the office on leave and that she will pass the letter to me on my return. I don't know if that will pause the juggernaut. But throwing myself on Gabriel's mercy, stopping the investigation?'

I stopped, thought about telling Sadie who Deirdre really was, then didn't.

'If I'm right about Gill, then I'm sure there are more girls out there that he's hurt, and that there will be more in the future. I don't know what I can do. I have doubts, Sadie. Every single minute I have doubts about what I'm doing. But I have to go on.'

'Okay,' she said. 'I'm worried for you, really worried. And you're going to have to be careful. But I'm glad you're not walking away, Finn.'

She paused.

'The way you described Gill, the narcissism, the bullying, the being whoever he needs to be to suit any situation, the volcanic temper when he senses he's been found out. And, at the same time, how he's elusive, manipulative, impossible to pin down, and that thing you said about how it feels confusing when you're around him. There's a name for all that.'

Sadie sank the last of her beer and leant across the table.

'How you're describing Gill? You're describing a psychopath.'

22

This time last week I hadn't known that I'd had a sister, and I hadn't met Jeremy Gill. Now, I was parked on the north side of Dublin's inner city, across the street from the twelve-foot-high red sandstone wall that surrounded the Convent of the Blessed Eucharist: Rhona Macbride's old school, and the place Jeremy Gill had made his first short film.

I had parted from Sadie at around ten o'clock the night before and had finally replied to Davy's texts when I got home, to say that I'd had a bad day, couldn't talk, and was turning off my phone. Later, when I was on my yoga mat, unsuccessfully trying to bring my attention to the breath, the doorbell went.

'I didn't want to let things rest the way they were this morning,'

Davy had said, over the intercom. 'I thought we should at least *try* to talk about what happened.'

I buzzed him in and met him halfway down the stairs on the landing. We stood facing each other in silence. Then I undid his shirt and led him into my bedroom.

But as we were both leaving the house this morning I said, 'This can't happen again.'

'It can,' he said. 'Though I think you're right. It probably shouldn't.'

He kissed me on the cheek and ran out the door into the black winter morning and he didn't look back so he probably didn't notice I'd stopped breathing.

By 7 a.m., I was driving up the M8. I had intended to hit Dublin around 10.00, just after the morning rush hour, but the traffic had been rainy day bad and it was well after eleven by the time I arrived at the convent.

I'd have to conceal my reasons for being there but the dishonesty wasn't going to come as easy as it had of late. Lying to a graduate on work experience was one thing, but lying to a nun? After finishing primary school, I went to St Angela's Convent Secondary on Patrick's Hill. Most of the classes were taught by lay teachers, but not all. I found out fast that nuns are human lie detectors, Sister Attracta, the history teacher, especially. I had been studious, mostly, but on any occasion I hadn't done my homework, unfailingly she had called on me to read my answer to the class. Still, it had been good training. I had learnt that, when lying, it was best to tell as much of the truth as possible.

I crossed the road and pressed the doorbell, my breath misting the brass plate on the door. It could do with a shine, I thought. But there were few nuns now, and most of those were geriatric, well beyond such duties. Many convents had closed, and there was a real risk that Sister Bernadette was dead, or had moved to a retirement home. I was about to press the bell again when the door was opened by a small, chubby, orange-tanned woman in a neon green velour leisure-suit. Times had changed, though surely not this much? But the woman was much too young to be a nun, I realised.

'Good morning, I'm here to visit Sister Bernadette, if she's available,' I said.

'I'll check,' the woman said.

She sounded like a local.

'What's your name, love?'

'Nola Fitzpatrick.'

Almost nobody calls me 'Nola' – I don't encourage it – and Sister Bernadette was unlikely to be on Twitter, but you never knew. I wasn't prepared to give a false name. That was a step too far, but a rarely used diminutive might provide some cover. At least the nun was still around – if it was the same woman. It was a common name, after all. I was regretting that I hadn't asked Tiernan more about Sister Bernadette.

The woman showed me into a narrow passageway and directed me to a row of plastic chairs placed against the left-hand wall. Then, without a word, she disappeared through a second larger door, and locked it behind her. The passageway looked like a recent addition. A weather protector? Or a security measure?

More likely the latter, I reckoned. Their centuries-old raison d'être meant that the nuns couldn't close their doors to callers – but they could be sensible. These were tough streets, had been since the Act of Union had abolished the Irish parliament and led the moneyed classes to London. Their great houses had become slum tenements, entering a cycle of dereliction, demolition and replacement with council flats, the poverty of the local residents the only constant. Convents in areas like this had been socially radical, educating the children of the poor. But these were less respectful times and it looked like the nuns had had to beef up their security as a result.

I checked my watch. I had been waiting more than forty-five minutes, which might mean that I'd been forgotten. Then I heard the Angelus bell toll. Presumably the nuns had prayers around now. If that was the case, I'd be waiting another while. Any other time, I'd be scrolling through Facebook and Twitter to pass the time. But I'd vowed to keep off the internet for a few days, hoping that the Gill furore would have died down by the time I returned. I did a breathing exercise and rehearsed my story in my head.

The smell here was the same as it had been in St Angela's convent, a mixture of furniture polish, cooking and mothballs. Comforting, in an odd way. By the time I got to secondary school, I had been adopted and my name had been changed to Fitzpatrick. It had been Whelan for most of primary school, until my birth mother had died. That had been a scary time, but Mam and Dad had said that they would fight to keep me if they had to. As it turned out, they didn't have to fight very hard. All of my birth mother's relatives, country people, had said no-thank-you-very-much to the social worker's suggestion that one of them might want to take me in. After a couple of months, or years, it had seemed like a long time, but it might not have been, everything was settled.

In St Angela's, a lot of my classmates didn't know that I was adopted, and most of those who knew assumed it had happened just after I was born. There were a few from Gardiner's Hill School who knew my original name and my whole story, but I eased them out of my life as fast as I could. They hadn't been nice to me in primary. I might as well have had a label around my neck, or a bell to ring. The kids hadn't known the difference at first. Their mothers were the ones who wouldn't let me come for sleepovers, who told their own children about how, when my birth mother brought me to school, I had had scabies and lice and a nose that never stopped running, and how they had had to complain to the teachers about it, and how I was often left hanging around on the side of the road, and if my mother showed up to collect me, which half the time she didn't, she was drunk, if that's all she was. And hadn't any shame about any of it, which was the worst thing nearly, and how in the end the school had had no choice but to call in the Health Board, and wasn't that the lucky day for the poor misfortunate because weren't the Fitzpatricks only after applying to become foster parents because they weren't able to have children themselves, sure God help us.

The stories followed me right through primary, and whenever lice came into the school, the mothers and the children stared at me. Secondary with the nuns at St Angela's had been my great escape from all that, from the knowing looks of outsiders, even if I was never able to silence the voices in my head.

Just after 12.20, I heard the jangle of a bunch of keys behind the great door and, instinctively, sat straighter in my chair. I might be about to tell a pack of lies, but the 'no slouching, girls' rule was harder to break. The door opened, a crack at first, then wider. I stood as a rail-thin, silver-haired woman in a calf-length grey wool skirt and what looked like a hand-knitted grey round-necked jumper, with a starched white round cotton collar inside it, came into the passageway. She wasn't wearing a veil. She didn't have to. She had nun written all over her. I caught a flash of neon green. The other woman was there too, watching from the inside hall. The nun looked to be in her late sixties, but nuns often looked a decade or more younger than their age. This one might be pushing eighty.

'Thanks for seeing me, Sister Bernadette,' I said, taking a chance with the name.

'Well, yes, I haven't agreed to anything yet,' the nun said. 'Yvonne told me you looked as if you wouldn't eat me so I thought I should come and check. But we don't know each other, do we?'

Her voice was strong, and her gaze was intelligent. I wouldn't have had a chance of deceiving the woman in her prime. But there had been a hint of the uncertainty that old age brings. That might be enough.

'No, Sister. And I realise that I should have written or phoned first. But I was in the area and, honestly, I thought there's no time like the present. Memories are so easily lost.'

'Well, yes, I suppose. But you're not a past pupil?'

'No, Sister, I'm sorry, I'm making a hopeless job of explaining. I'm here about the film that was made here. I'm an amateur film historian, and I was lucky enough to see Jeremy Gill during his recent visit to Cork Film Festival. Afterwards, I had lunch with, not with Mr Gill, I wouldn't have been so privileged. No. I had lunch with Tiernan McDevitt, the arts journalist. He worked on Mr Gill's first film, I don't know if you remember? No? Anyway, Tiernan told me about the filming, how it took place here. And I realised that I hadn't known that at all. It's such an important part of the Gill story and it's almost completely unknown and I just thought it needed to be recorded. So here I am. Cheeky, I know. Sorry again for the short notice, Sister, and for being a terrible pest.'

I waited.

'I see,' Sister Bernadette said. 'It's not known, you say? But isn't it in the credits that it was filmed here? I thought – no, I definitely remember that it is.'

'Well, of course, yes. There's a thank-you to the convent in the credits. But the circumstances aren't known – for example, that the park in the film is the convent's own garden. And what it was like for the community. Any special memories, all that.'

'I see,' Sister Bernadette said again.

After a pause, she continued.

'What would you want to do?'

'Talk, record an interview, take a few photos of the garden, the other locations, that kind of thing. As much, or as little, as you want. I'd put the information into the Film Festival archive, so that it would be preserved. And let you have a copy for your own archive, too.'

Most of it was true, though my amateur film historian status had only been dreamt up in the car on the way up.

'Yes, I see what you mean,' Sister Bernadette said. 'It's the kind of thing that might be forgotten, and so much has been forgotten, so much has changed, so much *will* change soon. The convent can't continue, not like this, not for much longer.'

She looked wistful, and I nodded in what I hoped was a sympathetic fashion.

'Come into the parlour and Yvonne will bring us a cup of tea.'

'Thank you *so* much, Sister,' I said.

Sister Bernadette remembered little about the filming, or how it had come about, though she said that Jeremy Gill's mother had been a past pupil. She thought that, perhaps, the initial approach had come by way of Jeremy's mother, and spoke at length about Gill's kindness and generosity to her and all the sisters, both during filming and, in particular, afterwards. The weight given to 'afterwards' left me in no doubt that a substantial donation, perhaps more than one, had been made to the convent's coffers. I listened closely to everything Sister Bernadette said. I took notes, in addition to my iPhone recording, and deliberately avoided all mention of Rhona Macbride until we got to the garden. The bench, the location for most of the film's scenes between Gill and

Rhona, was still there. I started by taking a few photos of Sister Bernadette on the bench from various angles, and then sat beside her.

'It's such a thrill to be here,' I said. 'I think you're in Mr Gill's spot and I'm in Rhona's.'

'Oh yes, I do believe you're right.'

She blushed, and laughed, but coyly, as if I had made a slightly risqué joke.

'Was there much of an audition process for her role, do you remember?'

'Oh my goodness, I don't remember a great deal about the auditions. From what I *do* remember, I think Jeremy saw nearly every girl in the school. He was marvellous with all of them, but once he saw Rhona, he made up his mind that she was the one. I'm sure she'd remember more about it herself.'

'Fabulous, it all sounds like such fun. But you know, you're right. You've just made me realise that I should talk to her too. She's a big part of the story.'

'Ye-es, I suppose. Though she changed schools, you know. Not long after the film, just upped and left. I needn't tell you, I was disappointed. A lot of media people came to take pictures for the papers and the news when dear Jeremy was nominated for the Oscar for the short film. They wanted to take a photograph of Rhona, too. And we had to tell them that she wasn't here. Well, it didn't look good. And that's it, I suppose, that's the way it goes. I could *never* understand it. I was dean of students at the time, out of active teaching since they brought in the compulsory retirement age, which is a terrible nonsense. But I had held on to that honorary role, and I knew Rhona Macbride very well. She *had* been an excellent pupil, but she changed all of a sudden, they often do at that age, was absent for a while and then the request for the transfer came in. She went from here, so convenient for her home on Wickstead Street on the other side of the Basin, to Stanhope Street School. Really, from every point of view, it seemed the wrong move. I said it to her mother at the time. But she was adamant that if Rhona wanted to move, she could. And I spoke to her father Tom too. But it was no use, no use whatsoever. Girls can be so wilful at times. That's what I've learnt these fifty-seven years. Wilful and stubborn, and if they don't get discipline at home as well as in school, if they're allowed to do what they like ...'

I had stopped listening. As soon as I could, without being rude, I thanked Sister Bernadette, and left. I had a father's name and a street address. It was enough to be getting on with.

I had been in the convent more than two hours, an hour more than my parking permit allowed. As I crossed the road to my car I saw that I had been clamped.

'Shit,' I said, under my breath.

The clamper van was still on the street, further along. I ran after it. There was no prospect of getting away with the fine – but I might persuade them to release me, provided I paid fast, over the phone. After a hurried conversation, more lies and a lot of pleading, the attendant agreed to come back. I ran ahead of him, called in my credit card details, and sat in the car while he unlocked the clamp.

My phone pinged. It was a text message from Aifric Sheehan.

Mentioned D to Eoghan MacG. He never knew her. Definite. You sure he did?

I typed a reply to Aifric.

Must have got it wrong. Thanks Aifric

But the Carneys had been absolutely sure that Eoghan Mac-Giolla, though he hadn't been teaching at her school at the time she was there, had known Deirdre from the area. I made a note: I'd have to arrange another chat with him when I got back to Cork.

I looked again at the convent, at the rows and rows of windows, lighting rooms long vacant of people and purpose. I saw what looked like a grey figure watching the scene from a window on the first floor. Was it Sister Bernadette? I waved, but got no response.

Maybe it was a trick of the light.

23

Eighty euros poorer, I drove in the direction of Phibsboro. Some friends and I had shared a house there, on Geraldine Street, when we'd been students at the Law Society. We used to go the Basin, a quiet green place with a pond and a few benches, to loll about after summer lectures. Only ten minutes' walk from O'Connell Street, the park felt like a local secret.

Seeing a space on the left side of Wickstead Street, the address Sister Bernadette had given me, I pulled in, making sure to text my parking fee before I did anything else. I wasn't going to get clamped twice in one day. Then I got out of the car and started knocking on doors.

I had no story concocted for my meeting with the Macbrides. If I started out on a lie, I could never regain their trust. But I had to be discreet: I couldn't assume that Rhona had told her parents anything about what had happened with Gill, *if* anything had. I was keeping the question open as a formality, a sop to my legal training, even though, by now, I was sure that Jeremy Gill had attacked both Deirdre and Rhona. Sister Bernadette couldn't understand Rhona's change of behaviour and decision to move schools, but to me it made perfect sense. If Gill had sexually assaulted Rhona, it was only natural that she would have wanted to move away from the memories she had of him, and of the filming, at the school.

Number 17 Wickstead Street was a two-storey Victorian red-brick, typical of the area, with steps up to a holly-green front door, and a well-tended front garden. The woman who lived three houses down had said she was 'nearly sure' that this was Macbrides'. But the door was answered by a child, a sturdy fair-haired boy of nine or ten.

'Hello,' I said.

'Hiya,' the boy said.

'Is this where Thomas Macbride lives?'

'That's my grandad. But he's called Tommy, not Thomas. And he's not here.'

'Oh, I see. Is there anyone else home maybe?'

'My granny.'

'Could I talk to her, please?'

He turned and roared into the house.

'Granny!'

'All right, all right, Shane,' a voice said. 'No need to tell the whole street.'

A glamorous blonde woman of about sixty came to the door. Her hair was styled in soft curls. Either she had just had a blow-dry or she had a way with heated rollers. I had imagined another Ann Carney, someone spare, someone haunted. Not this.

'Mrs Macbride?'

'Yes, my dear. How can I be of assistance?'

She had a confident, seen-it-all air, like a senior Aer Lingus stewardess. I had the feeling that, if I stood around long enough, Mrs Macbride might offer me a G&T.

'Actually, it's Rhona I'm looking for.'

'You're looking for Auntie Rhona? Not here,' the boy said.

'That's right. Rhona doesn't live here, hasn't for years,' Mrs Macbride said.

'I know,' I said, winging it. 'But I really need to talk to her.'

'Are you a friend of hers?'

'Not a friend, exactly. Look, I don't expect you to just give me her address or phone number. But maybe you could ring her for me and tell her I need to talk to her. That it's very, very important, it's vital, actually, that I do. This is my driver's licence and here's my business card. I can wait out here if you'd prefer. I'm parked just down the road.'

I handed my card to Mrs Macbride. She took it and read it.

'You're a solicitor?'

'Yes,' I said. 'I want to talk to her about when she was at the Convent of the Blessed Eucharist. Just before she changed schools. I know it must seem unusual.'

Mrs Macbride's face changed, as if something was clicking into place.

'Wait here,' she said.

She closed the door and went into the house. Moments later, she was back. She handed me a piece of paper.

'Here's Rhona's address. I'm sure with the internet you'd have found her sooner or later anyway. It's better if she doesn't know you're coming, she won't answer the door if you give her warning in advance. And she definitely won't answer if she knows I sent you. We – well, we don't get on. We talk, but not much. I'd prefer if you didn't tell her you were here. She's at work now but she should be home some time after five. Don't get your hopes up, she never talked to us. I can't tell you more because I don't know anything. Goodbye.'

Without warning, she shut the door, leaving me alone on the step. I almost rang the bell again, but stopped myself. There was no need, I realised. I had got more information than I could ever have expected from Mrs Macbride, and from Sister Bernadette too.

Winding my scarf more tightly, I walked quickly towards the car. Though she wouldn't be home for another hour at least, I wanted to locate Rhona Macbride's house before dark. The day was dark enough already. Cars had their lights on, and it had started raining again, a drenching downpour that might never stop. The wet and the heavy traffic made driving almost unbearable. And dangerous.

I turned off Skreen Road and drove south in the shadow of the walls of the Phoenix Park and, further on, McKee Barracks. Rhona lived on Rossbeigh, a few turn-offs shy of the North

Circular. I pulled in across the road from the small development. I conceded that you could just about see the tops of the trees from Park View Mews, but calling it a view was pushing it. More significantly, there was a locked gate and an intercom and a coded keypad. Maybe that was the reason Mrs Macbride had given out the address so easily: I wouldn't be able to gain access to the front door unless Rhona agreed to press the buzzer.

Before I did any more, I needed to go to the loo. I wanted to catch Rhona soon after she came in from work, before she settled in for the night or went out again. And if she *did* agree to see me, I didn't want 'where's the bathroom?' to be my first question. I pulled off and drove around until I saw a coffee shop. Then I ran in, grabbed a bottle of water from the fridge and left it on the counter with the assistant, saying I'd be back to pay in a moment.

But sometimes you can move too fast. On the way out the door, I collided with a heavy-set man in a suit, pulling a copy of *The Herald* out of an inside pocket.

'I'm so sorry,' I said. 'I didn't see you. The glass, it's all steamed up.'

Ignoring my apology, he muscled past me, brushing the rain off his jacket. He marched straight to a table, sat and opened his paper with a snap. By now, I was the aggrieved one. Didn't people say Dubliners were friendly, that Corkonians were supposed to be standoffish? I shrugged and left. Then I did a U-turn and headed back towards Rhona's place. She should definitely be home by now, according to what her mother had said.

*

I rang the buzzer.

'Yes, who is it?'

I started at the voice from the intercom.

'My name is Finn Fitzpatrick. I'm a solicitor. I've come up from Cork today. If it's all right, I'd like to talk to you.'

Silence.

'How did you get my address?'

'Please can I talk to you, Ms Macbride? It's about ...'

'I know what it's about. And I don't want to talk to you.'

'I understand, Ms Macbride, Rhona, if I can call you that. But maybe it's time.'

More silence. Then, at last, a buzzing noise.

I pushed open the gate and hurried in before Rhona could change her mind. A door opened on the right side of the car park and a lone figure stepped into the rectangle of light. An outdoor lamp flashed on automatically as I approached.

'I need to see ID,' Rhona Macbride said.

She pushed the door almost closed and I handed my driver's licence and card through the gap. The door slammed shut. The sensor light clicked off and I was in darkness. I moved and it flicked back on. Then the door opened again

'You can come in,' Rhona Macbride said.

'Thanks.'

She nodded towards the rear of the house. I went down the narrow hallway and came into a white-painted kitchen with white cupboards and a mid-century-style round white table and four white chairs. I waited until Rhona came into the room, then sat at the table. She handed me my driver's licence, but put the card into a white fruit bowl on the counter. She sat down in the chair furthest away from me and sighed. Eventually, she spoke.

'I've been expecting this for ever. Not you. Someone. Doesn't make it easy.'

'No,' I said.

'I won't say anything, you know. You can sit here all night and I won't talk.'

'Okay. I understand. But is it all right if I ask why you let me in?'

She got up and leant against the counter. For the first time, I could see her properly. Dressed in leggings and a slim-fitting grey tunic, with thick black socks on her feet, she looked like a ballet dancer. Her hair, tied up in a high ponytail, was long and thick and naturally blonde. Rhona Macbride had been pretty onscreen as a schoolgirl. She had grown up to be beautiful.

'I saw your name in the paper at work today,' Rhona said. 'Some Twitter thing in Cork at the Film Festival. A row between you and Jeremy Gill. I thought that if you went from that hassle to coming up here you'd be hard to get rid of so I thought I'd better see you and explain, face to face, that I am *never* going to talk. Get that? *Never*.'

'I missed that article,' I said. 'Where is it that you work, by the way? Is it far?'

'Not that it's any of your business, but seeing as you found me here I suppose you'd find that out too. I work in the Department of Defence.'

'Near enough, so. On Infirmary Road?'

'Yeah.'

'I've sued your department once or twice. Soldiers' personal injuries claims. I remember one of my clients went for medical examination in St Bricin's Military Hospital.'

'That's not my area.'

'No?'

'I work in ... Don't think you can soften me up with this chit-chat.'

'I didn't think I could.'

'It's still *no*. I am *not* going to talk to you. And I'd like you to leave. *Now*.'

'You're not the only one, Rhona. Gill hurt you, I know he did, or I think he did, at least. But there was another girl, from Cork. Gill met her in 1998, when he was visiting the Film Festival. I represent her parents. She died, in January, earlier this year. It was suicide.'

'Suicide?'

'She was raped, had a nervous breakdown and never recovered. She alluded to Gill in her suicide note. Said that the academy mightn't like him so much if they knew what he was really like.'

I paused.

'I went to your old school today, spoke to Sister Bernadette. She told me about you, about how Gill chose you for the film role, how you changed schools afterwards. That was when I knew for sure. Her description of you. It was like listening to Deirdre's parents.'

'Deirdre?'

'Deirdre Carney, that was her name.'

Rhona sat at the table again and dropped her head, and I couldn't see her face.

'Anything you say to me would be between us, Rhona. Off the record. I promise that I won't tell anyone else, not without your authority.'

She looked at me then.

'Off the record? Bullshit,' she said. 'You want me to talk to the Gardaí, I know you do, and I can't do it. I won't.'

'No,' I said. 'You going to the Gardaí is not what this is about. I'm telling the truth. An off the record conversation with you would be extremely valuable to the work I'm doing for Deirdre's parents. You could tell me about Gill, about how he operates. You might be able to point me in the direction of new evidence for Deirdre's case.'

Silence.

'Do you want to think about it? I could go away and come back?'

It was my last try. I wasn't going to hound the woman any more than I had already. Unless Rhona agreed to talk, I would let her be. She took a long time before she spoke again.

'All right. I'll tell you my story. Off the record. But no more questions. And no recording. I talk, you listen, and then you go. Take it or leave it.'

'I'm grateful for anything you say, any way you want to say it,' I said.

24

'I remember the first day he came to the school, he was like nothing we'd ever seen,' Rhona said. 'He was funny and loud and the teachers were running around after him, giving him whatever he wanted. He was so cool. We thought he was fantastic. And I remember the audition. After I finished mine, an Emily Dickinson poem "Because I could not stop for death", he came over to me and put his hand on my head and said "I've found my girl," and I thought my heart was going to burst with pride. And this feeling I had. That was the main thing. He made me feel special – no, more, it was like he treasured me. I was fifteen. I'd never felt like that before. Or since.

'The filming was, well, it was brilliant. Learning my lines, the different takes and set-ups. I'd thought about acting, but by the end of the film I was sure that it was what I wanted to do. And he, well, he encouraged me, talked about my potential, said he'd help me. And I believed him. We became friends, or so I thought. We had private chats and he told me how he found me so easy to talk to and how sincere and genuine, how unspoilt I was, how women were usually a pain in the neck, how they always wanted something from him, and how our friendship was pure and good, and how he was so glad he'd found me. That kind of thing. He gave me gifts. Small things he must have got through his job. Advertising stuff. A couple of pens. A T-shirt. Nothing much. I see that now. At the time though … Anyway, he said we'd keep in touch after filming ended, that I needn't worry about that, and he'd arrange a special treat, and I was to tell nobody, because by rights he should be doing something for the school, for the whole school, and Sister Bernadette, because only for her he wouldn't have been able to bring in the film on budget. He used all those kinds of movie terms like "on budget" and "rough cut", and I felt like I was learning at the feet of a master. And that everyone else was a waste of my time. My family. My school friends.'

'Did anyone apart from you know what was going on?'

'No. They knew I was in the film, and that he had chosen me, but beyond that it was our secret. He was careful. He told me that nobody else could know, that they wouldn't understand, that if they did our friendship would have to end. And all this time he was a perfect gentleman, he never touched me. But I was dying for him. To kiss me, that's what I was thinking about. Him holding my hand. Us being together. He made me fall in love with him. I know now that it's called grooming, but you have no idea how I felt at the time. As far as I was concerned, it was love.

'Then, the filming ended and he was gone, back to his day job and I was devastated. Bereaved, even. But he came back, seven weeks later, to show us the final cut of the film, the whole school in the Assembly Hall, and I was thrilled and he made time for a quiet word with me and said: "Private treat?"

'And I remember nodding, and my mouth was dry, and I was exhausted from loving him, so the thought of being able to see him again, to have him to myself was, it was intoxicating.

'"Tell your parents you're going on a sleepover but I'll meet you instead. We'll have dinner at a hotel and I'll book you a room. You're going to be a famous actress. This is the start of the rest of your life."

'That was more or less it. And I agreed, was delighted to agree.

'He gave me the arrangements – where to stand so that he could pick me up in his car, what to bring, and I obeyed. Went willingly, lamb to the slaughter.'

Rhona got up, went to the sink, and got a glass of water. Then she went back, got a second one, and put it in front of me. She took her time before she spoke again.

'The hotel was spectacular. The Gustav. It closed for a while, went bust during the recession, I was never so happy about anything. But a Chinese consortium, some chain or other, bought it a few years ago and relaunched it under a new name. Anyway, that was where we went. He picked me up in an ordinary car, a Toyota something. In my imagination I'd been expecting an open-topped sports car or a limousine, but he wasn't super-rich back then. And I realised later that he only had the suite at the hotel because he'd used it on an advertising shoot, and had the keys till the following day. We didn't have to go through reception – we went straight from the car park in the lift, he had some kind of card or passcode that got us upstairs.

'The suite, yeah. There were two bedrooms and he made a big deal of showing me mine, my own bathroom. And he said I could pick what I wanted off the room service menu and he told me to go and have a bath, there was a jacuzzi bath, and a rainwater shower, and when I came back out, dinner had arrived. Of course now I see that he didn't want the staff to know who he had in the room.

'So we had dinner and I ate, and he ate, and he got me a drink. Coke, at first. And then, he was having a rum and Coke, a Cuba Libre, he said, and where was the harm in me having one, and he wouldn't tell if I didn't, and why would I? So I had one, and then a second one, a third. He had a bottle of rum with him, and a big bottle of Coke. He wasn't paying for drinks from the minibar. He was too cheap. I didn't think of that till later, and it shouldn't bother me, considering what happened, but it does ... So, yeah, we were sitting there drinking and laughing and picking things to watch on the movie menu and that's the last I remember until I woke up.

'To this day, I don't know if he drugged me, or if it was the alcohol or a combination of the two. But I knew something had happened. I knew straight away that he ... he'd had sex with me. He didn't deny it. Told me I loved it, that I was the one who wanted it, that I'd forced myself on him, and that he was a man, and what could he do? And that I was a bitch for doing it, and that I was the same as all the rest of the bitches, and that he should have seen I would be, and that we were finished, and that I had myself to thank, and that I needn't think about telling anybody because if I did he'd kill me and, just to make sure I understood that, he hit me. Not on the face, on the belly, all around there, the back, and then he threw me on to the floor and raped me again and kept telling me that I was a bitch and fit for nothing. He dropped me home then, to the end of the street. The last thing he said to me as I got out of the car was that he'd kill me if I told. I believed him. I still do.'

She paused, picked up her glass with both hands, took a sip, and slowly replaced it on the table.

'I knew that he had used a condom, at least when I was awake, and I'm fairly sure that he used one while I was passed out as well. But when my period was late I thought ... So I bought a pregnancy test. Negative. I bought two more. Negative again. But I didn't believe the results. I had myself convinced I was pregnant. I couldn't go to the family GP, or I felt I couldn't, so I made an appointment with the Well Woman Centre. Mitched off school. Gave a false name and address and pretended I was over eighteen. I was already stressing about how I'd get the money to get the boat to Liverpool or the plane to London and how I'd find my way to an abortion clinic ...

'Anyway, it turned out I wasn't pregnant. But while I was in the clinic I broke down. I didn't say what had happened. But the woman, she was a nurse, I think, she knew it was something bad. She was very nice. She told me that, whatever had happened, counselling would help. I had a follow-up appointment with her, but I never went back. I couldn't face it.

'I changed schools. Changed my ambitions. I didn't want to act any more, I wanted to hide, to be safe. But I wanted to be healed too, I wanted the pain gone. And I kept remembering what the nurse at the Well Woman had said. So eventually I went to the Rape Crisis Centre, and they got me a counselling appointment, and I went, and kept going. But I never named him, never once all these years. I got on with things, worked hard. I've been promoted a couple of times. And I work even harder at being normal, at just being. I live quietly, but this is my own house. I bought it, I pay the bills, the mortgage. I have a life. To spite that evil fucker Gill. He couldn't take that away from me, no matter what he did.'

'Your family must have known there was something seriously wrong?'

'My mother knew something had happened. She kept pushing for information but the more she pushed, the more I pulled away from her ... So that's it. The End. There's no more to be said. Now you go, like you agreed.'

'I will, I promise,' I said. 'I just need a minute.'

I took a long drink of water.

'I don't know what to say.'

'Don't say anything,' Rhona said. 'That's not part of the deal. I've told you my story. Off the record, just as you asked. Please leave. Please let me be.'

'I will. But your story has ... well, it's made an impact on me. A lot of the details fit with what I already know about Gill. But to hear you describe it, that's something else.'

I was trying to use neutral language, trying as hard as I could to stay separate from the horror of Rhona's story. And it *was* her story, she owned it, she told it powerfully. But it was Deirdre's story too. And it was a story that needed to be told. Gill was a dangerous sex offender who had to be stopped. What Rhona had said, about Gill putting his hand on her head at the audition, had sent a chill through me – if I hadn't spoken up, might Carmel from St Al's school in Cork have been his next victim? It didn't bear thinking about. But I remembered that Rhona had said that the more her mother had pushed for information, the more Rhona had withdrawn.

I got up from my chair. I took a page from my bag with my private email and phone number on it, and left it on the table.

'I want to thank you for telling me. I'll go now, like I promised. But that's my email address, my private email, and my mobile number. If you ever change your mind, some day, some year, just email me. And you have my business card. Any time, just send me a message. About anything. If you want me to go to the Gardaí, help you with a statement, arrange an appointment. They'd come here, I'm sure, you wouldn't have to go to the station, not at the beginning anyway. And there are experts who could help you before you even talk to the Gardaí. Please feel free to contact me, even to talk about what you might or might not do. And I want to remind you that everything you've said to me is confidential.'

'The answer is still no,' Rhona said. 'But I'll think about what you said about Deirdre. And the others. There are others?'

'There are. I don't know who or where, but there *are* others. I'm sure of that.'

25

I sat in my car for as long as it took to make a detailed handwritten note of what Rhona had said. Then I signed and dated it, read it into my phone and saved it to my iCloud account: my legal training had taught me the importance of a contemporaneous note and this was as close as I was going to get. There was one other procedural matter to be dealt with. As Rhona was a potential witness, I had had the Carneys' implied consent to disclose their confidential client information to her. Still, I'd call to see them when I was back in Cork to obtain their explicit consent and I would do a back-up note for the file. All I could say for now was that I had interviewed a potentially useful witness, and that it had been necessary for me to reveal some information to her. I couldn't yet disclose Rhona's identity, or the details, to them.

As I was writing up my notes, the missing information, the questions I would have liked to ask, the corroboration that would be needed if Rhona's case went to trial, came into sharp relief. Dates and times. Where he had collected her. The Toyota car he had used to collect and drop her back, could she recall the model or any part of the registration? Or the room number? How had she known it was an advertising shoot, had he told her or had she found out some other way? And more. I noted down anything I could think of that I needed to ask the next time we met. If we ever did. There mightn't be a second meeting, though I didn't want to think about that possibility. Either way, there was no point in staying up in Dublin now. I pulled out. If I got going, I'd be back in Cork before midnight.

I crossed the Liffey and was on the motorway in twenty-five minutes. I travelled in silence. No wittering radio presenter. No music. What happened to Rhona had happened to my sister, too. But Rhona had been stronger than Deirdre. People had different levels of resilience; it was a lottery, it seemed, who got enough to survive, and who came up short. It was like the way some alcoholics went into treatment and recovered, and some didn't. The way Davy did. The way my birth mother didn't. And what about me? Had I enough strength to cope with all of this? Or was I as weak as I felt in that moment?

I tried to focus on exposing Gill. For my own protection, I couldn't get sucked into the foul vortex that he had created. And I had a sense that something in the pattern of behaviour Rhona had described might help with Deirdre's case, even if I couldn't see it yet.

*

After Naas, I couldn't see much else either. A thick fog descended and traffic slowed to a crawl. Hunched over the steering wheel, I gave all my attention to staying on the road but, by the time I got to Cashel, I had to stop for a break. The driver behind me had the same idea, I saw, as he or she exited the motorway behind me and followed me along the unnecessarily complicated system of loops that led finally into the motorway service station. I filled up with petrol, paid, got a large coffee, and went upstairs. There was a nasty seating area with a couple of black fake leather sofas. Uncomfortable, as it turned out. I had intended to rest for a while. But that feeling I had had all day, that I was missing something, wouldn't leave me. After no more than five minutes, I gulped back my coffee, went to the loo, and drove on.

It was almost 12.30 when I got home, jittery from the tension of the drive and the strain of the last few days. With no work to go to in the morning, and no hope of sleep, I flicked on the television and surfed half-heartedly through the TV channels. I perked up. *Night of the Hunter*, one of my favourite films, was just starting on Film4. I watched to the end, then switched off, and sat for a while in the dark, 'Leaning' and Robert Mitchum's voice, going round and round in my head. For the first time in years, I had missed most of the Film Festival and wouldn't see the rest of it either. All because of Jeremy Gill. Which I might call ironic, if I wasn't so dog-tired.

I woke from a half-sleep at seven and went down to my study, where I typed up a to-do list for the day, scanned my note of the night before, and updated my connections file. Assuming I got back to work some time, it would be easy to download it to the firm's system later. Then, I pinged an email to Tina, asking her up to my house for lunch, and to bring the exhibit box from my desk (she had my spare desk key but not the key for the box).

At 8.15, I checked my Gmail and found a message from Rhona, sent at 8.01.

Hi Finn,

I have been thinking about what you said all night, about Deirdre and the others. I am not making any promises but I will think some more and talk to my counsellor. Do not put any more pressure on me or ask anything else of me at the moment. Please. I was very upset after you left last night and I need time to recover. I will contact you when I am ready, if I ever am.

Rhona

This was progress, the progress I had hoped for. I should have been happy. But there was no timescale, and there was an express prohibition on further contact from me. Should I reply, or would that be a breach of Rhona's terms? It seemed rude not to reply at all. In the end, I sent back a short neutral email:

Thanks Rhona, I will wait to hear from you, Regards F.

Then, overcome with a wave of exhaustion that felt a lot like dread, I went back to bed and fell into a deep sleep.

*

Awake again before ten, and feeling more energetic, I rang Ann and Sean Carney and arranged to call out to see them at 11.30. I needed to update them on what had been happening, and get their retrospective consent to my disclosures to Rhona. And I needed to obtain a sample of Deirdre's DNA for the case I was trying to make. It had occurred to me overnight too that, if I asked the lab to test my own DNA simultaneously, I would be able to find out if Deirdre and I shared a father as well as a mother, although I wasn't yet sure if I wanted an answer to that question.

I made a few more calls. Tomas de Barra was the one who picked up. A barrister, he specialised in criminal defence work: he was sure to know of a private forensic lab where I could get DNA and chemical constituent tests done, along with a report that would stand up in court. I had used a brilliant London-based scientist as a DNA expert in the past and, usually, if I had to do a paternity test for a client, I would use one of the local labs and get a DNA kit sent to a GP. But, in this case, the DNA I hoped to find was on a drinks coaster. Something different was needed. Tomas gave me the name of a specialist lab and started up with the questions about had I seen Twitter and the *Examiner*, and how I'd even made the *Irish Times*, and what was going on with me anyway?

'Not talking about, Tomas,' I said. 'But, hey, great to know my fame has spread.'

Next, I rang the lab, explained what I had, and told them what I wanted: tests for every possible sedative that might have been used fifteen years before, along with alcohol and cola and DNA. Then I asked for a cost estimate.

'You're looking at nearly four for everything you've mentioned there,' the lab representative said.

He didn't mean four hundred.

'Let me think about that and I'll get back to you,' I said.

At this point, any money I spent was going to have to be my own. For now, I couldn't run any of this as an expense through the office: I was suspended in all but name. And, for the same reason, I couldn't seek payment of the expense from the Carneys either – if I wasn't officially working, they weren't really my clients. Yet, to move the case forward, I had to do the tests. Like I had all along with this case, I felt compelled.

But there was more to it than that. Getting the tests done contained an element of self-preservation. If the tests revealed what I expected then, even though I was still a long way from proving Gill's culpability, arguably I would have objective justification for my work on the case. I would be able to show the partners at work that there was real substance to Sean Carney's suspicions. And, even though this first set of results would be inadmissible in any court proceedings, they would give me the solid ground I needed to pursue the case officially, with the full backing of the partners and access to the firm's funds and resources. If I could show Gill's DNA and Deirdre's on the same coaster, I had a plausible argument to make that I had been right all along. And I'd no longer be at risk of dismissal.

Looking at it that way, even though I couldn't afford it, the huge financial investment was the easy part. If I was right, I'd get a refund of the costs so far from the firm. If I was wrong, I was out of a job, but at least I would have given the case everything I had. And nobody would ever know about the tests.

But, coming at it another way, I was edging close to being disbarred for misconduct by getting the tests done at all. Gill could argue that I had planted the DNA. He might be believed: taking DNA without his consent was unethical, procedurally faulty, and illegal. Lastly, and most importantly, it was unconstitutional, in breach of his fundamental rights, his rights to privacy and bodily integrity, to start with.

Though Gill hadn't cared about Deirdre's constitutional rights, or Rhona's, hadn't cared about anything except getting as much as he could from them, discarding them afterwards like broken dolls. I told myself that the circumstances were exceptional – and that exceptional measures were called for.

Which was *exactly* the argument used to justify torture and extraordinary rendition. And the death penalty.

What had possessed me to use a stupid pen to steal Gill's DNA without his consent? What I had done was legally and morally wrong. I would have to wait, make a formal request for the DNA, and obtain it by court order. Going ahead with the tests now was absolutely not the right thing to do.

And yet, it was the *only* thing to do, if I was to find out for sure.

'Fuck it,' I said.

On the walk over to the Carney house, I thought through the specifics again. I'd need to search for Deirdre's DNA. Probably all I'd have for that was a hair sample from the brush I had seen in her bedroom. And I was also looking for male DNA that I hoped would belong to Jeremy Gill. I knew that there was a good chance he hadn't touched the coaster, but if he had touched Deirdre, she might have transferred his DNA.

After talking to Rhona, I knew that I should be testing for alcohol and possibly a sedative too. DNA was remarkably persistent, as all the cold cases solved in recent years showed. I didn't know how long alcohol and sedative traces might last but I knew enough to surmise that they could have deteriorated, and possibly disappeared, unless they had been refrigerated and kept at an optimum temperature. But if I could get proof of Gill's and Deirdre's DNA together, it would damage Gill, I was sure of it. The very request for Gill's DNA *might* be the catalyst I'd need to force him to the settlement table.

I decided to bank on the DNA and forget about the drug and alcohol residue tests for the moment. It was worth a try. And it would cost a lot less than four grand.

While I was waiting for the Carneys to answer the door, I checked my phone. I had had it on silent and in the twenty minutes it had taken me to walk to Turners Cross, I had got seven missed calls from Sadie. Normally, if she wanted me to contact her, she sent one text, and never, ever, repeat-called. I walked backwards towards the garden gate, simultaneously phoning her. As Ann answered the door I mouthed 'Just a sec' and turned away.

'What's up?' I said.

'Something's happened,' Sadie said. 'Something bad.'

She paused.

Darkest Truth

'You can't say it yet, the name hasn't been cleared for public release. Word came down to us from Dublin this morning. I'm sorry to be the one to tell you but it's Rhona Macbride. She's dead. And, Finn, it looks like murder.'

26

Later, I would wonder how I had done it, how I had managed to carry on a conversation with the Carneys, collect DNA samples (as well as the hairbrush, Ann had kept a toothbrush) and give them a highly edited account of my progress. Rhona's death meant I was able to say a lot less than planned. I had gone to the bathroom and thrown cold water on my face. Everything else had been pure autopilot. Or the ability to compartmentalise. Or guilt. Rhona was dead. Murdered. I didn't know what had happened but I was sure of two things. That Gill had killed her. And that, somehow, I had led him to her.

After I left the Carneys, I texted Tina to say that I'd meet her in the Long Valley pub instead of at home and that I would email her with more instructions. It wasn't good for her if she and I were seen together while I was on 'holiday' but, after what had happened to Rhona, meeting in a public place was safer. Maybe Gill had followed me to Rhona's house. Or maybe he had had me followed. Or maybe he had always kept tabs on Rhona, but hadn't felt the need to do anything about her until I had started asking questions.

The Long Valley is famous for its sandwiches, but I couldn't eat. I ordered a pot of tea and sat at the large round table that, it was said, had come off a ship run aground by Roche's Point on the outer reaches of Cork Harbour.

As soon as I saw Tina, Supervalu carrier bag in hand, I went down the back to the ladies and waited for her to join me. Tiny and cramped, there was barely room for two, but the door was lockable and, once Tina was inside, lock it I did.

'Jesus, what's going on, Finn? This is weird, if you don't mind me saying.'

'Did you bring the box?'

'I brought it, and the rest of the stuff you asked for. But what's it for?'

'A lot has happened since yesterday. I didn't want you to be seen with me, for your own sake – work and all that. And there are, ah, other reasons as well.'

Your life, for one.

'I want you to chase up Deirdre's medical records,' I continued. 'They're more important now than ever and the sooner we get them the better. You've already sent in the request, I know, but you need to follow up.'

'No probs.'

'Good,' I said. 'But be careful, be discreet. I know it's odd but I want you to go in a minute – get a sandwich somewhere, not here, and go back to the office. I'll go out first and sit back where I was. You come out then and walk past me, as if you don't know me, pretend you were just at the loo. Now – I need to get one of the exhibits out of the box and I'll take all the documents you prepared. When you get back to the office, lock the box back in my drawer immediately. Do it before you eat your lunch. Please. I'll explain everything later.'

'It's like fecking *Tinker Tailor Soldier Spy*, Finn,' Tina said.

I couldn't smile. I had to tell her about Rhona before she heard it elsewhere.

Five minutes after Tina had gone, I got up, paid for my un-drunk tea and left the pub. I crossed Oliver Plunkett Street to the GPO. Once inside, I walked at speed to the far door, exited on to Pembroke Street and crossed the narrow street to Mayne's. The seats at the end of the bar, just inside the front door, were free. I ordered an Americano, left €2.50 on the counter, and sat in the second seat out from the wall. I could see whoever came in and went out. But, more importantly, I had space to deal with the package Tina had given me. I took the bagged coaster exhibit and labelled it with the sticky labels Tina had brought 'DC1'. Next, I labelled the items that I had got from Ann with 'DC2' and 'DC3'.

I tugged some of my own hair out by the root, put it in a bag, and labelled it 'FF1'. Waiting for Tina in the Long Valley, I had realised that I had to submit a sample, in case Deirdre's hair and toothbrushes didn't yield enough DNA to extract a reading. As a fallback, my own DNA – that of a sister or a half-sister – could identify Deirdre's. I would find out if we had the same father by default after all.

I had the pen that I had given Gill to use bagged up already. I labelled it 'JG1'. Then, I used a clip to attach all five exhibits to the covering letter Tina had typed for me, and signed the covering letter and my credit card payment authorisation. Finally, I put everything into the A4 padded envelope, pre-addressed by Tina to Setanta Forensic Laboratories, and sealed it. I fitted the envelope back into my handbag and wound the long strap around my wrist a couple of times. For all my precautions, it was impossible to tell if I had been followed into the pub. After all, I didn't know who I was looking for.

I went to the back of the bar and entered the smoking area that connected Mayne's with the Crane Lane, a permanently packed seven-night-a-week late bar, live music club and pick-up joint. Sadie says that there should be a motorway sign in the lane outside: 'Wrong way, turn back'. But around midnight, if you're still out on the town, the place has an irresistible draw.

Standing, back to the wall, I waited. Seconds later, the door swung open and a man burst through. He must have seen me, but he strode quickly past and on to the lane without looking in my direction. I only got a side view, but I recognised him instantly: the man I had collided with the previous evening in Dublin, the *Herald*-reading rude man, though now he was wearing a black leather jacket instead of a suit. It struck me then that he seemed vaguely familiar, and not just from the coffee shop.

I doubled back through Mayne's and crossed Pembroke Street to the GPO, hoping I'd make it before the man had a chance to follow. I went straight to the parcels section, and registered the letter to Setanta Forensic. I had intended to drive but, after what I'd heard about Rhona, registered post seemed safer. Gill was powerful, but even he couldn't have his tentacles in An Post, surely?

From the GPO, I crossed Oliver Plunkett Street and went into Penneys, via the back door. The shop was heaving, as usual. Good luck to anyone trying to follow me through that. I dashed out the front door, on to Patrick Street and hailed a cab to take me the short trip to Coughlan's Quay Garda Station to meet Sadie O'Riordan.

By the time I got there, I had remembered where I'd seen the man before.

27

'Don't worry,' Sadie said. 'We won't be disturbed here, not between shift changes.'

I cradled the cup of machine soup she had given me and tried to breathe. We were in the briefing room, off the station reception area, though reception wasn't the right word. It wasn't a waiting room, either. Coughlan's Quay was Cork's detective HQ. No traffic cops. No overnight drunk and disorderlies. But if you'd done something bad, you'd probably end up here. And you'd probably be coming in the back gate.

'So this is what I know,' Sadie said. 'Rhona left her house ...'

'At Park View Mews.'

'Yeah, that's right. At approximately ten past eight this morning intending to walk to work.'

'On Infirmary Road.'

'Exactly. You've been busy since I last saw you, by the sound of it. But she barely got outside the gate of the development. An unknown assailant attacked her – we're working on the theory that he might have got out of a car and come up behind her. He had a weapon – believed to be a screwdriver – and he stabbed her with it in the side of the head, the right temple area. He took her bag and walked, not ran, away. Nobody heard anything.'

'No scream?'

'He probably put his left hand over her mouth and used the right hand to stab her. Nobody saw anything either – the wall blocked the view from inside Park View Mews.'

'The houses across the road, though?'

'You're right, the attack could have been seen from across the road, but no one's come forward so far. The team in Dublin aren't holding out much hope. People had either already gone to work or it was breakfast time and the kitchens are at the back in those houses. *But* a neighbour, inside Park View Mews, who was putting rubbish in her bin, saw a man in a dark hoodie crossing the gate, and then crossing back, a minute or two later at most. She thought it was unusual at the time but didn't take any notice until the Gardaí arrived. She didn't see the man's face – though she's sure it *was* a man. She thinks she remembers hearing a car driving off but doesn't know if it's connected. Another neighbour found the body – never regained consciousness – and called an ambulance. By the time it arrived, Rhona was dead. When our lads got there, they fenced off the immediate area and did a patrol car search of the surrounding district. Nobody answering the description of the assailant to be seen. That doesn't mean much.

He may be a local, might have had somewhere to go nearby. It's being treated as a random drug-related mugging. Timing fits, early morning, money needed for the day's supply. The extreme violence is less usual – but that depends on what he was on, and how desperate he was. The team in Dublin will check all available CCTV, but there's nothing in the immediate area. Rossbeigh Road is a residential street. They'll be able to pick up footage from traffic cameras on the North Circular and up on the Navan Road. Trouble is, if he escaped in a car, they have no idea what kind. Best hope is that someone comes forward. But at the moment the lads have nothing to go on.'

'And the weapon?'

'From the shape of the wound, it looks like a screwdriver, like I said, but as to what type or where it was bought, nothing yet. Maybe nothing ever. He might have had it for years. It's not CSI, Finn. We won't be checking every Woodies and B&Q in Ireland.'

'It's not a random mugging,' I said.

'I thought you might say that,' Sadie said. 'Talk to me. Fast.'

'There's a lot to tell – come up to my house? It's all on my computer.'

'I'll get a car to drop us,' Sadie said.

'Great.'

If Jeremy Gill's security guard was still following me, a Garda car might frighten him off for a while.

'I think you're on to something big,' Sadie said. 'Coincidences happen, of course. But, based on what you've told me, I need to pass on this information to the murder team in Dublin. Jeremy

Gill is a suspect in Rhona's murder. Has to be. You'll have to pull back now, though – this is an active investigation, Finn, and you can't do anything to prejudice it.'

I said nothing.

'Are you listening to me, Fitzpatrick? I said you're going to have to back off.'

'I will. I know I can't have anything to do with the criminal investigation – but I have to keep on with my own work, my civil case for the wrongful death of Deirdre Carney.'

'You've spent the last hour telling me that Rhona's murder is inextricably linked to Deirdre's death. You've told me Gill had a man following you up to Dublin and back again. How can you possibly think it's okay for you to continue with your investigation? A woman is dead, Finn. You're out of your depth and you're too stubborn and pig-headed to admit it.'

'I see your point.'

'Thank God.'

'But I have just a few more things to do. Cork-based, mostly. Backgroundy things. I can't just let it drop.'

'Come *on*, Finn. What about your job? Your job that you were so worried about on Wednesday night? Has it even crossed your mind today?'

'It's less of a priority, actually.'

'You're impossible,' Sadie said.

'I know,' I said.

'If you're right about Rhona and Gill … what I'm saying is that if Gill's killed once, he could kill again. You could be in danger.'

'I don't see it that way. Now that I think about it, I'm in no danger whatsoever.'

'I like your confidence.'

'Look, this Twitter debacle is like health insurance for me. I've been all over the web, and the newspapers. I'm connected to Gill. So is Rhona. She's been killed in a so-called random attack. If something happens to me, it's going to look a lot less random. It's going to point a finger at Gill. I'm not going to take any stupid risks. But I reckon he needs me alive.'

'Assuming that's how he thinks. The guy's a psychopath, remember? Arrogant. Egotistical. Above the law. As far as he's concerned, normal rules don't apply to him. By the time he figures out they actually do, you might be dead.'

'Okay. That *is* a good point,' I conceded.

'Which you're going to take no notice of.'

'I promise that if I find myself straying into territory that might be part of the criminal case, I'll call you immediately. And I'll back off, for definite.'

Sadie sighed.

'Remind me why we're friends again? I've forgotten.'

'Sadie,' I said. 'Rhona's death ... her murder ... I have blood on my hands. Not literally, I know. What I mean is, it's my fault.'

'Oh, Finn. It is not your fault. It's whoever killed her, it's their fault.'

'Gill.'

'It might be. But whether it's Gill or someone else ...'

'I can't help thinking that, if I hadn't started all this, she'd still be alive.'

'Maybe she would, and maybe she wouldn't. It's terrible that she's dead. It's an awful thing. But you didn't kill her.'

'That's all well and good,' I said. 'I didn't wield the actual weapon. Doesn't matter. I'm the one responsible.'

'You're not. Look, I understand where you're coming from. It goes with the territory. At home at night, if I'm on my own, if Jack's out, or working late, I've got dead bodies piling up around me, fighting for room on the couch. The people I could've saved. If I'd done my job right. If I'd been a bit faster. A bit cleverer. A bit some fucking thing that I'm not. This one woman, though.'

Sadie stood up from the table, and walked to the kitchen island.

'I've told you about her before. She'll haunt me for ever. Jacqueline Delaney. It was when I was working over in Gurran station. If we'd answered the call a couple of minutes sooner, then, maybe ... But we were sick of her by then. The husband had a barring order against him. Timmy Delaney, a weed with one of those bum-fluff excuses for a moustache. A horrible man. And she kept saying he was going to kill her, barring order or not. She kept calling the station. We'd go and investigate. It was a cat one time, a bird on the Velux another time. The wind blew over the washing line one night, one of those roundy twirly things, and she heard the bang and called us in a panic. And it was nothing. It was always nothing. Until the night he killed her. I'd started at ten, it had been busy, and it was coming up to one in the morning, and we were in the patrol car eating our supper that we'd just got from the chipper on Baker's Road. A sausage and chips with curry sauce I was having, I remember. We moved when we got the call, we did, but we weren't killing ourselves with speed, we took it handy. Lost a couple of vital minutes. Only down along Cathedral Road and off to the left, a short spin, but by the time we got there Jackie's head was half hanging off and Timmy was sitting on the floor in a pool of his wife's blood, still holding the shovel he'd battered her to death with. Crying, he was, penitent, the fucker. He found God in prison after. He's out now on licence, did his twelve years. I see him sometimes in town handing out leaflets for that dopey church he's taken up with, whatever it's called, some born-again shower of gobshites. So when you talk about Rhona, I know what you're feeling. Or something like it. But the thing that keeps me sane, the only thing, is that I know I didn't kill Jackie Delaney. Like you didn't kill Rhona. You have to keep remembering that, Finn, or you'll go mad.'

28

I didn't bother with breakfast. The Law Society had provided a convenient resting place for my Friday night flit but I didn't know who I might meet in the dining room and what questions I might have to answer.

After Sadie had left the previous afternoon, I had booked the non-stop Aircoach to Dublin, and a taxi to take me to the bus stop on Patrick's Quay. A call to the Law Society had secured a reservation for the night. The rooms weren't much cheaper than a mid-range hotel or B&B, even at members' rates, but there was a permanent security presence and I hoped that I'd be adequately protected there. When I got off the bus at Bachelor's Walk, in Dublin, I hailed a taxi to Blackhall Place, instead of walking as I normally would have. I had taken the non-stop bus instead of the train for the same reason, banking on there being less chance that

I'd be intercepted by person or persons unknown. I hadn't been as confident about my safety as I had pretended to Sadie.

I had spent my time on the bus thinking about Rhona and I wasn't able to let go of the idea that I had played a big part in her death. Talking to Sadie had helped, but only up to a point. I had all those extra layers of guilt and shame that she knew nothing about; that none of my friends did.

But if I've learnt anything in my life, and at times I think I haven't, it's that going over and over something in my head only makes it worse, and prevents me doing anything that might improve the situation. So I put all of it away as best I could: it would still be there when I got back to it, which was another thing I'd learnt.

On the LUAS now, heading for Connolly Station, I didn't know if I was being followed. I scanned the tram carriage. No familiar faces. Maybe Gill had changed personnel. Or maybe he wasn't bothering to have me watched any more. That seemed more likely: that he reckoned he was off the hook. Untouchable – now that Rhona had been disposed of.

Especially as he had an alibi for the time of her death.

I thought back to the conversation I had had with Sadie the previous night. I had been sitting on the bed in my room at Blackhall Place, running through notes, when I'd got the call.

'It's not him,' Sadie had said.

'Not Gill?'

'No. He's got an alibi. The murder team took what you said seriously. At first. They went out to his house in ... doesn't matter where. But at the time Rhona was being murdered, Gill was at home having breakfast with his mother. He showed the team the security tapes. He has CCTV covering his front door and his cars. He's got two, a Range Rover and a Mercedes SLK. He lives in a terrace, and there's no back gate, so he couldn't have got out that way, and the cars never moved from the front. The gates are electronic, they leave a digital trail. It's incontrovertible proof that they stayed shut until he left the house at around eleven, when he brought his mother to the hairdresser's. He had a pot of tea and a scone and read the papers in a cafe across the street, then he drove her back home and stayed in until the Dublin lads arrived to interview him.'

I was stunned into silence.

'That's not the behaviour of someone who's just committed a brutal murder, is it? Em, there's something else. He mentioned you, asked if you'd been the source of the complaint. He said he'd been having trouble with you. That he's had to take legal advice. That you're obsessed. He showed the team a copy of the letter his lawyers sent you.'

'Fuck,' I said.

'Yup.'

'What about his security guard? Did they ask him about that?'

'He denied having you followed.'

'How can he? I recognised the man from the workshop at the Firkin Crane. I saw him in the coffee shop before I went to Rhona's house. Unfortunately it was only after I saw him again in Cork that I realised who he was. If only I had recognised him sooner ...'

'Gill says that if you saw his *temporary* security guard again, it was either paranoia or coincidence. His name is Pawel Zdziarski, by the way, a freelancer, originally from Gdansk, living here eight years, squeaky clean, fully registered with the Private Security Authority, no convictions of any kind. Gill said he had no reason to have you followed. He said he was confident he'd be able to deal with any threat from you to himself, but was worried you'd target his mother. That's why he cancelled his appointments for a few days. Stayed home with her. So as he could see how dangerous you were. But he made it clear that he doesn't want to make a criminal complaint. He actually said that he would prefer if you got the help you need.'

'Jesus Christ.'

'He and Mammy are going to go away for a while to his home in LA. He's sorry that he's going to miss Rhona's funeral, though of course he'll send flowers. Ireland has always been his home but he's very upset by all this and blah blah blah.'

'So as far as the Gardaí are concerned, Gill's out of the picture for Rhona's death? Are they not even going to *talk* to his security guy? What's his name again?'

'Pawel Zdziarski. Nope. Gill's not on the radar. In fact, the edict from on high is that he's to be left alone. All loose ends to be left unfollowed. Jeremy is *absolutely* not a suspect. Not now. Not ever. So we're back to the mugging-gone-wrong theory. Though, to be honest, only that you were in Cork at the time, you'd be in the frame yourself.'

'What?'

'Yeah. They found your business card in Rhona's kitchen and her mother told the investigation that you'd been looking to talk to Rhona the day before she got killed. And there's what Gill said about you and all the Twitter stuff. You're famous, and not in a good way, trust me. We've all been told to keep an eye on you. To watch for erratic behaviour.'

'This is getting worse. I mean, it's completely ridiculous.'

'I know. Best to lie low all the same. Where are you, by the way? At home?'

'Maybe.'

'Don't tell me you're in Dublin. Please don't tell me that.'

'Okay I won't tell you so. Better you don't know where I am, anyway. Don't worry. I *am* lying low.'

'Be careful,' Sadie said.

At Connolly Station, I got a flat white from the kiosk and sat on a bench, waiting for the DART. The platform was bright, bustling with shoppers and suburban kids in town for the day. But normality felt distant. I was inhabiting a different space now, my reputation in tatters, in pursuit of a quarry who was a lot cleverer than I had given him credit for. I couldn't attack him head-on. Rhona's death had proved that beyond doubt. I needed to go around him, to head in a direction he mightn't expect.

In this case, south. I got off the DART at Sydney Parade and made for the seafront.

29

Sandymount was popular with writers, perhaps because the suburb lies next to the beach where Stephen Dedalus had strolled. But it was popular with lawyers too and it hadn't been hard for me to find out exactly where Christopher Dalton lived. I had seen him, and his house, in a Sunday newspaper magazine feature, and knew it was somewhere in Sandymount. Before leaving Cork, I had phoned Ronan Teehan, a gossipy senior counsel that I'd briefed a few times, who lived facing the strand. It was close to five on a Friday. Which meant, I calculated, that he had been for a late lunch and a bottle or two of very expensive red wine, and that he might be receptive to questions. He was. At the end of twelve minutes, I knew not only where Dalton lived, I knew the time he walked his dog and the breed. That was another thing about Sandymount. It was *really* popular with dog-owners.

I reached the seafront as Christopher Dalton was turning for home. He looked preoccupied, and I wasn't surprised. By now, he would have heard about Rhona Macbride. He had to have known her. He had been friends with Gill back then, had worked on his short film too, co-wrote the script, and acted as 'Best Boy', according to the credits, whatever that meant. Another one of Gill's little jokes, I assumed.

I fell into step beside Dalton.

'You've a gorgeous dog,' I said.

'Thanks,' he said.

'A long-haired German shepherd, isn't he?'

'Yeah. It's a she, though.'

'What's her name?'

'Brünhilde.'

'Great name. What's her temperament like? I've heard they're aggressive.'

'Not at all. A real family pet. I think they've bred out those traits.'

'Good to know.'

'I'm crossing here, so, em, nice talking to you,' Dalton said.

'I'm crossing too.'

'You are?'

'Yes, Mr Dalton, I'm sorry for bothering you. But it's urgent.'

'Excuse me, do I *know* you?' Dalton asked.

'No, you don't. But I'm hoping you'll talk to me about Jeremy Gill.'

Dalton took a step back.

'I'm not talking about Gill to anyone, least of all you, whoever you are. That's in the past. I've never spoken about it before and I'm not going to start now. What newspaper are you with? I'll complain to your editor. This is *completely* out of order.'

'No, Mr Dalton, you've got it wrong. I'm not a journalist. I'm a solicitor.'

'Oh.'

I held out my business card. He bent his head to read it, but didn't take it.

'I know that name from somewhere.'

'If you're on Twitter, you probably know me as hashtag lawyerbitch.'

'That's it. You got into some spat with Jeremy down in Cork. I couldn't quite get what it was about.'

'It makes sense only if you know the truth about Jeremy Gill. That's why I'd really like to talk to you. I think you know the truth.'

'I don't know what you mean.'

'I think you know *exactly* what I mean.'

'What are you trying to do, subpoena me for something?'

'If you talk to me now, maybe I won't *have* to subpoena you.'

'Talk on or off the record?'

'Off the record, until you say otherwise.'

'I don't know,' Dalton said.

'Please,' I said. 'For Rhona's sake.'

At the mention of her name, Dalton winced and shut his eyes. When he opened his eyes again, he nodded.

We crossed the road together in silence.

*

Christopher Dalton's house was an estate agent's dream: a recently decorated double-fronted, double-bay period house in mint condition with a sea view and off-street parking. I hadn't had any idea that writing paid quite *this* well.

'Fabulous house,' I said.

'I have Jeremy to thank for it, actually,' Dalton said. 'He gave me a percentage of the back-end of his second movie, the one that really broke him into the big time.'

'*59 Seconds.*'

'Yeah, that one. I bought the house with the payout. I'm still making money out of it, in fact. And meanwhile, the writing's gone all right as well. So we're doing okay.'

We were sitting in Dalton's study, a downstairs room that opened into the left front bay window. Muffled noise was barely audible from the rest of the house and I wondered if the room had been soundproofed.

Dalton handed me a coffee from a Nespresso that he kept on a marble-topped antique side table, within reach of his writing desk.

'Black okay?'

'Perfect.'

I didn't want to give him an excuse to leave in search of milk.

'Me too,' he said.

'Lovely place to work.'

'Why are you here and what do you want to know? Saturday is family time, the kids off school and all.'

I knew that Christopher Dalton and Jeremy Gill had been contemporaries at UCD, that they'd collaborated artistically for a while, but had had an oft-reported, though mysterious, falling-out and had never worked together again. Dalton was rich and, by the look of his house, he enjoyed a lifestyle out of reach to most. But it didn't sit well with him. He had a pot belly, and despite daily dog-walking, he didn't look fit. His hair was thin, in need of a wash and he was sickly-looking, pale except for a few red patches of psoriasis on his face and another few on his arms that he scratched every so often. For all his wealth, he looked like a man under severe stress.

'I'm instructed in a civil case by the parents of Deirdre Carney,' I said. 'She met Jeremy Gill at Cork Film Festival when she attended a workshop given by him. I have come into evidence that leads me to suspect that Deirdre was raped by Gill some weeks after the festival.'

'You're instructed by this girl's parents?'

'Yes. You see Deirdre had a severe nervous breakdown and never identified Jeremy Gill publicly as her assailant during her lifetime. But in her suicide note ...'

'She's dead?'

'Yes. And so is Rhona Macbride, as you know. I spoke to her the night before she was murdered and she confirmed my suspicions about Jeremy Gill. Told me that Gill had raped her, savagely beaten her, too. She was too frightened of him to speak out. Now, as you know, she'll never be able to.'

I watched Dalton take in the implications of what I had said.

'I'm here about the Deirdre Carney case,' I continued. 'But from what I know about Gill's behaviour with Deirdre and Rhona, I suspect that they're not Gill's only victims. I think you know that too.'

'I don't know anything about Deirdre Carney. I wasn't even in Cork for the festival that year.'

'What *do* you know, Mr Dalton?'

'I read in the *Irish Times* that the Gardaí are treating Rhona's death as a random, drug-related crime.'

'That's right,' I said. 'It's not what *I* think, but you're right, it's what *they* think.'

He stayed quiet, but he was tearing at the rash on his arm again.

'Christopher, two women are dead,' I said. 'Rhona told me she'd been expecting someone like me to call for years. For ever, she said. It's the same for you, isn't it?'

I waited for Dalton to fill the space.

'You said that Rhona Macbride told you that Jeremy had raped her.'

He paused, then continued.

'I didn't know it was rape, but I knew that he'd met her, some time after the film wrapped. That they'd been intimate, sexually intimate.'

'How did you know?'

'Because he told me.'

'What did he say?'

'He boasted that she'd forced herself on him, that he hadn't been able to keep her off him, that eventually he'd had to submit to her advances and that they had had sex.'

'Is that how he described it, that they'd "had sex"?'

'Not exactly. He told me he'd fucked her hard, taught her a lesson. Said that that's what these girls needed, except he called her a slut. He said she'd fooled him for a long time but she was the same as all the rest of them.'

'What do you think he meant by that, "all the rest of them"?'

'Females in general. Jeremy doesn't like women. He has some in his films, depending on the script, but not many. And he doesn't employ women in any responsible roles. It's one of the reasons he never uses a casting director, it's a female-dominated profession. But there are other reasons he doesn't use a casting director.'

'The casting couch?'

'Yes. He's old-fashioned that way. He always had a Neanderthal approach. Whoever was available. Anybody would do. When we were in college, he was a legend. Any night out, Jeremy always scored. He boasted about his method. He'd spend time doing a recce of the party, or the pub or club, until he found the drunkest woman in the place. He used to say it was an art: to be able to find the girl while she was still mobile and transportable. In other words, before she collapsed or started vomiting. He was much the same when he was working in advertising, as far as I know, though I wasn't out much with him then. I was trying to write, on the dole, didn't have the money to go to Lillie's or wherever he was hanging out back then. Once he started making films, starting with *Another Bad Day at the Office*, he got back in touch with me. I was thrilled. Jeremy's always been great to work with. He's a gifted film-maker, truly gifted. But when he gave up the day job, he didn't need to target drunk women any more. He held auditions and private callbacks. Once shooting started, he could have any woman on set. Droit de seigneur.

Actresses. Extras. Catering staff. Make-up artists. Costume department. You get the picture. No repeats, though. For him it was always one night only. There was something mechanical about it.'

'You're talking about adult women in all this?'

'Yes.'

'But not always.'

'No.'

He took a deep breath.

'His real passion was for schoolgirls. He liked them young. Not too young, either. He was quite specific about it. After puberty, but before they got to seventeen. Sweet sixteen, even sweeter fifteen, he used to say.'

'Oh.'

'What?'

'Nothing,' I said.

But I was remembering how he'd used that word with Carmel, the girl in the green uniform, at the workshop in Cork on Wednesday. When she'd confirmed her age, he had said 'sweet'. He had said it a second time. I felt sick at the thought of what might have happened if I hadn't intervened, but I had to continue.

'Please go on,' I said. 'About his specific interest.'

'Well, yeah. He had a real thing, a detailed fantasy. He said that all women were bitches but that if he could get a girl at the right age, the right kind of girl, if she showed potential and if she measured up, she would be a fitting mate for him. He actually used that word. Mate.'

'Apart from Rhona, were you aware of other underage girls?'

'Not aware, as such, but I had my suspicions. I don't want to give a name. It wouldn't be fair on them, to tag them as a victim or whatever when they may not want that.'

'Gill told you about Rhona, not about anyone else?'

'No. I didn't know anything about that girl from Cork you mentioned. I think he knew from my reaction to what he told me about Rhona that I wasn't that comfortable with it.'

'You were okay about all the adult women, just not the younger ones?'

'Kind of that, yes. Though, I was starting to get uncomfortable about the women as well. Maybe I'd always been uncomfortable about it. I think I was beginning to see that maybe there was undue influence, maybe not quite full consent.'

'You think?'

'I do. It probably sounds odd to you, that I was only starting to realise it then?'

'A bit odd, I suppose, all right.'

Bile rose from my belly and my throat burned.

'Yes,' Dalton said. 'But Gill has this power over people. I don't know if you noticed. He brings people with him, like a boat with shoals of fish and dolphins following. Everyone's too busy watching Jeremy, trying to see if they're in or out of favour with him, to notice what he's doing, to have the distance to make a judgement call on it.'

Reluctantly, I had to admit to myself that I knew what Dalton meant. I recalled my meeting with Gill in the Opera House, and how I had felt when he'd moved on from me. And the audience. How they had been mesmerised. It was easy to condemn Dalton for his inaction, and condemn him I did, but with Gill, everything was complicated and ambiguous.

'I have some idea what you mean,' I said. 'But you said that you had suspicions?'

'I did say that, didn't I? Yes, you could say I had suspicions. I don't know where to begin. *Another Bad Day at the Office* opened a lot of doors. We both went to the Oscar ceremony. Jeremy was totally focused on that. Win or lose, it was about where it could get him next. The nomination wasn't an end in itself, like it would be for some people. He kept saying to me that it was small potatoes, it was about what it could lead to. He had his eye on the future, not the past, he said. Used the trip to Hollywood to set up meetings, make contacts, sell himself, and his next project. Which just happened to be a feature that I'd co-written with him, so I got brought along to all the studio meetings and played my part. But I was kind of along for the ride. Jeremy was the engine of it all. So – he got money to make his first feature *Giveaway*, a small caper movie. Smart, pacy, funny. It was a good script – but it was the direction that lifted it above the ordinary. I wasn't under any illusions. You've seen it, right? *Giveaway* did well – made its money back, and then some. Won lots of critical acclaim and the audience prize at Toronto. New is good in Hollywood. They're always looking for the next big thing. Jeremy got a lot of money for his second feature, *59 Seconds*. Another co-write credit for me, though I wrote most of it, in fact. Actually, I'd intended it to be a novel but Jeremy persuaded me to make a script of it instead. So, em, shooting started . . .'

'And your suspicions?'

'Yes. This is where it gets more awkward because it involves an individual I don't want to name.'

'A young girl?'

'Yes.'

'There's no young girl in the film, though.'

'No. But *59 Seconds* was a full production, not low budget. Not the highest budget either, but there was studio backing, plenty of money. So, of course, Jeremy had a Winnebago. I suspected that he used it for ... no, it was more than a suspicion. I knew that he took women there for sex. We were on location, multiple locations. The story had been set in Ireland originally, but we adapted it for the States. It was better, actually. More convincing. We filmed in and around Boston, New England, upstate New York. Wherever we went, Jeremy used to make a big deal of going to visit the local diner. And the school. Wanting to give back, he said. I knew there was probably more to it but I didn't ... well, I didn't do anything about it.'

'But you had your suspicions, you said.'

'Well, we were in a small town called Winterville, in upstate New York. Near the Adirondacks. It was the town in the movie where the first bank robbery happened so we were there a while. Yeah, we were there too long. Jeremy was doing his ambassadorial stuff, talking to the mayor, visiting the high school, all that. But then he started bringing this one girl on set. She was fifteen, sixteen at most. I didn't get involved. He was training her in as his assistant, he said. Giving her an opportunity. He met her parents, took them to dinner and ... well, what I'm saying is that he wasn't hiding anything. And, of course, he was busy, making a film, and we were going to be moving on. I didn't think too much of it. Until, well, our last night in town I was in my room at the hotel, doing rewrites and I went for a walk and ...'

'You saw something?'

'Yeah, I saw the light on in Jeremy's trailer. We were having an early start the following day, some dawn shots in the town and then moving out, heading to the next location, so when I saw the light I was surprised but I thought it was typical workaholic Jeremy stuff. I went over to the trailer and just walked straight in, to say hello. Or, I don't know, maybe I knew, maybe some part of me knew.'

At this, Dalton paused, sighed, rubbed his hands over his face in a scrubbing motion, then clasped them together in front of his chest, like a schoolboy preparing for first confession.

'Christopher, what did you see?'

'I saw Jeremy having sex with someone. I couldn't see her face. He was on top of her. He was being rough, yeah I think anyone would say that. But she wasn't making a sound. He didn't hear me, not then. I saw, I saw a half-empty bottle of vodka. And a Tropicana carton. And I saw a bag. It was the same bag the girl used to carry around all the time.'

'The schoolgirl, his assistant?'

'Yeah. It was a patchwork kind of thing, looked home-made. I recognised it.'

'And you think it was her.'

'I do. But I didn't stay long enough to find out for sure. And I thought there was a chance she had left it there earlier, that it hadn't been her he was with when I saw ...'

'But you suspected?'

'Yes, I suspected it was her. I said as much to him the next day, when we were finished shooting. He asked me to drive with him to the next location. I agreed so that I would have the chance to talk to him about it.'

'And what did he say?'

'He said he knew there had been somebody, that he'd heard the door closing, that he'd wondered if it was me. And he said it was voluntary, that she'd wanted it.'

'But at her age, she couldn't have consented. It would have been statutory rape, whatever her wishes. And if she was drunk, if he got her drunk, that's even worse.'

'I know that. I said that to him.'

'And what did he say?'

'He said that I was all righteous now but that I'd done nothing about it when I could have. And that if he was having sex with an underage girl, that my behaviour made me an accessory. And he said that, if I said anything, she would deny it. And that he would too. He said she was the one who came on to him, she had suggested it, had come to his trailer after everyone else had gone. And if I said anything, that an allegation like that would ruin her reputation, even if it was shown to be false. And it would be. They'd both make sure of it. And it's always the girl who suffers most in these kinds of situations. Mud sticks, he said. He said that, if I spoke out, I would destroy her life. He said a lot more than that, too. And I thought about it, and in the end I decided to keep my mouth shut.'

'He gave you a percentage of the film's takings, didn't he?'

'I never asked for it. I know what you think. But I *didn't* ask for it. He gave it to me. You think it was hush money, but it wasn't. I had already decided not to talk before he gave it to me. So I don't see it that way. It wasn't related. But I knew I couldn't work with him again. There was no way I could. From that moment, it was over between us.'

But you kept taking the money.

I waited until I could speak calmly. There was more information to come, and I didn't want to mess up my chances of getting it.

'Thanks for telling me,' I said. 'I'm sure it can't have been easy to revisit after all this time. But what I can't understand is, you've described a pattern of exploitative and criminal behaviour that Gill engaged in consistently over many years. With so many girls and women involved, how did he keep it a secret all this time?'

'He didn't. Everyone knew, everyone in the film business, they all knew what he was like. It was common knowledge. It *is* common knowledge,' Christopher Dalton said. 'Don't you get it? The biggest secrets are the ones everyone knows.'

30

I stood in the bay window. Outside, the sand stretched for mile after empty mile, and the tide ebbed silently. Behind, on Dalton's writing desk, lay the sprawl of notes I had made of my meeting with him. I had expected to feel better, had hoped for a sense of achievement now that the truth had crawled its way to the surface. Instead, I felt like screaming. Dalton had confirmed that I was right about Gill. But the truth had come too late. Too late for Deirdre. Too late for Rhona. Too late for the nameless girl from New York State.

Now, I awaited Dalton's decision. Unbelievably, the weasel was procrastinating still, in another room with his wife and his solicitor, mulling over how and when to make his disclosures about Gill, if ever. Dalton had known about Gill for twenty years. Now that he was finally thinking about speaking up, I had told him he needed independent legal advice, and that he had a duty to report Gill to the Gardaí, but he could do so in a way that minimised his own exposure. He had every entitlement to exercise the privilege against self-incrimination but, as far as I was concerned, he had to talk, and talk fast. Most of what he knew was background information and hearsay evidence that would be inadmissible in court. But it was no less valuable for all that. Corroborating what I already knew, it gave Gill a credible motive for murder.

I heard the door open, and turned. It was Richard Hawthorne, Dalton's solicitor. I had met the man for the first time an hour and a half ago, when he'd swept up to the house in a Mercedes the size of a flatbed truck. A third generation commercial lawyer in his late fifties, Hawthorne wore tasselled Italian loafers and a Hugh Grant *Four Weddings*-era floppy hairstyle. He was going to fit right in down at the Garda station.

'Finn, thank you *so* much for your patience,' Hawthorne said. 'Well, I've told Christopher that he's under no reporting obligation here, none at all.'

'I'd have to disagree with you on that one, Richard.'

Now wasn't the time for the traditional ceremonial dance between opposing lawyers, where typical opening gambits required mutual disparagement of the other's position.

'Well, yes, indeed, I suppose there might be a *moral* argument to be made, and quite possibly even a legal one, but as it happens and in any event Christopher is most desirous of making a full and frank statement to the Gardaí. He is—'

'Glad to hear it,' I said, cutting him off. 'I'll make the call,'

I had already talked to Sadie O'Riordan and obtained from her the mobile number of the lead investigator in the Macbride murder. Sadie had said she would tell Detective Inspector Pat Lenihan to expect my call.

'I wouldn't have thought there was any need to do this today, surely,' Hawthorne said. 'This has been extremely difficult for my client and his family. He needs time to—'

I was out of what little patience I had left.

'Time? *More* time? From what I understand, Jeremy Gill is leaving for LA, may even be gone already. I would have thought that your client has had quite enough time.'

'I see. In the circumstances, perhaps you're right. I'll go and talk to him again.'

Hours later, after Dalton had been interviewed and made a statement, and I had done the same, in a different interview room, I sat in DI Lenihan's office trying to force down a tepid cup of tea.

'Hope the tea's all right,' Lenihan said.

'It is, if you like bogwater.'

'It's not Barry's, I'm afraid.'

'No shit, Sherlock.'

'You're a bit of a comedian, Miss Fitzpatrick,' Lenihan said.

He was trying to give the impression that we were settling in for a friendly chat that I knew would be no such thing. He would be watching my every move, and I knew it. Ostensibly welcoming of my input into the investigation, I sensed deep hostility from him. I had disliked him on sight. Clean-cut and handsome, with pale green eyes, freckles and a sulky mouth, Lenihan had the lithe strength and economy of movement that came from years spent on a hurling pitch. A Kilkenny man, he was young for a DI, which meant he had to be smart, but it was his ruthlessness and cunning that had won him early promotion, I reckoned. Lenihan needed the information about Jeremy Gill like a double yellow in an All-Ireland Final. Still, now that he had it, I knew he couldn't, and wouldn't, bury it and that whatever needed to be done would be, as clinically and efficiently as possible.

'Actually, I was hoping to catch the last train home, if that's all right.'

'Might be,' Lenihan said, but he could keep up the nice act for only so long. He sat up in his chair and ran his fingers through his short red curly hair.

'Okay, let's cut the crap. I don't need to tell you that what you've brought here today isn't going to win either of us any popularity contests.'

'I know that.'

'And so fucking what. I didn't join the guards to be popular. I think it gives us enough to interview Gill again. But we've talked to him before about Rhona's murder, on your say-so, remember. And there's the teensy-weensy little problem of his cast-iron alibi. So I know you want us to throw everything including the kitchen sink at Gill, but he's only one of a number of investigative strands we'll be pursuing.'

'Go down your blind alleys if you want, Detective Inspector Lenihan. But Gill did it. You know that and I know that.'

'I know no such thing. And neither do you. What are you saying – that Gill was at home eating his porridge with his mammy while a contract killer was out doing the needful for him on the mean streets of Dublin? The guy isn't a fucking crime boss. He doesn't have those kinds of contacts. Even if he did, planning a hit takes time. *And* you're saying that Rhona Macbride only became a threat to him *after* his security guard saw you visiting her house. The same guy you say you saw in Cork the next day, which implies that he followed you down the night before, so that means *he* wouldn't have been able to murder Rhona either. The fact is that Rhona Macbride was killed only about twelve hours after you left her. How could Gill have had time to plan a murder in so short a time? And why was he worried, anyway? She'd kept quiet for fifteen, sixteen years. Why would he think she'd talk now?'

'He couldn't take the chance that she wouldn't. And no, I don't think it was his security guard who killed Rhona. You're right, he was in Cork following me. And I don't think Gill took out a contract. You're right about that too. No, I think Gill did it himself. He used a weapon that he had to hand. He waited outside the only place he was halfway sure she'd be. He either knew she'd be leaving for work, or he banked on it and took a chance and waited for her. The guy is a film director. He's used to orchestrating scenarios, and executing them. He knew to keep it simple. So that's what he did. I know he killed her. You just have to break his alibi.'

'Ah stop it, wouldya, you've been watching too much *Miss Marple*,' Lenihan said. 'Listen to me now. Go for your train, go home, *stay* home and we'll take it from here. Leave it to the professionals.'

Dismissed in every sense of the word, I dragged myself towards Heuston Station, along the north bank of the Liffey, a walk I had done a thousand times before, to and from the Four Courts and the Law Society. As I ran my hand along the black cast-iron railing of the Croppies Acre, I thought about Rhona and I thought about my sister and I thought about Jeremy Gill. And I didn't care how, but I was going to bring him down.

31

The last train to Cork was as slow as a hearse and, as was usual for the last train, it had no dining car or tea trolley. Pre-prepared, I ate a bag of Tayto Cheese and Onion, bought on the platform, for main course, and chased it with a bag of Salt and Vinegar for dessert. I hadn't bought a big enough bottle of water though, and thirst kept me half awake, and staring out the window into the blackness, as the train alternately hurtled through the dark countryside, then shunted in and out of every nowhere town and station until the announcement for Cork came at long last. Another fifteen minutes and I would be in my own bed. But my phone rang as I alighted on the platform at Kent Station at ten past midnight. No caller ID.

'Am I speaking to Finn Fitzpatrick?'

'Yes,' I said.

'Bridewell Gardaí here,' the voice said,

'Is there news?' I said, thinking of DI Lenihan and the Macbride case.

'Are you the owner of motor vehicle 03C____?'

'Yes, I am, is something wrong?'

'Could you furnish me with the make of the vehicle, please?'

'VW Golf. Please tell me what's wrong.'

'And the last known location, if you wouldn't mind?'

'Fort Street, Off Barrack Street. But what is it?'

'Finn, I'm afraid I've bad news for you about your car. It's after being set on fire.'

There were no taxis left at the rank, but I hailed one on the slope down into the city centre and was across town in minutes.

A swarm of passers-by and locals had gathered to view the inferno. I stood well back until the flames started to weaken, after they had been doused by the fire brigade, which took longer than I might have expected, if I had ever expected anything of the sort.

As the crowd started to thin, I made my way over to the firefighters and introduced myself to a man who looked like he was in charge: ruddy, big, and strong enough to carry most people of normal weight down staircases and through smoke and collapsing masonry.

'Chief Wilson,' he said and shook my hand. 'This is unpleasant for you.'

'Horrible,' I said. 'Though it could be worse.'

'That's true. Things could always be worse.'

Some folk memory or superstition meant that no matter how bad the circumstances, people were always giving thanks that they weren't worse. Which annoyed me, usually.

'Are you sure it was deliberate?' I asked.

'Definite. We'll examine her properly tomorrow. But the way the flames spread, it looks like someone sprinkled an accelerant over the seats and threw in a lighter.'

'A cigarette lighter?'

'No, something burning, a rag, paper, even a match would have done it.'

'Any idea who did it?'

'Could be vandals,' Chief Wilson said. 'Or somebody with a grudge against you. Or maybe just some head-the-ball who likes starting fires. We've had one repeat offender over the last while, haven't caught him yet. Though this looks a bit different to his usual modus operandi. Could be a copycat, or could be him trying something new. That's why we always check through the crowd. Have a look yourself. These guys like to watch their handiwork.'

I did, but recognised nobody.

'How did you contact me so fast?'

'One of the residents in the Gregg Road flats. When he rang to report the fire, he said you're parked in the same spot nearly every day, so he knew your car number. Once they had the reg, the guards were able to track you, I don't know how.'

'Maybe they got my mobile number from the phone company?'

'Dunno, to be honest, girl, you'll have to ask them yourself. They're over there.'

He moved his chin up and his head to the right. I walked across to where two young Gardaí in yellow high-vis jackets were standing, and identified myself.

'Hard luck,' the bigger one said. 'It must be a terrible shock altogether.'

Her eyes shone in the flames like it was bonfire night, and someone had just produced a pound of sausages. Not long out of Templemore, I reckoned.

'A shock all right.'

The Garda said I could call into any station to get my car insurance claim form stamped. I nodded, and turned again to look at the fire.

'Thanks for contacting me so fast,' I said.

'It was no bother. Once I had your name via the car registration, it clicked with me. You're a solicitor. Your name and number are on the custody sergeant's list.'

'Mystery solved. By the way, what did you say your name was?'

'I didn't,' the Garda said. 'But it's Ruth Joyce. From the Bridewell. It was me who rang you. I'll be in touch about making a statement.'

Once the flames had died down, the fire truck pulled off and the guards left and the crowd drifted away. Eventually, I was left all on my own, beside the smouldering wreck that had once been my car. Was Gill responsible? Or someone else? But how? And why? Though the why was easily answered. Someone had intended to frighten me.

In that, they had succeeded, I thought later, as I locked my bedroom door and wedged a chair under the handle, and placed a carving knife under my pillow.

32

'Jesus Christ! Why didn't you call me last night?' Davy asked.

'Good question,' I said. 'I don't know. Didn't want to bother you, I suppose.'

The truth was that it hadn't even crossed my mind to contact Davy, or my parents, or Sadie, or any of my other friends. I had retreated behind the walls of my tower and recovered as best I could. On my own. Like I always did.

Davy shook his head.

'That's bullshit, Finn,' he said. 'Promise me, next time, you'll call.'

'Next time my car is burnt out, I'll definitely call,' I said.

Davy's face was like granite.

'That's not what I meant and you know it. I know our relationship has got more complicated in the last while but ...'

'It's not a relationship,' I said.

'Whatever it is.'

'It's not going to happen again.'

'That's what you said last time,' he said.

'It's what you said too, if you recall.'

'I recall.'

Davy had messaged me around 10 a.m. to ask if I wanted to go for a run. I had replied, saying that I was still in bed but awake and that he could call by for coffee if he wanted. We didn't bother with coffee, as both of us had probably known we wouldn't, and I didn't bother telling him about my car until he was putting his jeans back on. I didn't want to make a big deal out of it. Anyway, I was due at my parents' house for Sunday lunch and I needed to get going. By now they knew that I was on an unscheduled holiday from work and, as usual, my mother was worried. Her anxiety levels would go off the scale once she heard about my car.

'Do you want me to drop you over to your parents' house?' Davy asked.

No, Davy, that's the last thing I want.

But I've just had sex with you for the third time in a week.

'Yes,' I said. 'You can drop me over. Thanks.'

My words came out in a whisper, and Davy said nothing but I think he knew how hard it had been for me to say yes. He took my hand as we walked out of the lane and on to Barrack Street. I let go first as we approached his car.

*

My parents lived halfway up Gardiner's Hill, on the left side of the road. It was so close to the primary school that, when I was a pupil, I could be home for lunch almost before the bell stopped ringing. And it was near enough to the corner shop for my mother to stand at her gate and watch little me walk there and return with a litre of milk or my dad's *Evening Echo*.

'You have to give the child a bit of freedom,' my dad used to say, as I got older.

There was no talking to her. In time, I realised that she was different to other mothers, that her anxiety about me was bound up so closely with love that she was no longer able to tell the difference.

Dad was an electrician with the ESB, a well-paid secure job. With an only child and a small mortgage, my parents could afford to take the ferry from Ringaskiddy to Roscoff every summer for a fortnight in France, when many of my school friends would have thought themselves lucky to get a week in a caravan in Youghal.

But the job had risks. On stormy nights, when Dad was called out on repairs, Mam would bank up the fire with coal and she and I worried together. No matter how late it was, we would wait up, for the sound of the key turning in the door, and for her to help him out of his yellow oilskins and towel-dry his hair in front of the fire. I wondered about that, about how it was that these were my happiest childhood memories. Not Christmas or birthdays, but times when tragedy was imminent, and averted.

When I got to the front gate, Dad was in the garden, though it was November and there was little for him to do. He had a pair of secateurs and was snipping at a square-cut box hedge. Grey-haired and blue-eyed, he moved like a much younger man even though, like Mam, he was seventy-two. Living on Gardiner's Hill kept them both physically fit.

'I thought you'd be inside setting the table,' I said.

'No need. Sure you're here now. How's my girl today?'

'I'm great, Dad. How about yourself?'

'I'm as good as ever. Divil a fear o' me. Though I can't say the same for herself.'

'The form is bad with her?'

'Not *too* bad. Sure you know yourself. But who have we here?'

He was looking over my right shoulder. I turned around to find that Davy had followed me. Without being invited. This was going too far, I thought, but I didn't want to cause a scene in front of my father.

'Dad, this is Davy, a friend of mine. He's just dropping me off, he can't stay.'

'Ah, I'm not in that much of a rush,' Davy said.

I wanted to give him a kick.

'That's great altogether. Sure if you're in no rush, come in and meet herself.'

Dad turned and walked towards the front door.

'I'd love to,' Davy said.

I made a face at him and went into the house. He followed me, laughing softly.

My mother was in the dining room at the back: west facing, it had double doors giving out on to the garden. The house was on the part of the hill that shelved higher than the houses below it, so the garden had a southerly aspect too. Sometimes I wondered why I'd moved to the other side of town when the mountainous northside had all the best views, and a lot more sun. A visit home always reminded me why. I loved my parents, but having the river between us was healthier.

Mam saw Davy, but said nothing until she had kissed me. Once that was out of the way, she started to scold me, but for show, rather than with any real intent.

'Finn, you're very bold, why didn't you tell me you were bringing a visitor?'

'Mam, this is my friend Davy,' I said.

'Pleased to meet you, Mrs Fitz,' Davy said.

I choked back a laugh. Mam wasn't going to like being called 'Mrs Fitz'.

'My *name* is Doreen.'

'Pleased to meet you, Doreen,' Davy said. 'I just dropped Finn over, don't worry, I won't be staying long, I don't want to intrude.'

She smiled.

'Intrude my eye. Nobody ever intruded in this house.'

Which wasn't quite true.

'You're staying for your lunch and that's that,' Mam said. 'Tell him, Jim.'

'I wouldn't argue with her, if I were you,' Dad said. 'Many a man has tried and failed. I gave up years ago myself. 'Twasn't worth it.'

'Would you listen to what I've to put up with, Davy? Sit down there and Jim will get you a drink.'

'No thanks, Doreen, I'm driving and, em, I don't drink anyway. But I'd love lunch.'

I could see my mother weighing up what Davy had said. On the one hand, being a careful driver was a positive. On the other hand, being a teetotaller raised questions. If you want to find the alcoholic in the pub, the old joke went, look for the man drinking soda water. Her mouth tightened by a few millimetres, and she double-blinked. She was thinking about it. But when it came down to it, women liked Davy, and Mam was a woman with an eye for a good-looking man.

'That's settled so,' she said.

She smoothed her thick, grey, curly hair, the only part of her she had never been able to control, and nodded. She had decided to approve of this development. For the present.

Davy had that easy way about him and, with him as my wingman, the laser was off me. I batted away questions about my job easily enough, and slipped in the burnt car as something that was conceivably accidental or, at worst, the work of a serial arsonist. Having Davy there also meant that I could defer telling my parents about Deirdre. And I could defer asking them the question that had been gnawing at me since I'd found out about her: had they known that I had a sister? I had been in the care of the Health Board. It was inconceivable that the social worker responsible for me didn't know that my birth mother had had another baby. But had she told my parents – my foster parents, as they then were? And, if she had, why had they never told me? I didn't want to think about what the answer to that question might be.

Like I didn't want to think about what I was going to do with the information the DNA test would throw up on whether Deirdre and I shared a father.

The same way I didn't want to think about what had been happening between Davy and me, and how feeble my 'we're not in a relationship' protests had started to sound.

I didn't have the headspace to think about any of that. And I didn't have the time.

At around four, Davy drove me into Coughlan's Quay Garda Station. Mainly I wanted to meet Sadie, if I could, but it was also a good opportunity to get my car insurance claim form signed and stamped by the duty Garda.

I didn't say much to Davy on the trip in, but I had a lot on my mind. For all my bravado, the arson attack had left me seriously rattled. And, along with the fears for my own safety, I had money worries. Between the cost of the DNA tests, and getting a new car, and my various trips to Dublin, I was going to be flat broke unless I managed to persuade Gabriel and the rest of the partners that I was safe to let back to work. And tonight was the Film Festival closing ceremony, the first time in years that I wouldn't be there. Knowing I wouldn't be welcome made me sad. But I felt worse about the loss of my friendship with Alice. I hadn't heard a word from her since our fraught encounter after the Jeremy Gill workshop. I would send her an email, try to mend fences.

Grumbling along underneath everything was the guilt I felt about Rhona's death. No matter how often I told myself that Gill was the perpetrator, that he carried all the blame, I was certain that, if it hadn't been for my investigation, Rhona would still be alive.

'I'll wait for you,' Davy said.

'Thanks but best not,' I said. 'I don't know how long I'll be. I might have to wait a while for Sadie. I know she's on duty but she might be busy.'

And she still knew nothing about my non-relationship with Davy. I was waiting for the right time to tell her, if there would ever be a right time to tell my best friend that I'd been having a thing with an ex-cokehead with a criminal record.

'You sure?'

'Yeah, go on. And, you know, we have to try and get things back to normal between us.'

Davy replied with a kiss that reminded me why that wasn't going to be easy.

33

'It must have been a fairly bad one,' the young Garda said, after he'd stamped my form.

'What do you mean?'

'You're smiling a lot for someone whose car has been burnt out is all.'

'You know, so much has happened over the last week or so, this is actually way down the list,' I replied, realising it was true as I said it.

It was time to let last night go. The car-burning was either targeted at me, or it wasn't. But it was done. Dwelling on it would get me nowhere.

'Is there any chance Sadie O'Riordan's in the building?'

'She was in earlier, all right. Have a seat there and I'll check for you.'

*

I sat and worked through my plans for Monday and Tuesday. There was the car insurance stuff. Get that out of the way. Check with Tina what progress she'd made on Deirdre Carney's medical records. And, top priority, ring Setanta Labs to make sure they had got the DNA exhibits and to see if they could expedite the results. Then, track down Lorcan Lucey, who had been on the youth film jury with Deirdre, though any evidence he might give seemed less important now, after Rhona's and Christopher Dalton's revelations. Start putting together a brief for counsel, in anticipation of positive results from the DNA tests and medical records. Which was counting my chickens, I knew, but I needed to start the process. Find time to update the Carneys. That was low priority. Better to work towards something tangible first. Finally, arrange to talk to Gabriel about coming back to work, if possible. At least Christopher Dalton's statement to the Gardaí meant that the partners would see that I wasn't a complete crank and that I'd had just cause for my actions.

But I had been acting on my own, without authority, far outside my job description so, arguably, I *was* guilty of gross misconduct. Which was a firing offence. I thought – hoped – that Gabriel McGrath would swing back to my side, would be able to see why I'd acted as I did. He was fundamentally decent, with a strong moral code. But that snake Dermot Lyons would leap at the chance to be rid of me. If he got a few of the other partners onside, I'd be in real trouble.

I checked my phone. There was a missed call from a number I didn't recognise, and a voicemail. I rang 171. It was a message from Marie Wade – I had nearly forgotten about her – asking me to give her a ring. Maybe she had remembered something about Daniel O'Brien, the ex-education officer? I'd call her later, but it wasn't important any more. My focus was Gill, and Gill only.

'A penny for them,' Sadie said, and flung herself on to the seat beside me.

'Only a penny? You're going to have to do better than that. I'm in a rather precarious financial position or hadn't you heard?'

'I *just* heard about your car from Eamonn in the Public Office. You're in getting a form stamped following an arson attack? I knew there was a car burnt. Didn't realise it was yours. Foolishly, I'd assumed you might tell me if something like that happened.'

'Sorry, Sadie – it was late. And I'm telling you now, sure. Anyway, the fire chief said there's some guy going around the place torching cars so maybe my poor old Golf was just in the wrong place at the wrong time.'

'Yeah, maybe.'

'Though I'd bet anything it was Gill's bodyguard. We know he was following me, though I thought he had stopped. Still, it wouldn't have been any bother to Pawel to fit in a spot of light arson as Gill's parting gift to me.'

'Pawel has to be a suspect,' Sadie said. 'If it isn't some randomer.'

'Or the arsonist the fire chief was talking about.'

'Of all the cars to pick, though?'

'Exactly,' I said. 'But, hey, Sadie, is there any news from Dublin? I didn't think much of DI Pat Lenihan, by the way. Didn't like him at all.'

'Huh. You should be his number one fan. There's a strict news blackout on it, but Lenihan brought in Jeremy Gill and the mammy this morning.'

'Arrested them?'

'Not quite. The two of them presented themselves voluntarily with their solicitors in tow – Lenihan told Gill it was either that or flashing lights at home in Clontarf at 7 a.m. When they got to the station, they were detained under Section 4 and they're still being held. For the moment. But the word is, there hasn't been much progress. He's admitting now that he had you followed, but he's saying that it was for his own protection. He says that his security guard Pawel will make a statement that Gill told him to follow you after the incident at the workshop. Gill is saying that he didn't say that sooner because he was embarrassed to admit that he was frightened of you. He says he's had experience of stalkers in the past ...'

'Oh come on!'

'That's what Gill is saying. That that's why he reacted so quickly. I'll tell Lenihan about your car, though. Having a potential criminal charge against Pawel might oil the wheels a little, get him to spill the beans.'

'What's Gill saying about Rhona?'

'That he had a friendly relationship with her in the past, but no contact for years. She lost interest in acting as far as he knew, he thought it was a shame but the idea that he in any way interfered with her is a figment of your imagination. He's made no specific comment on the Dalton allegations, except blanket denial. But the fact is, Finn, none of what Dalton said is admissible. And the experts have examined the CCTV again. They say it's good, definitely not tampered with. Gill lives on a terrace, one way in and out. The CCTV shows for sure that he didn't exit his house by the front. He didn't take one of his cars out for an early morning spin. *And* the mother is absolutely adamant that he was with her all the time while Rhona was being killed. I know it feels like he did it, it feels like that to me too. And he is certainly guilty of something, but it looks like the one thing he's *not* guilty of is Rhona's murder. You're going to have to accept it: Gill's alibi is watertight. You must let this go. You've done enough, Finn. It's known now, the kind of man he is, he's not going to be able to get away with what he did before. But it's time for you to stop.'

'Gill's guilty,' I said. 'And I'm not letting it go.'

'Christ, Finn, you're an almighty pain in the arse, do you know that? Look, promise me you'll sleep on it, promise me, please.'

'I promise,' I said. 'And I'm sorry for being a pain.'

'No hassle. You've been under a lot of pressure. Rest is the best thing for you.'

I nodded my assent. But rest was the last thing on my agenda for the evening.

34

I sat in front of my computer, welded to my chair. I planned to stay there until I found something, anything, that might chip away at Gill's alibi. I was starting from the premise that Gill had murdered Rhona Macbride. In other words, that what Gill was saying was a lie. And that what his mother was saying was a lie. Two lies. And big lies are often made up of a collection of little lies, of all different kinds of lies. Lies of commission and lies of omission. Things said and things unsaid. And the most successful lies of all were the ones that blended seamlessly with the truth. To isolate and identify what was false, I needed to test the truth of every element of the Gills' story. The same as if I was cross-examining them in the witness box, I would have to go through what they were saying and take down the wall they had constructed, brick by brick.

What did I know already? His house. Everyone in the country knew that, when in Dublin, he lived with his mother Esther in a Georgian house in Clontarf. I googled 'Jeremy Gill Georgian house Clontarf' and found an article from a three-year-old property supplement describing painstaking restoration of the house at Clontarf Crescent using best conservation practice, his membership of the Irish Georgian Society, how he was a proud northsider born in the Rotunda and would never move to the southside. Same old, same old.

But what did I know about the mother? Not so much. I checked Gill's Wikipedia entry and followed links to press articles on Esther Gill. Esther had grown up dirt poor in the flats off Dorset Street, near the Convent of the Blessed Eucharist. She had had Jeremy when she was eighteen, and in everything I had read before, and in what I was reading now, there had never been a mention of Gill's father. Esther was a single parent, never married. Based on my calculations she was sixty-six or sixty-seven now, and Jeremy was forty-eight. She lived in the Clontarf house, but that was as far as entries on Esther Gill went: a life of total devotion to Jeremy, serving her only child in every possible way. I went into Google Images and studied photograph after photograph of Esther Gill. No lavender-scented silver-haired little old lady, she was wiry and glamorous in a hard, cheap, fake tan, fake nails kind of way. Esther looked tough. And she had the same eyes as her son. Was she capable of lying to protect him? My gut said yes.

Next, I checked the Property Registration Authority website on the house where Gill lived. Did he own it or was it held in his mother's name? Nothing turned on it, probably, but my search confirmed Gill's ownership. I kept the PRA window open and went into the Ordnance Survey to compare the PRA and OSI images. The sites looked identical, but it was easier to read the Ordnance Survey maps. I wanted to check the back gardens. If he didn't go out the front, he must have gone out the back.

Sadie was right. There was no rear exit. The OSI map showed that to get access to the road, Gill would have had to cross through the next-door neighbour's garden. Though, as the house next door to his was at the end of the terrace and had a boundary that abutted the public road, in theory, Gill could have scaled his fence, crossed through the next-door garden and climbed their side boundary to reach the road. Google Street View didn't help much as to whether it was a wall or fence. Whichever it was, having Gill climb two obstacles to reach the road seemed too risky.

Unless Gill knew for sure that the house next door was un-occupied? I clicked back into the PRA window. Gill's neighbour's house was owned by a company called ProProperty Limited. Some kind of property development company? Strange. All the houses on Clontarf Crescent were listed buildings so there wouldn't be much scope for redevelopment. Unless it was an executive lettings agency? I ran a Companies Registration Office search but the CRO link was down. Yet something about the name seemed familiar. I'd come back to it.

I decided to accept for now that Gill had got out somehow on to the public road without being seen. If he had, he'd have needed transport to take him to Rhona's house. So I started thinking about Gill's cars. And that there had been no mention of *Esther's* car. Maybe she used his? But her son's success had come relatively late in her life. Ten, twelve years ago, she would have been in her mid-fifties. That was late for a woman born and brought up in dire poverty to get used to driving a Range Rover or an SLK. I brought up pictures of the cars from Google Images. I am a confident driver but I would be terrified of scratching them. No. I reckoned Esther had a runabout, something manageable, if she drove at all. If Gill had got out the back, unobserved, and if Esther had her own car, parked on the road, he could have borrowed hers. For now, I had no way of checking if Esther even had a car. But DI Lenihan could. I'd talk to him in the morning. And if Esther didn't have a car, maybe Gill had hired or borrowed one?

I liked that theory less. It complicated things, and that didn't ring true. He had kept it simple. I had said it to Lenihan, and I was even surer now. I needed to strip away everything extraneous. The truth was bare and unadorned. It had to be.

It was heading on for 9 p.m. and I needed to pee. Just one last thing? The CRO window was still open. I might as well complete the search on ProProperty Limited, if the CRO link was back. It was.

As I read the results, I sat back in my chair and smiled.

Upstairs, confident for the first time in days, I flicked on the kettle. I remembered that I needed to call Marie Wade but my phone rang before I could. It was a blocked number.

'Finn, sorry for calling so late, but there's been a development in your case.'

'Who is this, please?'

'Jesus, sorry, did I not say? It's Garda Ruth Joyce. About your car?'

'Great,' I said. 'I can meet you tomorrow if you want.'

'Well, actually I could see you now, if it was convenient,' she said. 'It's just that I'm on nights at the moment and I came in early to view the CCTV footage and I think I've found something.'

If it shows Pawel Zdziarski burning my car, that's the beginning of the end for Gill.

'I'll come straight to the Bridewell.'

'Em, I'm actually on Barrack Street. I downloaded the footage to my laptop so as I could come to see you, but you'll have to tell me exactly where your house is.'

I buzzed her in and met her at the inside door on the ground floor.

'We can go to my study, which is a mess, or the living room, which is two floors up. Your choice,' I said.

'This is an *amazing* house,' Ruth Joyce said. 'I'd love to see the living room.'

'Come on,' I said.

I ran ahead of her, flicking on the lights as I went. I like rambling around in the dark but I didn't want Garda Joyce to have an accident.

'Wow,' she said on reaching the top of the stairs. She blushed.

'Em, well, em, as you know, I'm here about the CCTV.'

She removed a laptop from the messenger bag she had hanging from her right shoulder and put it on the table. She sat in front of it, tapped a few keys, and asked me to sit beside her. When I was in place, she clicked play.

The suspect walked down Gilabbey Street past the Abbey Tavern in the direction of Fort Street and out of coverage. Six minutes later he walked back, moving faster but not running, going out of view again as he headed in the direction of College Road. The timing dovetailed with the burning of my car. And the figure was male and bulky. It looked like Pawel Zdziarski, but because he kept his hood up and head down, it was hard to tell.

I played and replayed the video and tried to tune out Ruth's running commentary in my left ear. There was one section where it was almost possible to see the suspect's face but only for a microsecond. Every time I went back over it I missed it. I slid the laptop across to Ruth and asked her to try. She went back and forth repeatedly, grimacing, until she got a freeze-frame on the face. Then she passed the laptop back to me.

'Holy shit,' I said.

'Do you know him? Do you?'

'I can't believe it.'

'Who is he? What's his name?'

'He's on your system. He has previous. He works in his dad's garage on the Kinsale Road. His name is … it's Joey O'Connor.'

35

I woke with a start.

Remembering.

Last time I saw her.

Her coming to collect me for a visit. Mam letting her in.

'Come in, Nora, good to see you.'

Me in the dining room, hearing her voice.

Her rushing in, standing, looking.

'Hello you,' her saying. 'Bigger every time I see you. Come here for a hug.'

Me. Nine years old. Staying back, standing, far side of the table from her, the door to the garden open behind me, sunny day. Me watching. Her. Summer dress on. Pink with black lace. Bracelets jangling. Pink lipstick. Hair high, all fresh blonde, dark roots

Catherine Kirwan

*hidden, flowery scarf around her head. Pretty today. Like Barbie.
Like Madonna.*

Won't last.

*'No hug?' she says. 'Plenty of time for hugs in our new home,
that's where we're going, our own house, two bedrooms, a little
garden, we can plant sunflowers, look?'*

*Her taking a packet of seeds out of her bag, pushing them at
me, teeth smiling.*

*Her putting the seeds back in the bag, the purple bag, always
full of her stuff.*

Books.

Ciggies.

Vodka.

Me saying nothing.

'That's okay,' she says. 'We can decide later.'

'I don't want to go,' I say.

'Now, Finn,' Mam says. 'We talked about this.'

'I don't want to go,' I say again.

*'I didn't say it right,' she says. 'We're only visiting today. Just
for a look. We'll go as slowly as you want. The judge says I'm
nearly ready to get you back, and I know I am, but I want you to
be ready too, so we'll be really gradual, won't we, Doreen?'*

'We will,' Mam says.

'She's my real mother,' I say, pointing at Mam. 'Not you.'

'Finn,' Mam says. 'Be kind. Please.'

I'm not kind, though, I'm bad.

'I hate you,' I say to her. 'I never want to see you again.'

Her face.

Darkest Truth

Her tears.

So sad.

So what.

Her head down, running away, door slamming, Mam after her, loud words out front.

Then quiet.

Me in the garden.

Mam coming out to me.

'Oh, Finn,' Mam's saying. 'Poor Nora is very upset.'

'I don't care,' I say.

'I don't want to see her any more,' I say.

And I never did.

The mistake I made.

And.

Not straight away. A few weeks, a month, later.

Her dead.

She tried so hard, then stopped trying.

Because of me.

My mistake.

The biggest mistake I ever made.

Didn't know the full story till later.

But always knew the truth, deep down.

That it was my fault.

All my fault.

And now Rhona.

Two deaths.

My fault.

My fault.
My fault.

I got out of bed and opened the blind. The moon filled the room with a cold hard light. I scrunched myself into the window seat, knees drawn up to my chin, my body twisted, my hands pulling at my hair, my forearms in front of my face, my breath coming in wet gasps.

Then sleep.

Awake again, with a sore neck, I unpicked myself from the frozen knot I had become. I went to the other side of the room, and checked the time on the ancient luminous travel clock I keep on my locker. 5.40 a.m. Monday. No work to go to.

And the investigative work I *had* been doing? A disaster. How could I have messed up so badly? When I met Joey O'Connor, I saw what he was like, the spurned boyfriend, the obvious candidate for what had happened to Deirdre. Almost everything he had said had identified him as the man responsible for the vicious attack on Deirdre, everything had fitted, but I had ignored him and gone chasing after Jeremy Gill. Who had an alibi for the time of Rhona's death. Maybe I had been wrong about that, too. Maybe it *was* a random mugging, like the Gardaí thought. Random or not, it was my fault. Normally so security conscious, Rhona must have been distracted by what we'd talked about. She had told me how upset she had been as a result of my visit. And she had sent me an email only ten or fifteen minutes before she was killed.

Or was it possible that Joey had something to do with Rhona's death? My head said no, that it was too far-fetched, but then so was the idea of him burning my car. He was capable of extreme violence. Was he capable of murder? But there was no evidence that he knew Rhona. Even if he did, what would his motive have been? I discounted the idea.

Yet what had become abundantly clear was that I was looking at two unconnected crimes: Joey *had* to be the one responsible for Deirdre's rape and Gill, though he had raped Rhona, *hadn't* killed her.

I checked my clock again. 6 a.m. My head was exploding. And there was something I needed to do but I couldn't remember what.

Jesus.

The bins.

I stepped barefoot into my Birkenstocks, pulled a hoodie on over my pyjamas, ran down the stairs and opened the front door. I grabbed an umbrella, left it on the floor between the door and the jamb so that I wouldn't be locked out, and ran out the door to the yard. First, I opened the yard door wide and hooked it back on the stone wall, then went to the bins. Recycling or rubbish this week? I couldn't remember. But the recycling bin felt heavy, it had to be that one. I pulled up my hood and started down the lane towards Barrack Street, dragging the bin after me.

When I got out as far as the street, I realised I'd picked the wrong bin.

'Fuck,' I said aloud, and turned back down the lane, the blue bin even heavier than on the way out, it seemed. I shoved it back into place and dragged out the other two bins, the brown and the green ones, and wheeled them in front of me, the lane just wide enough for both if I staggered them, kept one arm long. At the end of the lane, I parked the two bins and walked across the road, opened the brown compost bin opposite. It stank like there was a dead body inside, but it was full, so they hadn't been around with the lorry yet. Retching, I headed home. I unhooked the gate, closed it quietly, went into the house, kicked the umbrella out of the way, and let the door shut behind me.

In my en-suite bathroom, I washed my hands, had a quick pee, then washed my hands again and went back out to the bedroom, and checked the clock. It was 6.15. I picked up a pair of tracksuit bottoms and socks off the floor, put them on, and went upstairs to the living room, flicking on the heating as I went but keeping the lights off, relying on the street yellow of the city, not wanting to admit that morning had come, hoping that yoga and a cup of camomile tea might warm and relax me enough to win me a couple of hours' rest. Upstairs, I walked to the kitchen island and started to fill the kettle.

'Are you making me a cup of tea? Ah that's lovely,' a voice said, a male voice, a voice I recognised, coming from the direction of the armchair. I hadn't looked when I came into the room, I hadn't thought, couldn't have imagined, and I was dizzy now, my mouth dry, a buzzing in my ears, black spots in my vision, my stomach churning. I stayed very still.

'Lovely place you've got here,' Jeremy Gill said. 'But you should be more careful, Finn. There are a lot of bad people in the world, you know, and leaving your front door wide open is never a good idea, is it?'

The kettle had overflowed. I tipped out the excess water and put it back in its place. It clicked on automatically. I was still standing with my back to Gill. I looked to the right, in the direction of the knife block. It was empty. And my phone was on the coffee table at the far side of the room.

Jesus Jesus Jesus.

'Now, now, not looking for a knife, Finn, are you? Come on. Knowing how you feel about me, I'm hardly going to leave lethal weapons lying around in easy reach, am I?'

'Get out of my house,' I said.

'Get out of my house,' I said again.

'No need to shout, Finn,' Gill said. 'I'll go. But not yet. I want us to have a little chat first. But I can't talk to you when you've got your back to me. So would you like to turn around? Or would you like me to do the turning for you?'

In the silence that followed, I heard one slow footstep, and then a second, coming towards me. Then he stopped.

'Are you going to look at me, Finn?'

'Yes,' I said, but softly.

'I can't hear you, Finn, I should probably get closer to you.'

I heard him take another slow step.

'So, are you going to turn around, Finn?' Gill asked, almost conversationally.

'Yes,' I said, louder this time, and I turned to face Gill, keeping contact with the worktop with my left hand, swivelling slowly on one foot and pressing my right hand back on the worktop as soon as I had completed the turn.

'That's good, Finn.'

He was standing in the middle of the room, his hands in the pockets of a short zipped black jacket, hood up, that he wore with black jeans and black boots. Behind him on the coffee table, scattered around my mobile phone like a bad student sculpture, the knives from the knife block glinted. How many were there? I couldn't remember, and I was afraid to check the block again. Did he have one of the knives in his pocket? Or a screwdriver? He was going to use something, it didn't matter what, and I was going to die, of that I was certain.

'Now we can have our little talk.'

'I have nothing to say to you,' I said. 'Anyway, I thought you were in custody.'

'Oh I was,' Gill said. 'But they let me go. Had to. No evidence, you see. No evidence because I'm innocent. That's what I wanted to talk to you about, actually. To ask you personally what is your fucking problem, you fucking cunt?'

I tried to press myself further back into the worktop but there was nowhere to go. Behind me, the kettle was coming to the boil as if nothing was wrong, as if my world hadn't started to implode. I held on to the counter with both hands but it felt like the edge of a cliff.

'Oh dear, Finn, you don't like that word? Funny, it's one of my favourites. And it's never been more fucking appropriate, let me tell you.'

Gill took a step closer. Two more steps and he would be able to touch me. Three more and I would feel his breath on me. Four more steps and I would die.

'They kept me longer in the station than my mother, wouldn't even let me drop her home, get her settled. I had to get my solicitor to employ an agency nurse to stay with her. She's a tough bird, but she *is* old now, an OAP, and you put her through that. I wanted you to hear it. *You* put my mother in a cell like she was some kind of junkie whore. All because of your deluded obsession with me. But I've told them about you, they know, the guards know what you are, you mad stalker bitch. And it's only the beginning. I'm having a meeting with my lawyers later today, and we are going to rain down vengeance upon you, Finn. Your days practising law are over. And this house? It will please me no end to take it from you. Maybe I'll keep it as a pied-à-terre.'

He paused.

'Hang on, wait a minute, sorry – did you think I was here to *kill* you? Or *rape* you? Did you think that? Finn, *when* will you learn that I don't *do* those terrible things.'

He smiled.

'What I have in mind for you is going to be a lot worse. Slow and painful. In the end, you'll pray for death, you'll fucking beg for it.'

He took a step closer.

'On the other hand. It would be *so* much kinder to put you out of your misery now.'

He leant forward. His long hair brushed against my face. He pressed his mouth against my left ear.

'You're the same,' he whispered. 'Ye're all the fuckin' same when ye're stripped.'

I felt his gloved hand on my neck. Then his fingers tightened around my throat and I heard his breath, faster than before. I was paralysed.

Until I remembered Rhona's story. Reaching behind me, I grabbed the handle of the kettle and swept it forward between me and Gill. I felt the heat of it through my clothes. He would feel it too.

'Take your filthy paw off me, you fucker, or you'll be peeling burnt skin off your dick for the next six months. I'll burn too.'

He loosened his grip. Straightening, he looked down at me.

'Oh, please. You're too much. It's like a game of Cluedo. Miss Fitzpatrick in the kitchen with the kettle. Do you *really* think I'd let you hurt me?'

His hand tightened again briefly. Then he let go, stepped back and walked slowly towards the stairs. He stood at the top for a moment and looked at me.

'This was surprisingly good fun,' Gill said. 'Goodbye, Finn. See you soon.'

He took his phone out of his pocket, and he must have made a call as he went down the stairs, because I could hear his voice talking softly to someone, though I couldn't hear what he was saying. The front door slammed and I sank to the floor.

36

Once my terror had subsided, I was utterly confused. Had Gill driven to Cork to frighten me? The idea that he had would have made a lot more sense if I hadn't known about my car: I was still trying to come to terms with the fact that Joey was responsible for that and possibly – no, probably – for what had happened to Deirdre. As for Gill, there was no doubt that he was a rapist – Rhona had confirmed that – but he had insisted that he was innocent of killing her. Was that why he had come? He had an alibi. The guards believed him. I was starting to think that I had been wrong all along.

But what if I had been right? What if Gill *was* guilty? The fact that he had come down all the way to see me might mean that he was losing control, and if he was losing control, he might start to make mistakes. Was that what his visit was? The start of an unravelling?

And what next? Should I make a formal complaint? Report this morning's incident to Lenihan? But what had I to report? I looked in the mirror. Gill had been clever, he had left no bruises or marks on my neck. He had walked into my house through an open door, had told me he *wasn't* going to rape and kill me, but that he was consulting his lawyers and planning to sue me. I had never been as scared of anything or anyone in my life, but none of it would translate into a charge that would stick. My credibility was hanging by a thread. I didn't want to risk compromising it further.

I wrote up what had happened, and went back over my notes from the previous night. The facts were there in black and white: Gill was still a suspect in the murder of Rhona Macbride, he had to be, and I had valuable new information I needed to pass on to the investigation team. I rang Lenihan. He was his usual polite self when he answered.

'I'm in the middle of my fucking breakfast. What do *you* want?'

'It's Gill,' I said.

'Of course it's fucking Gill,' Lenihan said. 'It's never anyone else with you.'

'What I mean is, last night I found out that he owns the house next door to where he lives. Or, more precisely, his trust company, ProGill Trust, owns ProProperty Limited which, in turn, owns the house next door. He got out through that house, the garden of it, and I think Esther has a car, and that he used it to drive over to Rhona's place and kill her.'

Lenihan wasn't saying a word.

'Gill's no longer in custody,' I said.

'That's an operational matter. As a civilian you are not entitled to know that information. But, yeah, we let him go. That info about the other possible exit is interesting, though. We'll take a look at it when we get a chance.'

'Are you watching Gill's house? Make sure you watch it front and rear.'

'That's another operational matter,' Lenihan said.

Which meant that they weren't. But after hearing about the second exit, they would be watching from now on. And if they could catch Gill going in the back way after his visit to Cork ...

'Don't forget about the car, Esther's car.'

'We thought of the car ourselves. We're not as thick as you seem to think. Nice idea, Finn, but Esther Gill has no car registered in her name. We checked Gill's insurance too. She's not registered as a named driver on his insurance either. And there's no third car in his name, he only owns the two you already know about.'

'Fuck no,' I said.

'Fuck yeah,' Lenihan said. 'Welcome to the real world. So, thanks for your input anyway, like, and we'll take it from here.'

'Gill didn't go home after he left Garda custody, did he?'

'That is the last question of yours that I am answering, Fitzpatrick. He went for a consultation at his solicitor's office. He's still there, last I heard. Good. Bye.'

It was the opening I needed to get in the information about Gill's morning visit.

'He's not at his solicitor's office,' I said. 'He's—'

Lenihan had hung up. I tried calling back but he didn't take my call.

I threw my phone on the sofa and reviewed the conversation. Ultimately what it amounted to was that Esther had no car *registered* in her name. I thought it through again and again and came up with an alternative possibility. I reckoned that whatever income Gill was paying his mother had to be through one of his companies. By calling her an employee, his Dublin PA, say, he'd get a tax write-off. And the more I thought about it, the more certain I became that his mother's car, *if* she had one, was owned and registered the same way. I emailed my thoughts and a list of Gill's companies and directorships to Lenihan, saying I had more important information on Gill's movements and that I needed to talk to him. Then I texted him and tried phoning him again. I gave up after the fourth go.

I went to my bedroom, took off what I was wearing, and the sheets on my bed, and the towels from the en suite, and threw everything down the stairs. I went to the storage and laundry room on the ground floor and dumped the towels and linen in the washing machine. There was no knowing what he had touched. My skin crawled from the memory of him. I smelled my underarm. I stank. I ran the shower in my en-suite as hot as I could bear, scrubbed myself nearly raw and shampooed twice. Then I dried off and threw on leggings and a giant black sweatshirt. I had just started to comb through my hair when I heard the doorbell ringing.

'Who is it?'

'Me,' Sadie O'Riordan said.

I buzzed her in the gate and, combing my hair, ran down to open the house door.

Sadie's face was white.

'What did you do?'

'What do you mean?'

'We've had a complaint about you,' Sadie said. 'From Jeremy fucking Gill.'

'What? Oh my God.'

'Oh my God goes nowhere near how I felt when I heard it.'

She stomped upstairs, followed by me. Then, leaning against the table, she took out her notebook, flicked through it, and started talking, intoning, like she was giving evidence at a trial.

'Complainant states that he was upset after being released from custody, that he decided to try to talk things through with you, that he left his solicitor's office via the basement car park, where a hired vehicle had been left for him.'

She looked up from the notebook.

'We'd been watching the front door, didn't see him exit,' she said, in her normal voice, then looked down at the notebook again.

'Complainant states that he had planned to go home, but on impulse he came down to Cork to see if he could talk some sense into you.'

'Sadie, how is this complaint even being tolerated, let alone investigated? Isn't he intimidating a witness by coming anywhere near me?'

'He hasn't been charged with anything, remember? And the fucker is saying it was the natural thing to do in the circumstances, given how you've been stalking him, and making up stuff about him. Poor lamb blames you for all the shit he's had to put up with in the last week or so, but he's a reasonable guy, he says, jaw jaw better than war war and all that, so he rings your doorbell, and you very kindly *invite* him in and all is going great until you threaten to castrate him with knives from your knife block which he says you had scattered all over a coffee table.'

Sadie paused.

'That would be those knives, on that table, I imagine.'

'It wasn't like that,' I said. 'He was the one ...'

Sadie continued.

'And then, this is my favourite bit actually, Complainant states that you produced a kettle of boiling water and told him he'd be peeling burnt skin off his prick ...'

'Dick,' I said. 'That's the word I used. That part is true, but the rest is lies. Well, he was here, okay, but I didn't let him in, the door was open while I was putting out the bins, and he was waiting here when I came back in. And I never threatened to castrate him, just the boiling water. He was the one who ... I told him to leave and he wouldn't and ...'

'All right,' Sadie said. 'He let himself in. And you didn't think to ring me, or any Garda station, to report this? You allowed *Gill* to be the one to do it?'

'I didn't think. I was going to tell you, and Lenihan, but it seemed kind of lame, and I let it sit for a while, only an hour or so, probably a bit more, while I thought about it. Anyway, I wasn't able to … not immediately. I was in shock. But I was on the phone to Lenihan earlier, I was trying to tell him, and the arsehole hung up on me, and wouldn't take my call when I tried to get him back. I've tried ringing him four times.'

'He was probably taking a call from us in Coughlan's Quay, telling him that Gill was in making a complaint about you. Jes-*us*, Finn, I know you say you were shocked but I can't understand why you didn't call 999 while he was here, or straight after he left. Why you didn't call me, for Christ's sake.'

'I couldn't get to my phone while he was here. He was blocking my way. And, after, I … I felt like a fool, the woman who cried wolf, after Gill had been interviewed for the second time and released, despite everything.'

'I know you must have been terrified but most people would've called the cops straight away, in all fairness. Christ. The main thing is that you're okay, I suppose, and you'll have to make a full statement, but you needn't do it today. The DPP will decide ultimately if there's a case to answer. It'll all depend on what happens next, if Gill follows through with the complaint, or withdraws it. It'll be a swearing match between the two of ye, your word against his. He may just want to torture you for a while. We'll see. Go on, make me a cup of coffee for God's sake, and there had better be biscuits or I will scream because let me tell you, I am so fed up of you and Jeremy fucking Gill.'

'No biscuits. Cheese and oatcakes are the best I can do.'

'Jaysus. All right. Just coffee so,' Sadie said. 'Now tell me again what happened. And slowly. I want to take notes.'

I walked to the worktop, picked up the kettle.

'*Are you making me a cup of tea? Ah that's lovely.*'

I dropped the kettle.

'You're going to have to make the coffee,' I said. 'I have to sit down.'

Then I vomited into the sink.

'You don't need to dump the chair,' Sadie said, after I had finished telling her what had happened. 'From what you've told me, Gill was sitting in it for ten or fifteen minutes, max.'

'I have to get it out of here. I'll never sit in it again.'

I grabbed the back of the chair and started pulling it towards the stairs.

'Come on,' I said.

'This is idiotic,' Sadie said, but got up anyway, and started to help.

We half lifted, half dragged the chair down the stairs, marking the paintwork in places, and I couldn't have cared less. On Barrack Street, I wrote a sign ('*Free to take away*'), stuck it in a plastic folder and Sellotaped it to the leather. In the ten days since I'd met Sean Carney, I had lost a car and now the armchair. If things kept going like this, I'd have nothing left. And yet, the idea was a lot less terrifying than it might have been a couple of weeks before. When you were close to death, as I felt I had been that morning, possessions didn't matter all that much.

'Scary thing to happen, all right,' Sadie said as we walked back along the lane.

'Yeah.'

'But he's gone, at least for now. Chances are, he won't pursue that complaint against you. If he does, you have a cross-complaint against him for assault. If any marks show, make sure you photograph them and go to your GP to put it on the record.'

'Don't worry, I will. At the time I was sure he was going to kill me but I don't think I'm going to bruise,' I said. 'I think he knew what he was doing. It's what I was saying to you before, if anything happened to me, he'd be the number one suspect.'

'I'm nearly more worried about Joey,' Sadie said. 'He's local. And he's highly dangerous.'

'And I *knew* he was, from his record and the way he behaved when I met him.'

'You barely mentioned him to me at the time, though.'

'I know. He just didn't fit with the story I'd constructed in my head about Gill.'

'Rookie mistake,' Sadie said. 'Ignore the facts, stick with the theory.'

'You're all heart. Hopefully he's on his way to being arrested for my car, at least.'

If he had raped Deirdre – and I still wasn't convinced he had – he would never serve prison time for that. All the same, it would give me some satisfaction to see him put away. He'd probably argue that he was upset after I'd reminded him of Deirdre's death, but hopefully the main influence on his sentence would be his previous convictions for violence.

'I'm sure he is. I'll check what's happening when I'm back at base,' Sadie said.

'Thanks,' I said. 'But Gill is still the one taking up most of the space my head.'

'And it's pretty crowded in there at the minute,' I added.

'Rhona, you mean?'

'Rhona, and the girl from New York State, and all the others he's hurt and damaged, and that he's going to in the future. Rhona's dead now, so she can't give evidence against him. And all Gill's other victims seem to have stayed schtum so far. In the end, what we have on him amounts to nothing that would get him prosecuted for anything. The trouble is, he's so clever. If he walks away scot-free from this, I don't know what I'll do.'

After Sadie was gone, I emptied the washing machine and transferred the bed linen and towels into the dryer. Then I left the house.

I needed to check something before I could get my head clear on anything else.

37

I didn't bother making an appointment this time. I walked through the main hall, up the stairs and past his astonished secretary, and into his office.

'What on earth are you doing?' Eoghan MacGiolla shouted.

He leapt out of his chair and made for the door but I blocked his path.

'You lied,' I said. 'And I want to know why.'

'I'm going to call the guards.'

'Please do. Or you could tell me the real story about you and Deirdre Carney.'

I kicked the door shut behind me, walked around MacGiolla, and sat in his chair.

'Take a seat,' I said. 'And start talking.'

*

The truth, when it came, was pedestrian and contemptible.

'Yes,' MacGiolla said. 'I knew Deirdre from the area where I grew up. Sad what became of her. But suicide is bad news, for many reasons. Morale. Staff and students. Not to mention the publicity. She was a past pupil and … Well, give a dog a bad name, etc. etc. I was thinking of the institution. I thought it best to keep my distance, minimise any connection between the school and the, em, event. We sent two teachers to the funeral, but that was as far as we went.'

'You go on about your students. But, unless they perform how they're supposed to, you don't care. I've been in that rotten little room. Do you even *have* a school counsellor?'

'The role has been vacant for some time. Other funding priorities seemed—'

'Deirdre was in trouble when she was here and this place did nothing to help her.'

'I'm sure that's not true. Anyway, I wasn't working here at the time.'

'You wouldn't have made any difference,' I said.

As I walked west along the Mardyke towards Fitzgerald's Park, my anger receded. MacGiolla was a despicable creature, and his attitude stank, but he hadn't hurt Deirdre. Which didn't mean that I knew who had. The questions raised in my mind in the last twenty-four hours about Joey O'Connor and what he might have done to Deirdre, and about Gill's culpability, or innocence, in Rhona's death, had served to let one truth float clear of the wreckage: that Deirdre had killed herself without knowing that our mother had done the same thing. Had the rape been responsible for Deirdre's mental illness? Or had she inherited it?

The park was empty apart from a few well-swaddled children and their minders. I sat on a bench facing away from the river, but I felt its great power and the pull that had been inescapable for my mother and my sister.

Back home, the chair Gill had sat on was gone from the side of the street, which cheered me, but only for a moment. I went to my study and tried to work, rereading my notes, seeking patterns or details I might have missed. The words swam on the screen in front of me. I remembered that I had intended to call Marie Wade the previous night, just before Garda Ruth Joyce had called around with the CCTV. Just before the bottom had fallen out of my case. I hadn't the energy to call her now. I couldn't even remember why the former education officer Daniel O'Brien had seemed important.

I went up to the living room. With the remote in my hand, I skipped through my music library, playing snatches of different songs I liked. But I couldn't settle, not even when I got a text from Sadie to say that Joey had been detained for questioning, not even for Merle's 'Mama Tried'. I paced the room like a prison cell until, at last, a lock opened in my mind.

I grabbed my phone and rang Sadie.

'Good news about Joey O'Connor, right? And are you feeling better?' she asked.

'Yeah, good. I'm fine. No, I'm agitated. This morning's been bothering me.'

'I'm not surprised,' Sadie said. 'Like I said, it was—'

'That's not what I meant. I need to check what time Gill came to the station to make the complaint about me. You were up here about half elevenish, right?'

'Yeah. He called in about 9.15, was gone a little after 10.20. I went up to you as soon as I could, after we'd done the paperwork and talked it through with the boss.'

'Okay. He was gone from here by seven, no later. That means there are two hours unaccounted for. Sadie, he couldn't have known in advance that I'd be putting out the bins at 6 a.m. or that he'd be able to gain access to my house so easily. It was pure chance.'

'So what are you saying?'

'What if he only called by here for a look and took the opportunity, when it presented, to come into my house? But what if it *wasn't* me he came to Cork to see? And what was he doing during those missing two hours?'

38

Bottle green is the uniform of St Aloysius's Secondary School, but that was as much as I knew about it, though I live not ten minutes from the place. I'm a northsider. While I was at St Angela's, we had little or no contact with St Al's. I didn't know any of the teachers or any of the current pupils, apart from Carmel, the blonde girl from Gill's film workshop, and I didn't even know her last name. Other than loitering around on the street outside the school, or across the road outside St Maries of the Isle Primary, I had no fast way of making contact with her. The headmistress wasn't going to allow me to chat to 'Carmel X from Transition Year'. Sadie could have gone into the school and said she was investigating something or other, but she wasn't going to, not unless I came up with something more than a hunch. I could tell she wasn't taking what I'd said seriously. Or that she didn't want to. Being my friend couldn't have been easy for her this last while.

'The delay between leaving your place and going to Coughlan's Quay isn't conclusive of anything. Gill had been up all night, remember? He might have had a kip in the car. Or gone for breakfast – a fry-up in Tony's Bistro? He delayed going to the Garda station. It doesn't follow that he was having an assignation with a schoolgirl, surely?'

'He phoned someone as he was leaving my house, Sadie,' I said. 'I didn't hear who it was. I assumed initially that it was his security guard, or his assistant; possibly his solicitor. But what if it was Carmel he was talking to? Maybe he was arranging to meet her.'

'I think your first impression was the right one, Finn, that it was probably his security guard or his assistant,' Sadie said. 'There was definitely someone with him in Cork this morning.'

'How can you be sure? Did you see who it was?'

'No, I didn't see anyone, but whoever it was must have been the one doing the driving. When Gill was leaving, he rang and arranged to be collected outside the door.'

'Right,' I said. 'Gill could still have met Carmel, though.'

'With a witness in tow? I doubt it,' Sadie said.

'I don't know,' I said.

That was the truth. I didn't know, not for sure, though I felt it in the way my head pounded. I couldn't let the day go by without seeing Carmel and checking that she was safe. Lunchtime was past already. Was there a way of seeing her after school? I'd have to try to meet her at the gate. There was nothing else for it. But what if I missed her in the crowd? It was wet out – they'd be wearing hats or hoods and one girl looks much like another in the rain. Or what if she wasn't there? What if she was with him?

And then I remembered that I had a way of contacting her, after all.

It was five days since I'd checked Twitter, and I wasn't looking forward to it. There weren't as many tweets as I'd feared. Social media had moved on and refocused their outrage several times over. I searched under #lawyerbitch. Within a minute I'd found Carmel: Carmel McMonagle, @CarmelaMcMocha, whose twin missions in life, according to her profile, were to locate and consume the ultimate mocha (#idreamofmocha) and to win an acting Oscar by the age of twenty-five (#onlytenyearstogo). She was so young.

And so dumb. Apart from the #lawyerbitch tweets, she didn't do much on Twitter but there were some cross-posts from her Instagram account. I clicked through. Her profile was public and had an impressive 2,347 followers. It looked like her mocha comments were popular. Or maybe the recent controversy had boosted her numbers? Carmel's profile revealed a trail of movements in a quest for coffee and chocolate beverage perfection over the previous eight months. There were almost daily posts and photographs, and a link to a blog (Carmela McMocha's House of Mocha, 923 subscribers) where she provided tasting notes and star ratings for anywhere she'd been, on holidays and school trips as well as locally.

There weren't that many places in Cork. Some of them she never returned to after scathing one or no star reviews. Others were more frequent haunts. I sat at the kitchen table with my laptop and a note-book and wrote down the names of the cafes she had visited more than once that were in walking distance of St Al's. The rain was spilling down now. If she was going to go somewhere after school today, it would have to be close. I narrowed down the options to two places, pulled on my rain-jacket and ran out the door.

I had no luck at the first cafe, Tiramisu on Proby's Quay, in the shadow of the cathedral. I headed down Sharman Crawford Street, past the Art College and St Al's School, and crossed the bridge on to Lancaster Quay. By the time I got to Cafe Depeche, my leggings were stuck to my knees and shins, and the band of sweatshirt that hung below my jacket was flapping against my thighs like a wet flag. I had a black knitted cap on under my hood, and the front of it was soaked, but at least most of my hair was dry. I entered the cafe, peeled off the beanie, wiped my face and hands with it, and surveyed the room as best I could, head bent, from beneath my hood.

I heard them before I saw them, the unmistakable high-pitched squeal of a group of female teenagers. I looked up. There were a few tables of Pres boys but, at the far end of the counter, three girls coiled themselves on high stools. The middle one was Carmel. She looked well. She looked like nothing bad had hap-pened to her. Not yet.

And she hadn't noticed me yet either. Moving quickly to retain the element of surprise, I went up behind her and rapped her on the left shoulder.

'You,' I said. 'We need to talk.'

I walked backwards and stood by a table, arms folded.

'Here,' I said. 'Now.'

I watched Carmel register who I was. For a moment, she looked scared. But her expression changed fast.

'Fuck off, you weirdo,' she said. 'She's the one I was telling you about, girls, the woman at the workshop who—'

'I'll fuck off in a minute. Gladly. But I think you'll want to hear what I have to say directly from me. And I'd hate to have to go through your parents or the school or, how can I put this, other more *official* channels.'

Carmel's top teeth closed over her bottom lip.

'I suppose I can spare a minute,' she said, after a pause.

She climbed off her stool, sulked her way over to me, and sat down.

'What do you want?'

'To talk to you,' I said. 'About you know who.'

'I don't, actually,' she said. 'This is getting weirder and weirder,' she said then, more loudly, looking back in the direction of her friends.

I leant across the table.

'Do you want me to say his name? Because I will, you know. And I won't just say it to you, I'll—'

'Okay, okay,' Carmel said. 'I know who you're talking about. The man we met at the workshop.'

'Thank you,' I said.

'Are you, like, *obsessed* with him or something?'

'In a way I am,' I said. 'But not for the reasons you might think. And not for the same reasons you might be.'

I waited for a denial or a retort, but none came, and that was the moment I knew for sure that Gill had been communicating with her, that he had been grooming her. I was less certain if he had met her. He might have. But he hadn't touched her. I was sure of it.

'He's forty-eight years of age, Carmel,' I said. 'And you're fifteen.'

'And your point?' she asked, but she spoke quietly. 'You *do* have a point?'

'My point is that, like I said at the workshop, any private communication between a forty-eight-year-old man and a fifteen-year-old girl should only be with parental consent. And I'm not a parent, and I don't know yours, but I can't imagine any circumstances where they *would* give consent.'

She made no reply but something like doubt crept into her face. I should have said nothing, let her talk next. Instead, over-confident, I asked a question that alerted her to just how little hard information I had. I knew it was a mistake the second it left my mouth.

'Has he been contacting you?'

She tilted her chin upwards, and smiled slowly.

'Of course he hasn't been contacting me, you pervert,' she said. 'That would be illegal. You know, you're the sick one, not him. You're the one with the dirty mind. Oh my God you're so fucking pathetic, do you know that?'

She stood and pushed back her chair. Without looking at them, she called to her friends at the counter.

'Girls, we're *so* out of here. Get my bag and coat and I'll meet ye outside. The air quality in this place has deteriorated all of a sudden.'

They left in a flurry of schoolbags and indignation. I was left alone, staring at the slammed door, kicking myself.

39

If I had said less, Carmel might have opened up and admitted that Gill had been in touch with her. I could have persuaded her to talk to Sadie, or I could have helped her make a Child Protection report to a social worker, and the mandatory investigation would have started; I could have seen to it that Gill was arrested and charged. And now I could do none of that. Forewarned, probably in touch with Gill again already, Carmel would deny everything.

I left the cafe and headed in the direction of the university, taking the long way home, facing into the rain, the drops like whips on my cheeks, and night falling as fast as a stone in a lake. Back at the house, I tore off my clothes in the hallway, wrapped myself in a towel and sat on the stairs. How had I let it happen? How had I thrown away the chance to catch Gill in the act of committing a crime that would have got him locked up and unable to hurt anyone else?

But, after a time, the hot rage I felt at myself and at my own stupidity turned cold. Carmel was going to be Gill's next victim. There was nothing surer. The only way of preventing it was to put him away for Rhona's murder. I needed to get back to the investigation.

And yet, I didn't trust myself as much as before. I had been wrong about Joey. I had completely mishandled my meeting with Carmel. What if I made another mistake, a bigger one this time? Exhaustion coursed through me, spread out from my belly, up my neck to my head, and down my legs, and all the way to my fingertips.

I leant my head against the bannister, and closed my eyes.

The doorbell woke me.

'Thank God you're here,' I said.

I took Davy's hand and led him upstairs.

'Come on,' I said, and threw the towel over the bannister.

He laughed.

'Shit,' I said, at my bedroom door. 'No sheets.'

'No matter,' Davy said, and pushed me on to the bed.

'So I've a little surprise for you,' Davy said.

'I don't like surprises. I hate them, in fact.'

'You'll like this one. I've booked Paradiso for dinner.'

'Tonight? It's Monday.'

'Exactly. Which is why I could get a reservation at such short notice. Get dressed or we'll be late. The table is booked for 7.30.'

'Davy, I can't,' I said.

'Why?'

'I just can't. I'm not in the form. I'm distracted, I spent a lot of the day on the sofa listening to country music and the rest of it …'

'You love country music,' Davy said.

'I know,' I said.

'So where's the problem except that your day got even better because your wonderful friend – your "just good friend", nothing more – booked your favourite restaurant?'

'Davy, I appreciate the gesture …'

'Whoa,' Davy said, and sat up in bed. 'Gesture? Is that what this is to you?'

'I don't mean it as an insult. I'm just not up to it. I want to do a bit of work, if I can, I haven't been able to all day, but now I think I could, I have to, there's so little time …'

'Great,' Davy said. 'Glad to have been of service.'

'That's not what I meant. But you know how important this case is to me.'

'I do,' Davy said. 'But I thought we were important too. Or is this how it's going to be? You working, and fitting me into your schedule when you feel like a quick shag?'

Then would have been the time to tell him about Gill's visit, and about Carmel.

'I'm not going to be controlled by you, Davy,' I said instead. 'Or emotionally blackmailed. I've said I'm not going out, and I'm not.'

'So I'm blackmailing you now, is it, just because I've booked a fucking restaurant for dinner? Where we could actually talk, for a change, or would that be so wrong? Jesus Christ.'

Davy got out of bed and looked down at me.

'I've news for you, Finn. Label it what you like, be it "friends with benefits" or "just good friends". But whatever this is, it's not going to cut it with me. We're either fucking each other and having a relationship, or we're not. And when you decide what you want, let me know and I'll see if I'm still available.'

He got dressed in silence.

'Don't go,' I whispered. 'Not like this.'

'Oh I'm going all right,' Davy said.

He left the bedroom without saying goodbye and I heard the front door shut behind him with a soft click. He was gone, he couldn't be, but he was. In my mind's eye, I saw him walking away and never coming back. I jumped out of bed and ran down the stairs, pulling on my robe as I went. By the time I reached the gate, he was most of the way down the lane.

'Davy, stop,' I shouted. 'I can explain.'

He turned.

'Explain what?'

'Explain why I can't go out tonight,' I said. 'Come back.'

He thought about it, then walked halfway back.

'I'm listening.'

'I had a bad day,' I said. 'Starting with my visitor this morning.'

'Who?'

'Who do you think?'

'Haven't a notion.'

'Him.'

'Gill?'

I nodded.

'I'll kill him.'

'Don't kill him,' I said. 'Just don't leave me. Not tonight.'

40

How hard could it be to call and update me on what was happening? It was over twenty-four hours since I had told Lenihan that Gill owned the house next door, and emailed him my theory about Esther Gill's car. I was doing Lenihan's job for him. The least he could do was keep me informed. I hoped that he was following up on the leads, but who knew?

I spent the morning, after Davy had left for work, intermittently reviewing the file I had on Deirdre's case. I didn't get far. There was no sign yet of the DNA results or the medical records. The longer they took to arrive, the more pessimistic I became. The drinks coaster was probably hopelessly cross-contaminated and the medical records were probably silent on anything that might identify the rapist, be that Joey O'Connor or Jeremy Gill. My case was hopelessly stalled, and it was impossible for me to concentrate while I was waiting for news on the murder investigation.

The doorbell rang at 10.15. I jumped.

'Morning, Finn, is it?' the voice on the intercom said.

'Who's this?'

'Andy O'Mahony, electrician, your fella sent me up to fit the security light on the gate, like.'

I buzzed him in. I had mentioned to Davy that I agreed with him now that I needed a security light. Had there been one, Gill wouldn't have been able to conceal himself unseen, where I assumed he had been, in the recess to the left of the gate, while I took out the bins. But I hadn't asked Davy to organise it for me, and part of me was annoyed that he had; the part that didn't like people taking care of me, the same part that liked being in control of all things at all times. But another part of me had wanted Davy to be with me last night, had asked him to stay.

So I scowled at Andy O'Mahony, but I let him do the job. I even brought him down a mug of tea with the three spoons of sugar he had specified.

'He's not my fella, by the way,' I said.

'Who?'

'Davy Keenan.'

'Oh right,' Andy said. 'What is he so?'

'I'm not sure any more.'

'That sounds interesting.'

'Yeah,' I said. 'That's one way of putting it.'

*

After Andy left, I remained in the garden. I took a brush from the shed and swept the paths clear of snipped electrical cable and leaves. For a time, I leant against the stone wall and remembered the previous Tuesday night, when Davy I had stood in this place in the rain and, later, slept together for the first time.

Since then, Rhona had been murdered, and so much else had happened. And yet, in the middle of all the chaos, Davy and I hadn't been able to keep our hands off each other. Worse, he had been to my parents' house for Sunday lunch. Now he had started organising home improvements for me. It had to stop, I knew that. And soon.

But not yet.

Upstairs, I started thinking about the case again. I was going to make no progress here. And I had to get out of the house before I started kicking the walls.

Now, I was walking towards UCC, looking for Lorcan Lucey who had been on the festival youth jury with Deirdre. I had left a couple of messages for him but he had never returned my calls. According to his timetable, he was giving a lecture in the west wing of the Quad right now. I wasn't expecting much from him but I had to cross him off my list. Going by Fort Street was the more direct route, though, if I went that way, I would be confronted with the charred corpse of my car. Instead, I walked up Barrack Street, the ancient road in and out of the city from the west. At one time, almost every house had been a shop or pub. Now, many were derelict or vacant, while others had been converted into rough living quarters for students and other renters.

Dotted amid the wreckage were well-cared-for owner-occupied homes. And the few remaining businesses traded with pride and defiance. Halfway up, Tom Barry's pub glowed like a sapphire.

At Denroches Cross, the road divided. I took the lower fork and looked behind me before turning sharp right through the gap on to Wycherley Terrace. If anyone was going to jump me and drag me into a car or split my cranium with an axe, this was where they'd do it, a short low passage underneath and between two houses. But the road was clear.

The closer I got to College, the more stolen road signs and heaps of empty beer cans were visible inside grubby windows. Formerly a leafy suburb, most of the area had been colonised by students now. For eight months of the year, the ordinary residents had to endure the horror of Thursday nights in term time, and Rag Week, and Hallowe'en, and the 'Twelve Pubs of Christmas' vomit fest. It was all very far from Newman's *Idea of a University*.

But at weekends, and out of term, and coming up to exam time, the streets were as quiet and pleasant as they had always been, and the student presence meant that there were cafes, well-stocked local shops, hairdressers, even a bank, that might have closed otherwise.

I skirted the edge of the Quad – the abiding superstition was that to cross it would result in certain exam failure – and entered the stone corridor. Leaning against the wall opposite the door to W5, I could hear the lecturer's voice. Though I was unable to make out the words, his timetable had told me that today he was talking about the philosopher George Berkeley who, two centuries or more before, had been bishop of Cloyne, half an hour east of the city.

Within a couple of minutes, the cold of the limestone had permeated my jacket. I stood out from the wall and shook myself warm as students began to file out of the lecture theatre. I went against the flow, not wanting to miss the elusive Dr Lucey. He was standing by the lectern, being subjected to the anxious attentions of two students. Presumably no older than his early thirties, Lorcan Lucey was prematurely grey, with tired-looking white rabbit eyes behind wire-rimmed glasses. I waited until his glance fell on me.

'Are you waiting for me?' he asked.

'Yes,' I said.

'You are?' he said, after the students had gone.

'Finn Fitzpatrick. I left you a couple of voicemails.'

'I don't listen to them. Waste of time.'

There was no point mentioning the message left with the department secretary. Before I had a chance to speak again, Lucey fired another question.

'You want to talk to me because ...?'

'It's about a workshop that I think you did in 1998 at Cork Film Festival, with the film director Jeremy Gill. I represent the parents of one of the other participants, Deirdre Carney. Do you remember the workshop and do you remember her?'

'I remember both,' Lucey said. 'Is that it? Are we done?'

'No,' I said, through gritted teeth. 'If I can buy you a coffee I'll explain.'

'Well, as long as it doesn't take too long, I suppose I *could* go for coffee. Though when I say coffee, I mean tea. Earl Grey, to be precise. Come along now. Let's go to the staff common room. That's our best bet at this time of day, methinks.'

Lorcan Lucey sped off like a beetle, his black gown billowing after him. He dodged around the corner into the north wing, under the stone arch, past the Ogham Stones and up the stone steps. I had to keep up a good pace to stay with him. By the time I got to the common room, he had already taken a seat at a window table. I loved this room, the vaulted ceilings and wood panelling, the views onto the wooded heights of Sunday's Well. Lucey made no move to join me at the counter. It looked like he was used to being waited on. By his mother, presumably.

'You're fit,' I said as I laid the tea things on the table in front of him.

'Fencing,' Lucey said. 'I was auditor of the Fencing Society when I was an undergraduate, and I've kept in practice. *Mens sana in corpore sano.*'

'Dead right,' I said.

Tosser, I thought. Lorcan Lucey was so self-obsessed, he wouldn't notice anything beyond his own nose. This was going to be a complete waste of time.

After Lucey had poured his tea, he spoke again.

'I'm intrigued,' he said.

I repeated the history that I'd given to other potential witnesses, told him about Deirdre's death and asked about his recollections of the workshop. As expected, he had nothing to add to what Jessica Murphy and Joey O'Connor had told me.

'Thanks for your help. I take it that you didn't keep in contact with Deirdre?'

'No, not at all,' Lucey said.

'Different schools, of course,' I said. 'And her life changed considerably after she became ill.'

'So sad, really. I had no idea. I think I only saw her once after the festival, and that wasn't very long after it.'

'Can you remember where you saw her?'

'Out at Muskerry Castle Hotel. We were there for a family occasion, my grandfather's birthday in fact. His seventieth.'

'Did you talk to her?'

'No I didn't. But it stuck in my mind. I was in the lobby and she was walking upstairs towards the bedrooms. I thought it was unusual because I knew she was from Cork. I remember wondering why she was staying in the hotel but I can't say I thought much more about it than that.'

'Was she with anyone?'

'No, she was on her own.'

'Dr Lucey, do you remember when this was?'

'Well, my grandfather's eighty-five now, so …'

'The date, Dr Lucey? Can you remember the date? It's very important, or at least it *might* be.'

I held my breath.

'Well, he has the same birthday now as he always had. That hasn't changed,' Lucey snorted. 'So, yes, it was the 12th of December. The 12th of December 1998.'

41

'Need big favour! Call me ASAP.'

I had sent the text to Davy as I was leaving the university campus, but I was home a while now, and still hadn't heard from him. He was probably at meetings or teaching classes. It could be hours before he saw my message. Still, it was worth waiting for him. He had an 'in' at Muskerry Castle with Ned Foley, the concierge, who could check the hotel's records for the 12th of December 1998. If they still existed. Though they mightn't. But *if* there were records, and *if* they showed a room reservation for Jeremy Gill, or for his then employers Thomson AdGroup, or for Joey O'Connor – he would have had enough money to pay for a room too – then that, along with Lorcan Lucey's sighting of Deirdre at the hotel, was a breakthrough in identifying her rapist. That was something to take to Sean and Ann Carney, something real.

Eventually, Davy called back. When I told him what I wanted, he was matter-of-fact.

'We can't do this over the phone,' he said. 'Meet me at the end of Barrack in ten.'

He was the same when we got out to the hotel.

'Leave it to me,' he said. 'I'll do a bit of preparation work with Ned. He wasn't too fond of you last time we were here, as I recall.'

I bristled, but I knew Davy was right. I went to the bar and ordered a pot of tea for three, hoping that he would be successful in getting Ned to join us, though I had no real doubt that he'd get somewhere with him. People did things for Davy, often without being asked. Ned Foley would roll over and let Davy tickle his belly, but if I asked the same questions he'd double-lock the door and call security.

I looked out the window into the misty, mossy, grey-green of the day. I was close now, I could feel it. But what about Lenihan? Was he following up or ignoring the leads I had given him? He hadn't called me back. And I had been forced to stop texting and calling him after my conversation with Sadie O'Riordan a couple of hours earlier.

I winced at the memory. I was just home from UCC, waiting for Davy to call, when she rang.

'Hiya, listen, Finn, one of the Macbride murder team was on to me to say that Lenihan, well, he wants you to stop contacting him. Except he didn't put it as politely as that. He said you were to let him do his job or he'd have you arrested and charged with interfering with an active investigation.'

'That bastard. He'd have no investigation only for me.'

I stopped then, realising how true that was, in more ways than one. Sadie didn't notice my pause.

'Leave it, Finn, for fuck's sake.'

I knew that I had to. For now, at least. It was just as well that a new avenue had opened up in Deirdre's case or I would have been seriously depressed.

Davy's charm seemed to be deserting him. The tea was stewed and there was still no sign of him, with or without Ned Foley. But, just then, Davy came to the door of the bar. He raised his eyebrows and signalled me to follow him. In the lobby, I found him standing by an open door at the far side and down a short hallway. I crossed to him and shut the door behind me.

We were standing in the library. A fire blazed, and standard lamps illuminated armchairs and sofas set in cosy groups. Ned Foley stood to one side, before a glass-fronted cabinet. Gone was the professional bonhomie of our previous visit. Foley looked serious and determined.

'It's better if I don't know any more than Davy told me. But what he said is enough. I can't get you the room reservation records. They're all archived. Anyway, I don't have that kind of access. But you'll find what you need in here. Make sure to close the case when you're finished and drop the key back to me at the concierge desk. This never happened. But at least you'll know where to look if you come back with an official request for information. Good luck to you.'

Ned Foley glided out of the room in silence, a silence Davy and I didn't break. I made my way towards the cabinet. If there was something in there, it could take days to find it. But, as I got closer, I saw that the leather-bound books had years etched in gold on their spines. They were guest books, I realised. I ran my finger along the row until I reached 1998. There were three volumes. I plucked the third one from the shelf and paged through it until I got to December.

The 11th.

The 12th.

A few entries. Then a full page of angled signatures and autographs.

Thanks for a fantastic shoot, we'll be back.

Thanks Muskerry from Thomson AdGroup.

T.A.G. says TA.

Gill's name or signature wasn't there. Nevertheless, I photographed the page. I could check if any of the comments were in his writing – but it wasn't what I'd hoped for. I turned the page.

The 13th.

Brilliant few days folks. Thanks. Jeremy Gill 13/12/98.

I exhaled slowly. The 13th. Evidence that he had stayed overnight on the 12th, the same night that Lorcan Lucey had seen

Deirdre walking up the stairs to the bedrooms. It hadn't been Joey O'Connor. Jeremy Gill was the one who had raped Deirdre. And his pattern of behaviour was an almost exact copy of what he had done with Rhona. I photographed the page and took a close-up of Gill's message. I felt Davy at my shoulder.

'Who'd believe it?' he said. 'A guy rapes a schoolgirl and takes time to write in the Visitors' Book next morning. Unreal. But, hey, you've got proof now.'

It was a fair point. Who *would* believe it?

'I've got proof of nothing. It's only another piece of circumstantial evidence.'

Davy stepped back from me.

'I'm sorry,' I said. 'What I should have said is that thanks to your efforts ...'

'Thanks to me you've got nothing worth talking about, by the look of it.'

'That's not what I meant. All I meant is that I need more. When you said who'd believe it, it brought it home to me. That's all I meant.'

'Come on, let's go. This place seems to bring out the worst in us,' Davy said.

'The worst in me, maybe,' I said.

Davy didn't say anything to contradict me.

'I didn't mean it the way I said it,' I said, on the way back to town.

'I know,' Davy said. 'I understand. I do. You were talking professionally. I wasn't.'

'That's not what I meant either,' I said. 'You made a good point. A point I should have seen, and instead of accepting it with good grace, I got mad with you.'

'I told you it's fine so would you leave it? You're nearly there. Just be happy.'

'Okay,' I said, but it wasn't fine, and I wasn't happy.

'You're too hard on yourself, you know,' Davy said.

Why was he being nice to me? I didn't deserve it. But I was saved from further self-flagellation by the sound of my phone ringing. It was Garda Ruth Joyce.

'Hi, Ruth. Are you calling to tell me you're charging Joey in relation to my car?'

'Not quite,' she said. 'It *is* about him, though. I wonder if you could come into the Bridewell as soon as possible?'

'Is something wrong?'

'I'll explain when I see you.'

The arson attack on my car had looked like an open and shut, and relatively minor, case, headed for a guilty plea, after I'd fingered Joey on CCTV – so why the urgency?

'I'll be there in fifteen minutes,' I said.

42

There has been a house of correction at the Bridewell since 1731. The old wall of the city stands to the rear of the station and the river flows past the front door. But if Joey O'Connor felt hemmed in by the landscape or the weight of history, he was showing no sign of it.

'This is snug,' he said. 'And we're in out of the rain, I suppose.'

I gave Joey's solicitor, Mark Henchy, an 'is this guy for real?' look.

'Joey, Ms Fitzpatrick is here at your request. She's a busy person. Maybe you could tell her why you asked for her. It's something I'm curious about myself, I must say.'

We were in a small interview room, the three of us. Ruth Joyce was outside. All she had said was that Joey's solicitor had promised his client's full co-operation with her investigation – provided he had a chance to talk to me first. She didn't know what it was about. Neither, it seemed, did the solicitor.

'You don't have to meet Joey,' Ruth had said. 'There's no obligation whatsoever. But, if you like, I could get someone from Victim Support to talk to you to help you decide?'

'I'll be grand.'

Joey was smirking to himself and glancing back and forth between his solicitor and me. Mark Henchy didn't do much criminal defence work. Quietly spoken and unfailingly polite, he was probably the O'Connor family solicitor, possibly even a friend of Joey's parents.

'Joey,' he said. 'Come on.'

'Okay, okay.'

Joey looked at me.

'I want a deal,' he said.

'That isn't the sort of thing you ...' Mark Henchy said.

'What kind of deal?' I asked simultaneously.

Mark looked at me in surprise.

'I want you to drop the charge against me,' Joey said.

'I'm sure what Joey means is that a sum of compensation will be available,' Mark said.

I kept my eyes on his client.

'Doesn't sound like much of a deal,' I said. 'My car was worth about five euros.'

'True,' Joey said. 'I did you a favour by burning that piece of shit.'

Mark Henchy put his head in his hands. I waited for Joey to talk. The mistake I'd made with Carmel, asking the wrong question at the wrong time, I wasn't going to make again.

'You're looking for info,' Joey said. 'If the charge disappears, I'll tell you what I know.'

'Talk first,' I said. 'If the information is of use to me, I'll certainly consider it.'

'Write it down,' Joey said, addressing his solicitor. 'If my info is good, she says I'm out the gap.'

He turned back to me.

'It's good,' he said.

I nodded. My heart was racing. Maybe Joey had seen Deirdre with Jeremy Gill? If so, he could provide the corroboration the case so badly needed. Like I had told Davy, the Visitors' Book entry with Gill's signature was circumstantial evidence at best. More facts were needed to make the Muskerry piece of the jigsaw truly valuable.

'You know how Deirdre told me there was someone else,' Joey said. 'I told you that already.'

'I remember,' I said.

'Yeah, well, I didn't tell you the full story.'

'Joey, where is this going?' Mark Henchy asked.

'It's going exactly where I want it to go, with me walking out that door over there. If I took your advice, I'd end up in Cork Prison. Now let me talk, for fuck sake.'

He paused.

'Where was I? Oh yeah. I said I don't know who she was with. That was a small bit true. I didn't know his name. But I saw him.

I was, ah, I happened to be, em, passing her house. Oh fuck it, I may as well come clean ...'

He laughed bitterly.

'I passed by there a fair bit. A lot.'

He paused again. He had been stalking her, I realised. That was why he hadn't said anything about it before. He stared at me, daring me to make a comment. But I didn't and, after a time, he started talking.

'I cycled by, any chance I got. Before school. After school. During school, sometimes. Going to and from rugby training. And at the weekends. All the time hoping to see her, praying that if I bumped into her, if she saw me, she might change her mind. Anyway, one of the days, I saw her getting dropped off.'

'Dropped off?'

'Yeah. From a car.'

Rhona had said that Gill drove a Toyota.

'Do you remember the make?' I asked.

'Course. A yellow Fiat Cinquecento. 96C. I don't remember the rest of the reg.'

Not a Toyota. And there was no way in hell a card-carrying Dubliner like Gill would drive a Cork-registered car.

'It was a girl's car,' Joey continued. 'But it was a guy driving it.'

'Did you recognise him?'

'I didn't, but he did seem kinda familiar.'

'Can you remember what he looked like?'

'Fat fucker. Brown, light brown hair. Harry Potter glasses.'

I took my phone out of my bag.

'What the fuck she was doing with a loser like him was beyond me,' Joey said. 'I couldn't believe I got dumped for *that*. I told no one. Seriously, it's even hard talking about it now. Only for where I am, I'd have been happy to leave that particular memory buried.'

'Will you take a look at this photo and tell me if this is the man you saw?'

He took the phone and replied immediately, 'Yeah, that's him. But where'd you get the photo?'

I expanded it and handed him the phone again.

'You're in it too,' I said. 'That man is the former education officer of Cork Film Festival. His name is Daniel O'Brien. Do you remember meeting him?'

'No. Maybe. I was so bored at that fucking workshop thing, I remember very little. Hey, he was a good bit older than us, though, like eight or ten years? Maybe he *wasn't* the new guy after all. Maybe she was with someone better.'

She was with someone far worse.

'Was it soon after the festival you saw the drop-off, Joey? Could it have been something to do with Deirdre's work on the festival, her stuff with the youth jury?'

'Coulda been soon after, coulda been later on, coulda been any day of the week,' Joey said. 'It was definitely him, though. So is that enough for me to walk?'

'It's enough for me,' I said.

What Joey had told me did little for my case against Jeremy Gill, but it was new information nonetheless, evidence of a closer bond between Deirdre and Daniel O'Brien than anyone seemed to have realised. I would definitely have to talk to him and find out what he knew. My only link with him was Marie Wade. I needed to shake that tree again.

But first I needed to tell Garda Ruth Joyce that I wasn't proceeding with my complaint against Joey O'Connor. And I wasn't looking forward to the conversation.

As I left the Bridewell, the sky was clear. I decided to walk to the Opera House to see if I could catch Marie Wade after work. On the way there, I passed the steps where Deirdre had walked to her death, but I didn't stop, and I tried not to think about how she must have felt.

I should have paused to pay my respects. Marie had left by the time I arrived.

'Sure, accounts always closes at five,' the box office assistant said in a way that suggested this was a well-known fact.

'I'll know the next time,' I said. 'Thanks. I'll give her a ring.'

But when I stepped back out on to Emmett Place, the rain had started again. I nabbed a taxi on the quay, got in the back as quickly as I could, and sent Marie a text asking her to call me as soon as possible.

Back home, I checked my email. There was a message from Gabriel McGrath requiring me to attend a meeting the following day at the office with him and Dermot Lyons, the partner designated to deal with 'issues arising' from what Gabriel referred to as 'recent unhappy events'. My bad relationship with Dermot was well known. The fact that the rest of partners had chosen him to investigate implied they were against me.

The message invited me to bring a fellow employee to the meeting. An 'investigatory meeting', the message said. It would have been more accurate to call it a preliminary step in a disciplinary process that could end in my dismissal. I leant against the kitchen worktop. Now that it had come, I was surprised by how unafraid I felt.

'Let them try,' I said aloud.

I would go alone to the meeting. I would make an excuse about not being able to get anyone at the last minute or, even better, wanting to keep things confidential. But with me there alone, Dermot would be forced to make an effort to be polite and maintain a veneer of fairness. Otherwise I might be forced to walk out in protest. Or start crying, and then walk.

There was another email. From Alice Chambers. I hoped that it might be a response to the olive branch I had sent. But there was no personal message. Alice was forwarding a letter from the festival chairperson, asking me to a meeting to explain my behaviour during the recent Film Festival and, in particular, my interest in the festival's 'honoured guest'. It was never a good idea to fight a war on two fronts. I composed a two-line letter of resignation from the board and emailed it to the chairperson, cc'ing Alice. I sent a second email to Alice saying I hoped that, in time, we would be able to meet to talk about what had happened. I wouldn't push it. I would wait for her to contact me.

Next, I sent a text to Tina: 'any news on med recs?' and found the number of Setanta Labs. I was about to phone them when Tina's reply came through.

'Got FOI acknowledgement, asked them to expedite. But!!! Lab say DNA tests ready! They're doing report. Heart in mouth here waiting for email. Will forward when thru. ETA 4pm.'

All I had to do was wait an hour. One twenty-fourth of a day. Sixty minutes. Three thousand six hundred seconds.

I ran downstairs to the bathroom and tried to distract myself by brushing my teeth. When that failed, I took the Cif from under the sink and started to scrub the bath. Only fifteen minutes gone. I got an old toothbrush from under the sink, doused it with Flash liquid and started to work my way along the grout around the tiles in the shower. By the time I had finished rinsing off the tiles, shower head in hand, I had almost convinced myself that I could live with a negative result. That a negative result was, in any case, inevitable. And that I had been foolish to think otherwise.

I took off my clothes and stepped into the shower. I remembered that the DNA results would show, too, if Deirdre and I were full or half-sisters, though it didn't much matter any more what the answer was. No more than a spectre at the start, the case had made her real to me. As the water washed my body clean, it came over me what we had missed, what we had lost, by never knowing each other.

I felt a whole new kind of lonely.

43

'Miss Fitzpatrick.'

'It's Finn, Dermot. It's always been Finn until today. What's changed?'

'What's changed is that, prima facie, you've brought this firm into disrepute. Unless you can show grounds for your, to say the least, odd behaviour.'

He adjusted his yacht club tie with one hand and, with the other, smoothed his thinning fair hair. We were in the boardroom at 17–19 MacSwiney Street: first floor, high ceilings, original restored Georgian sashes, enormous marble fireplace, a gracious drawing room in days gone by. Dermot was trying his best to restrain himself, but it was proving difficult. Over the collar of his blue-striped shirt, his fat neck bulged red and a blood vessel throbbed under his left ear.

'What Dermot is saying, Finn, is that we're seeking an explanation from you,' Gabriel said. 'And we're entitled to it, I think you'll agree.'

'I do,' I said.

I leapt to my feet and went to the projection screen at the side of the room.

'I thought it might be easier if I did this visually.'

I smiled at Dermot. He tore a page out of the barrister's notebook on the desk in front of him, crumpled it into a ball and threw it with force on to the long antique table. It rolled on to the floor at my feet. I kicked it out of my way and started the presentation. An image of Jeremy Gill, holding his Oscar over his head, flashed up.

'This is outrageous,' Dermot Lyons said. 'A joke. Abuse of process.'

'It's not meant that way,' I said. 'I'm hoping it'll save a bit of time. I want to make all this as clear as it can possibly be so that you and Gabriel understand exactly what I've been doing for the last while. And why I've been doing it.'

'Make clear? It's abundantly clear already. You've taken on a frivolous and vexatious claim without authority and without any regard for the consequences for this firm.'

'As I said, I want to explain in full what I've been doing. But, in summary, my investigations ...'

'It's not your job to investigate anything,' Lyons said.

'Let her talk, for God's sake, Dermot, or we'll be here all day,' Gabriel said. 'I'm in favour of anything that shortens the matter. It's all terribly unpleasant, I must say.'

'As I was saying, my investigations have led me to the inescapable conclusion that Jeremy Gill is a serial sexual predator. I base this mainly on two statements. The first is from Gill's former friend, the writer Christopher Dalton.'

I clicked into a photo of Dalton.

'The second is from this woman.'

'Who is she?' Gabriel said. 'Her face looks familiar.'

'Her name is Rhona Macbride. She was murdered last week, the day after I met her, after she'd told me that she'd been brutally raped, beaten up and put in fear of her life while she was still a schoolgirl. She acted in Gill's first film. That's how he got to know her.'

I clicked back into the photo of Jeremy Gill.

'*He's* the one who raped her, and he's a suspect in her murder. I need hardly add that this is highly confidential. You can't tell anyone outside this room any of this.'

I paused.

'Any questions so far?'

'*If* any of this is true, which I very much doubt, I must say,' Dermot Lyons said, 'Where's the civil case you're supposedly pursuing? Any murder, any *alleged* murder, is a matter for the Gardaí. And as far as I'm aware from the news reports, it's a drug-related mugging. The idea that ...'

'I agree that Rhona's death is a Garda matter,' I said. 'But the civil case that I've been, yes, Dermot, *investigating* is a wrongful death suit by the parents of a deceased woman, Deirdre Carney, against Jeremy Gill. She died in January this year. She committed suicide following—'

'Preposterous! No claim!' Dermot said, thumping both his fists on the mahogany.

'Be quiet, and listen, Dermot, if you are at all interested in what I have to say.' I made a point of looking at Gabriel before I bent to scribble in my notebook.

'Sorry, I just wanted to note these repeated interruptions.'

Dermot blushed an ecclesiastical purple, took a deep breath, shifted in his chair.

'Go on, please, Finn,' Gabriel said. 'Though I fervently hope you haven't spent office funds on this extremely speculative case.'

'I haven't. Very little. I did a few searches in the CRO and the Land Registry using my office access code. A tiny outlay. My intention was to reimburse the expense on my return to work, if you decide not to support the case further. My hope, of course, is that you will see that there *is* a legitimate cause of action, and that the firm will opt to fund the case, in the usual way, on the basis that the costs will be recoverable ultimately from Gill.'

Before either of them could respond, I clicked into a bullet-pointed summary:

- **Workshop Photograph**
- **Muskerry Castle**
- **Dr Lorcan Lucey**

I took them through a series of slides on the evidence that I had found linking Gill and Deirdre. They weren't convinced. I clicked through to the final slide. It contained just one word:

- **DNA**

'The lab report came back yesterday.'

'I *thought* you said there was little or no outlay,' Dermot said.

'I paid for it on my credit card,' I said. 'It's a private expense.'

Dermot's eyes narrowed.

'And?' Gabriel said. 'Have you a result?'

'Deirdre Carney's DNA is on the drinks coaster. There are two other female DNA samples on it. Not mine – the control sample I gave didn't appear on the coaster. It may be cross-contamination from a hotel employee, or possibly a classmate: she hid the coaster in a mechanical instrument box that she used at school. But there's male DNA too. And it matches the male DNA on the pen that Gill used to sign my programme at the Opera House.'

Silence.

'It's inadmissible,' Dermot said. 'And a breach of his constitutional rights. Not to mention being unethical and an invasion of Gill's privacy. DNA from a pen he used. Utterly out of order. You could be struck off for this.'

'I told you, Dermot. It was a private expense. I never had any intention of using these results against Gill. But the DNA sample I get via discovery in the course of the civil proceedings will be an entirely different matter. If it ever gets that far. I'm inclined to think that Gill's legal team might be keen to enter into early settlement talks with me.'

'It's not enough,' Dermot said. 'Even if we accept all that you have to say, even if we accept that Jeremy Gill sexually assaulted this unfortunate girl ...'

'It was rape and her name was Deirdre Carney,' I said.

'Okay, okay, even if we accept, for the sake of argument, the alleged rape of Deirdre Carney deceased,' Dermot said. 'It was fifteen years ago. How on earth can Jeremy Gill be said to have caused her death?'

'Just a moment, please.'

I went to the phone on the side table and rang Tina's extension.

'We're ready for the medical records.'

'You have medical records?' Gabriel said.

'I collected them in a taxi this morning. There are a lot of them. Two banker's boxes, in fact. Deirdre had a long psychiatric history that started in the months *after* the 12th of December 1998, and none before it. Frequent readmissions. Self-harm. Serious depressive episodes. And a lot of therapy. I was worried that she wouldn't give any details of the attack. As it turns out, my fears were groundless. Her version tallies almost exactly with Rhona Macbride's. How the incident took place in a hotel room, unnamed hotel unfortunately but, as you saw earlier, Lorcan Lucey puts her in Muskerry Castle on the 12th of December, the same night Gill stayed there, according to the guest book, with him leaving on the morning that Ann Carney found her daughter bruised and bleeding, having been out all night. The medical records describe alcohol, and possible sedative use. A threat to kill her if she reported the rape. And the name she refers to him by throughout is 'J'. There are *hundreds* of pages of notes detailing her severe trauma secondary to rape and violence at the hands of her assailant, her inability to pursue a criminal complaint as a result of ongoing psychiatric disability, and her fear for her personal safety if she were to do so. Near the end of her life, she was working with her therapist towards making a report about 'J'. But his Oscar nomination seems to have made her change her mind. That's what her suicide note said. That he's too strong now. She must have thought she'd never be believed.'

There was a knock at the door. I let Tina in.

'Thanks,' I said, and took the box from her.

'These are some of the records. I didn't have time to prepare slides. And I haven't yet obtained a formal psychiatric report but once I get it I'm certain that I will have enough evidence to draft and file the Carneys' claim against Gill. Absent the full psychiatric report, maybe you'll bear with me, Dermot, as I read out a few extracts.'

'Is this necessary?' Dermot said.

'I think it is,' Gabriel said. 'Go ahead, Finn.'

'Before you start, Finn, Detective O'Riordan is in reception for you,' Tina said.

'What does she want?' I said.

'All I know is she's here to collect you. You're wanted in Dublin immediately.'

44

'You're not seriously expecting me to believe that you don't know what this is about?'

'Finn, that's the twentieth time you've asked me and the answer is still the same. Like I said, I was called into Divisional HQ in Anglesea Street to see the Chief Super. And when I met her, worried sick, let me tell you, she tells me that she has a special request from DI Lenihan. And that, because of that request, she wants me to secure your co-operative attendance in Dublin today, soon as. Grand says I, as if I'm going to disagree ...'

She paused, then continued.

'So, I started tracking you down. When you weren't at home or answering your mobile, I said I'd try Tina to see if she knew where you were.'

'And you don't know why he wants me?'

'Well unless Lenihan is suddenly after taking on another case, I'm assuming it's to do with the Macbride murder.'

'Duh. I know that,' I said. 'But what?'

'Look, with cutbacks and everything, there's no way I'd be put doing this job unless there was something big happening. And you'll find out soon enough. Now stop talking and let me concentrate.'

At that, she accelerated through an amber light. I shut my mouth and closed my eyes, and allowed my mind to drift. Sadie was right. There had to be a major break in the case, otherwise we wouldn't be careering at 120 kph through Dublin's outer suburbs.

If the case was really over, then what came next? Probably, hopefully, I'd get my job back, though there were no guarantees. And I would have a lot more time to think, no excuses left. I would have to start facing up to what I had known in my heart for a while now, that I couldn't bear the thought of Davy and me finishing. But if what Davy and I had going on wasn't friendship any more, then what was it?

My phone pinged – a 'Free for a call?' message from Marie Wade. When I'd checked my phone earlier, apart from the missed calls from Sadie and a couple from my mother, there had also been one from Marie, replying to my text message of the evening before. I hadn't yet had a chance to reply, but I did need to talk to her.

'Hey, Sadie, I have to make a call.'

'As long as you're not bothering me with questions I can't answer, work away.'

*

'Hi, Marie. Sorry we've kept missing each other. Have you remembered something?'

'Not exactly. But I've seen something, and I don't know if I've got it right.'

'What did you see?'

'You'll think I'm stupid.'

'I won't, Marie. I promise. What did you see?'

'I think I saw Daniel O'Brien last week. He looked different so that's why it took a good while for me to realise.'

'Where do you think you saw him?'

'At work, in the Opera House,' she said. 'I'd nipped downstairs for a few minutes to have a look at the Jeremy Gill interview, I can't remember which day it was.'

'Wednesday, at noon.'

'That's right,' she said. 'But it was taking ages to get started, it was all applause and stuff, so I had to go back up to my office and when I was on my way out the door of the dress circle, your man was coming in against me.'

'Daniel?'

'Yeah, or the guy I think is him. He said "hi" and smiled and I knew his face but I couldn't remember from where. I thought no more about it until it dawned on me ...'

'Can you describe him?'

'I'll give it a go. He was wearing contacts or he's had laser done on his eyes because he wasn't wearing glasses. He's lost *tons* of weight and he's a lot blonder, but that might be the sun, because he was really brown so maybe he's been living abroad.'

'Can you remember what he was wearing?'

'No, sorry.'

'Can you think of anything else?'

'Not really,' she said. 'It was the smile that brought him back to me. He was always so pleasant, always joking and laughing. That's what made me remember.'

'That's great, Marie. And if you think of anything more at all, will you text me?'

'Okay,' she said. 'But I probably won't. I'm not even sure it was him.'

I was trying to sort through the repercussions of what Marie had said when Sadie veered left into the Garda station car park, drove at speed to the far end and came to a sudden stop just before she hit the wall.

'Come 'on,' she said. 'Come on, wouldya? You know, for the one who was all talk on the way up you're awful reluctant to get out of the car. Why so?'

'That last phone call. I ...'

'Get your arse out of the car, Fitzpatrick.'

'Sadie, I just found out ... Oh, what the hell, I suppose it can wait.'

'O'Riordan and Fitzpatrick to see DI Lenihan,' Sadie said at the public office window.

'I'll buzz yiz straight in. Youse are to go to Interview Room 3.'

'Interview room?' I said to Sadie. 'That doesn't sound very promising.'

'You're a member of the public, Finn. Where else is he going to see you? The Shelbourne Hotel? Don't be getting above yourself, now.'

'Being with you is a real confidence booster, O'Riordan.'

Sadie laughed.

'Don't want you getting a big head is all.'

'I won't make the mistake of offering tea,' Lenihan said as we walked into Interview Room 3. 'I know it's not up to Fitzpatrick's high standards. Anyway, we've no time for pleasantries.'

Lenihan was standing, arms folded, his back to the only window. Apart from a laptop on the table beside him, and three chairs, there was nothing in the room. No files. No notebooks. I tried to work out what was going on, but Lenihan's expression gave nothing away. Grey in the face, there was a nervous caffeinated energy about him. He had been working all the hours. But to what end?

'I was busy over the last few days. I didn't have time to, em, take calls or anything.'

It was the closest I was going to get to an apology from him.

'So did you follow up on the tips I gave you? I deserve to know,' I said.

'Why the fuck do you think you're here? If you stay quiet for two minutes, I'll tell you. The house first. We looked into it. So, yeah, Gill owns it, you were right about that. We got a warrant to search the two houses. Next door is vacant mostly, used only rarely by him as a guest house for when he has visitors in town, apparently. Also, it has a separate basement flat. And the interesting thing is that there's a connecting door between Gill's kitchen and the basement next door ...'

'So Gill *had* rear access to the garden next door.'

'The connecting door was hidden by a dresser that was pulled in front of it when we called there the first time,' Lenihan said. 'We did a full-scale search the second time. Once we found the connecting door, we started looking closer at the place next door. Turns out there's a garage at the end of the garden that opens on to the public road.'

'Which is where Esther keeps her car,' I said.

'Well that's what we were hoping, but the garage was empty so ...'

'Does she have a car? Did you prove that? If she does, it's hidden somewhere.'

'Not so fast. We found that Gill's *company* Gill/Direct owns a Mini Cooper and, when we did another insurance search, we learnt that Esther is insured to drive it.'

'We need to find that car,' I said. 'It *has* to be the car he used. He drove the Mini to Rhona's house the morning of the murder and then dumped it somewhere, and got back into his house via the basement next door, and got an alibi from the mother. Now that you know the car, surely you can find it on traffic cameras and CCTV. There must be footage of him driving it when he's supposed to be at home with his mother.'

'That's what we thought too. Turns out we were wrong. Your pal Jeremy Gill didn't drive anywhere that morning ...'

'What are you saying?'

Lenihan grabbed a chair, sat at the table, and opened his laptop. Sadie and I pulled up the other two chairs either side of him.

'We found footage of the Mini at various points on the route between Clontarf and Rhona's place. See this, where the Mini turns off by Peter's Church. We got a good shot of the driver there.'

'Jesus,' I said.

'I always knew that an Irish mammy would do anything for her son but this is beyond the beyond,' Sadie said.

'It's Esther? Esther killed Rhona?' I said.

'Wait,' Lenihan said.

He clicked into the next photo. It showed a hooded figure in the passenger seat beside Esther Gill.

'She drove him,' I said. 'She drove her son and *watched* while he killed Rhona.'

'He kept his head bent most of the time so we haven't got a good image, apart from this one. This one was taken near Gaffneys' pub in Fairview, he looks relaxed, job done.'

The enhanced photo showed a close-up of Jeremy Gill's blond assistant.

'Boyband,' I whispered.

I couldn't believe it. I got up from the table and walked to the window and pressed my forehead against the cool of the glass and closed my eyes.

45

Lenihan and Sadie were talking about Esther's Mini when I turned around again.

'It's with the Technical Bureau,' Lenihan said. 'They're going over it with a fine-tooth comb. We found it parked two streets away. We reckon Esther parked it in the garage when she got back first but that it was moved from there later, just in case.'

'Either she was confident it'd never be traced,' Sadie said. 'Or she didn't want to draw attention to it by burning or dumping it somewhere.'

'Exactly,' Lenihan said.

'Are they under arrest?' I asked.

'Esther is,' Lenihan said. 'She's at this station. Gill is too. Voluntarily. Boyband, as you call him, has disappeared. That's why

I got you up here. To see if you have any idea where he might be. Cos I fucking don't.'

'Is Esther saying anything? Is she admitting ...?' I asked.

'She's admitting very little. She's claiming she was forced to drive him. That he had a carving knife as well as the screwdriver he used to kill Rhona. She says he looked and acted like he'd lost his mind, either drugs or a breakdown, she says. He came into her kitchen from his basement flat next door. She says the connecting door was never locked and that's why they had to pull the dresser in front of it later, to keep him out, not to hide the connecting door. She says he left straight after the murder. That she was terrified, alone, vulnerable and that Gill was asleep up in bed all the time. He's backing her up 100 per cent. He says he only found out about the murder afterwards and that all he's guilty of is giving his poor old ma an alibi, he was just trying to keep her out of jail. He says she's in poor health, and he was afraid she'd die in prison.'

'He's still an accessory after the fact,' Sadie said.

'Is he?' I asked. 'Would a jury convict him for trying to protect his mother? If they believe that Esther acted under duress, under the threat of being killed herself, she might be acquitted. And, if she's acquitted, Gill might walk too.'

'I agree,' Lenihan said. 'We need to concentrate on the primary—'

'I'll be back in a minute,' I said. 'I have to make a call.'

I went out to the street for air, found Tiernan McDevitt's number in my phone, and sent a text, asking if he was free to take a call. He replied 'who this?' which I took as a yes and rang him.

'Hi, Tiernan, it's Finn Fitzpatrick, we met last week in Cork Opera House.'

'Yes, and you bought me lunch. It's nice to talk to you again, I …'

'Remember the blond guy you were talking to, you said he was Gill's assistant?'

'Well, yeah, I do, but …?'

'Do you know his name?'

'It's Donnie. His last name is, um … let me think …'

'Might it be O'Brien?'

'I'm not sure,' Tiernan said. 'It could be something like that.'

'How long has he worked for Gill?'

'Years, like ten years, twelve years, probably more. He wasn't involved when we were making the short film. But he was hanging around a lot when Jeremy went to the Oscars that first time.'

'That was about six months after the short had been shown at Cork Film Festival the previous October?'

'Yes. I was on the periphery by then, but I recall seeing him at a cast and crew celebration when Jeremy got back from Hollywood, some time, maybe around the end of March? I wasn't talking to Donnie, but I couldn't help seeing him. He acted like he was Jeremy's devoted puppy. He looked a lot different back then, though. He was fatter, wore those Harry Potter glasses, and his hair—'

'How did Donnie and Jeremy know each other?'

'They were both working in Thomson AdGroup. At least, I *assume* that's how they got to know each other. Maybe they were friends before that. Then Jeremy got super-successful, needed an assistant and Donnie got lucky. He and Jeremy are extremely close. Donnie's a minder as much as an assistant. If Jeremy goes a little too far, like he did with me in the interview at the Opera House in Cork, good old Donnie swoops in to sort things out.'

'Sort things out?'

'He's diplomatic, gets on with everyone. Jeremy rubs someone up the wrong way, Donnie makes everything okay again. It's a job I wouldn't want no matter how big the pay cheque was. But Donnie likes it, I presume, or he'd have left a long time ago.'

'And he knows all about Jeremy for the last ten, twelve years, maybe longer?'

Tiernan gave a hollow laugh.

'Oh yeah,' he said. 'Donnie knows where the bodies are buried.'

I tried to process what I'd discovered. The former Film Festival education officer Daniel O'Brien was now calling himself 'Donnie' and had been working for Jeremy Gill for a decade plus. They might or might not have met for the first time in Cork, but somehow Donnie ended up working in the same ad company as Gill six months after the 1998 Film Festival. Maybe Gill got Donnie the job, or maybe he applied for it himself? And Daniel/Donnie had no presence on LinkedIn or any other social media because he didn't need the profile, and there was probably a strict privacy condition under his contract of employment. But none of that mattered.

What *did* matter was that, according to Tiernan, Donnie cleaned up Gill's messes.

And that Gill and his mother were saying that Donnie had forced Esther Gill to drive him to Rhona's house where he had murdered her.

I thought it through. It was certainly plausible. From what Tiernan was saying, Donnie had to know about his boss's sexual appetites. And it was highly likely that Pawel the security guard reported to Donnie rather than to Gill directly – Lenihan would need to check that to be sure of it. But assuming that's how it had happened, Donnie could have heard from Pawel about me visiting Rhona. He could have seen the danger and taken the initiative. And killed Rhona. To protect his job, his position? To protect Gill? A jury might go for that story.

Then I remembered what Tiernan had said: 'He wasn't involved when we were making the short film.' How would Donnie have known the significance of me visiting and talking to Rhona Macbride unless he had discussed it with Gill? He might have put it together eventually. But so fast? She was murdered barely twelve hours after I'd met her.

Gill, on the other hand, would have spotted the risk immediately. The three of them – Esther, Donnie and Jeremy – had to have planned Rhona's murder together.

But how was I ever going to prove it?

When I went back inside, Lenihan and Sadie were still in the interview room. They'd been joined by two other members of the murder team that Lenihan didn't waste time introducing.

'Well, Fitzpatrick,' he said. 'Any idea where we might find Bryant?'

'Bryant?'

'Christ,' Lenihan said. 'Rhona Macbride's murderer, remember him? Donnie Bryant. US citizen. Still in this fair land, for now at least, as far as we know.'

'Why do you think he's still in Ireland?'

'Because we found his passport. One of ye lads show her, for fuck sake.'

The taller of the two detectives pulled a plastic evidence bag from his suit jacket and handed it to me. The bag contained a blue American passport issued to Donnie Bryant, date of birth 4th March 1978.

'Is it real?'

'First thing we checked. It's real but ...' Lenihan said.

'Good,' I said. 'Then the date of birth could be real too. But he must have an Irish passport as well. Look at the place of birth: Ireland.'

'That's the second thing we checked. There's no record of a Donnie or Donald or Donal Bryant born in Ireland on the 4th of March 1978. The passport's real but he must have got it under an assumed name. We've put in a request and we're waiting for info on him to come back from the American authorities. But I reckon he built up a false identity. He could have done it over years, maybe.'

'It makes sense,' I said. 'He changed everything about himself. Of course he'd have changed his name too. But you need to be searching for him under his original name now. Donnie Bryant may have acquired US citizenship, but he's not American. He's Irish. He's the ex-education officer of Cork Film Festival. And his real name is Daniel O'Brien.'

46

Marie Wade had been right in her recollection: the former education officer was from Clare, from the Gort Road in Ennis. Estranged from his family following his parents' acrimonious separation, he had studied art in Limerick and worked a succession of short-term jobs before meeting up with Jeremy Gill in Cork in 1998.

The guards found Donnie Bryant at Shannon Airport, in the queue for a Ryanair flight. If he had made it to Lanzarote, he could have lived very comfortably at Esther Gill's holiday apartment for a long time without being caught. He had enough cash on him to last several months and he had dyed his hair dark brown. He had on Ray-Ban Wayfarer sunglasses and a 'Dodgers' official merchadise baseball cap turned backwards. But his Irish passport gave his name as Daniel O'Brien. And he was going nowhere.

*

Disappointingly, the station didn't have one of those two-way mirrors you see on the TV cop shows. Instead, Sadie and I were hunched over a laptop in Lenihan's office, watching a live feed from Interview Room 3, now occupied by Donnie Bryant and his solicitor, and Lenihan and one of the detectives Lenihan hadn't introduced me to.

I was glad that Donnie had been caught, but I wasn't at all happy with what he'd been saying ever since. Still talking in that ridiculous Californian accent, he had made a full confession, taking on all responsibility for Rhona's death; for everything, it seemed. Lenihan hadn't yet asked Donnie if he knew where Shergar was, but I had a hunch he'd admit to the horse's kidnap if he thought it might help Jeremy. Donnie absolved the Gills of all guilt, including the allegations of sexual misbehaviour made by Christopher Dalton. Donnie had never seen any of that: Jeremy was a gentleman who never laid a finger on anyone. That part would be easy enough to disprove, and would damage Donnie's credibility, but he was sticking solidly to the story that he had acted alone, and that Esther had driven him in fear of her life.

'Why did you kill Rhona, Donnie?' Lenihan kept asking.

'I did it,' Donnie kept replying. 'It's none of your business *why* I did it. Jeremy and Esther had nothing to do with it. It was *my* idea. They just got caught up in my madness. I want to do everything I can to make it up to them. They've been so good to me. I don't want them to spend another second in this awful place. I want you to charge me with the murder of Rhona Macbride. I know my rights. You have to charge me or you have to release me. You can't keep a suspect here indefinitely when you have enough evidence to charge.'

Unfortunately, Donnie was right. The clock was ticking. If there wasn't a break soon, he'd be heading for court, charged with Rhona's murder, and Esther and Jeremy would be released and their file sent to the DPP. They might end up being charged with nothing. The DPP only brings forward charges where there's a reasonable chance of conviction. The way Donnie was talking? I wouldn't bet on ever seeing the Gills in the dock.

In fairness to Lenihan, he was dogged. He was walking Donnie back through his story for the tenth or twelfth time, excavating any inconsistency, hoping he might start to become complacent.

'Tell me again how you got to Shannon.'

'You know this already.'

'Humour me, Donnie. I'm just doing my job. And this is the last time, I promise.'

'Okay, Inspector Lenihan,' Donnie said. 'As you *well* know, I drove to Shannon.'

'What kind of car do you drive?'

'As you *well* know, I drive a 2013 Alfa Romeo Giulietta Sportiva.'

'Small,' Lenihan said.

I sat up. Lenihan was going off script.

'It's a beautiful car, Inspector Lenihan. Beautifully designed. Anyway, I'm not here in Ireland much. I drive a bigger car back home in Los Angeles.'

'Another Alfa?'

'Yes, as it happens.'

'I drive a Passat,' Lenihan said. 'Very reliable.'

'Reliable but dull,' Donnie said.

'You can't beat the Germans, though. When I've some money, I'm getting a Merc.'

'You've no romance in you, Inspector. I've always driven Italian cars.'

'Yeah?'

'Even when I hadn't a bean, I had style.'

'Yeah?'

'My first car was a Fiat, a yellow Cinquecento,' Donnie said.

'*Hang* on,' I shouted. 'A yellow Cinquecento. That's the car Joey O'Connor saw him driving. Dropping Deirdre off at her house …'

'What?' Sadie asked. 'What has this to do with anything?'

'Where did I put my fucking phone?'

'Here's your fucking phone,' Sadie said. 'Are you okay? You look …'

I grabbed the phone from her and started scrolling through my pictures until I found the one I was looking for. My fingers shaking, I enlarged it.

'Thanks be to God,' I said. 'Poke your head in the door of the interview room, Sadie – I can't do it, Donnie would recognise me – and tell Lenihan I've got something and that I need to talk to him *now*.'

'What have you got?' Sadie asked.

'Proof that Daniel "Donnie" O'Brien stayed in Muskerry Castle with Thomson AdGroup in 1998. He signed the guest book. I have a photograph of his signature. The 12th of

December 1998. The same night Jeremy Gill raped Deirdre Carney. Joey O'Connor saw Donnie – Daniel O'Brien, as he was then – dropping Deirdre Carney home in his Cinquecento. Joey can't say when he saw it happening, but Donnie doesn't know that. And I know in my heart and soul it was the morning after the rape. That fucker Donnie, he's not just protecting Gill now, he's been protecting him, enabling him, all along. For *years*. Donnie's the organiser, the manager. He *must* want to tell that story.'

It took a little longer than I'd hoped to convince Lenihan, and it took even longer than that for Donnie to start talking. Sadie and I were watching the interview on-screen in Lenihan's office and for a while we were losing hope.

'I know you've explained before,' Lenihan said. 'But I still can't figure out what your job was.'

'Assistant, like I've told you about fifty times.'

'Like some kind of a secretary?'

'No. I was Jeremy's personal assistant.'

'Picking up his dry-cleaning kind of assistant?'

'That was *not* my job. I had no domestic duties.'

'O-kay,' Lenihan said. 'Putting petrol in the car, maybe?'

'No.'

'I don't get it. Not a secretary. No domestic duties. No general duties. Nothing that sounds like anything. Oh, hang on, am I missing something here, was it some kind of a Rock Hudson scenario?'

Donnie sighed.

'I might have expected you'd be homophobic as well as stupid,' he said. 'For the record, Jeremy Gill is not gay and neither am I.'

'For the record could you tell me what the fuck you were getting paid for, so?'

'We had a strictly professional relationship.'

'Professionally doing sweet fuck all by the sound of it.'

'No no *no*,' Donnie said. 'I worked hard. Nothing happened without me.'

'You mean you were like a producer or something?'

'It's a simplistic analogy but you could put it like that, I suppose.'

'Have you a better way of putting it?'

'Maybe first assistant director is a better analogy.'

'Sounds menial.'

'Only someone who knows *nothing* about the film business would think that. A first A-D runs the set, the logistics, the whole fucking thing, you fucking dope.'

'And that's what you did?'

'Yes.'

'But for Gill *personally*.'

'Yes.'

Lenihan sat back in his chair and scratched his head.

'I still don't understand it,' he said. 'But it sounds like some cushy number.'

'*Cushy* is the *last* thing it was, you fucking ignoramus,' Donnie said. 'Jeremy would have been caught years ago only for me. He thinks he's invincible and that he can do anything but he needs a support team. Genius is genius, but genius needs help. His mother knew that too. You know, right at the beginning, Jeremy didn't understand why Rhona had to die. With the arrogance that makes him a great director, all that certainty, he was sure she'd keep quiet, like she had done all these years. But the risk was too great. Eventually he saw that, eventually we persuaded him. Well, his mother did. She made him see that Rhona had more on him than any of the others. He was still doing it DIY back then with Rhona, doing the collecting in his own car, that old Toyota, doing the drop-off after. That was the *very* first thing I changed. Right from what's her name, the girl in Cork in that great hotel, Muskerry Castle. It was really nice being back there recently, actually.'

'The girl from Cork? You're talking about Deirdre Carney?'

'Yes, Deirdre, that was her name. She was a fighter. All talk about reporting Jeremy on the way back from the hotel. Until I explained to her that no one would ever believe her. And told her what would happen if it ever went to court. In intimate detail. You know, all the usual stuff, about how it's the victim who's on trial, really.'

He paused.

'Tell me I'm wrong.'

Lenihan shrugged.

'You see, you can't,' Donnie said. 'That's what I told Deirdre, how she'd never recover, all of that. I was good at it and I got better over the years. I had to. I learnt on the job. A steep learning curve *that* was, I can tell you. Jeremy, well, he's a handful. Once he gets a fixation on one of them, he has to follow through. That Carmel from the workshop, she was next in line, once the coast was clear. He wasn't going to do anything until it *was*, obviously. He's got his, em, well, weaknesses, but he's not a fool. He was able to wait, he was *always* able to wait once he knew that it was going to be worth his while.'

'And Rhona? Her death?'

'She would have ruined everything if she'd talked. That's why she had to go. He knew we were right. He saw it. He was grateful. And Esther ... We were, we *are*, so close.'

'Who planned it?'

'What?'

'Rhona's murder?'

'Well, Jeremy did, of course. Something big like that? I know my limitations. No, Jeremy was reluctant at first but once he'd decided, he swung into action. And it worked with *military* precision, right down to the last detail. I was really nervous. But having Jeremy on speakerphone in the car all the way to Rhona's house and back, my nerves disappeared. He's a great actors' director, you know. Everyone says that.'

'I'm sure he'll be a great addition to the prison drama group,' Lenihan said.

47

Stone built, with classic proportions, Ionic columns, and black cast-iron gates and railings to the front, the place looked innocent enough, if you didn't know better. But Green Street Courthouse was a fortress, set squat on a narrow street, easily controllable at both ends. There were two small front doors, but only one was open to the public, and that could be closed fast at the first hint of trouble. The side yard was surrounded by walls too high to climb and topped with metal spikes in case anyone was foolish enough to try.

Inside, the bitter tang of disappointment tainted the air. If you were in the dock here, you were probably going down. In the old days, that meant hanging, transportation to Van Diemen's Land, or maximum security in Portlaoise Prison. More recently, since the Special Criminal Court had moved to

Parkgate Street, the place had gone soft. Drug Court was held here now, where judges and probation officers worked with long-term addicts who wanted to get clean, stay out of jail, and live a better life.

But Drug Court had finished for the day. It was after five, and it was night. I gazed through the Georgian windows at the black of the sky. There is a very particular atmosphere in a courtroom after dark. During regular daylight hours, anyone might ramble in for a look: tourists, schoolkids, nosy pensioners, under-employed lawyers, time-killers of various kinds. When it's late, it's different. All the people in the courtroom have a stake in the proceedings. At a special sitting, a case that can't wait till morning, everyone knows that something important and extraor-dinary is about to happen. I could taste it, that peculiar combination of anticipation and privilege. We would know the story before anyone else, see it, and hear it. Along with a small number of favoured reporters and court staff, legal teams and guards shuf-fled papers, exchanged looks, or talked quietly in the body of the court, but the scene wasn't as Gill would have directed it. There had been no waiting supporters, no cheers, no rounds of applause. I had watched the Garda van as it drove into the side yard. Televi-sion cameras had filmed its arrival, but there would be no shot of Gill walking in, and no photography was permitted in the build-ing. There wasn't even a court artist, though there would be one at the trial. For now, Gill had lost control of his image. He would enter the court the same as any ordinary accused person. I sat alone on a bench, in a high corner of the public gallery, and waited.

Darkest Truth

At about ten past five, the door at the far side of the court opened and a female Garda in uniform walked through, followed by Esther Gill, and Sadie O'Riordan. A hush fell over the room. Whoever had chosen Esther's court clothes had done her no favours. She must have asked for a suit, but she couldn't have meant this one, a baby-blue spring wedding coat and dress with a thin flower print chiffon scarf that did nothing to protect her from the biting cold. Despite the make-up, her skin was almost the same colour as her outfit, but she had two faint spots of pink blusher on her cheeks, like an antique china doll. Her hair, normally big and over-styled, was so flat and thin that I could see her skull. The crowd parted before her. The first Garda helped her up the steps to the dock, and sat behind her. Sadie stood on the floor below, in silence.

A few minutes later, Gill climbed the stairs from the cells and emerged in the dock. He was wearing a dark grey business suit, with a mid-blue shirt and a navy and red striped tie. Were it not for his trademark long hair, he would have been indistinguishable from the male lawyers present. He took his place beside his mother. I had a side view of his face. His jaw stiff, he stared straight ahead at the vacant judge's chair. His mother whispered to him, he nodded, and resumed staring at the same spot. His solicitor left his seat at the front of the courtroom below the judge's desk, walked down to the dock, and muttered something to Gill. He bent to listen, but didn't reply. It was unnerving, the silence, the fixed gaze, so different from his garrulous public persona. Proceedings hadn't started but, when they could bear to drag their eyes away from him, the journalists were already scratching at their notebooks.

Finally, as Gill had, Donnie entered the dock from below. He was dressed, as he had been at the station, in sun holiday clothes. He shivered in his seat, holding his baseball cap in his hand, and stared at the floor. Gill and Esther ignored him entirely.

At twenty past five, the judge took his seat, and the hearing began. Evidence of arrest, charge and caution was given by the guards who had been tasked with formally arresting Gill, Esther and Donnie. Lenihan stood at the side watching for any errors or forgotten details, ready to prompt the prosecutor if needed. But there was little to be done. There would be no bail hearing, as bail in a murder case can only be granted by the High Court, though the various defence solicitors confirmed that applications would be filed as soon as possible. The judge nodded, took a note for the court file and remanded Jeremy Gill and Donnie Bryant in custody to Cloverhill Prison. Sure to be considered a flight risk, they would have a hard time getting out again before the trial. Esther was remanded to the Women's Prison at Mountjoy. She'd get a comfortable berth in the Dochas Centre, given her age.

'Any further applications?'

Gill stood and opened his mouth. The judge spoke first.

'Mr Gill, I think that's what your solicitor is for.'

Gill's solicitor shook his head, but his client started to speak. I wondered if this was what the lawyer had said before court, that Gill should stay quiet and refrain from speech-making. If that's what it was, he was ignoring the advice.

'I'll be very, very brief, judge. Thank you for the time. I want the people of Ireland to know that I love them and I love this great country still, even after what has happened today. The establishment has never liked me, and they've tried to bring me down before. They didn't succeed then, and they won't succeed now. I put my faith in the constitution and in the jury of my fellow Irishmen and women that I will be happy to have stand in judgment over me, and I want every one of them to know now that I am completely innocent of this abominable charge, this travesty of justice, as is my mother. *I* am the victim here, and I will fight this horrible calumny, this stain on my character until my dying breath and I ...'

'Mr Gill, you would be far better advised to save that kind of talk for your consultations with your solicitor and your counsel. I'll rise now.'

When the judge had left the room, Gill looked in the direction of the press benches, half raised his left arm and fist in a gesture of defiance, then turned his back on them and the courtroom. The show had finished, and the journalists knew it. As one, they leapt to their feet and started to make their way outside.

Donnie went back down to the cells immediately and I saw Esther mouth the words 'good job, son' to Gill and he bent to kiss her before she was taken away. But after she had left, as the courtroom emptied, he seemed to turn in on himself for a moment. He held on to the railing, his skin dull with fatigue. I remembered how he had been on that morning in my kitchen, and how frightened of him I had been then.

No longer. I saw him now for what he was, and I saw what he would become. It was over for him – his power, his riches, his great success, all of it. He would never admit his guilt, and it didn't matter. He would fully contest the case against him, and he would fail.

The attending Garda touched Gill's elbow, but he made no move towards the stairs. I stood to go, and he must have heard something because he glanced up at the public gallery, empty except for me. He hadn't known I was there, I think, and when he saw me his eyes widened, very slightly.

Almost instantly, he straightened and his face became a mask again, hard and unyielding. He turned towards me, his back to the guard and the people in the well of the court below, and the rest of the world fell away. Gill brought his left hand to his throat and drew his index finger right to left across the base of his neck. He smiled at me then, and kept smiling as the custody guard put his hand on his shoulder and guided him down to the cells.

I stood my ground and kept watch until Jeremy Gill had vanished, as completely as if he had descended into hell.

48

10th March 2014

'If you'd held out, you could have done better,' I said.

'We wanted it over,' Sean Carney said. 'And what we got is worth more than any money to us.'

'It's a symbol,' Ann said. 'Even if we can't tell anyone about it until after the criminal case.'

'And maybe never,' I said. 'If Gill isn't convicted in the murder trial, the terms of the settlement mean you'll have to stay silent for ever.'

'I know,' Ann said. 'And he's never going to be convicted for what he did to Deirdre. Still, it's some recognition. It means more than I imagined. And he *will* be convicted, I know he will.'

*

The Rhona Macbride murder trial was fixed to start in early May. I wouldn't be involved much, I reckoned. Even though I had been listed as a State witness, it was likely that the Gills' legal teams would argue that my evidence should be excluded for fear of prejudicing the jury. If they succeeded, *Another Bad Day at the Office* would provide evidence that Gill knew Rhona but, as with all criminal trials, the jury would have to adjudicate on the basis of the evidence before them, and nothing else.

The background about Gill and Deirdre would come out only after the trial. There would be more prosecutions too, and civil cases. After he was charged with Rhona's murder, other victims had felt safe enough to come out of the shadows, in Ireland, and also in the United States. I hoped that one of them was the girl from Winterville in New York State, the girl Christopher Dalton had told me about, though I didn't know. The upcoming trial meant that a lid was being kept on publicity about additional complaints. But once the trial was over, there would be no way back for him. I had had new client enquiries already in relation to personal injury claims against Gill, and in other similar cases. I had even received a few referrals courtesy of DI Lenihan, which surprised me no end. Though when I rang to thank him, he didn't take the call, which surprised me less.

Garda Ruth Joyce's tenacious investigation had led to the solving of the string of arson attacks that had plagued Cork during 2012 and 2013. After I had dropped my complaint against Joey O'Connor, Ruth had re-examined the footage from previous burnings and found that Joey had an unfortunate and inconvenient habit of being in the neighbourhood of several of the attacks. When confronted with the evidence, he admitted finally that he had been responsible for torching not just my car but all the rest as well, his only selection criteria being that the car owners had visited his car showroom and not bought a car. And that he hadn't liked them. He wasn't prosecuted for my car, but he was done for the rest. He pleaded guilty and, unlike after his previous prosecution, got jail time. But, with a discount for his co-operation and plea, he could be out in as little as eighteen months.

We walked down the steps of the courthouse and on to Washington Street. The settlement discussions hadn't taken long in the end. The Carneys had pressed me to seek an admission from Jeremy Gill of what he had done to Deirdre, rather than a larger damages payout without an admission. Soon after Gill's arrest, I had obtained a Mareva injunction, preventing him from dissipating his assets pending the resolution of the Carneys' claim. Understandably, as he didn't qualify for legal aid, Gill and his legal team wanted the order lifted, and I was able to set up early settlement negotiations as a result. There was a gagging order on the Carney settlement until after the criminal trial, but it was enough for Sean and Ann that the concession had been made. For them, the case had never been about the money.

At the foot of the steps, Sean turned to me.

'All I ever wanted was to warn others about Jeremy Gill. To make sure that he wouldn't hurt another girl, like he did Deirdre. I blame myself, you know. Right back at the very beginning, if

I'd listened to Ann, maybe the two of us could have persuaded Deirdre to go and report what had happened. But I didn't even try. I didn't want her hurt any more. I thought we could mind her. I thought we could make her better. There was a time later, too, when she might have … It was only a few weeks before she died, she came to me and she talked around in circles but, as I look back on it, I think, no, I know that's what she was saying, that she wanted to go to the guards then. If I'd been brave enough, I could have helped her. And she might still be alive. You could have met your sister. And we would still have our daughter. I didn't want her to go through the pain and the public shame of a trial after so many years had gone by. But I was wrong, so wrong.'

It fitted with what Deirdre's psychiatric records had said – that she had been building towards naming her assailant and making a report. There had been no mention in the notes of a conversation with her father, though. Maybe it hadn't been as important to her as it seemed to Sean in retrospect, but there was no way of knowing.

He started to cry, and I remembered the November night that we had met, and how he had wept on the street in front of my office. I looked at Ann. Her eyes were filled with tears. She shook her head. She knew about regret. I did too. I knew it didn't help anyone and that it never went away.

'You did your best, Sean,' I said. 'And at least Gill is a danger to nobody now. He's on remand in Cloverhill. Assuming he's convicted, he's facing a mandatory life sentence. He'll be inside for a long time.'

Ann took hold of my hand.

'Don't be a stranger, Finn,' she said.

I walked in silence with the Carneys to the corner of South Main Street, the same street Sean and I had taken together that first night on the way to Forde's pub. We stopped for a moment and both of them hugged me. Then we parted without a word. There was nothing left to say.

Legally, the case had ended successfully, but Deirdre was never coming home.

EPILOGUE

29th May 2014

I was at my desk, staring out the window at the rooftops and the sky, and waiting, waiting. When the call came at last, I messaged Davy to let him know the news and said I'd talk to him more when I met him later. We saw each other most days. In my mind, I still wasn't calling what we had going on between us a 'relationship'. But the rest of the world probably would.

My feet took me down the stairs to MacSwiney Street, along Liberty Street and on to Castle Street. Had Deirdre walked this way on the last evening of her life? I thought about her all the time, and about Rhona, who would still be alive if I hadn't visited her that one time.

Darkest Truth

By the time I got to the Roundy, other people knew the news too: it had come through on their phones. Early evening drinkers waved at me from sunlit tables, and gave me the thumbs-up. I'm famous now. I had had to give evidence after all. Cornered, Gill had gone on the attack – on Donnie and on me. I had spent three whole days in the witness box being cross-examined by his very expensive silk. Allegations of unprofessional behaviour were the least of it. He tried to target my mental state, brought up again the allegations he had made that I had threatened him and put him in fear, tried to suggest I had planted evidence.

And the jury had bought none of it. Their verdict was unequivocal: Donnie Bryant and Jeremy Gill guilty of murder and Esther Gill guilty too. The truth about the twisted dynamic that had bound the trio together for so many years would remain a mystery, but special supplements were planned for the weekend's papers, a 'tell all' television documentary was in production, and a hastily assembled true crime book was almost ready to go to press. I had been asked to give interviews, to tell my side, to write my own book. Several ghost writers had offered their services. My star had risen in the office too, now that I was bringing in more high-paying work, and getting publicity for the firm. Dermot Lyons greeted me civilly whenever we met on the stairs or in the coffee-room. I had even been asked back on to the Film Festival Board.

I had declined all invitations.

But I had put out feelers to the Macbrides, had said that I would like to meet them. Word had come back, via Sadie, that Mrs

Macbride wasn't ready to meet me, and that she might never be. I knew about that kind of unready, knew it all too well, had known it since I was sixteen, when I had first found out about my mother's suicide.

Now, that knowledge was no longer enough. After all this, I needed to know more about where I had come from. I needed to know about my birth mother, about who she had been before she had been an alcoholic, a diagnosis, a label. The search might take a long time, and wouldn't be easy on me, I knew. But it would be equally hard on my mam and dad. What I had told them about Deirdre had come as a shock at the start. They hadn't known that I had a half-sister, hadn't been told about her by my birth mother. They hadn't found out either from the social workers during the adoption process. At first, I hadn't fully believed that, though I hadn't said anything to them about my doubts. I had gone away and investigated on my own, had asked a colleague who worked in Child Protection about a hypothetical case involving a double adoption, preceded by fostering. She had told me that not only was it possible, it was likely that foster or adoptive parents wouldn't know about a later sibling. She had said that things like that happened all the time. I had left it at that, tried to get on with things. I didn't know how long it would take for me to get used to being alive while Deirdre was dead. Maybe I never would.

I went down Cornmarket Street and, as I had often done those long months since November, on to the Coal Quay. Along from the footbridge, at the place where my sister had gone with the river, I looked down into the Lee, its waters still and quiet now. I counted the steps of the stone staircase, exposed to the air by the low tide. But, after a time, I turned my back to the river and leant against the quay wall. Hearing a ping, I checked my phone. It was a message from Davy.

Good news about the trial. Great excuse for me to cancel a couple of yummy mummies. See you at your place around 6.30. OK?

Smiling, I sent him a one-word reply.

Yes.

Acknowledgements

I want to thank everyone who encouraged and supported me on the road to *Darkest Truth,* particularly my agent Luigi Bonomi and all at LBA Books; my publisher Selina Walker and all at Cornerstone, Penguin Random House UK and Penguin Ireland especially my editor Sonny Marr (Sonny, Selina and Luigi knocked the book into shape and allowed me to be far braver than I could ever have been on my own); my copy-editor Beth Humphries, Grace Long, and cover artist Emma Grey Gelder; the judges and organisers of the Penguin Random House UK and Daily Mail First Novel competition; my friends, colleagues and clients at Finbarr Murphy Solicitors and throughout the Cork legal community (by the way, everything in the book is completely made up, including a few locations, and not based on real people or legal cases; also the errors in the book are my own – and some are intentional); Nick Daly who, with great fortitude and kindness, read chunks of the earliest version of this book as it was going along; all the members of the Ulysses Reading Group whose ridiculously positive reactions to my weekly posts boosted my confidence enormously; Cork's amazing reading, writing and creative community and its arts and literary institutions including Corcadorca, the Munster Literature Centre and Cork International Short Story Festival, the Cork World Book Festival, the City Library, the County Library, the 'From the Well' competition, Fiction at the Friary, Crosstown Drift (and Cork Midsummer Festival), West Cork Literary Festival, UCC School of English and Waterstone's Cork; Cork's various film festivals and film organisations (especially the oldest of them, Cork Film Festival, to which the Film Festival in this book bears much resemblance, though there are some differences); my book club friends who helped me to read better; and Alison Bonomi, Ann Luttrell, Anna Kelly, Billy O'Callaghan, Brian Murphy, Carol Quinn, Carys Davies, Christine Moore, Claire Connolly, Claire Kilroy, Colm Roberts, Danielle McLaughlin, Deirdre Kingston, Diarmaid, Miah and Nora Falvey, and Mary Jones, Dr Denise Syndercombe-Court, Eimear O'Herlihy, E.R. Murray, Fin Flynn, Ger Kenneally, Harry Moore, Helen Boyle, Helen Guerin, Jane Moore and John Strachan, Jean Kearney, Joan Sheehy, Joe Kelly, Joe McNicholas, John Breen, Jon Gower and Sarah Hill, Jules O'Toole, Katie Dinneen, Kerry Dineen, Kieran O'Connor, Lily O'Sullivan, Lynn Sheehan, Madeleine D'Arcy, Maggie Kennedy, Marguerite

Phillips, Maria O'Donovan, Marie Gethins, Mary Doyle, Mary Stanley, Michelle Nagle, Miriam O'Brien, Natalia Cacciatore, Norma Burke, Olan and Paul O'Donovan, Oonagh Montague, Peter, Nicola, Laura and Alex Byrne, Pat Cotter, Pat Kiernan, Patricia McVeigh, Paul McVeigh, Rachel Andrews, Sally Kearney, Sile Ni Bhroin, Siobhan Lankford, Sophie Dwyer, Stephen Darcy Collins, Vanessa Fox O'Loughlin and all at Inkwell Group and writing.ie, William Wall and Zsuzsi Gartner; and my family – Marcia Kirwan and Rob, Michael and Molly Regan, and Neil, Nicola and Elizabeth Kirwan and, for everything, my parents Michael and Breda Kirwan.